Fifteen years have passed since the eve~
dos, where our four heroes, Bill)
entered adulthood and a period of
us the beginnings of a new series, Ch   ᴜᴋ One,
Song of the Ovulum, is grittier than tl   ᴠooks—part spy
novel, part underground church/concentration camp novel.

Mr. Davis didn't just drag out a complete story; he started afresh
with the twin children of legacy and five-thousand year-old
teenagers from Genesis six. Most of Joran and Selah's arc is from
Joran's perspective, and he's very well-developed and carries his end
of the plot well. He's hurting and angry, but beneath all that he's
a good kid who matures as the story progresses. His arc is one of
redemption, a theme Davis develops beautifully.

Song of the Ovulum has beauty, intrigue, and grit all wrapped in a
package. I'm looking forward to its sequel.

—**Kaci Hill** (Co-author of *Lunatic* and *Elyon*)

Outstanding! *Song of the Ovulum* is a masterpiece without com-
parison! This breathtaking saga will take you on a journey along
with new characters and old characters, from before the great flood
to the present time. When you read *Song of the Ovulum* you will
feel like you are walking among dragons, Oracles, and Listeners,
right in the thick of the action. You cry in times of pain and smile
during times of joy. The pages keep turning, no matter the time.
Bryan Davis has created yet another wonderful chronicle for us to
enjoy and learn from. Keep reading. You won't regret it.

—**Melanie Sue** (Age 15)

WOW! *Songs of the Ovulum* is amazing! The imagery has to be
some of the best. Mr. Davis had me ducking when fire was spewed
at the people, jumping when someone was injured, and wincing
when the candlestones shone. The detail is also fantastic! I can picture exactly what Tamiel, the other demons, the dragons, and most

of all the humans look and act like. This book is amazing, and I can't wait for the next in the series.

—**Val Chapman** (Age 15)

When I began reading *Song of the Ovulum*, my heart raced with excitement. As the plot continued to unfold, I was laughing and crying, anxious to find what part all the characters would take in this new series. *Song of the Ovulum* left me enthralled. It was filled with the qualities of friendship, sacrifice, and God's love. Children of the Bard is off to an amazing start, and my high expectations were not only fulfilled, but exceeded. I am delighted by *Song of the Ovulum* and overjoyed with the opportunity to continue this journey even more!

—**Skyeler Syrek** (Age 16)

From the moment I started, I found myself pulled into a separate world of dragons, Listeners, and Oracles. I would find myself alongside the characters, in the Healers' room with Bonnie, fighting atop dragons with Walter, or in a deep, dark dungeon with Billy. Wherever it took me, I found myself feeling their emotions. Mr. Davis has done it again! Bringing us into a world we have never known before or feel like we've known all our lives, his magic with words makes us feel as if we are there in the midst of what's happening. We are fighting the battles, feeling the pain, or thanking the Maker. Thanks, Mr. Davis, for another exhilarating experience.

—**Naomi Hesterman** (Age 16)

Song of the Ovulum transfixed me from the first word of the prologue to the final word of the last chapter. Mr. Davis has whipped up another great fantasy/Christian story. With new characters and old characters, this book was like none other I have read. This book keeps you on your toes, flipping through page after page, and it leaves me satisfied, yet craving for more!!!

—**Dan Lupo** (Age 13)

Bryan Davis has done it again with *Song of the Ovulum*! This wonderful book is filled with action and packed full of spiritual truths. Watching the characters grow in their faith and risk their lives for each other has inspired me to become a better person and closer to God. Every page in *Song of the Ovulum* is filled with page-turning events that make you never want put it down.

—**Rebecca Blome** (Age 17)

I went into this book wondering what new adventures could befall our heroes and heroines. Immediately, I was swept into the action and couldn't wait to start a new chapter. *Song of the Ovulum* is another fantastic story of faith, discovery, loyalty, and inspiration. With both new and old characters, the story flows seamlessly from one world to the next. This book keeps Bryan Davis at the top of my list of favorite authors.

—**Kristen Twomey** (Age 16)

I loved *Song of the Ovulum*! Once again Bryan Davis has woven a masterful tapestry of love, sacrifice, and the never-ending power of God's mercy and compassion. This amazing tale of Lauren and Matt will take you on a thrill ride you will never forget!

—**Cassidy Clayton** (Age 14)

Song of the Ovulum not only brought back nearly all the familiar faces, it introduced still more characters just as captivating and endearing as the originals—perhaps, in some cases, even more so. The stakes seemed so high, I often found myself thinking that there was no possible way out this time, but I was again proven wrong. Dragons, at least those that serve the Lord, really can take on almost anything. From the days of the flood, all the way to the up to the current world relations with Second Eden, Mr. Davis has shown his amazing ability to create memorable characters to fill fantastical worlds where anything and everything might happen: plants may turn to people, voices may be stolen, and songs of mercy have power incomprehensible. For those of you who thought the ride was over with *The Bones of Makaidos*, buckle your seat belts and get ready to dive in even farther, because you ain't seen nothin' yet.

—**Alisha Lavender** (Age 15)

I loved the array of songs that spanned throughout the book. This book rivals even *The Bones of Makaidos*. The previous series never shied away from God, and in Oracles of Fire the passion strengthened. This book carries on that passion. It was a wonderful story about God's redeeming love, mercy, and forgiveness. This book will leave you hungry for more.

—**Kathleen Clifton** (Age 16)

Song of the Ovulum is beautifully composed; definitely a page turner. I've developed a habit of staying up late reading. Thanks Mr. Davis for writing another fantastic book!

—**Nichelle Phillips** (Age 16)

Fans of the Dragons in Our Midst and Oracles of Fire series have waited a long time for this book, and I am happy to say they will not be disappointed. *Song of the Ovulum* took me on an exhilarating ride from cover to cover, alongside characters I quickly came to love. This book has it all: fast-paced conflict, heart-stopping plot twists, and a beautiful message that left me feeling inspired and refreshed. There were moments where I wished I could leap through the pages and join in the action! Bryan Davis is a master storyteller. Book Two cannot come fast enough.

—**Gina Garavalia** (Age 17)

When I finished *The Bones of Makaidos*, I thought it was all over. Boy was I wrong! Mr. Davis has entered the world of Billy and Bonnie again. *Song of the Ovulum* lets you reunite with old characters, plus meet many new ones. See Walter and our old friends back in action! Travel back to Bible times to meet Methuselah's kids. And to top it all off, give your spiritual walk a boost. What a great ride! Congratulations on another great book, Mr. Davis. This book is a MUST read!

—**Jared Besse** (Age 13)

In *Song of the Ovulum*, Bryan Davis revives a world familiar to those who have experienced his adventurous books before; he has crafted a tale that brings readers the sensation of being encompassed within the tumultuous and exciting events, journeying along with their beloved characters who manage to give constant hope in times of despair. It is scarce for avid readers to find books that not only contain innovative and original storylines, but are spiritually edifying as well. *Song of the Ovulum* is a rare find in today's world, and is well worth anyone's time.

—**Sarah Halbrook** (Age 19)

A captivating read! I was enamored from page one. Bryan Davis has once again produced a tale filled with extraordinary adventure and thrill. Readers will fall in love with our new hero and heroine as they follow along in their incredible triumphs and perils.

—**Katie Larink** (Age 18)

Dragons in our Midst readers, be prepared for a lot of surprises – and thrills. Whether or not you've read the eight books in the previous storyline, *Song of the Ovulum* will twist your mind and pull you in before you can even realize what's going on. Brick by brick, Mr. Davis builds up his most shocking story world yet, along with an epic yet smoothly-constructed storyline that will keep you fully engaged even after you've turned the last page.

—**Ian Hancock** (Age 18)

Song of the Ovulum has a very strong message of redemption and mercy. From the first page to the last, it draws readers in and they feel like they are there with the characters. Bryan Davis has presented in each of his books a strong Christian message that challenges the readers' faith and encourages them in their Christian walk.

—**Emily Hancock** (Age 18)

I had a lot of fun reading *Song of the Ovulum*. It's a really great book, and I'm definitely going to be reading it again!

—**Christine Elliott** (Age 11)

Well, Bryan Davis has done it yet again. An excellent read. He captures readers with the first word, holds them until the last word, and leaves them aching for more. Just as with Dragons in our Midst and Oracles of Fire, there is action, adventure, and of course the ever present power of God's love and mercy. I can't wait for the next book in the series. I know the rest of my family will love this book as much as I do.

—**Tammy Whiting** (Parent)

As a parent who reads over the shoulder of his pre-teens, I appreciate the battle between good and evil and the chance to exercise discernment between the two. Thanks, Bryan, for writing books I am thrilled to hand to my sons. *Song of the Ovulum* resonates in my house.

—**Mark T. Hancock** (Parent)

I love how Bryan Davis has seamlessly integrated a new storyline and characters into the existing world of Dragons in our Midst. I look forward to sharing the adventures of Billy and Bonnie with my children as they grow up.

—**Rebecca Rasmussen** (Parent)

Children of the Bard 1

Song of the Ovulum

Bryan Davis

Living Ink Books
An Imprint of AMG Publishers
Chattanooga, Tennessee

Song of the Ovulum
Volume 1 in the Children of the Bard® series
Copyright © 2011 by Bryan Davis
Published by Living Ink Books, an imprint of AMG Publishers
6815 Shallowford Rd.
Chattanooga, Tennessee 37421

Printed Edition ISBN 13: 978-0-89957-880-4
Printed Edition ISBN 10: 0-89957-880-2
EPUB Edition ISBN 13: 978-1-61715-107-1
Mobi Edition ISBN 13: 978-1-61715-043-2
ePDF Edition ISBN 13: 978-1-61715-185-9

First printing—June 2011

CHILDREN OF THE BARD, ORACLES OF FIRE, and DRAGONS IN OUR MIDST are registered trademarks of AMG Publishers

Cover designed by Bright Boy Design, Inc., Chattanooga, Tennessee

Interior design and typesetting by Reider Publishing Services,
    West Hollywood, California

Edited and proofread by Susie Davis, Sharon Neal, and Rick Steele

To hear a performance of the song on page 361, access this web link:
http://www.daviscrossing.com/ItIsYou.mp3

Printed in Canada
17 16 15 14 13 12 11 –T– 8 7 6 5 4 3 2

A whip never draws love from those who kneel. Only mercy can penetrate a heart, soften it with healing balm, and set it ablaze with devotion. This story is for those who wish to learn the mercy song— the melody of grace, the harmony of forgiveness, the rhythm of a heart set free. After your chains are broken, perhaps someone will ask you, "What is your mercy song?" Then, you will be able to pass the liberating music on to another imprisoned soul.

ACKNOWLEDGMENTS

Special thanks to Jason Waguespack who helped me come up with the idea for this book. Without your help in brainstorming, this series might never have come to pass.

Thank you to my wife, who also happens to be my editor. You are amazing. Even after reading the entire manuscript multiple times, you never fail to find a new way to improve the story. Most of all, I appreciate your emotional and spiritual support. I couldn't do this without you.

Thank you to the folks at AMG. You have done a great job once again. I trust that your work for God's kingdom is being noticed by the King.

As always, I give thanks to God, the great musician who composed and taught me my mercy song. I look forward to singing it in your presence when my time as your minstrel has come to an end.

AUTHOR'S NOTE

When I completed *The Bones of Makaidos*, I thought the adventures of Billy, Bonnie, Walter, and company had reached an end. In that book's epilogue, however, I left hints that a new adventure with new characters might be forthcoming. Still, I didn't want to continue in this world of dragons, anthrozils, and slayers unless I came up with a really great idea. Well, after a round of brainstorming with contributor Jason Waguespack, an idea took shape, a cool concept that gave birth to *Song of the Ovulum*. I am excited about this new series, Children of the Bard, four books that will continue the excitement and heart of Dragons in our Midst and Oracles of Fire.

Although it will be helpful to read the eight books in the previous two series before reading *Song of the Ovulum*, it isn't essential. This story can be enjoyed without knowing the history behind these pages. Yet, if you choose to take the leap into *Song of the Ovulum* without reading the other stories, I highly recommend that you first check out Jason's recap at the end. It should provide all the information you need to embark on this new adventure.

With that said, I invite you to turn the page and explore a new world of fantasy and adventure. Ladies and gentlemen, prepare to draw your swords. The heroes and heroines within these pages are going to need all the help they can get.

CONTENTS

xvi

Bonnie's Chains

Some nights I lie awake and reach
For hands I would enfold,
To feel my friend's familiar warmth,
His lovely eyes behold.

Yet when my fingers stretch for his,
I grasp but empty air;
I rise and search the silent room.
Alas! He isn't there.

Oh will this nightmare never end?
This pain, this lonely war?
Will dawn arise and bring you back
To arms that ache for yours?

We battled foes of ghost and flesh
In fields of sky and sod.
You bore my soul on paths through hell;
I carried yours to God.

My soul I stitched to yours alone;
I wrapped you in my wings.
You set my heart aflame with love,
And now my spirit sings.

To God who hears my every prayer
This orphan's outcries burn;
On wings to altars filled with light,
I beg for your return.

As long as you are out of reach,
My heart is never free.
These hands, these arms are tightly bound
By chains I cannot see.

Come back to me my hero friend!
And tear my chains in two.
Restore the warmth, inflame my heart,
And fill my arms with you.

PROLOGUE

A winter storm is brewing. I can tell by the damp chill in the air. I hope we get blankets. Last year the guards told us they had to save the coats and blankets for the soldiers, but I don't believe them. Malice spices their words, as chilling as last February's blizzard. It was so cold one night, Ashley nearly froze to death. If not for wrapping her in my wings, I'm sure she would have died. Summer breezes thawed our bones, but autumn breezes portend another storm. Will we survive this time?

It has been fifteen years since I last wrote in a journal. In spite of the miserable conditions, I am thankful for Walter's courage in sneaking this little notebook and pencil to me. It will be difficult to keep them hidden, but Ashley and I managed to dig a small crevice in the wall behind the toilet. Since it's near the rat hole, I doubt that anyone will look there, but when Stella's on duty, you never know. Sometimes I think her piercing eyes can see through concrete.

Ashley is asleep, curled on our mat in the corner. Poor thing. The experiments are getting more invasive. Of course, I grew accustomed to the never-ending needle jabs when my father tried to learn the secrets behind my dragon ancestry and the reasons my blood brought healing and youthful vigor. The Healers, or so they call themselves, are determined to unlock the secrets, and morning will dawn with my turn to face the electric shocks and specimen-collecting needles. My faith will have to remain strong.

I have used much of our candle, so I must join Ashley in slumber soon. Yet, I fear the dreams. Of late they have been dark, foreboding, mysterious. It seems that they are a movie trailer—a montage of scenes that cast more shadows over this present distress. I know, of course, that God is with me even in the darkest of prisons, so the dreams, though piecemeal and fractured, have helped me feel his presence in inexpressible ways, as though he is calling me to more intimate fellowship than ever before. The darker the night, the brighter the flame, and the more precious it becomes to those who wait for the dawn.

I am sure a new scene will enter my dreams tonight, a story from long ago that will provide another puzzlement. Maybe if I write the dreams, all will become clear. I pray for clarity. This cruel, twisted world is void of it.

At one time, our plight seemed unimaginable. When Billy and I celebrated the birth of our twins, all was well. The people had accepted the existence of dragons and anthrozil hybrids, and the relationship between Earth and Second Eden was blossoming into an alliance of cross-dimensional worlds. Who could have predicted that rumors of war would begin to flourish only a year later? Who could have guessed that Billy and I would be forcibly separated and our children taken away before they were even weaned?

I apologize for the smudges. My tears are smearing the pencil marks.

If only they would allow my children to visit me! A glimpse is all I ask. What do Charles and Karen look like? Did they ever develop dragon traits? If not, have they been brainwashed to hate dragonkind? Are they even alive? Do they know I exist? And what of my husband? Is Billy suffering the same brutality I have to endure? Will we ever be together again on this side of Heaven's gates?

At least Walter brings us news now and then, much of it dark and fearful, especially concerning the disease spreading among some anthrozils. The details are sketchy, and Walter can't give us more than a few coded messages. Since he is not dragonkind, he is able to spy out our persecutors, but he does so at great risk. If they learn he is merely pretending to be on their side, what will they do to him? And does this pretense violate his conscience? But I leave that dilemma to him. I am not his judge. And now that I think about it, if the guards become suspicious, I should erase this paragraph. If they find this journal, Walter's life will be forfeit.

I must end now. Stella will come on duty soon, and if she is in a foul mood, she will likely torture me again.

I hear footsteps. And chains.

Help me, Lord!

Bonnie Bannister

3

CHAPTER

THE LISTENERS

Joran set an arrow to his bowstring. The giant lay on his back only a few paces ahead, quiet and motionless. He was a clever one; his pose could be a ploy. If this Naphil's heart still had life, he wouldn't be able to hide it for long.

Surrounded by curtains of smoke, Joran tiptoed over fallen branches, scorched leaves, and blackened evergreen needles littering the carpet of thin grass. Narrow fire lines crackled here and there, looking like sizzling orange serpents as they gobbled the debris. Pools of thick tar dotted the area, less-than-subtle evidence of the recent battle between a dragon and the demon that got away. Unlike the Naphil, the demon, one of the lesser Watchers, seemed no smarter than a pomegranate, so Makaidos, though an inexperienced dragon, would likely catch him eventually.

Joran leaped over one of the black pools and halted, holding his breath to avoid taking in the noxious fumes. The giant hadn't moved a muscle. Even the arrow protruding from his chest stayed perfectly still. A single arrow rarely slew one of these beastly humanoids, and they had been known to swim underwater for more than a league, so he might be holding his breath.

While Joran's sister crept up behind him, her sword in one hand and their captivity lyre in the other, he listened for the slightest noise. Even from a distance, and even with the surrounding fires emitting pops and snaps, the Naphil's heartbeat would be easy for his sensitive ears to detect. Still, nothing sounded, not a thump or a breath. He was either dead, or the pools of darkness had slowed his heart to an imperceptible level.

"Is the lyre detecting anything?" Joran asked.

Selah slid her sword into its scabbard and held the lyre's wooden frame with both hands, lifting the strings close to her eyes. "The G string is vibrating slightly. It's the only one not housing a demon."

"That's a good enough sign for me. The ovulum has to be around here somewhere."

A fly landed on the giant's bulbous nose, but his pale, bearded face didn't twitch. As the sun eased toward the western horizon, its rays broke through a gap in the trees and struck the giant's closed eyelids. Still, he remained motionless. Dead or not, he wasn't about to start a fight anytime soon.

Joran looked up. The smoky sky revealed no winged creatures at all, no demonic Watcher or warrior dragon, but the Watcher could return at any moment to retrieve the ovulum, if the Naphil still had it.

"No signs of life," he said as he released the arrow from his string and pushed it into the quiver on his back. "But no other sign of the ovulum either."

Selah stepped around one of the black pools and pointed at the giant. "He has a supplies bag on his belt, but we should be able to hear the ovulum if it's in there."

"I'll check." Joran eased up to the giant's body and listened to the goatskin bag. No song of the ovulum emanated from within. After sliding his bow up to his shoulder, Joran untied the bag's leather drawstring and pulled it open. Inside lay several black scarabs, each one the size of his palm, but since their eyes lacked any hint of fiery redness, they had not yet been activated as weapons. They posed no threat.

As he retied the bag, a faint melody reached his ears, but it seemed warped, troubled. He followed the sound to a spot under the giant's meaty arm. Using both hands, he shoved the arm out of the way, revealing a pool where blood had collected and blended with black resin to create a thick slurry. A glass egg lay half-submerged in the mire.

While Selah again skulked closer, Joran slid his hands under the ovulum and lifted it carefully. The demon's ammunition, sticky dark resin it shot from its eyes, still adhered to the surface and slowly oozed onto Joran's fingers. No wonder the ovulum's song sounded so troubled. This liquid curse, this evil spell of hopelessness, must have distorted the holy sound. Apparently the demon planned to keep the ovulum's rescuers from hearing its call.

Joran looked up again. Since Makaidos wasn't around to burn the spell away, he would have to risk a song. It could draw the demon back, but it was the only way to restore the ovulum.

He eyed the resin as it began crawling from the glass shell to his wrists. The ovulum wasn't the only one needing to be saved. This stuff could take over his mind if he didn't hurry. "Selah, I need a rhythm."

She pressed close from behind and peered around his arm. "A cleansing song?"

He nodded. "If you add a harmony, it might go faster. We need to get out of here as soon as we can. Makaidos will find his way home … if he survived. He's not exactly experienced in demon hunting."

"You'd better fight those doubts." Her voice carried a calming tone. "If you let that darkness spell affect you, you won't be able to sing."

"I remember Seraphina saying something like that." Joran mentally cringed. Resurrecting grief over Seraphina wasn't the best way to counter negative thoughts.

Selah's eyebrow twitched, a sign of hurt, but a smile brushed it away. She played the lyre, alternating between two high notes. Following her upbeat rhythm, Joran began singing.

> Dark begone. Doubt depart.
> Light restore. Faith restart.
> Cast away the gloom and fear;
> Heed my words, let sight be clear.

As he repeated the lyrics, the music intermixed with the resin, diluting it and forcing it to stream down the transparent shell, clearing its smooth surface. A bluish glow blossomed at the center and feathered out toward the inner edges. With every pulse, the ovulum emanated a musical note of its own, part of its signature melody, now unhindered by the demon's curse and the giant's smothering weight.

Letting out a relieved sigh, Joran shook the leftover resin from his fingers and turned to Selah. "It's alive."

She hooked the lyre's bracket to her belt and took the egg, cradling it in her palms. "Thanks be to Elohim!"

"Perhaps." Joran jerked the arrow out of the Naphil's chest and wiped the point clean on a clump of grass. "We have the ovulum. We'd better go."

"Perhaps?" Selah squinted at him. "Are doubts from the demon's curse still lingering?"

"Not really. I'm just thinking about what happened. With the angle I had, it seemed like an impossible shot, especially from a dragon's back. I suppose divine guidance had something to do with it."

"Then why *perhaps?*"

8

Joran shrugged. "I'm confused about the inconsistency. Why would Elohim help us today when he plans to kill us tomorrow?"

"I know. I know. We've been over all that before." Selah slid the ovulum into her own leather bag, tied the end closed, and attached it to another hook on her belt. "Speaking of dying tomorrow," she said as she looked at the sky, "we have the ovulum, so why the rush to get home? I think we should wait for Makaidos."

"And risk facing the Watcher again? Are you sure?"

"Today we live. Tomorrow we die." Selah gripped her sword's hilt. "That demon sang the foulest song I have ever heard. If we can silence him forever, it will be worth enduring his obscenities. We have no guarantee that the flood will kill those monsters."

Joran gazed at Selah's youthful face. Sweat streamed down her smudged cheeks, and dark hair flew about her bronzed forehead in spite of her carefully tied braid, stark contrasts to her sparkling eyes. Her loosely fitting earth-brown battle tunic and ankle-length trousers also acted as contradictions. Strong and lean from her training, her frame looked almost as athletic as his own, though she stood three inches shorter, one inch for each year younger. She had proven her skill time and again, but it didn't seem right to allow a thirteen-year-old girl to endure the evil songs of the Watchers and fly into danger on the back of a dragon. Yet, what else could they do? The ark had to be protected. The ovula had to be preserved.

9

He caressed her dirty cheek with his hand. "I'm sorry about the Watchers' obscenities, but I can't track their songs without you."

"I know." She pressed his hand closer and kissed its heel. "Don't worry about me. Elohim has put a shield around my heart."

Joran imagined a tough dragon-scale hide surrounding Selah's heart. Her faith was so strong, so certain. Of course, no daughter of Methuselah could doubt Elohim's existence, but how could she know for sure that a distant deity cared for her ... or for anyone besides the few who would be allowed to ride to safety on the ark?

Breaking their locked gazes, he turned to the west. The Watchers' song, a dissonant assortment of notes, drifted into his ears. The filthy demon cried like a spoiled child, another sign of stupidity. He was nothing like the Silent One, the Watcher of legend who controlled his sound environment. It would be a great adventure to confront that demon, but he had kept himself scarce lately.

"I can still hear him," Joran said, "so if we follow the sound on foot, maybe we'll find Makaidos."

"The Watcher is close." Selah nodded toward the setting sun. "The rhythm is wild and inconsistent."

"Chasing or being chased?"

"I can't tell."

"Do you want to hide or face him?"

Her brow bent low, and an uncharacteristic growl spiced her voice. "Face him!"

"Then we'd better get ready." Joran set his bow on the ground. "How close is he?"

"It's hard to tell." Selah detached her scabbard and laid it next to Joran's bow. "But he's definitely coming this way."

"How do your lungs feel?"

She unhooked the lyre and held it at her waist. "Tired, but I can manage."

"Good." Joran scanned Selah's body. She had removed all metallic items from her clothing, as always. With the exception of the rods themselves, the sound barrier would destroy any metal it touched. "We'll need to use standard base range. Have you detected the rhythm?"

Taking faster breaths, she nodded. "It's the same Watcher. He has murder on his mind."

"I hear his threats." After stripping off his quiver, Joran reached into a pouch on the side of his trousers just below his hip and withdrew a pair of metal rods about the width of his finger and as long as his forearm. "You set the beat," he said as he gave a rod to

Selah. "I'll do the probe. I won't know the exact notes until I hear how the Watcher reacts to my guesses, so you'll have to adjust as I do."

"Okay." She swallowed hard. "We've never tried a face-to-face wall before."

"Today we live. Tomorrow we die." Joran positioned himself to her left, both of them facing west. As he raised his rod over his head with his left hand, she lifted her rod with her right. They hooked their free arms together, supporting the lyre, and listened. The demon's song grew slowly louder. The terror their father called "unholy wrath" would soon arrive.

Selah's body trembled. Joran tightened his lock on her arm. Her anxiety wouldn't last. The upcoming clash would bring about her usual battle-hardened poise.

Inhaling deeply, he took note of the sparse collection of sycamores in front, many of them stripped of leaves. The recent battle between Makaidos and the demon had transformed this part of the forest into a clearing, leaving only a few unbroken trees within a range of twenty paces.

Ahead, the dark orange sun bathed them in warmth, but it also posed a threat. Fully illuminated and partially blinded, he and Selah stood as easy targets, but that couldn't be helped. They needed an unobstructed line for their voices.

He cleared his throat, hoping to quell any sign of nervousness. "Now, Selah. Interpret the demon's song. Replace the obscenities with something else."

"With what?"

"Anything. Just use the same word over and over. I'll under-stand."

Blinking, she gave him a nod and turned toward the sunset. "Closer … closer … closer." Her words flowed in a moderate rhythm, taking on a hum as she stretched them out. "Hatred … evil … murder … closer … closer … closer."

11

Joran sang out, alternating notes in time with Selah's rhythm. The music rippled through the air, probing the path ahead. Seconds later, an echo sounded, his own voice, yet warped and off-key.

His rod vibrated. The captured sound entered his hand, shot down his arm, and coursed through his and Selah's bodies. Her rod did the same. As they absorbed the altered music, a new tune entered Joran's mind, the solution to the demon's attack, and the key to his undoing.

He pulled Selah closer. "I have it. Are you ready?"

Her lips pressing together in a thin line, she nodded.

"I'll wait until the last possible moment. We don't want to give him any warning."

Another growl rumbled in her reply. "Let's make him shrivel."

As the roar of a dragon pierced the air, the Watcher flew into sight, his dark form looking like a winged smudge at the center of the sun. Another winged form took shape behind him, Makaidos giving chase, his red eyebeams clear even from so far away. The Watcher zipped around trees like a weaver's thread, and the young dragon dodged every obstacle while shooting fireballs that either missed or grazed the zigzagging demon.

The Watcher's eyes shifted toward Joran and Selah, turning black as he drew near. His flight path straightened, and Makaidos's flaming blasts stopped, apparently to avoid striking his human allies.

Joran tried to loosen his tightening throat. At this speed, the Watcher would arrive in seconds. "Start the rhythm again. Use the demon's words."

Selah's voice erupted in a rapid singsong chant. "Strike them, kill them, shatter their spindly bones. Beat them, grind them, hurtle them to the stones."

Joran let out a wailing song, a series of connected notes that followed Selah's rhythm. She joined in with a perfect harmony, still interpreting.

12

"Closer … closer … cut their throats … spill their blood."

The rods vibrated so hard, they seemed to churn the colors in the air. A wall of sound spread between the metallic poles, thick and warped, making the sun and forest ripple in their view.

"Human fools … closer … closer … now you die."

Dark beams shot from the demon's eyes. Joran pushed all his energy into the song, strengthening the wall. The blackness splashed against their shield. Gooey resin splattered from one rod to the other and disintegrated.

The Watcher slammed into the barrier and froze in place, the wall of sound absorbing his momentum. As big as the Naphil, he jerked and squirmed. His huge bare feet slapped the ground, his white robe and golden sash sizzled against the barrier, and his massive reddish-black wings beat the rods, but Joran, Selah, and the shield held firm.

As Makaidos angled away and landed with a slide, Selah shouted, "Let's wrap him!" She unhooked her arm from Joran's and set the lyre on the ground, plucking the G string before rising again. The note flowed up toward the barrier, visible as a serpentine ripple in the air, and attached to the barrier's bottom edge. The active connection between the barrier and the lyre kept the string vibrating, allowing the G note to continue feeding sound upward.

13

Still singing, Joran ran around the demon. Like a banner flapping on a staff, the wall of sound encircled their captive and hemmed him in. When Joran completed his orbit and reached Selah's opposite side, she shifted her rod to her other hand and again locked arms with him, the lyre standing to her left.

After taking a quick breath, Joran continued the song. His lungs ached, but the job was almost finished.

The Watcher screamed. The barrier captured his shrill voice, thickening it. With every grunt and groan, the demon's limbs thinned, his face wrinkled, and black vapor flowed from his mouth into the lyre's G string. Like a predator serpent, the barrier constricted, squeezing the substance out of its victim.

Soon, the Watcher shriveled into a wisp, leaving only a prunish head and a gaping mouth. With a final scream, his frame dwindled to a black string and flowed into the lyre.

Joran exhaled. Selah did the same. Both gasping for breath, they unlocked their arms and set their rods on the ground. The barrier of sound wiggled and writhed, stirring up leaves and twigs until it settled and faded away.

Taking in a cleansing breath, Joran picked up the lyre and allowed himself a gratified smile. "It's full now. Seven demons locked up."

"*Now* will you sing them out?" Selah asked, her expression hopeful. "I'm sure Makaidos would enjoy greeting them with fire when they show their ugly faces."

Joran let his smile wither. Selah's emphasis on *now* wasn't meant to be a slap, but it stung all the same. He looked at the strings. This lyre, one of only two in the world that could entrap a living being, had been passed down by Adam himself, the first human on the face of the Earth. And Joran, the elder of the two surviving Listeners, was the only living human who had the power to extract the demons … that is, until that fateful day.

"I can't, Selah."

"Why not? You said—"

"Never mind what I said." He set the lyre on the ground and backed away. "Let's just burn it where it stands. That will kill the demons and save a lot of time."

Selah gasped. "Burn Father Adam's lyre?"

"We're all going to die tomorrow anyway, and Noah's family doesn't know how to use it." Joran turned to Makaidos. "Good dragon, will you please do the honors?"

With a flap of his wings, Makaidos scooted toward them. When he stopped, he sat on his haunches between the lyre and

Joran, looking him in the eye. "Since I perceive no need to save time," Makaidos said, a sparkle of red in his pupils, "I wonder if there is an alternative reason for this decision to destroy a family heirloom."

Joran stared at his sandal as he brushed a toe across the leafy debris. This dragon had no idea how many times he had tried to sing a demon out of a string, and Selah had heard only excuses for years. Even she had never seen a successful singing extraction, only a few executions by fire. Finally, he firmed his jaw and shifted his gaze back to Makaidos, his tone assertive but controlled. "Just do as I say, or I will have to report your insubordination to Arramos."

"Joran?" Selah leaned close and whispered, "His question is reasonable. Why are you threatening him?"

"He is a servant to humans. It isn't his place to question me." He met her gaze. With a fist on her hip and her brow bent low, her stance was clear. She was right, and she knew it. She wasn't about to back down.

15

Heaving a tired sigh, Joran gave both Selah and Makaidos an apologetic nod. "I shouldn't have been so terse. I'm exhausted, and it takes a lot of energy to sing a demon out of a string, and extracting seven is just too much. The lyre will be destroyed in the flood anyway, so, if you don't mind, Makaidos, I would appreciate it if you would make up for my weakness."

Makaidos bowed his head. "Very well, Joran. Your weariness is quite understandable." He curled his neck and aimed his snout at the lyre. "Stand back."

"One word of warning," Joran said. "When a demon comes out, he'll be enraged. The screams will be nothing like you've ever heard before. Don't let the noise distract you, or he'll get away."

Makaidos puffed a plume of smoke. "A blast of fire will silence any escapees."

"You think it will," Selah countered, "but this is your first execution. You have no idea how resilient these demons can be."

"It seems that I will have to learn quickly. Your brother has made his decision." With his pointed ears pinned back, Makaidos gave her a firm nod. "Let us proceed."

Joran scooped up the sonic rods and slid them into their pouch. Taking Selah's hand, he backed away slowly. With their sensitive ears, the screams would be horrific, but they couldn't retreat too far. If one of the demons escaped, they might have to corral him again.

Twin streams of fire shot from Makaidos's nostrils. They encircled the lyre and engulfed it in flames. As it burned, a squeal erupted, then another, both cries saturated with obscenities. Selah covered her ears, wincing. Joran glanced at the rods' pouch. He probably should have kept the sound barrier active, which would have allowed him to shield Selah from the verbal onslaught and quickly capture an escaping demon, but it was too late now.

While Makaidos continued blasting the lyre, several thin trails of black mist rose from the strings.

"Makaidos!" Joran called, pointing. "The mists are the demons. Scorch them!"

The dragon's river of flames shifted to the rising trails, intermixing tongues of orange in a violent swirl. One trail broke away and expanded into a body, dark and winged. As the demon took shape, it slowly solidified. Its robe smoldering and its face blackened, it let out an ear-splitting scream as it beat its wings and tried to escape from the swirl.

Makaidos's eyes darted toward it, but he couldn't move the fire again lest he allow the other six to escape.

Silence deafened every sound, even the Watcher's cries. The lyre exploded noiselessly, shooting flaming shards in every direction. Joran and Selah flew backwards like hurled stones. They landed on their backsides, tumbled into reverse somersaults, and sprawled prostrate.

Joran scrambled to his feet and helped Selah to hers. Makaidos blew a raging river of flames at the escaping demon. Now a

16

winged, fiery silhouette, the Watcher swelled in size and straightened to his full height. He staggered toward Joran and Selah, waving his flaming arms as he cursed in his hellish language.

"Run!" Joran grabbed Selah's wrist, but just before he could turn, the Watcher burst open. Black-streaked flames spewed from his side. Joran threw Selah to the ground and covered her with his body. Sizzling lava-like globules rained down, some pelting his back. Scalding heat bit through his tunic. He clenched his teeth, but he couldn't roll away. He had to protect Selah.

Something swiped against his back. The burning pain eased. Angling his head, he looked around. Makaidos stood over him, batting the smoldering flames away with a wing.

"I apologize," Makaidos said. "I miscalculated the Watcher's capacity. If you wish to report my inadequacies to my father—"

"That won't be necessary." Joran climbed to his feet and helped Selah rise. "I'm the one who said we had to burn it."

Selah brushed off her trousers. "No need to blame anyone. All is well."

Joran flapped his tunic, allowing cool air to waft over his scorched back. A flurry of reasons why all was not well died on his lips, including his usual complaint that he and Selah were risking their lives to protect an ark that would soon float away to safety without them.

After glancing at the lyre's remains, a pile of gray ash and scattered strings, he offered Makaidos a conciliatory head bow. "The Watchers are dead, we're alive, and we rescued the ovulum. That's all that matters."

"I appreciate your mercy." Makaidos's ears perked up. "But I am not sure all is well."

Selah scanned the clearing. "Do you sense a Watcher's song in your scales?"

"That is my mother's talent," Makaidos said, keeping his voice low. The tip of his tail twitched, and his head swayed. "I am able to detect danger, not songs."

17

Joran followed the dragon's line of sight. Up until recently, they had ridden Shachar, Makaidos's mother, and her ability to detect the evil songs had been helpful. This young dragon had more deficiencies than expected. "Can you tell if the danger is close?"

"The sensation is weak," Makaidos said, "so I assume it is far from us. I will let you know if it increases."

"Then we have a spare moment." Selah withdrew the ovulum from her pouch and displayed it again in her palms. Its glow emanated beyond the glass exterior, painting her hands blue. Its song rode the smoky air, inaudible to most dragons and humans, but loud and clear to angels, demons, and, of course, the two Listeners.

As the energetic tune pumped through his mind, Joran hummed along. The vigor seemed out of place. One day remained before Elohim would send a flood to kill every creature with the breath of life. This was a time for sadness, a day of grief.

Letting his hum wither, Joran swallowed through the tightness in his throat. Without a doubt he, himself, deserved to die. His sins had been many, especially the one great sin that likely cost him his soul. Even Father and Arramos seemed unable to forgive him for what he did to Seraphina, and if she were still alive, she probably wouldn't forgive him either. He didn't deserve forgiveness, only death. But Selah? She deserved life, eternal life beyond this doomed world. She, like their sister Seraphina, possessed a flame that could not be extinguished.

As he looked at Selah's eyes, they reflected the ovulum's radiance. With her love and purity, she was more like an angel than a human, and every bit as righteous as Noah.

Joran shook his head. No. It just wasn't right. Somehow he would convince Father to use his prophetic influence and get Selah on board the ark. At this point, nothing else really mattered.

Another sound rode the breeze—a voice, elongated calls of "Joran" and "Selah."

"Did you hear that?" Selah asked.

Joran stilled his body, trying to identify the voice, a deep tone, fragile, like that of an elderly man. "Father?"

"That's what I thought." She returned the egg to its pouch. "We'd better get this back to him. Maybe he's calling because the anchor ovulum needs support."

"Although I heard nothing," Makaidos said, "I agree that leaving is a good idea. The danger sensation is growing."

Joran kept his ear trained on the wind, but no more calls drifted their way. Selah was right. Father's ovulum was the most important of the seven ovula, but its energy shield couldn't protect the ark by itself for very long. Although Arramos and his dragon family even now pursued the Watchers who stole the other five, who could tell when or if they would succeed in time to augment the protective anchor?

A low groan sounded from somewhere nearby. Selah sidled up to Joran and nodded toward the giant. "He's alive."

Joran let out a shushing sound. "Mount. Immediately." While he backed toward their weapons, Makaidos lowered his head to the ground, and Selah quietly climbed his neck, dodging the spines protruding from the central ridge.

Stooping slowly, Joran collected his bow and quiver, grabbed Selah's sword and scabbard, and attached each one to his belt. The giant sat up and shook his huge, hairy head, as if casting away a dizzying spell. Makaidos straightened and curled his neck, ready to shoot fire, but Joran jumped in front of him and shook his head sharply. They couldn't risk another battle. Time was short, and they had accomplished their mission.

As the Naphil rose to his feet, Joran ran to Makaidos's flank, leaped up his scaly side, and with help from Selah's outstretched hand, vaulted to his seat in front of her.

The giant charged. Makaidos launched from the ground and smacked him with his tail as he zoomed toward the sky.

Joran clenched a fist. Yes! Victory! Although this Naphil survived the arrow's plunge, he lost the battle and the ovulum. Now he would have to face his demonic father with news of his failure.

As wind whipped across the burns on Joran's back, pain returned with a vengeance. Selah had been kind not to press close as she usually did when they flew together, but her body contact might have been less excruciating than the barrage of stinging air.

After several minutes of flying above the lush forests surrounding the Tigris River, they passed over the remains of Eden's Garden. Below, misshapen trees bent toward the ground like crippled men bracing for a fall. Leafless bushes made up the square boundary of what Father called *The Odious Orchard*, and only weeds and thistles grew alongside short trees with thorny vines and shriveled produce. Then the cursed tree came into view. Still lush and heavy with red, oval fruit, it stood as an odd survivor, a plant that, being a curse itself, resisted the blight.

Finally, they passed over the holy tree, a gorgeous evergreen with hefty branches that effortlessly carried a bounteous supply of ivory fruit. An angel robed in brilliant white stood at one side brandishing a sword that emitted a beam of light. Waving the blade back and forth, he stirred the light into a semitransparent shield that covered the tree, similar to the way their rods formed a wall of sound.

As they flew past Eden's boundary, Joran looked back at the desolation. It seemed as if it might be easy to land in that forsaken garden, but every dragon and human knew what would happen if someone tried. The guardian angel would attack with his sword of light and disintegrate the intruder. Such was Elohim's wrath against anyone who dared to challenge his edicts.

Joran licked his dry lips. What would it be like to taste the guarded fruit? No one knew, of course, but stories abounded. No more thirst? Eternal life? Deliverance from the coming flood? If any of those legends were true, might it be possible to sneak past the angel, snatch one, and give it to Selah? Of course, stealing the fruit would probably spoil its powers, maybe even turn its flesh into poison. Such was the way of Elohim. No one was allowed to take mercy without it first being offered.

His mind drifted back to a day when he actually dared to approach. At the age of twelve, cocky in the vulgarity of his youth, he strolled up to the cherub and demanded some of the fruit. The angel sternly warned him to leave, but young Joran's foolish stubbornness held sway, and after analyzing the sound the protective sword made, he sang a note that he thought might neutralize it. When tiny holes began appearing in the shield, the angel lowered the sword and aimed it at Joran. "Foolish boy!" the angel shouted. And Joran ran, never looking back and never returning to the tree to this day.

Foolish boy. The rebuke rang so true. Not satisfied with this transgression, that very day he went on to carry out his darkest deed, and the scars from his wickedness still remained. He hadn't been able to sing a demon out of a lyre string ever since, no matter how many times he tried. Even now his gifts diminished at a nearly imperceptible rate, as if the evils of that day continued to strangle and squeeze life out of him.

He breathed a silent sigh. No matter. Today we live. Tomorrow we die. He needed his gifts no more.

Biting his tongue, Joran turned toward the front. His thoughts of theft both then and now were juvenile, stupid. And Selah wouldn't touch the fruit anyway. Still, he had to rescue her from the flood somehow, and very little time remained.

21

2

CHAPTER

Reading Minds

Bonnie, wake up."

The whispered call knifed into her dream, and Makaidos and his two riders dissolved and crumbled. The adventures of Joran and Selah had once again ended.

Bonnie opened her eyes. How strange. She was sitting upright against the wall with her wings spread behind her. Had she dozed off in this position, or had she sat up while sleeping?

Ashley knelt on the thin blue mat they shared during the colder months, her stare fixed on the iron bars that separated their jail cell from the hallway—a concrete corridor lit by fluorescent ceiling lamps. From a high window on the opposite side of their cramped quarters, the rays of approaching evening cast yellow beams, painting a silhouette on the linoleum floor—more dark bars, another symbol of their captivity.

Yawning, Bonnie blinked to clear her vision. After a morning of torture, an afternoon nap had been a blessing. With the Healers taking her and Ashley at seemingly random times, day and night, they grabbed a few hours of sleep whenever they could. At least the guards had let them stay together the past few years, supposedly a reward for good behavior, but in reality they had probably decided it wasn't worth the effort to closely monitor two cells.

Ashley pushed her fingers through her shoulder-length mop of brown hair, a signal that something troubled her mind. Her thin lips and bent brow added to the effect.

Bonnie sighed. If only she had Ashley's mind-reading abilities, Ashley wouldn't have to verbalize her thoughts and risk the danger of being overheard. Even an errant whisper might be picked up and cost them exercise or shower privileges.

"What do you sense?"

Ashley raised a finger. "Just a minute."

Bonnie looked at the camera mounted on the windowsill just above head height. Ashley had probably turned down its microphone range before waking her up. Her electronics expertise often came in handy. The silent battle against their captors' spying ways never seemed to end. Of course, the guard who monitored them might eventually notice a lack of ability to hear whispers, so Ashley always turned the volume back to normal before anyone checked the camera for malfunctions. After much practice, she had become adept at avoiding the lens while drawing close to manipulate the settings.

Fortunately, the guards still allowed them to draw a curtain in front of the toilet for privacy, but either she or Ashley had to be in sight at all times, such was the guards' fear, or perhaps hatred, of those with any trace of dragon blood in their veins.

Touching Ashley's hand, Bonnie focused a thought in her direction. *Why did you wake me up? Any news from the men's block or the dungeon?*

"Bits and pieces," Ashley whispered. "It's always like a jigsaw puzzle. Sometimes I think Billy's somewhere nearby, and other

24

times I get the impression that he's not. Stella guards her mind well, but some of her cronies let a few things spill. I woke you up, because someone's thoughts mentioned a name I haven't heard in a long time."

Bonnie smiled. Ashley was being dramatic, waiting for the obvious question. But that didn't matter. They didn't have any other entertainment, so an occasional bit of drama helped them exercise their minds. *What name?*

Ashley turned away from the camera and mouthed, "Mardon."

Mardon? Bonnie stared at Ashley's newly morose expression. The name conjured so many images! Mardon, the son of King Nimrod thousands of years ago, wandered as a spirit in Hades before traveling to Second Eden. A brilliant scientist, he once tried and failed to bring Earth and Heaven together with a cross-dimensional connection. Later, with help from his mother, Semiramis, he used his prowess as a geneticist to weaken Acacia, one of the Oracles of Fire. Although he failed in the long run, he did great damage, including indirectly bringing about Acacia's death. Since he and his mother continued to exist in a post-dead state, imprisoned in Second Eden, they could still potentially cause problems.

25

Bonnie cast another thought at Ashley. *Any context to the mention of Mardon?*

"No. I'm just piecing the puzzle together."

Do you think Mardon is behind the recent spike in the anthrozils' disease?

"Maybe. He's smart enough to do it. He has the know-how."

True. Have you heard anything new about the disease? Does my mother have it?

"No word on that at all." Ashley rose to her feet and hugged herself, shivering. Her arms wrapped around her threadbare navy sweatshirt all the way to her back. "I just wish Walter would visit."

Bonnie nodded. Even lacking Ashley's mind-reading ability, it wasn't hard to guess her thoughts. It had been a month since her beloved husband last came by. She had smuggled prison security passwords to him during his most recent visit, hoping he could use them to break into the facility, but since the prison administration frequently changed the codes, would they be out-of-date already? Not only that, Walter's latest coded message included dire news about the strange disease. It had infected the original anthrozils, the humans who had once been dragons. He didn't provide many details, only that some were getting weaker, as if constantly exposed to candlestones, though the energy-draining gems hadn't affected them since their transformations.

As Ashley stretched, her sweatshirt rode up a notch, exposing her wasted frame. Bonnie cringed. Ashley was so thin! So pitifully thin! The radioactive tracers their captors pumped into her bloodstream brought about a nightly vomiting session. No matter how bland the food she ate in the evening, she lost it all before bedtime. Fortunately, Stella hated the odor, so she provided a toilet brush and cleanser. Thank the Lord for small favors.

Leaning forward, Bonnie extended a wing. "Come. Sit close."

Ashley sat, scooted into the wing's embrace, and leaned her head against Bonnie's. They extended their jeans-covered legs and lined up their Nikes, new pairs the jailers had recently provided. Before the replacement, Ashley's right sole was half detached, and a big toe protruded from each shoe. With a rip across a Nike logo and multiple knots splicing her laces, Bonnie's weren't much better, but she didn't try to run in place as often as Ashley did, opting instead to keep her wings in shape by hovering in the room. If she had to run very far, she might be in trouble, but Ashley would have no problem. Even as sick and thin as she was, she probably could outrun any of those skirted cows patrolling the prison floor.

"So," Ashley said, now whispering without moving her lips, "Catherine dropped some thoughts about anthrozils. I guess the other guards haven't given her tips on how to keep me from reading her mind."

"She's been here, what? Three weeks?"

"Something like that. Anyway, her rookie brain leaked that—"

"Wait." Bonnie added a thought. *Do your Catherine imperson-ation. That is, if it's something you can tell me out loud.*

"My pleasure." Ashley put on a dour expression and lowered her voice's pitch. "Before I came to this God-forsaken pit of a prison, I was a patrol pig, an evil sister of the devil who hunted down children and sent them to labor camps." She sneered at Bon-nie. "Just because I like to see dragonkind suffer."

Bonnie laughed. *Your impersonation is perfect!*

"It might come in handy someday, so I've been practicing."

Bonnie looked at the window and imagined the patrol pigs, the Enforcers, as they called themselves. Some sat at computers using the latest spy technology, and some went door-to-door in the middle of the night, all for the purpose of tracking down her children, as well as other anthrozils, such as Thomas and Mariel, who might still roam the earth. She had already heard through the prison grapevine that Catherine had been one of the Enforcers, so Ashley's monologue revealed nothing new. The arrival of a rookie guard, however, resurrected hope that news from the outside world lay only a careless thought away, prompting questions in Bonnie's mind, questions she hadn't asked in a long time.

Any news on Thomas or Mariel?

Ashley shook her head. "I suppose their mothers are still searching, assuming the disease hasn't sapped their strength."

"You're probably right." Bonnie ran her fingers across her abdomen, focusing her thoughts on the womb that once carried Charles and Karen. A mother can never forget. Kaylee and Dallas would never give up their search for their babies, no matter how sick they were. *How about Tamara? I've been worried about her.*

"Same here," Ashley said. "How long has she been missing?"

A year, I think.

A tear sparkled in Ashley's eye. "She's an easy target. Too easy."

27

Bonnie nodded. *I know what you mean. I hope Listener is coping.*

"Don't worry. She's as tough as nails."

So did Catherine leak any other information?

Ashley brushed the tear away and put on her Catherine-like sneer. "I had a lead on a male anthrozil, but I'm not about to mention his name. That brilliant Ashley is bound to hear it. Since it was a dead end, and since they spent a lot of money and manpower on my 'sure thing,' I got busted to jail duty. Anyway, those scoundrels at headquarters won't let me follow up on a female who has a suspicious talent. She can hear things beyond any reasonable limits. If someone else finds her and takes credit, I'll throw a hissy fit! That'll teach them!"

Bonnie gave the camera a furtive glance. Ashley was being less cautious than usual.

"Anyway," Ashley said, reverting to her own voice, "Catherine created an image in her mind of a rival that made my skin crawl— a pale, winged, emo-looking freak wearing black. I suppose he's the one who might take credit for what she learned through her snooping."

So this female has super hearing? I have never heard of that as a dragon trait.

"Neither have I, so maybe it's another dead end. Anyway, the girl is the right age to be Karen, but Catherine didn't communicate any traits for the boy she was looking for, only that he's also a teenager."

Aren't you concerned about saying all this out loud? You might never get any information out of Catherine again. Besides, no showers for a week makes for smelly anthrozils.

"I'm hoping to get her in trouble. Anything to bust that patrol pig down to garbage duty. You remember what those monsters do. I'll take a month without showers if we can flush that slime out of here."

Bonnie leaned back against the wall. The night the federal marshal stole Charles and Karen still haunted every hour. As he

28

and a social worker hauled her babies away, they screamed. She cried. One of the marshal's goons had already clubbed Billy, rendering him unconscious, and held a gun to his head to make sure no one tried to stop the government-authorized kidnapping. It was a dark night, indeed.

Yet, hope remained. Word came from Walter that Sir Patrick of Glastonbury, England, a former dragon who exercised great influence in foster-care circles, later managed to alter their records and hide their identities so that no one knew their origins. Apparently Patrick had a spy in government circles, but Walter never learned how the spy managed to lose Charles and Karen in the system, since they were lost to Walter as well.

As she had a thousand times before, Bonnie imagined what their faces looked like now. If Charles and Karen had dragon traits, what might they be? They wouldn't know why they had them or how to hide them. Still, since the official persecution of anthrozils was no longer a secret, and so many had joined the insane hunt for anyone who had strange abilities, people with a trait that appeared outside the norm now tended to hide the ability, fearing the persecutors. Maybe Charles and Karen would be careful to do the same.

"Catherine also regurgitated some of the usual tripe," Ashley added, "but I think that was intentional, kind of like a taunt."

"The usual tripe?" Bonnie asked out loud.

"You know. If our escape attempts ended, we could get out of maximum security, get transferred to a cushy dorm, have more contact with the outside world. That sort of thing."

Bonnie let out a huff. Escape attempts. What a laugh! Sure, someone from the outside had apparently tried to break in and set them free. One night, a note tied to a stone sailed through their window. Its laser-printed message said, "Be ready at three a.m." But when that hour arrived, no rescuer showed up. The next morning, the guards transferred them to another cell, this one with a surveillance camera. It seemed like a manufactured reason to increase their punishment.

"Catherine is coming." Ashley kissed Bonnie's cheek. "I'll pray for you."

Bonnie unwrapped Ashley and rose to her feet. Having a mind reader as a warning system had proved helpful hundreds of times over the years.

"How's your neck?" Ashley asked. "I see new abrasions."

Bonnie rubbed her throat. "Stella stretched me pretty far. If this keeps up, I'll be a giraffe."

"If the stress tests don't end soon, we'll both look like half-starved zoo animals. I think they enjoy inventing new ways to make us suffer."

A metal-on-metal click sounded. Catherine, standing in her prim calf-length skirt, long-sleeved white shirt, and form-fitting navy blazer, pushed a key into the cell door's lock. "It's Bonnie's turn to see the Healers," she said without emotion.

As she turned the key, her brow furrowed, unusual for her, since bobby pins pulled her dyed-black hair into a forehead-stretching bun. "It's unlocked. How did that happen?"

Bonnie glanced at Ashley and sent a thought her way. *Is that the third time?*

Ashley nodded but said nothing.

Catherine slid the door open and stormed inside. Stocky, muscular, and sporting a baton in a sheath on one hip and a taser on the other, she was more of a pit bull than a patrol pig. "What is the meaning of this?" she bellowed. "How did you unlock the cell?"

"We have no idea how it got unlocked," Ashley said in a matter-of-fact tone. "If you'd think about it for half a second, maybe even you could figure out that there's no benefit for us to unlock it and then sit here and take the punishment for the offense."

Catherine whipped out her baton and pointed it at Ashley. "Don't patronize me! I won't take any guff from a vile dragon woman! You and your kind are all alike. If I had it my way, you

30

would all be executed on sight, including that treasonous husband of yours. He might have everyone else fooled, but not me. You infected him with dragon poison, so he'll never be pure again. As soon as I can prove he's a double agent, I'll make sure he joins all the other dragon sympathizers in Hell."

"I apologize." Ashley rose to her feet and walked up to Catherine until they stood nearly nose to nose. With her tone smooth and calm she said, "I didn't mean to patronize you. I meant to insult that bigoted, egotistical wad of slime you call a brain. Your vomitus ramblings make a UFO conspiracy theorist sound like Einstein."

Catherine swung the baton and smacked Ashley across her face, sending her staggering. Bonnie jumped up and caught her with a wing.

Glaring at Catherine, Ashley touched an emerging purplish lump on her cheek.

"That'll teach you to stay in your place … dragon." Catherine waved the baton toward the hallway. "Bannister, it's time to go."

After steadying Ashley, Bonnie pulled in her wings. There was more method to Ashley's insult than madness. Getting the guards to open their minds to her probing sometimes required a stoking of their passions.

Bonnie cast a thought at Ashley. *If you picked up anything new from her mind, let me know later.*

Ashley gave her an almost imperceptible nod. "Remember to sing your psalm. It always helps."

"I'll remember."

With Catherine's baton pressed against her spine, Bonnie shuffled down the hallway, wincing at the light. The fluorescent lamps in the ceiling were always harsh here, but not as brutal as in the lab. Everything seemed brutal there. From the needles to the electrodes to the probing pill cameras, there was nothing gentle about that overly sanitized chamber. Even the white-smocked Healers' condescending smiles were enough to make anyone barf. That is, of course, if one happened to be observing from the sharp side of the needle. The so-called scientists often chattered with glee about their new findings, ignoring the fact that they extracted their plunder through government-approved torture and the blood, sweat, and tears of their victims.

Bonnie let out a silent sigh. Yes, force the few to suffer so the many could benefit. All in the name of science. All in the name of progress.

After traveling through a series of ninety-degree turns and similarly harshly lit corridors, they halted in front of a thick steel door. The sign on the front provided its usual warning—*Healers and Specimens Only.*

Catherine punched a red button on a wall-hanging box and barked into it. "I have Bannister."

A tinny voice responded. "We're ready. Send her in."

A buzzer sounded. Catherine jerked the door open. With a final shove from her baton, she pushed Bonnie through. The door clicked shut behind her, the signal that torture would soon begin.

Ahead, three women stood in a row, smiling as they clutched their clipboards against their chests, like charlatan preachers shielding their Bibles from those who might see what it really says. Three windows lined the far wall with the head of a hospital-style bed under each one. Leather straps hung from the side railings, another foreboding sign.

As the woman in the middle—Dr. Myers, according to her perfectly lettered plastic name tag—stepped toward Bonnie, her instruments of torture came into view on a pristine paper-covered bed behind her. With wires and electrodes attached to a metallic hat sitting on the pillow of the rightmost bed, and an IV stand ready with a hanging bag of sedative-spiked saline, it seemed that the evening promised another electrical nightmare. The Healers planned to light up the specimen with cell-shocking probes, callously looking for clues that would unlock the answers they craved.

"Come, Mrs. Bannister," Dr. Myers said with a mechanical smile. "Your bed is waiting. We turned down the power, and the sedative will be stronger, so it shouldn't hurt as much this time."

One of the other doctors handed her a hospital gown, not bothering to offer a fake smile. "You know the drill," she said in a gruff tone.

After changing into the gown and laying her clothes on the middle bed's railing, Bonnie slid onto the prepared bed, spread out her wings, and laid her head on the half-sized pillow. She closed her eyes and mentally drew pictures of Dr. Myers attaching the metal cap and strapping her wrists to the bed frame, grunting as she pulled them. For some reason, she put extra effort into that task, probably a reflection of her sadistic nature.

Bonnie peeked at a strap—tight and pinching her skin. If all went as it usually did, the straps would be loose when she awakened, whether the Healers were around during recovery or not. It seemed strange that they would be so diligent now and so careless after the tests.

She closed her eyes again and let her body relax as she hummed her new rendition of her favorite psalm, allowing the words to pass quietly through her lips. In a way, it might be better if they would turn the power all the way up or give her a sedative overdose. Then she could fly back to Heaven and try to help Charles and Karen from there. If they really were being tracked by Enforcers, what good would it do to live through this ordeal, just to go back to her cell and rot?

As the needle pierced her arm, she winced. Would living in such pain, blinded by iron bars and concrete, be better than dying and going to Heaven where she could watch all three of her beloveds, where she could drop to her knees in front of the God of mercy and appeal for their protection and deliverance?

The sedative numbed her mind. Even the pinching straps seemed to relax. The shocks would come soon, as would another dream.

33

"I think she's under now," Dr. Myers said. "You can show yourself."

"Very well."

Bonnie tried to open her eyes, though without success. That was a man's voice, but the Healers had always been women.

"We will have to conduct the test quickly," the man continued. "I must get back to the weapons as soon as possible."

"Of course. We've already proven that the synthetic candlestones work quite well as a weakening agent, so we need you to examine the genetic code after we conduct a new stress test. We're hoping for more physical changes this time."

"I know what you mean. Darkening her hair is hardly proof that you have altered her code. Your foolish attempts to create stress have failed to produce results. I suggest that you stop the routine torture immediately, including the withholding of heat in their cell."

Bonnie forced her eyes open. The man stood at her bedside, looking at one of the monitors. Although burn scars covered his face, his identity was clear. *Mardon!*

Letting her eyelids drop, Bonnie shivered. How long had that mad scientist been involved with their experiments? What kind of weapons was he working on? Knowing Mardon, they would be powerful and designed for evil. And now he was doing experiments on her, somehow trying to alter her genetics. She had noticed her darker hair but thought it had come from aging. Now it was clear that he and the Healers were manipulating her traits.

"I think she saw me," Mardon said.

"No worries." Dr. Myers's voice sounded calm and confident. "The drug will purge the memory. The only images she'll keep are her dreams."

With unconsciousness looming, Bonnie let out a breath and silently prayed. *Stop this madman. Send a message to Billy or Walter. Help them save our children.*

Sitting on his bunk, Matt looked around the empty barracks. With his fellow cadets finally gone, he had a moment to himself, a chance to breathe. The afternoon drills had been fun but exhausting, especially the five-mile run with full gear. Dropping and shooting at robotic targets was a blast—a sweaty, muscle-draining blast.

He opened the newspaper, the latest edition of the *Hesperia Star*, and read the headline—DRAGON SIGHTING IN LOS ANGELES.

Shaking his head, he turned the page. Southern California was great, but so many loony birds roosted here, the dragon hysteria had gotten out of control. One letter to the editor after another railed about Second Eden and the dragons living there, that humans never should have trusted them and shouldn't trust them now. One letter writer called for a nuclear attack, but, of course, he was clueless. Most civilians didn't understand that Second Eden controlled the portals to their world. They assumed the military could do anything. Such was their false sense of security.

"Package for you, Fletcher."

The mail clerk stood at the barracks door and tossed a brown rectangular object. Matt pushed the newspaper off his lap and caught the package. He turned it until the lettering shifted upright, then read the name above the return address.

"Foley," he whispered to himself. *Who could that be?*

He tore away the wrapping paper, revealing a worn, spiral-bound journal with a floral design in pink, purple, and yellow pastels. Handwritten words at the bottom read:

Silver Tokens
My Hopes, My Prayers, My Dreams
December 2002
Bonnie Conner

He rifled through the journal. The same person had filled every page with flowing script, obviously a female, judging from the elegance and, of course, the design and name on the cover.

35

Footsteps sounded from the door. "Hey, Fletcher! Aren't you coming to the pizza party?"

Matt glanced up. Across the width of the barracks, Rick strolled to his bunk, the middle one of seven. He stood in front of a wall-mounted mirror and brushed his crew cut. Wearing civilian clothes—khaki slacks, long-sleeved sky-blue shirt, and a red tie—he looked almost human.

"I'm thinking about it," Matt said.

"Victoria will be there." A chuckle flavored his tone.

"Figures." Matt refocused on the journal. For some reason it carried an allure, a drawing power that begged him to read every word. "Victoria's a bit too … I don't know …"

Rick turned toward him, retying his tie. "Aggressive?"

"I guess that's part of it." Matt wanted to say *shallow*, but that was too blunt. Victoria was nice enough, and he had tried to engage her in stimulating conversation. Yet, when he asked her about history, philosophy, or anything unrelated to celebrities or popular music, she usually answered with a blank stare or somehow brought the topic back to the latest movie she had seen. She seemed no deeper than a layer of lipstick. Still, at least she wasn't cold and calculating … like Darcy. "I don't know why she's zeroed in on me."

Rick laughed. "Don't lie, Fletcher. You save a girl's life, she's gonna think you're a rock star."

"I suppose so." Memories of the previous "mingling," as the drill sergeant called the social events, came to mind. He and Victoria were paired up at random to go on an ultimate thrill ride at a traveling carnival. The ride drops two people from a hundred feet up and catches them in a net, but for some reason the net hadn't been raised when the floor opened. Just before the drop, he grabbed Victoria's wrist and the ride's frame. Then he hung there with her dangling in his grip until help could arrive. Everyone seemed amazed that he noticed the missing net in the dark,

36

because the whole idea was for the riders to drop without being able to see it.

And he didn't see it. Somehow he just knew it wasn't there. "I guess I got lucky."

"Lucky is better than good, I always say." Rick tossed his brush to Matt's bed, making it land on the newspaper. "Better tame that mess or the sergeant won't let you keep your hair that long. As hot as you stay all the time, you should get a cool buzz cut. Then you'll be as handsome as I am."

"Whatever." Matt waited for Rick to leave before combing his fingers through his hair. Of course, it wasn't more than two inches long, but to Mr. Crew Cut it probably looked like a stringy mop. Yet, the length of his hair was the least of his problems. Rick wasn't the only one to notice his body heat issue. All summer long, he had to drink twice as much water as the others did just to avoid heat stroke. Fortunately, with winter coming, it wouldn't be a problem. Being a human furnace made him eat more, but at least he always stayed warm.

He refocused on the journal. Now with every cadet at the pizza social, maybe he could get a few minutes to figure out this mystery. He turned to a page somewhere near the middle and began reading.

Dear God,

Tomorrow is my birthday. It's hard to believe that I'm going to be a teenager. One of my older acquaintances says that I will soon become more like her, that once I get exposed to the "real world," I will turn away from my "childish" faith and realize that no one is as obsessed with "religion" as I am.

Dear Father above, I pledge to you that I will not become like her—sullen, moody, and obsessed with appearance. I will cling to my faith, like a child in some ways—believing without seeing, hoping without visible proof, crawling into your spiritual lap, and luxuriating in your presence. Yet, in other ways, I have

already put away childish things, and I am learning that this world is a dark place, often a lonely place.

I know that even as I walk an obedient path, there is always more to learn, new wisdom to gather from your generous hand, more suffering to endure for the kingdom of Jesus Christ. Many are the tongues that tantalize with flattering words. Many are the hands that extend riches that come with a snare. And many are the hearts of my friends who willingly embrace the false offerings.

Alas, my Father! It is such a lonely path! I have no friends my age who understand. Even most adults think my "obsession with religion" is unhealthy, and no matter how many times I try to explain that what I possess is love—love for you and for them—they assume that my passion has overcome my senses. To them, I am a fanatic.

Not even Daddy understands. I overheard him say just two days ago, "No one could be that righteous. When the hormones kick in, she'll change."

I am thankful that Mama defends me. She said, "I pray with all my might that she never changes, hormones or no hormones."

Dear Father, I vow never to leave my first love. With your help, my love for you will never flag or falter. I will be a light to this world. I will be a shining city on a hill. I will be your friend.

Although tomorrow is supposed to be a day of celebration, I feel dark hours creeping up on the morn's horizon. Like spiders spinning a web, evil forces lurk at my threshold and fashion snares for my feet.

When comes my hour to face these dangers, will you be my friend, my comfort, my solace? I know you will, but I ask, knowing that you want to hear my requests. So I pray in faith, believing that you will honor your promises and stay by my side when darkness hides the light, for when I hold your hand, you are all the light I need.

Your friend,
Bonnie Conner

Matt brushed a tear from his eye. A twelve-year-old wrote this? Okay, she was turning thirteen the next day, but still, how could anyone so young be so beautifully expressive? And the sentiments seemed to flow from the page as if the words had come alive and pierced his heart with her cry for help. These words were as deep as the ocean. This girl, unlike so many others, understood what was valuable in life.

He looked at the cover again and noted the year. Bonnie Conner would be in her thirties now. Since she wrote so eloquently, this journal was probably a valuable keepsake. Why would someone send it to a high school guy who has never heard of her?

As he slid his finger under the page to turn it, an odd sensation stung his gut—turmoil, trouble—an alert. He snapped his head up. A ball rocketed toward him. With a quick snap of his hand, he grabbed it out of the air, letting it smack against his palm.

He rubbed the white ball's red stitches. A baseball? He looked at the barracks doorway. Dr. Carter, the school administrator, stood there with a man wearing camouflage from his pants to his shirt to his baseball cap.

39

"You were right," Dr. Carter said. "Matt will go with you."

"Only if he's willing." The visitor's voice was firm but friendly.

Dr. Carter glanced between the visitor and Matt. "Since when do we care if they're willing?"

"Just let me worry about that." The visitor kept his stare on Matt. "I don't think it will be hard to convince him. The alternatives are not appealing."

"Very well."

As Dr. Carter left, the man walked closer, smiling as he touched the bill of his cap. "Hello, Matt. I'm Walter Foley."

Matt tucked the journal under his arm and rose to his feet. "It's nice to meet you, sir," he said, extending his hand.

As they shook hands, Mr. Foley nodded at the ball. "That was a great catch you made. Very impressive reflexes."

"Thank you." Matt displayed the ball in his palm. "Were you testing me for some reason? I already play for the team, but the season doesn't start for a while."

"It was a test, but not for playing baseball." Mr. Foley took the ball and dug into a scuff mark with his fingernail. "Word around the school has it that your reflexes are, shall we say, more like intuition?"

Matt glanced at Rick's bunk. Who could tell what stories he and the other guys had been spreading? "If you mean when I dumped a rattler out of my boot, I always check my boots before I put them on."

"No." Mr. Foley nodded toward the front window. Approaching sunset had dimmed the military school's facilities, but the football field and marching grounds were still easy to see. "I mean when you jerked your drill sergeant to the ground just before lightning struck."

"We were in a thunderstorm, and I heard a sizzling noise."

"And when you pulled a buddy from a jeep right before it exploded."

"I smelled gas and thought I saw a spark."

"And when you insisted that another friend check his parachute again before his jump."

"Yeah. The way it was packed, it wouldn't have deployed." Matt shrugged. "A lucky guess. It just didn't look right."

Mr. Foley tossed the baseball into the air and caught it. "And I suppose you heard this coming toward you. Baseballs make a lot of noise, don't they?"

Matt scanned the stranger. His toned arms, bushy eyebrows, and square jaw made him look formidable. And the camo outfit just added to the idea that he probably wasn't a man anyone would want to rile up. "I see your point, sir, but why are you here?" He lifted the journal. "And why did you mail this to me?"

"First of all, you can cut the *sir* business. I'm not in the military. Just call me Walter. Second, my associates and I have been

40

scanning every news story in the world searching for someone who has a danger-sensing ability like yours."

"Your associates?"

"Actually, two computers I call Larry and Lois do most of the searching, but a techno-geek named Carly and my sister Shelly help a lot, too. They operate the computers." Walter tossed the ball to the bed. "Anyway, I didn't mail the journal. I brought it with me and asked it to be delivered. I watched you read it from the window to see how you'd react."

Matt bent the cover and let the pages flip across his thumb. "So I cried a little. Does that disqualify me?"

"Just the opposite." Walter clasped Matt's forearm. "I needed to know that you have a heart. It's going to take a lot more than military training and intuition to get the job done."

Matt stared at Walter. Somehow this soldier-wannabe-turned-stalker had convinced Dr. Carter that he was on the up-and-up, so maybe he wasn't a militia lunatic. "Okay. So you found me. What do you have in mind?"

"To find the truth and free some prisoners."

"Prisoners?" Adrenaline pumped through Matt's body. "You have friends in prison? People falsely accused?"

"I do, and one of them is more precious to me than life itself."

Matt tapped his finger on the journal. "Oh, I get it. The girl who wrote this is your friend, and you wanted me to see how wonderful she is so I'd get stoked about helping you rescue her." He pressed his lips together and nodded. "Good strategy. I could get excited about helping her."

"I hope so." Walter took the journal and set his finger next to the name on the cover. "I believe that Bonnie Conner is your mother."

"My mother?" Matt backed away a step. Heat filtered into his cheeks, angry heat. "My mother deserted me. She was a drug addict who left me at a church when I was barely one year old."

41

He jabbed a finger at the journal. "How could anyone who wrote that abandon a baby?"

"She didn't abandon you. That's just a story someone made up."

"A story?" Matt mentally counted to ten. Getting angry at this guy wouldn't do any good. He had to keep a lid on his emotions. "How would you know?"

Walter pointed at himself. "Because I invented the story. I wasn't the one who put it in place, but the basic idea was mine."

"It was your idea?" Matt shook his head. "I hope you don't mind me asking, but aren't we just playing cat and mouse with all the back-and-forth talk? Wouldn't it be better just to tell me everything you know?"

"I can't tell you everything." Walter glanced around as if nervous about who might be listening. "But I will as soon as I can." He leaned closer and whispered, "Have you ever heard of Bonnie Bannister?"

"Bannister?" Matt glanced at the barracks television sitting on a table in a far corner. "Sure. The woman with dragon wings. But she's kind of dropped out of the news lately."

Walter touched the name on the journal again. "Bonnie Bannister and Bonnie Conner are one and the same."

"Are you serious?" Matt said, raising his voice. "You think I'm the son of one of those anthrozils?"

Walter nodded. "In fact, now that I see your face and hear your voice when you're agitated, I'm sure of it. You are definitely the son of Billy Bannister."

"But they're … they're …" Matt grabbed the first word that came to mind. "Weird."

"Weird? Well, in some ways, but so are a lot of normal humans."

"Yeah, but anthrozils eat fish while they're still alive, and some of them need to drink human blood once a month to survive."

Walter rolled his eyes. "That's nonsense. You've been brain-washed by the bigots."

"Bigots?" The word stung. He had always tried to make friends with the outcasts, being one himself most of his life. "Well, I don't hate the anthrozils. It's just that they kind of … creep me out."

"Then get used to being creeped out every time you look at a mirror."

Matt glanced again at the doorway. So that was why Dr. Carter said what he did. He seemed ready to execute the newly found anthrozil. "Look, if you're really an Enforcer, you're going to need more proof than a baseball and a journal to put me away."

"I can arrange for more proof, but I'm not an Enforcer. Now that Dr. Carter thinks you're an anthrozil, you're in more danger here than with me." Walter withdrew a creased sheet of paper from his pocket. "Do you like adventure?"

"Well, yeah. That's one of the reasons I'm at the academy." One of the other reasons came to mind—escaping from his foster sister, Darcy. No use mentioning that.

43

Walter unfolded the paper and began reading. "Matthew Fletcher excels in every category of physical training. With superior scores in marksmanship, hand-to-hand combat, obstacle course drills, wilderness expeditions, survival skills, paratrooper training, and endurance tests, he will be an outstanding candidate for any branch of the military that requires extraordinary physical prowess and stamina." He refolded the note. "Your drill sergeant wrote that."

Matt let out a low whistle. "I had no idea he noticed. He just barks at me all day long."

"He noticed."

"Well, it's about time I got some credit for how hard I've worked. You wouldn't believe what we have to—"

"Credit?" Walter grabbed a fistful of Matt's shirt and pulled him close. "Listen, Fletcher, if you want credit, then go do an extra five miles on the track or turn in another book report, but if you want to help me, you're going to have to forget about credit. I live in the real world. My wife is rotting in prison because of bigots who think she deserves to die because of how she was born. She and your mother are tortured daily because of eggheaded fools who think their research is more important than two human lives, no matter how much they suffer. Credit or no credit, I'm in this to rescue my wife, or die trying. The question is, are you ready to grow up and put your life on the line for your mother?"

Keeping his head still, Matt looked at Walter's tight fist, then at his red face. It might be better to stay quiet than to risk saying something stupid.

Walter released him and let out a sigh. "If you want to come with me, then get your wilderness gear, including your rappelling equipment. I have rope and everything else we'll need in my vehicle. It's a blue Ford SUV with West Virginia plates. If you're not there in ten minutes, I'm hitting the road without you. It's a two-hour flight and a one-hour drive, so I can't afford to waste any time." With that, he turned an abrupt about-face and marched out.

44

Matt smoothed his shirt. Wow! That guy was intense! And he had reason to be. If his wife was being tortured, he had to move Heaven and Earth to set her free.

As he watched Walter stalk away, he backed toward the bed. Should he pack his gear? Risk his life for someone he didn't even know? The idea that a dragon-winged anthrozil might be his mother seemed so absurd. For years he had pictured an emaciated street hooker with stringy hair and dirty clothes, someone who chose to destroy her body for another drug fix, someone who sold her baby just to get her daily high.

And now? Now he was stuck. Should he stay here and try to convince Dr. Carter that Walter Foley was one of the loony birds, or should he go out on a wild adventure that promised nothing more than a ride with someone who might be the head loony?

He sat heavily on the bed. Something shifted near the newspaper. The journal lay next to his pillow. Walter must have tossed it there while he wasn't looking.

As he picked it up, it fell open to the same page he had read earlier. He focused on the entry's ending paragraph. *When comes my hour to face these dangers, will you be my friend, my comfort, my solace?*

The words stabbed his heart. An image formed in his mind, a crying girl in chains reaching out for help, dragon wings spreading out behind her. Then she changed into a grown woman, still reaching, still crying as she sat in a dim, dingy prison cell.

Matt rose slowly to his feet. It didn't matter. Whether his mother was a drug-addicted hooker, a crying twelve-year-old, or a grown woman in prison, it just didn't matter. Walter's friend, whoever she really was, needed help, and Matt Fletcher would give it to her.

45

3

CHAPTER

THE COLOR OF MERCY

Joran and Selah sat side by side, a camel blanket covering their legs. The evening air had brought a chill, and the campfire to Selah's left did little to warm their skin. A high rocky ridge hemmed them in, blocking a stronger wind from the highlands, which helped quite a bit. The nearby tent's canvas didn't flap at all, promising them a warm place to sleep when night fell.

Father sat in front of them, leaving an arm's-length gap in between. With Watchers always threatening, it seemed odd to be sitting out in the open without a dragon in sight. Yet, the scaly sentinels remained close, hidden in alcoves, watching, ready to fly to the aid of their human allies at the first sign of a demon's approach.

Playing a lyre with his leathery hands, Father closed his eyes and hummed with the song of the strings. Most of the notes stayed in the low range, and the slow rhythm added a sense of sadness to the tune.

"It settles the dragons," Father said in the midst of his dreamy humming. "The Watchers are near, and the great flood looms. The

47

dragons know they will die tomorrow, so I think we can forgive them for their melancholy."

Selah raised a pair of fingers. "Except for two."

"That is correct, my dear." Father strummed the strings and began a new song, this one even slower. "One blessed dragon couple will accompany Noah, and they will survive to repopulate the world with their kind."

Joran drew a mental sketch—the great ark with all the animals on board. He had seen it from the outside several times, as well as the plans for the inside. The streams of mockers who passed by daily, hurling insults and scoffing questions, kept him from drawing closer, despite Noah's invitations to explore the divinely inspired masterpiece. Besides, walking through the refuge would only deepen the sadness of being forsaken. How could he rejoice about the handiwork when he and Selah would soon be drowning under its hull?

This wrathful judgment was so wrong, so terribly wrong! Yet, as always, there wasn't anything he could do about it. He had to cast away the thoughts and focus on something positive.

Trying to keep his voice from cracking, he whispered the only question that came to mind. "Have the two dragons been chosen?"

Father continued the sad melody. "The last I heard, they had settled on Arramos and Shachar. They are the oldest, which is a drawback, but they are still able to bear young. Since they are also the wisest, they will be able to help and advise Noah and his family after the flood subsides. Not only that, Shachar has a special gift that will be quite useful."

"Her scales sometimes glow," Selah said. "Is that it?"

"That is not the gift I had in mind, but it still could benefit. Eve herself told me that Shachar's scales carry radiance that restores what was lost. I am not aware of the meaning of that phrase, and Shachar has not explained. Perhaps it is better that we do not know."

Joran looked at the western ridge, barely visible now in the failing light. Well beyond that boundary, the ark stood waiting for the coming deluge. "Are Arramos and Shachar on the ark now?"

"Not yet. Every dragon is needed for battling the Watchers until the last moment."

"What if one of them is killed by a Watcher?"

"Then Elohim will choose another pair." Father stopped playing and set the lyre upright on his knees. "Joran, your concern is valid. In your perspective, Elohim's plan rides on spindly legs, as if it could topple at the slightest breeze. His purpose seems harsh and vindictive, and when you and Selah inhale the killing waters tomorrow, nothing will be able to persuade you otherwise. Yet, I want to show you something that might provide a sliver of solace." As he plucked each string in turn, the vibrating note radiated a trembling aura of white. "Now watch carefully."

Joran leaned forward. Father's lyre was as much a part of their family life as hard work and baked bread, but now, on the eve of their final day on earth, it seemed more than a musical instrument that had accompanied their songs and laughter. Tonight it was a symbol of life itself.

"This lyre," Father said, "belonged to my father, Enoch. Like myself, he was a bard, but a much greater prophetic singer than I ever hoped to be. Since he was taken by Elohim long before you were born, you heard his songs only through my poor recitations, and you heard me playing his lyre in a vain attempt to recreate his prowess. In these final days, however, Elohim has allowed me to uncover one of Enoch's secrets." He strummed the strings, again making them radiate a white glow. "This instrument has been blessed as a visionary device. With it, you can see places far out of reach of your own eyes, and the strings are able to reproduce the sounds in those places, enabling you to hear every laugh and sigh."

Father's fingers played nimbly in spite of their age-inflicted bends, creating a melody of stunning beauty that only his experienced hand could produce.

"Can anyone in those places hear you if you call out to them?" Joran asked.

Father hummed as he replied. "Why do you ask?"

49

"Because Selah and I thought we heard you call us earlier. We had just finished battling a Watcher, and it seemed like your voice came to us from far away."

"Ah! Then you *did* hear my call! I could see you, but I could not tell if you could hear me." Father waved a hand in front of the strings. "Images appear in this area, including scenes from the past, but, of course, I could not hope to speak to people in those visions, because they are no longer there to hear me. It seems that the most effective melody for creating the images is our traditional love song, the one Enoch composed to encourage love among siblings."

Father again strummed the strings in order—E, F-sharp, G, A, B, C, and D—calling out a name with each note. "Adam. Seth. Enos. Cainan. Mahalaleel. Jared. Enoch. These are the seven patriarchs who taught me the ways of Elohim. All warned of the wrath that would come if people rebelled. Yet, Elohim provided a way of escape for the righteous, a symbol of a greater deliverance yet to come. Noah's ark is merely gopher wood that saves body and breath, while the greatest of all arks saves soul and spirit. All seven of my forefathers prophesied the deliverer's coming, and we look forward to seeing his arrival, though we will not be able to do so in person. We will bear witness from a higher plane."

Joran gazed at his father's face. He seemed so sad, yet joyful at the same time—a man filled with sorrow, yet hoping for the sun to rise on a brighter dawn.

"Now that you have heard what the lyre can do …" Father laid it at his side, reached into a saddlebag, and began withdrawing ovula, setting them in a circle one by one. With each placement, the song of the ovulum hummed. No two songs were alike, yet when arranged, they harmonized perfectly, as if gathering together to form a choir. After placing the seventh and completing the circle, he set the bag at his side, though something still weighed it down.

The choir sang a chorus that plunged deep into Joran's soul. He laughed, then his eyes welled with tears. His biceps flexed, ready to fight and defend. Then, as they relaxed, he slid his hand into Selah's and compressed it warmly. Whispered words spilled out unbidden. "I would do anything for you, Selah. You know that, don't you?"

With tears sparkling in her eyes, she raised his hand to her lips and kissed it. "Of course I do, and I will never desert you. I am your rhythm and harmony. We will live and die together."

"I see that their songs have affected you," Father said. "This is a good sign, for those with hearts of evil are too hardened to allow the influence to penetrate."

As the eggs continued singing, each one glowed with its own color—blue, a shade that matched the sky just after dawn; yellow like the down of a chick; the green of a grape leaf; violet as the fruit of grapevines; orange as brilliant as the sun's setting rays; indigo of a shade that nearly matched the violet, though not quite as dark, perhaps a grape of a different variety; and, finally, a red that shone like a scarlet ruby. The colors blended in a swirl at the center, painting a portrait of their perfect harmony.

"Now," Father said, touching the blue ovulum, "it is fitting that your heroic efforts restored the ovulum of valor and faithfulness." He shifted his hand from egg to egg as he continued. "And your songs washed clean the violet ovulum of generosity, the indigo of liberality, the green of diligence, the yellow of patience, the orange of kindness, and the red of humility. These seven virtues are safe, and even now they send signals that confuse the Watchers, thereby protecting the ark."

"What color is mercy?" Joran bit his lip. His question blurted out as soon as it entered his mind. Selah straightened and looked at him as if stunned, but she stayed silent.

Father slowly withdrew his hand. "Is this a sincere question, or are you casting a bait to hook old Methuselah?"

"Well …" Under the blanket, Joran kneaded his own leg. His father's counter question was the real bait, and now the son was the hooked victim. "I suppose I was making a statement. When talking about virtues, I think mercy should be near the top of the list."

"A wise observation, Son. In fact, we could list many virtues that are not individually represented here, but there is more on your mind. Speak it. In these times of trouble, there is no reason to withhold a heartfelt word."

Joran gazed toward the ridge where the sun had recently set. "Noah says the flood will come tomorrow, and only he and his family are allowed to be saved on the ark."

"That is true," Father said, nodding. "But you are telling me what we both already know. Again, be free with your thoughts."

"Well, I deserve to drown. I know that, but—"

"There are no *buts*, Joran." Father's tone took on a sharp edge. "What you did to Seraphina has been written in the books of Heaven. Only blood will wash away that stain."

Joran let his head droop. How well he knew this truth. No more reminders were needed, especially from Father. Yet, was forgiveness possible? If not, why not?

Inhaling slowly, he laid his arm around his sister's shoulders. "What about you and Selah? You're both righteous. You should be allowed on the ark. And I have listened to Noah's preaching, so I have been obeying Elohim, at least since after the day when Seraphina ..." He lowered his head again, letting the rest of his thoughts leak out in a long sigh. "Why isn't Elohim merciful enough to let us go as well? What color is his heart?"

It seemed that his words hung in the air for all to see. They were hard words, but honest ones. He had held them inside for so long, it felt good to get them out, a purging of the soul.

Father gazed at him for a full minute before responding. He lifted a finger and touched himself on his chest. "You say *I* am righteous? Joran, I was alive when Elohim declared Noah to be righteous, and he made no mention of me, so who am I to accept your declaration? Yet, Selah was born long after Elohim's statement, so I agree with your assessment concerning her. In any case, there is no need to be concerned about me. The flood will not be the cause of my death. I have been told that the demons will kill me, and I am prepared."

"Father!" Selah said. "Don't speak like this! It's too horrible to bear."

Father gave her a sad sort of smile. "What is the difference if I die at the hand of a demon or in the flood of Elohim? In either case, I will go to be with my fathers and wait for the great deliverer. I am content with that."

"Content?" Selah buried her face in her hands and wept. "How can I be content when the lives of my family and friends are about to be snuffed out?"

After a moment of awkward silence, Father reached over the ovula and patted Selah's head. "It seems that a daughter's tears are powerful. They are more than this old man can bear."

"Does that mean you will ask for mercy for Selah and me?" Joran asked.

"For Selah, yes. I can make an appeal to Noah, if that is your desire. She deserves to witness God's merciful hand."

Joran tightened his lips. The exclusion was worse than any piercing arrow. "It *is* my desire. I was thinking that Ham's wife died last year. Maybe he could marry Selah and—"

"No!" Selah jerked up and shook her head hard. "I would rather drown than marry that whoremonger!"

"Selah!" Joran said. "Mind your tongue!"

Father raised an eyebrow. "It seems that Selah's valor and temperance have waged a battle."

"And temperance lost," Joran added.

Selah crossed her arms over her chest. "This isn't a matter of temperance. I have seen the woman he visits in the village, and my words are justified."

"But Selah—"

Father lifted a hand. "That is enough. When Elohim is silent, we are called to trust. Whether the righteous one lives or dies, he or she will never be forsaken."

Ten vile retorts flashed through Joran's mind, but he resisted each one. Elohim would not approve of a harsh tongue, especially toward an elder, and the only way to appease a god who didn't know the color of mercy was to play the part of a righteous son, at least with his lips. It seemed to work for Ham. At least he would be able to ride above the water instead of sinking under it.

And Selah was justified in her brutal remark. The woman she mentioned was Naamah, a prostitute who lured her victims with Seraphina's stolen voice. Whenever he and Selah walked through the village while coming home from a demon-hunting expedition, Naamah's evening call to passersby provided a vivid reminder that the voice thief still used Seraphina's gift for evil purposes. Although she had directly participated in the crime, Father had said to leave her alone, that no one but the Listeners likely recognized Seraphina's voice, and Naamah would perish with the others under the waves. What was done, was done.

Joran shook his head. Yes, Naamah would die, but that harlot would take his sister's voice down to Sheol. By rights, it should be ripped from her throat before she drowned. Nothing else would satisfy justice.

Something fluttered next to a boulder that stood a stone's throw to Joran's right. He focused on the spot, but nothing moved. It had appeared to be a wing, maybe that of a dragon skulking closer to check on them. A Watcher would have alerted them with its song long before it could come that close. Joran returned his gaze to Father. He could check on the movement later.

Father's eyes took on an odd aspect. He touched the red ovulum, his stare wide and unblinking. "I have seen more sunrises and sunsets than any man or woman ever has or likely ever will. Yet, I learn something new before I lay my head down each night, and today is no exception. You see, for years I observed my father as he warned the people about learning the Watchers' ways, about obeying Elohim, and about avoiding the wrath to come. They despised him, spat upon him, and hurled stones and insults, like toddlers casting pebbles at a bull who could trample them to bits. Even as recently as today, I witnessed the parade of donkeys who daily come and mock Noah, braying at each other's trite and tired jests."

His fingers rolled into a fist. "In my heart I hated these fools, and I hoped for a slower, more agonizing death than the merciful drowning Elohim has planned. In recent months, however, as I watched the two of you wage war with the root cause of the wickedness, the Watchers who taught their dark arts to the sons and daughters of men, I came to see the scoffers less as enemies and more as lost and wayward friends. And now, as if whispering from his throne in Heaven, Elohim has given me a new song, an answer to your question about the color of mercy. As his bard, I will sing it for you, then I will tell you what it means to me."

Father picked up the lyre and played as he sang.

> You ask the color mercy shines,
> Expecting gold or silver hue;
> Yet one bare stripe is not enough
> It must be told in stripes of two.
>
> When light exposes sin in men,
> The humble souls turn red with shame,
> And kneeling low they bow their heads,
> Expecting blows and shouts of blame.
>
> Yet love compels such men to rise
> And view the red that sets them free;
> The blood of grace is shed by one
> Who wears the white of purity.

Repenting there, the soul then stands
And takes the cup of dripping red;
He drinks the mercy, draining half,
And pours the rest upon his head.

Within his soul the red turns white;
His hands the deeds of sin refuse.
And now he stands a righteous man,
Made pure by mercy's twofold hues.

When Father finished, the ovula hummed a fading harmony, as if singing a perfect amen, and the strings quieted with them.

New tears filled Joran's eyes. He reached for Selah's hand and took it into his lap. "I'm sorry."

Selah's brow lifted. "For what?"

"For doubting. If Father says Elohim will provide for the righteous, I'll just have to believe it." Joran laughed, hoping it would mask an emerging sob. "We have all night and all day tomorrow, right? A lot can happen between now and then."

"Indeed." Father climbed to his feet, walked around the ovula, and sat next to Joran. "And now it is my turn to say I am sorry."

"You're sorry?" Joran scooted closer to Selah. "For what?"

"For not recognizing the color of mercy." He covered their hands with one of his. "When Seraphina died, it seemed that my heart died with her. She was the first Listener, and her loving ways and her gifts made me wonder if she was an angel in disguise, especially since she was the only fair-skinned, yellow-haired child in our brood. When your betrayal led to her death, though you cried in repentance with many tears and I forgave you with my words, I allowed a wound to fester within, never bothering to treat it with the medicine of mercy. I wanted to hurt, and I wanted others to hurt as I did, to feel the pain I felt." As a breeze blew back his scant

56

white hair, tears flooded his eyes. "My son, I forgive you with all my heart, and I ask you to forgive me for the evil grudge I have held against you."

Joran stared at his father, his cheeks now wet and his chin trembling. The last time he looked like this was after hearing the news of Seraphina's death. His moaning laments filled their home for days, each one ripping at Joran's heart. And now his silent grieving threatened to do the same. Father's words were heartfelt and real, the words he had longed to hear for the past four years. They felt good but somehow not as healing as he had hoped. Something was still missing. Seraphina's stolen voice still rose from its thief, a wicked young woman who used it to manipulate men for her own benefit. And Father would do nothing to stop her.

After clearing his throat, Joran spoke with all the passion he could muster. "I forgive you, Father. Thank you for forgiving me."

Father wiped tears with his sleeve. "I will ask Noah about places on the ark for both of you, but I fear that it will not be possible. Noah was quite adamant that Elohim will close the ark's door on only eight humans."

57

"I understand." Joran bit his tongue. Did he really understand? Probably not, but at least Father's feelings would be soothed.

After returning to his place opposite Joran and Selah, Father picked up the ovulum bag and set it on his lap. "Now I will reveal what I have called you here to do." He reached into the bag and withdrew his open hand, but nothing sat on his palm. "Here is the purity ovulum."

As Father set the invisible egg at the center of the circle, the colors in the other eggs faded until they all disappeared. "You see, purity of heart and mind causes all other virtues to be holy. By themselves, every virtue can be feigned, often for selfish purposes, but a truly pure soul can allow all his attributes to be examined freely, and he will be found faultless."

A song emanated from the ovulum, too quiet to hear while it was in the bag, but now an audible tune, a sweet melody that wafted over their bodies.

Warmth seeped into Joran's cheeks. Just as the songs of the other ovula evoked a surge of emotions, the very presence of this one injected a feeling of guilt, a burden on his shoulders he couldn't shrug off. Even in the twilight, Father and Selah likely noticed the color of shame in his face. In the presence of such perfection, it seemed that he sat naked, dirty, his thoughts and motives exposed for all to see. His valor amounted to acts of vindictiveness. His kindness toward Selah always had his own interests attached. His virtues were falsehoods, feigned colors that combined to make his heart black.

Father lifted the purity ovulum and reached it toward Joran. "You must take it. Secure it so that the floodwaters will not be able to dislodge it."

His hands trembling, Joran extended his arms, his palms open. When Father transferred the ovulum, the space inside the glass turned light gray, making it easier to see, and the song faded away. Father and Selah must have noticed the change, but they didn't breathe a word about it.

"This ovulum must be set apart," Father said. "Each one emanates a song of virtue that evil cannot detect, but the purity ovulum is able to search out the others. They house refuges for souls who are able to escape this realm if Elohim so chooses, and the demons wish to destroy these places, for each ovulum is a shield against demonic influence."

Joran gazed at the glass egg. In the midst of the fog, a tiny light sparkled, a brief flash, like a glimpse one sees out of the corner of one's eye. "How do you know about these refuges? Have people been there and come back to tell you about them?"

"Only in a way. We have a prophetic dragon who has ventured inside the ovula in her dreams. She has told me that there are habitations within."

"Shachar?" Selah asked.

"You are perceptive, as usual." Father lifted the red ovulum, its color now restored. "The dragons and I will hide these and record their locations in a book. Since only Shachar will know the location of the book, it will be up to her to find it after the flood. Of course, one might think it most reasonable to stow the ovula on the ark, but there is one member of Noah's family I do not trust at all, so the safest option is to hide them for collection later. Then, the stewardship of these ovula will pass to another generation of protectors. Whether they will be dragons or humans, I do not know."

Joran imagined a dragon family—Arramos, Shachar, and a newborn youngling—standing in the shadow of the ark. It would be a great adventure to help reestablish a new world. Once again, exclusion from that opportunity brought a pang of regret. "Will I write the location of this ovulum in your book?"

"No. Its location must be your secret alone. Although a Listener can hear its song when close, Shachar can hear it from far away and search it out. Even if a villain finds the book with the locations of the seven, it will be useless for finding the eighth."

59

Joran focused again on the ovulum, hoping to catch a glimpse of another sparkle. "What could a villain do with it?"

"Most villains could do nothing. You see, when the Watchers came to Earth as fallen angels, they hoped to corrupt all of mankind with their vile teachings, thinking that ruining Elohim's created order would be a satisfying measure of revenge.

"To protect us, Elohim provided the ovula. The songs that emanate from them are like barricades the Watchers are unable to penetrate. That is why we have used them to protect the ark. The purity ovulum's song guards the hearts of men with its combination of virtues. Although people cannot consciously hear it, the song strengthens their inner beings to resist the Watchers' temptations.

"Enoch warned the people to guard the purity ovulum carefully, but they grew lax, and the Watchers stole it. While they held it captive in another realm, the people could no longer hear the song, allowing the Watchers to bring corruption more easily. Yet, during this time, we learned about another interesting property the ovulum possesses. Its song can break shackles that keep it imprisoned. It came back to us on its own, suddenly appearing in a shepherd's tent. The Watchers stole it again and covered it with their darkness spells, smothering its song and weakening its ability to return. It stayed in their possession until Arramos found it and brought it home."

A gust of wind flapped their blanket and sent ash billowing into the rising smoke. Selah snuggled closer to Joran. "Why didn't the Watchers destroy it?"

"The Watchers know that such an action would raise a curse beyond any they can imagine. The one who brings about its end will meet his own end in a horrifying way."

Joran looked at the foggy egg again. It seemed to reflect his own imperfections—cloudy, uncertain, doubting. The stripping of his façade was annoying, inciting an inner anger that threatened to grow. He swallowed down the feeling. He had to control himself and keep it from turning black.

"Since people were unable to hear the song," Father continued, "the Watchers tempted them more easily. They became so corrupt, Elohim decided to destroy them, which was the hope of the demons all along. They believe the flood will be a first step, a warning judgment that, if not heeded, will usher in the greatest of all judgments, one that will benefit the demonic horde. What that judgment might be, I do not know. Perhaps it is merely a myth, but since the demons believe in it, they have all the motivation they need to bring it about."

Still holding the red ovulum, Father nodded at the empty bag. "Selah, help your brother put the holy vessel in."

As she held the bag under Joran's hands, he pushed his arms inside and laid the ovulum gently at the bottom. After drawing the string at the top, she passed the bag to him, her countenance reverent, as if she were transferring her own heart to his safekeeping.

"We will sleep here tonight," Father said. "The dragons will keep watch. We expect a final assault from the Watchers in the morning, so we will leave this basin before dawn and hide the ovula, though I must keep the scarlet one free until the last moment, for it protects the ark, and Father Enoch might have a message for me."

Clutching the bag tightly to his chest, Joran nodded. Father had mentioned the red ovulum's uniqueness in the past. Dubbed the Eye of the Oracle, grandfather Enoch watched from a place unknown and gave Father advice when needed. Maybe that was how Father learned about what to do with these eggs.

While Father and Selah retired to the tent, Joran stayed near the fire. He looked at the boulder, hoping to see the wing again, but nothing stirred. Only a few embers crackled, spewing a bit of ash into the rising air. He used his sandal to rake dirt over the fire. Alone with his thoughts, he pictured himself in the midst of the flames, burning in agony as the tongues licked his melting flesh. What would it be like to die? Would he go straight to Elohim's judgment seat and be condemned eternally for his sins? Or would he see the colors of mercy, red and white, smeared across the Holy One's countenance? In only a few hours, he would learn the truth.

61

CHAPTER

Dreams

M att rested in the copilot's seat of an old Cessna Caravan, a pair of headphones covering his ears. Although there had been no traffic control chatter since shortly after takeoff from the Hesperia airport, wearing them made him feel like a pilot, or at least a navigator guiding the plane through dangerous maneuvers. The only other times he had flown, he and other paratrooper trainees just stood in the back, waiting for a signal to jump. Sitting in the cockpit behind a control yoke was far cooler than leaping into open air.

Watching Walter throttle up and send the plane into a wickedly sharp climb and then helping him program the GPS as they sped along at the engine's upper limits had been a rush. And the future promised more heart-thumping action. The destination on the dashboard's brightly lit map showed a grassy hilltop in northern Arizona, a short, bumpy runway that ended at a steep slope. Overshooting the target meant a wild plunge into a ravine. It seemed that every step in this adventure would be more exciting than the last.

63

Matt rubbed a silver engraving on the dashboard—*Merlin.* Just before they took off, Walter referred to the airplane by that name, saying that they had been through a lot of adventures together, including traveling to another world. Apparently this living-on-the-edge pilot had quite an imagination.

Walter slid off his headphones and tossed a box of granola bars onto Matt's lap. "Now that we're cruising, it's a good time to get some body fuel while I fill you in on the details. After we land, we'll be hiking like madmen, so this might be our last chance to talk."

"Sure." Matt pulled a handful of granola bars from the box. As usual, he was famished. A hike through a cold forest meant that his internal furnace would be running on high, so stocking up was a good idea.

"Still have the journal?"

Matt slid off his headphones and pulled the journal from his jacket's inner pocket. "Right here."

"Good. I want you to get to know your mother better." Walter tossed a folded sheet of paper onto Matt's lap. "Add this to your reading material. Study it and memorize it."

Matt unfolded the sheet—a facility layout with labeled buildings, interior rooms, and yard areas, including fences that divided the facility into sections. "Is this the prison?"

"Yep. And your mother's in the Healers' Room. Look for that in the research wing's first floor."

In the light of the dashboard's glow, Matt ran his finger along the building's hallway, searching for the label. It probably wouldn't do any good at this point to protest the reference to Bonnie Bannister as his mother. Walter had made up his mind. After a few seconds, he tapped the page. "Got it right here."

Walter peered at the drawing. "If our spy picked up the right schedule, she should be there all night. Like I said, it's called the Healers' Room, but that's like calling a gas chamber a spa."

Matt gave him a skeptical stare. "And you want me to use my danger-sensing ability to sneak in there and get her out."

"Not just her. Once you find Bonnie, I hope she'll help you dodge the guards so you can get back to her cell and spring my wife. Ashley has the ability to read minds, at least sometimes, so she'll be a big help when you're trying to get out without being noticed."

Matt resisted the urge to roll his eyes. "If you say so."

"And our spy will be listening in and trying to keep the guards away from you, so stay in contact as you go, so he'll know what's going on."

"How will I stay in contact?"

"I'll show you the transmitting equipment when we get there." Walter pointed toward the rear of the airplane with his thumb. "I have a radio and some other stuff in my backpack. The wire cutters for the fence are back there, too. We'll also have a giant who'll cause a diversion."

"A giant?"

"One of the Nephilim, to be exact. He's friendly. You'll like him."

Matt stared through the side window at the growing darkness. "This is sounding more like *Mission Impossible* every minute."

"Do you want to back out?"

Matt swung toward him. "Not a chance! It's just that we have to count on everything lining up perfectly for it to work, and the script isn't exactly carved in stone."

"More like scrawled in the sand." Walter grinned. "Don't you love it?"

Matt studied Walter's confident expression. This guy oozed adventure, but he might also be suicidal. "Yeah. I guess I love it."

"Good, because there's more. When you get into the Healers' Room, there should be a computer there. We're looking for records for Karen Bannister. If I'm right about you being Charles Bannister, she's your twin sister. Since the records could be under another name, you might have to do a search for any girl your age, especially a girl with blonde hair and blue eyes."

"Won't it be password-protected?"

Walter slid a metal band off his wrist and handed it to Matt. "I'm not sure if the embedded passwords are current, so if this doesn't get you in the research wing's back door, you're sunk. Just hustle back, and we'll bail. But if you get in, the passwords will probably get you the rest of the way, including into the computer files."

Matt put the band on and rubbed its smooth surface with a finger. It looked like the ID bracelet he had seen on a visiting General at the academy. "How did you get access to these passwords?"

"I have connections with someone very dear to me." Walter gave him a half smile. "And I have some computer power of my own that checked the embedding. If the codes are current, it'll work."

"I'll take your word for it." Matt drew a mental picture of a blonde-haired girl his own age. Escaping a deranged foster sister had been hard enough. Now he might have to deal with a flesh-and-blood sister. Who could tell how mentally unstable she might be?

"Something wrong?" Walter asked.

"Not really. My only experience with a sister was a disaster named Darcy."

"Darcy, huh?" Walter nodded. "I got a slice of sibling harassment for a while. But Shelly's a dream sister now. Maybe Darcy will—"

"No," Matt said, shaking his head. "If you knew her, you'd never say that. If the devil has a daughter, her name is Darcy."

Walter focused on the darkness ahead. "If you say so."

An awkward silence descended. Matt stared at the items on his lap—headphones, granola bars, Bonnie's journal, and the map. For some reason the presence of each item drilled a sense of reality into his mind. This wasn't a training jump. He was really going to a prison where he would risk his life to rescue the author of this journal, supposedly his own mother.

Shifting in his seat, he mumbled, "I'm going to study the map for a while."

"And the journal?"

Matt opened the front cover. "I suppose so. It feels like an invasion of privacy, though."

"I think …" Walter focused straight ahead, his voice breaking. "I think she would be thrilled."

Matt settled back in his seat and munched on granola bars as he read. After such an exhausting workout earlier in the day, his muscles ached and his eyelids felt heavy, but the beautiful words entranced him, inviting him to turn page after page. The suffering that Bonnie endured at the hands of her father pulled him in, a betrayal of trust he knew so well. That monster subjected her to more needle jabs and drew more blood than any loving parent would ever have allowed. If only he could have been there, he would have protected her—whisked her away to a loving home, far from the cruelty, far from the hypocrisy of lip-service love that came with stabs in the back.

67

Matt imagined Darcy, smiling while holding a dagger behind her. Living with her made such stabs almost a literal reality. His mind drifted to a night six years ago when she was fourteen and he was ten. He lay curled in bed, poking his nose out from under his blanket just enough to breathe. Although he should have outgrown night-lights, he always asked for one, still frightened by every shifting shadow. His danger-sensing hadn't kicked in yet, though his ability to stay warm had been with him for as long as he could remember.

In his mind's eye, the room turned into a movie scene with his younger self playing the part of the sleeping boy. An auburn-haired girl wearing a long nightgown tiptoed through the night-light's glow. Carrying a coil of rope, she opened a window next to the bed.

Of course, since he had been asleep during the first part of this event, his memory was little more than a dramatization of what Darcy must have done. Still, no matter how much evil intent he poured into her image, he could never overestimate her malice.

As the scene played on, Darcy pulled the blanket back carefully, uncovering the younger Matt. She slid the rope under him and tied a loop around his waist, gritting her teeth as she fastened it tightly. With a maniacal expression twisting her face, she tied the other end of the rope to the bed's frame.

Taking a step back, she called, "Matt! It's snowing! Come to the window and see!"

Matt sat up, blinking. Darcy took him by the hand and led him toward the window. Barefoot and wearing thin flannel pajamas, he walked in a meandering daze.

"Look!" she said, pointing outside. "You can build a snowman!"

When he leaned over the sill, she shoved him through the opening. The rope reeled out until it tightened and dragged the bed halfway to the wall.

Matt's mental perspective zoomed to the second-floor bedroom's window. His younger self dangled a few feet from the ground, his arms and legs flailing as he swayed, bumping against the exterior wall, but he stayed completely quiet.

Muffling a laugh, Darcy withdrew a steak knife from a nightgown pocket and sawed through the rope, glancing at the door every few seconds. When the final thread snapped, young Matt fell to the snow-covered grass with a thump.

Darcy leaned out the window and waved, her evil smile spreading from ear to ear. "Enjoy the snow, Matt!" she called in a whisper. "I'll unlock the door for you … in a few hours. Maybe even you will be cold by then."

Laughing, she pulled back and began sliding the bed into place. After she left with the rope, the room stayed silent for a few moments. Soon, the rays of dawn peeked through the window. Young Matt walked in, his pajamas soaked. Rubbing a bump on his head, he stripped off his top, grabbed a terrycloth robe from a hook on his closet door, and put it on. As he closed the window, his thoughts played out loud. *They'll never believe me. They always believe Darcy. And then I'm the one who gets punished for lying about her. One day she'll kill me with one of her pranks. Then they'll believe me.*

He crumpled to the floor and wept. *Why do I have to have a sister? If it wasn't for her, this home would be great. But Darcy ruins everything. I can't even eat without worrying that she put dog hair in my food ... or something worse. I wish I could go to a place where there weren't any sisters. Maybe the army. That would work.*

As young Matt cried on, the room darkened and became completely silent.

Matt blinked, bringing his mind back to the present. Would the wounds gouged by Darcy's evil pranks ever go away? And this was just one of many. The worst episodes left him bloodied, sometimes requiring stitches, causing his foster parents to label him as accident-prone in public and a klutz in private. Darcy was a sadist times ten to an infinite power.

69

He refocused on the journal. If he concentrated on Bonnie Conner for a while, maybe he could push thoughts of Darcy over a mental cliff where they belonged.

Soon, his eyelids grew heavier, and the words on the page jumbled. Images of Darcy swirled in his mind as she grinned at him from the bedroom window. Again and again he fell, the rope twanging as it tightened, and Darcy laughed each time, as if she could never see him suffer enough. After a while, a bump shook the scene, making it crumble and fade away.

Matt opened his eyes. The journal still lay on his lap, and an airplane cockpit surrounded him. He looked at the pilot's seat. Walter sat with a firm hand on the yoke, his stare riveted straight ahead.

"Did you get a good snooze?" Walter asked.

As the bumps continued, Matt straightened in his seat. "I guess so. I must have been more tired than I thought."

"Probably good that you caught some winks." Walter nodded at Matt's seat. "Better check your belt. The air's getting choppy, and we'll be landing in a few minutes."

Matt pulled the strap, his hands trembling. Even though that dream had recurred dozens of times, it never failed to shake him up. Darcy was the original twisted sister, the author of a two-year-long nightmare. And now he had to find a new sister. Prospects for brotherly love at first sight seemed dismal.

Walter pushed the airplane into a steep descent. "We'll be hopping out in a hurry. Are you ready?"

"I think so. I just have to grab my gear from the back."

"I don't mean to sound like a mother hen, but is that jacket warm enough? It's supposed to snow tonight."

"It's fine. I don't ever get cold." Matt shivered. The chill from the dream had lingered far too long. "Well, hardly ever."

"Really? Ever checked your temperature?"

"Sure. Lots of times. The doctor said I have a higher base temperature than most people. Nothing to worry about."

"Hmmm." Walter stroked his chin. "Interesting."

Matt shrugged. "Guess I'm just hot-blooded."

"If you say so." Walter flipped a few control switches. "Get ready. This landing might be rough, but the rest of the night will probably be a lot rougher."

Standing close to the bed, Mardon scanned Bonnie's motionless body. The Healers had left the premises, glad to travel home before the forecasted storm arrived. Normally, they would have taken Bonnie back to her cell, but tonight's schedule called for a longer stay.

He watched as her eyes darted beneath their lids. Unattended and unguarded, she lay dreaming about whatever goes through the minds of the naïve. Although courageous to a fault, she knew so little. Of course, she couldn't know that she was bait, a helpless guinea pig waiting for a heroic rescue, but she would learn soon enough. The draconic heroes would join her behind bars in due time.

Mardon glanced at the window. Wind buffeted the panes. The storm approached. Although the Colonel had allowed such an odd scheduling twice before, this attempt had the best chance of succeeding. Mother was right to suggest it. With a blizzard on the way, Bonnie's friends might think this their last chance of rescue for quite a while. Now if the Second Eden snobs would open the portal and send the dragons, restoration would come.

"Patience," Mardon whispered. "Mother and I will soon be whole." After reading a hanging IV bag, he walked to the closed door and passed through it.

71

5

CHAPTER

THE SILENT ONE

Joran, Selah, and Father lay together in their crowded tent. Their huddled bodies and two blankets served to keep them comfortable, though the pebbly ground was nothing like the feather-stuffed mat at home. Selah slept in the middle, warm and protected.

Joran held the bag close. Although the covering silenced its quiet song, the ovulum's warmth and shape constantly reminded him of its presence. As he lay there, his ears gathered every sound—the breathing of contented sleep, the songs of the seven ovula lying in an open padded box near Father's head, a gentle breeze caressing the tent's canvas, and the whispers of nearby dragons as they conversed in their odd, guttural language about their duties as guardians over Methuselah and the mysterious eggs. No Watcher lurked about. Not a trace of their evil songs rode the breeze. Still, the dragons seemed nervous, and for good reason. Except for Arramos and Shachar, their lives would end tomorrow.

Joran eased away from Selah, picked up Father's lyre, and crawled toward the tent flap, the ovulum bag still in his grip. Maybe he could play something that would soothe the dragons and make them forget their troubles. Makaidos's voice had come through, as had Thigocia's. They were both kind and talkative sorts. He could play while they told tales. Listening to their droning stories might lull him into a sleepy state, and seeing their powerful forms might provide comfort in spite of the prophesied darkness of the coming day.

After pushing through to the outside, he rose to his feet. A full moon hovering overhead illuminated their site. A string of smoke rose from the campfire embers, and the tall grass where he and Selah had sat still bowed lower than the surrounding blades.

Above, two dragons flew in front of the moon, one of them with glowing scales. "Shachar," Joran whispered. As Selah mentioned earlier, although Shachar appeared to be a normal dragon in daylight, she often glowed in the midst of darkness, sometimes so bright she could be seen from far away. At other times she was like a crescent moon, barely visible at all. No other dragon exhibited this trait, so the combination of her radiance and her ability to locate the purity ovulum made her unique indeed.

While Shachar flew away, the other dragon, Arramos, Shachar's mate and king of all dragons, descended toward him. Before Seraphina died, Arramos was her mount in battles against the Watchers, and his frequent visits made him a family friend. Ever since her death, however, he had remained aloof.

Seconds later, he landed gracefully in front of Joran, beating his wings in near perfect silence.

Joran bowed his head and whispered, "Greetings, King Arramos."

Arramos briefly lowered his head in return. "I saw you from above. Is all well?"

"I'm not sure about *all*, but considering what will happen tomorrow, I suppose *I* am well. I just couldn't sleep."

"That is to be expected." Arramos looked from side to side, his ears twitching. "As if you did not have enough worries, I must also inform you that a Watcher I battled today boasted that the Silent One has returned to our region. I assume he will be part of their final attack tomorrow. We hoped that you would be well guarded, but since he emits no song, he might approach without your notice."

"I haven't heard much about the Silent One. How dangerous is he?"

"Quite dangerous, though not in the way you have come to expect from demons. He has no ability to cast darkness spells, so he relies on cunning to disrupt Elohim's purposes. With his ability to deceive and blind the discernment of the unsuspecting, he convinces people to do what he asks. Sometimes he will threaten a loved one, which is his most common tactic, using your own love as a weapon against you."

Joran's skin crawled. "Such a beast should burn in Sheol's deepest pit."

"I agree. His tactics are truly evil. In fact, he can be so beguiling and persuasive, some of the patriarchs called him Lucifer's craftier brother."

Joran glanced around. "If I were to see him, what should I do?"

"Call for a dragon. Enoch told me that he fears us, though we are not sure why. Perhaps he is cowardly in the face of fire, but I suspect there is something more."

"What if no dragons are around or they can't get to me in time?"

"This is another reason I visited. You should not be alone. It is far more difficult for a beguiler to deceive more than one person at a time, because the tool he uses to mesmerize one person might not affect the other. Besides that fact, the songs of two Listeners should be effective on all demons, which is one of the reasons your father always insists on you and Selah going into battle together." Arramos's tone deepened, mixing with a low growl. "And why you and Seraphina battled together."

Joran nudged a pebble with his foot. This conversation had taken a bad turn. "I ... I'm not sure what to say. I know how close you and Seraphina were, so—"

"What is done is done," Arramos said. "I apologize for allowing my feelings to invade my words. My emotional turmoil was incited by my love for Seraphina and my grief over her loss. I hold no ill will toward you. You were young and inexperienced. I will say no more about that tragic day."

Joran's ears burned. If only youth and inexperience were the real reasons for the tragedy.

"In any case," Arramos continued, "I believe in an afterlife for humans and dragons alike. Seraphina lives again in another world. Perhaps I will be reunited with her soon."

"Soon? But you're going on the ark." Joran pointed at the ground. "You'll keep living in this world, and dragons live for so long—"

"I am not going on the ark, nor is Shachar."

Joran blinked. "You're not?"

"Makaidos and Thigocia will take our places. They are young and strong, so they are good choices. They have trained as a team in the past, and with the expected final assault from the Watchers, I will need them to protect your father while he uses the ovulum to protect the ark."

"But Makaidos is ... well ..."

"Inexperienced. I know. He told me of his failure during your most recent battle, and I commend you for your refusal to report his mistake." Arramos's eyes flashed, then slowly dimmed. "We all have needed second chances, have we not?"

Joran lowered his head. "Definitely."

"Then let us hope for a Second Eden, a second chance for all humanity." Without another word, Arramos beat his wings and launched into the sky. After orbiting the area once, his eyebeams sweeping the ground, he flew toward the western ridge and disappeared into the night.

Joran let his shoulders sag. Every hour seemed to bring another reminder of his dark past. Yes, Father had forgiven him, and Arramos didn't seem to hold an outward grudge, but what would Seraphina say if she stood in front of him now? At the moment of betrayal, she seemed so disappointed, her face a portrait of bafflement. Those wide eyes haunted every dream. Shame was his prison, and only Seraphina held the key.

Lifting his gaze toward the sky, he whispered, "Elohim, is there any way I can let Seraphina know how I feel? If she were here, I would beg her to forgive me. I was a stupid brat who wouldn't listen to her wise counsel, and she is the one who had to suffer."

Again, he let his head droop. Why would Elohim want to listen to a condemned sinner? His life would be over soon. It was too late to appeal to the executioner for a final apology to the victim of his crime.

He looked at the tent and listened to the rhythmic sounds of contented sleep. Although Arramos was right to warn against being alone, what harm could come from staying out a little while longer? Death awaited at dawn. Could dying at the hands of a demon be worse than drowning?

Holding the top of the bag closed with one hand and tucking the lyre under his arm, he strolled past two tall boulders and stopped near the campfire embers. In the midst of the faint sizzles, new dragon conversation reached his ears. The cool air must have allowed their voices to carry from the ridge, a bit unusual considering that the communications seemed to be whispered. Maybe they were closer, just out of sight. With the moon so brilliant, a shifting shadow would give them away.

A hint of movement caught his attention. Near one of the boulders, a shadow of what looked like a wing bobbed slowly, as if waving an invitation. Joran cocked his head and listened. Since no Watchers' songs spoiled the air, maybe this was the same dragon he had noticed earlier.

Stepping on the grass carefully so as not to arouse Selah's sensitive ears, he walked around the boulder and leaned against it. He set the ovulum bag next to his feet and began playing the lyre, using the tune that was supposed to summon images. Maybe, just maybe, he could gain a measure of Father's ability. Couldn't he have inherited the bard's talent?

After he played the family's tune several times, the white aura reappeared. An image took shape in front of the strings, a miniature woman in battle togs riding a dragon, a quiver of arrows on her back and a bow attached to her belt. Although the dragon appeared to be flying, its wings beating and its tail acting as a rudder, the image stayed in place about two handbreadths away from the lyre. As the woman's hair and clothing flapped in the wind, she smiled, apparently enjoying the flight.

Joran studied the pair. Although the white glow made the details indistinct, the woman looked a lot like Seraphina and the dragon like Arramos. Since they were inseparable as a battle team, the lyre showing them together made sense.

Ghostly trees appeared, and the dragon landed in their midst. The woman dismounted and hugged the dragon's neck, a lengthy embrace, much longer than a typical human and rider exchange. With his ears twitching and his tail swishing, the dragon seemed to enjoy the affection.

Soon, the dragon flew away, leaving the woman in the dim, foggy woods. She pushed her hair back from her ears and looked around, as if watching and listening for something. Then, moving slowly, she withdrew an arrow from her quiver and set it to the bowstring.

Although she was nothing more than a white semitransparent specter and no taller than a forearm, her identity became clear.

Seraphina stood ready for battle, apparently focusing on an out-of-view opponent.

Joran stared at her lovely face. Was this the past, a replaying of an old tale, or might this be a present event in her new world? Maybe that dragon wasn't really Arramos but rather a look-alike in another realm.

"Seraphina," Joran whispered. "Can you hear me?"

She took no notice. Her eyes stayed focused on her target. The lyre's strings began to vibrate, giving sound to the scene.

"Joran," Seraphina said, looking around as if searching for an ally, "why did you bring them here? I told you never to show anyone our hideout."

A boy appeared, followed by a petite woman and a winged man. Also glowing white, the boy was clearly Joran at the age of twelve, and the woman was Naamah, back when he thought of her as little more than someone who seemed unusually friendly to male villagers.

"We are no danger," Naamah said in a strained, raspy voice. "Do not chastise your brother. I convinced him to bring us here. Our presence is for good, not for evil."

Seraphina lowered her bow and eyed the strangers. "Is that so?"

"It is so," the winged man said as he bowed. "I am Tamiel, a Cherub who shares the duty of guarding the Tree of Life, and I have come to help you in your battle against the fallen ones."

Seraphina's face took on a skeptical slant. "And how do you propose to do that?"

"With this." Tamiel produced a fruit and displayed it on his palm. "Take and eat, and you will be indestructible."

Seraphina's face slackened, and her tone shifted to a whispered monotone. "Joran, did you eat any of that fruit?"

"No," the projection of Joran said. "He told me you and I should eat it together. That way—"

"Never mind. It is time to fight. We must begin the battle song."

79

"The battle song? But why? This is an angel. The Watchers all look like—"

"Do not judge based on appearances!" Seraphina barked as she aimed the arrow at Tamiel. "Sing now, Joran! Sing with all the passion in your heart!"

"Beware!" Tamiel raised a hand. "I am an angel of Elohim. Elohim's wrath against those who refuse his gift will be terrible indeed."

"You can fool a child, but you cannot fool me." Seraphina shot an arrow. It ripped into Tamiel and embedded in his chest.

"Seraphina!" young Joran shouted. "You shot an angel!"

Tamiel jerked the arrow out and looked at it, a blend of pain and annoyance in his expression. "Your aim is excellent, but your wisdom is sorely lacking."

Seraphina spewed her words. "Joran, if you don't start singing right now—"

"It is too late," Tamiel said. "Now neither of you will be able to sing." Dark vapor flowed from Tamiel's wound and spread toward Joran.

Silence fell upon the scene. Although Seraphina appeared to scream, no sound emanated from the lyre's strings. She lunged toward Tamiel, but Naamah tripped her, making her fall headlong. With a twisted smile, Tamiel plunged the arrow into Seraphina's back. She screamed again, and her lips clearly formed the words, "Run, Joran! Run!" Her neck slackened, and her face fell to the grass.

Young Joran shouted, "Seraphina!" but no sound emerged from his lips.

Tamiel reached deep into Seraphina's mouth, withdrew a shining sphere, and gave it to Naamah. Then, turning to Joran, he broke the silence. "I know you are unable to answer me, young Listener, so just hear and remember what I say. As I told you, I am an angel. You do not understand what I have done, but someday you will learn. Tell your father to retrieve your sister's body here. I will do no more damage to it."

Young Joran ran from the forest and disappeared. Tamiel and Naamah walked away together, leaving only Seraphina's corpse and the phantom trees in the scene. Soon, the lyre's strings stopped vibrating, and the image faded.

Joran sat down heavily, his back against the boulder. How many times had he relived that nightmare? How many times had he wept over ignoring Seraphina's orders not to bring anyone to their forest hideout, the only place Arramos would leave her unguarded? And why didn't he sing as soon as she commanded? When silence descended, it was too late.

Cocking his head, Joran replayed that part of the scene in his mind. At the time, the silence felt like a manifestation of his fear, but now, it was clearly real rather than imagined. Could Tamiel have created the silence? Might he be the Silent One? Of course, he had claimed to be an angel, but since the Silent One was "Lucifer's craftier brother," he probably wouldn't hesitate to lie about his identity.

Tamiel did tell the truth about one thing. He left Seraphina's body in that forest unmolested, though somehow he had robbed her of her voice, likely symbolized by the bright sphere he removed from her throat. It seemed so odd that he would give that precious treasure to a common prostitute who would soon die in the flood. The benefit he gained from stealing her voice seemed minuscule compared to the risk he took. Yet, if his only objective was to cripple Seraphina's brother, he had achieved that goal. Hearing Naamah sing never failed to enrage him, and it seemed that his own song suffered, smothered by grief and anger. It never held the same power again.

Joran strummed the lyre, taking care to pause after each string, giving it time to fully sing its note. If only he could find Seraphina in the other world Arramos mentioned. Then she could hear his grief and listen to his pleas for forgiveness.

Again, an aura coated each string, but no image floated next to the lyre. Instead, a strange glow emanated from an area about ten paces in front of him, a grassy plot between two sycamore trees. Like radiant fog, the glow floated a few inches above the grass and extended upward to the height of a normal human.

Joran rose slowly, picking up the ovulum bag as he straightened. The fog congealed into the shape of a woman. Her features slowly clarified, her skin taking on a pale hue and her hair turning yellow, as if gathering invisible sunlight. Moonlight shone through the arching tree boughs, making her face glow.

Still touching the lyre's strings, Joran stared at the amazing sight. Might Enoch's instrument be doing even more than he had wished for? Could it really be bringing Seraphina back from her new world?

After a few seconds, the process completed, and Seraphina stood before him. Dressed in the same battle clothing and gear she wore that tragic evening four years earlier, including a quiver on her back and a bow in her hand, she glanced from side to side, as if lost. "Where am I?"

82

Joran's throat clamped so tightly, he could barely breathe. She was alive! And her voice had been restored! He ached to rush forward and embrace her, but that might startle her. "You're …" He swallowed hard. "You're in the eastern basin, where Father likes to camp."

She stared at him, her head tilting. "You look very familiar."

He set the lyre and bag down and took a step closer, spreading out his arms. "I am your brother, Joran."

"Joran?" She marched toward him and stopped within reach, her expression and posture staying aloof. "Joran, my little brother?"

Now shaking all over, he nodded. "I guess I've grown up quite a bit, haven't I?" He leaned forward, hoping she would receive his embrace.

Her brow furrowed. "You needed to grow up. Your foolishness cost me my life."

Pain stabbing his stomach, he lowered his empty arms. "I know. And I *have* grown up." He clasped his hands tightly. "I was stupid. I shouldn't have brought Tamiel to our refuge. I should have obeyed the moment you told me to sing. I don't have any excuse. All I can do is say I'm sorry, and I beg for your forgiveness."

She crossed her arms in front and averted her eyes. "Words are easy. Deeds are difficult."

"Deeds? What deeds? There's nothing left for me to do here. Selah and I have been killing demons together ever since you died, and the flood is coming tomorrow. There's no time to do anything else."

"Maybe there is a way for you to prove your repentance, though perhaps not here." She refocused on him, her expression softening. "If you could come back to my world with me, you and I could battle evil forces there. Of course, I wouldn't put my life into your hands at first, but I would give you a chance to prove yourself."

He loosened his hands. "That sounds perfect, but how do I get there? And how did *you* get *here*?"

"I was chasing a demon who stood on the opposite side of a stream, and just as I raised my bow, I heard a call, a desperate song so real and powerful that it seemed to pull my body. Then everything around me turned dark, and this world appeared."

Joran picked up the lyre. "Could this have called you?"

Seraphina's eyes brightened. "Grandfather's lyre! I have heard that its notes can call across the worlds."

"But can it ..." As he stared at her, confusion swirled, as if the fog from which she appeared had entered his brain. "Can it take us to your world?"

Seraphina caressed the lyre's frame. "I don't think so. Only Father's ovula have such power. The purity ovulum, especially, is a gateway to other worlds, but it was stolen by the Watchers. Even if he had it, I don't think he would let you see it, much less use it to leave this world. In fact, I have never seen it myself."

83

"Well, seeing it isn't a problem. We got it back." He set the lyre down and picked up the bag, letting the ovulum at the bottom sway in front of her eyes. It glowed so brightly, light shone through the material. "It's right here. All we have to do is ask Father. Since he doesn't want Selah and me to drown in the flood, I think he'll let us try. And he'll be overcome with joy to see you again."

When he turned to go to the tent, she grabbed his arm. "Wait. There is no need to disturb him."

Joran swiveled back. "Why?"

As the glow in her face strengthened, her smile became dazzling. "I assume he suffered greatly at the news of my death. Why put him through the torture of separation again? We will see him in Heaven someday, and then we will all laugh about the trials of our earthly dwellings."

Confusion again fogged his mind. Even the simplest thoughts seemed almost impossible to hold in the forefront. "If we don't wake Father, how will we learn to use the ovulum?"

"I know how. Father showed me with his red ovulum when I was about your age." She wrapped her hand around the throat of the bag. The ovulum inside grew brighter than ever. "Give it to me, and I will show you. We will go together to a wondrous land. You will escape the flood, and we will once again battle evil forces together and purify a new world, free from the threat of drowning."

He let his fingers slowly loosen. "What about Selah?"

"What about her?"

She began pulling the bag away, but he retightened his grip. "She's the one who deserves to escape the flood, and the three of us would make the best demon-fighting team possible. Her gifts are amazing! She can hear almost anything, and she sets the rhythm for our songs perfectly. Without her, I couldn't have killed any demons at all."

Seraphina's eyes darted for a moment before settling. "Very well. Give me the ovulum. While you fetch Selah, I will see if I can open a doorway to the other worlds."

"Okay." Joran blinked. Something was wrong, terribly wrong. What could it be? "Maybe I should stay here and watch—"

Seraphina's tone sharpened. "Do you want to prove yourself or not?"

"Of course I do. I just—"

"Then give me the ovulum and let me open the door." Her brow lifted. "Or will you continue the stubborn disobedience that cost me my life?"

Her words knifed into his heart, and every muscle slackened. She was right, of course. His disobedience did cost her her life, but if she wanted him to earn his way back into her graces, why was she resurrecting his failures, stabbing him with a dagger of memories? How could mercy be so cruel?

"Okay," he said, loosening his fingers again. "Take it."

She pulled the bag away. "Take care to be quiet. We wouldn't want to disturb Methuselah."

Joran cocked his head. *Methuselah?* Why would she use Father's given name? Only the other elders called him that.

He glanced at the lyre. Its strings, now dark, didn't vibrate at all. Seraphina wasn't a vision, of course. Her ability to touch and hold things proved that. Yet, this slip of the tongue had to mean something. "Seraphina?"

"Yes?" she said as she opened the bag and gazed into it.

"Do you have a father in the other world?"

"An adoptive father." She looked up. "Why?"

"Do you call him by his first name?"

"Oh, I see." She gave him a disarming smile. "As a matter of fact, I do call him by his first name, Manichen. We are all on a first-name basis there. The authority structures are not the same."

85

Joran let her words and tone repeat in his mind. Earlier, there was no cause for suspicion, no reason to test the quality of her voice. But now? With such an odd alteration in her normal manner, it seemed right to measure everything, and she began to sound less and less like Seraphina with every word she spoke.

"Is something wrong?" Her eyes glittered in the moonlight. "Aren't you going to get Selah?"

"Well …" Again, Joran measured her words and countenance. Yes, he was delaying, but so was she. Why wouldn't she go ahead and take the ovulum out of the bag? Might her touch reveal something she wanted to hide?

The fog in his mind now dissipating, his old sharpness returned. "I was waiting to see what you would do to open a door."

She half closed one eye. "I am getting the impression that you lack trust in me."

"Should I? You look like my sister, but you haven't acted much like her."

"Seeing how you are begging me to believe in you after what you did to me, you should know that people can change."

"Of course, and our hope is that we change for the better. We want the sun to rise and dispel fog and darkness." He copied her skeptical pose, bending his brow and half closing an eye. "Darkness is a mask that will always be exposed."

"Perhaps, but a mask that has achieved its purpose is no longer needed." She put her hand into the bag and began withdrawing the ovulum. "Revealing the truth to you now will make no difference. I have what I came to acquire."

She dropped the bag and held the ovulum in both hands. As she stared, it darkened with each passing second. "Concealing its song is ineffective unless I take advantage of someone's carelessness. And you, dear Joran, cared more about yourself and Selah than about your guardianship of this ovulum."

Joran lunged, reaching for it, but she leaped to the side as he passed. He stumbled headlong, his chin and hands digging into the grassy turf. With a spin and jump, he leaped back to his feet.

"Still clumsy," Seraphina said, laughing. "Just as clumsy as when I met you at the outskirts of the Garden of Eden. You were a stupid twelve-year-old then, and you are a stupid sixteen-year-old now."

Tightening his fists, Joran growled. "Who are you?"

"As if you have not guessed." Like a cocoon, Seraphina's form stripped away and crumbled, leaving behind a familiar-looking man. Dragon-like wings emerged from his back, stretching out farther than his height. His scant frame appeared to be that of a preadolescent, calling to mind Selah's form, though as tall as some adults. His hair, dark and curly, touched the base of his neck, and his knee-length tunic, battle trousers, and sandals appeared weathered and dusty.

Now holding the black ovulum in one hand, he spread out his free hand, as if gesturing for Joran to look. "Now do you remember?"

Joran stared. Yes, he remembered. Tamiel, the so-called angel who killed Seraphina, had once again made a fool out of him.

He lunged, but Tamiel grabbed his wrist and slung him against the boulder, smacking his head on the stone. Pain ripped along his spine and down to his toes.

His vision blurry, Joran tried to focus on Tamiel. With such strength in a small body and with the ability to take on Seraphina's appearance, he had to be a supernatural being of some kind. Since he emanated no song, maybe he really was the Silent One.

"Staring is not considered polite with your race, son of Methuselah." Tamiel's voice resonated, taking on a deep, masculine tone. He caressed the ovulum's shell, peering at it intently, as if searching for a flaw. "I suppose you are wondering how I assumed your sister's form. I am able to take on the appearance of any human I kill. She is not the first."

Blinking away the mind fog, Joran rose slowly to his feet. How could he battle this demon? His sonic rods lay in the tent, but running there might endanger Selah and Father. "What are you going to do with the ovulum?"

Neither smiling nor frowning, Tamiel gazed at him with deeply set eyes. "You are going to die tomorrow." His lips barely moved, and the small nose on his narrow face flared slightly, as if sniffing. "Why should I tell you?"

Something stirred back at the tent. Joran forced his eyes to stay focused on Tamiel. He had to protect Selah at all costs. Yet, without her help, this wicked monster would escape with the ovulum. "Since I'm going to die, what harm would it do to tell me?"

With a soft flap of his wings, Tamiel glided closer. "There is still time for you to spoil my plans."

Joran stepped back, but the boulder blocked his way. Tamiel halted and settled on the ground, so close, the breeze from his wings wafted across Joran's face. "Perhaps I should kill you now. Waiting for Elohim to kill you in the flood is too great a risk."

Pushing as much venom into a whisper as he could, Joran replied with a hiss. "If you try, you despicable serpent, you'll be in for the fight of your life. I have killed demons a lot more powerful than you."

"Verbal courage ignites passion, but it makes the mouse clutched in the eagle's talons sound like a fool." Tamiel added a laugh. "Instead of killing you now, perhaps it would be better for me to store you inside the ovulum. Your gifts are valuable, and I might be able to use you at a later time. Besides, a battle would likely raise too much noise. I would have to create a shell of silence." He paused, glancing upward for a moment. "Creating one is likely a good idea no matter what happens."

Tamiel wrapped both hands around the ovulum. Completely black in his grasp, it veiled his face in a shadow. "If you do not resist, this will be easier for both of us. At least you will survive beyond tomorrow." As he stared at the glass shell, it began to wail softly like an awakening infant.

"Joran!"

He looked around the boulder. Selah ran toward him, the two sonic rods in her hands. "What have you done?" she shouted as she arrived. "Why did you give it to a demon?"

He pointed at Tamiel who now glared at them with a pensive frown, as if considering his options. "He was disguised as Seraphina!"

"Seraphina is dead!"

"I know, but if you had been here, you'd understand."

She shook a rod at him. "You should *never* go anywhere without me, not when demons might be around! Neither of us can overpower them alone."

"Silence!" Tamiel hissed as he extended the ovulum. "I have succeeded in opening the doorway. Now is your chance to escape Elohim's wrath."

A fierce wind kicked up, flapping their hair and clothes, but it made no sound, not even a whistle as the gust swept across the boulder. The ovulum's dissonant song quieted, and light swirled toward its shell.

Selah sneered at him. "I would rather be dead in Elohim's hands than live in a refuge that you hold."

Tamiel replied in a matter-of-fact tone. "Then you will come against your will."

"Makaidos!" Selah shouted as she scanned the horizons. "Come help us!"

"Your cries will not be answered. I have placed a shield of silence around us. Every sound will be absorbed."

"Then silence this!" Joran grabbed one of the sonic rods and held it aloft. Selah lifted the other. "Destruction!" he shouted. "Selah, start the rhythm."

Selah opened her mouth, but the eerie silence expanded and swallowed every word. Joran tried to sing, but the effort felt like

89

trying to blow down a tree. Something powerful blocked his breath.

Finally, a calm, quiet voice emanated from an invisible source. "Selah, the time has come."

Joran kept an eye on Tamiel. He didn't say that. Who could it have been?

Like invisible tentacles, the wind swirled around Selah and dragged her toward the ovulum. Screaming, but unable to produce a sound, she hung on to Joran's wrist.

He returned her grasp and pulled with all his might. The suction lifted her feet and drew her closer to the egg. With their left hands and wrists locked, Joran dug in his heels, but he managed only to plow a divot in the turf.

A blast of wind blew under Joran's tunic and clawed at his wounds. Yelling without a voice, he dropped to his knees. His fingers gave way, but Selah held on. As the vacuum continued its pull, drawing her legs into the ovulum, she mouthed a new call, phrases she had spoken not long ago. "I will never desert you. We will live and die together."

Her silent words pumped energy into his muscles. Using the same hand that held the sonic rod, he grabbed Tamiel's sleeve. The demon's eyes widened, but he didn't move.

Like a lion's maw, the ovulum expanded until it enveloped all three. An awareness of falling took over, a plunge into pure darkness. Then, Joran smacked into something solid, crumpling his body. Pain tore through every nerve.

Gasping for breath, he regripped Selah's wrist. She tightened hers in return. Selah was alive. They were together. All was well.

Exhaling, he gave in to the pain and drifted into unconsciousness.

6

HEARING THINGS

Matt skulked through a forest, his head low. Even though an overstuffed backpack and a coil of rope weighed Walter down, keeping up with him was more difficult than running PT drills. He was like a Navy SEAL on steroids.

At least this hike was better than facing Victoria at the pizza social. Dealing with a love-struck girl wasn't exactly part of his training. And since Dr. Carter hated all dragonkind, he'd be sure to persecute an anthrozil in his midst. There was no going back.

After scaling a cliff and negotiating two dry ravines, Matt tromped through thorny brambles in a bug-infested forest. Wearing boots, gloves, black cargo pants, and a hooded jacket, he was ready for anything, and today's revelations provided plenty of fuel to go on. The whole evening was like a *Twilight Zone* rerun, especially finding out that his would-be mother was trapped in a prison torture chamber because she's an anthrozil, and that he, himself, might have dragon traits. Getting to the bottom of all these mysteries couldn't wait.

Matt vaulted over a boulder and landed deftly on the other side. This wooded plateau near the Kaibab National Forest would have made his ecology teacher wax poetic. The trees thinned out, and deep ruts scarred the soil, sure signs of mankind's plundering of the forest ecosystem, or so he would say.

As Matt continued jogging, he sniffed the air. The scent of pine mixed with the odor of decaying leaves filled his nostrils, kicking in a memory from today's weather report. Late fall had brought a brisk wind that portended a blizzard by tomorrow, possibly beginning as light, frozen precipitation before midnight, which would arrive in about an hour. With heavy snow on the way, this might be their last chance to break into the prison for quite a while. It was a good thing there were plenty of granola bars aboard the airplane. Since he had stuffed himself with at least five, his furnace would probably stay stoked.

Ahead, the trees gave way to a precipice. Walter slowed his pace and glanced from side to side. Matt followed suit, staying several steps behind. One more factor spurred him to go on this insane mission. During the ride to the airport, Walter had said something about a second dragon trait, something even more valuable than danger-sensing. Learning what it might be could make all this effort worthwhile.

Finally, in the light of a bright moon, Walter threw the rope to the ground, dropped to his belly, and signaled for Matt to drop beside him. As soon as Matt slid into place, Walter pulled off his baseball cap, releasing a mop of hair that fell over the top half of his ears and partially hid the camouflage paint on his forehead. Shining a penlight, he unpinned a tiny chip from the cap's bill and pinched it in his fingers. "Open your mouth."

"What?" Matt squinted at the chip. "Why?"

"It's a transmitter. Remember what I said about staying in touch? If I'm going to monitor you, you'll have to wedge this between your teeth. If you get it in there right, you should be able to tap your jaw to toggle it on and off."

Matt shook his head. "Look, Mr. Foley, I've gone along with this crackpot story this far, but I don't want to plug in a silicon wafer and be your robot boy."

"First of all, like I said before, call me Walter. Mr. Foley makes me sound like an old goat. Second …" He pointed ahead where the ground and greenery suddenly dropped out of sight. "We're at the cliff that overlooks the research wing of your mother's prison, and maybe your father's, too, but I'm not sure of that yet. This is where we'll prove what I've been telling you about your heritage, so when you rappel down that cliff, we need to be in constant contact. And I can also use the chip to track your location. Your life might depend on it, and my life, too. Anyway, this is the only possible entry point, because in other places, the woods are loaded with tripwires that'll snag you like a bug in a spiderweb."

He stopped, took a breath, and smiled, using the pen to light up his face. His teeth looked gleaming white against the black and green paint. "You can do it. I've done lots of stuff more dangerous than this."

Matt half closed an eye. "Really? Like what?"

"Well, using a dragon's tail to mount his back while in mid-flight qualifies."

"What? How do you do that?"

"If you're falling through the air or standing on the ground, and a dragon tail comes by, you grab it, and the dragon flips you forward with the tail. Then, if your timing is perfect, you land on his back, but you have to be careful not to sit on one of his spines. That'll ruin your day."

Matt shook his head. "It sounds like you're reading a fantasy bedtime story."

"Everything I've told you so far has been proven right. Right?"

"Well … not exactly. The danger-sensing stuff is on target, but Bonnie's journal doesn't prove she's my mother. One of her entries says she lived in Montana, and my records say my mother was born and raised in Detroit."

93

"Listen," Walter said, pointing at him, "the reason Sir Patrick, God rest his soul, had one of his agents hack into the computer to alter your records and your sister's records was to protect you from dragon haters, but the agent was killed before he could report what he did, and we lost track of both of you. Everything you know about yourself is a lie. And I know about lying. I've been posing as my own worst enemy for a while. And it made me feel like a Judas when I stopped visiting your mother and my wife. When I heard about your carnival-ride escapade, I couldn't risk seeing them."

"Right. Your wife and the mind-reading thing."

"Exactly. They say when they're under sedation, the Healers are getting information, so if I leak anything, the quack doctors might eventually hear it."

"I get all that, but it doesn't prove that I'm Charles Bannister."

"I couldn't take the time to do a genetics test. I'm hoping when you see your mother, you'll be convinced. Besides, I'm risking my life to protect you. And since you could report me to the Enforcers, I'm putting everything on the line. Doesn't that mean anything to you?"

Matt grinned. "It could mean that you've played soldier in the Holodeck a few too many times, if you know what I mean."

"Okay," Walter said, returning the grin. "You get points for humor, but you have to give me a break. After following me for six miles, you know I'm more than a couch potato. I am who I say I am, and you are who I say you are."

"Maybe, but what parent these days calls their kid Charles? I mean, seriously. What were they thinking?"

"Charlie, Chuck, Chucky, take your pick." Walter shifted the light away from his face. "On second thought, throw out Chucky, but you could use your middle name. It's Reginald."

"Reginald?" Matt winced. "Where did they get those names? From a medieval phone book?"

94

"Closer than you realize. But you could go with Reggie. That's not so bad."

"No, but I'll stick with Matt, at least for now."

Walter pointed his penlight at his watch. "We have fifteen minutes till my friend shuts down the power."

"You mean, the giant?"

"Right. Another name you won't like. Yereq. Giants are good at absorbing power."

"If you say so." Matt rolled his eyes. "Fairies are probably good at it, too."

Walter's face hardened. "What does your sergeant do when you pull that eye-rolling excrement?"

"I don't do it in front of him. I'd be marching the grounds till doomsday."

Walter climbed to his feet and pulled a Glock from a shoulder holster. He popped out the ammo clip, glanced at it, then slapped it back in place. "I didn't risk my life to bring you all the way out here to play parent versus spoiled brat." He shoved the gun back to the holster and glared at him from under his bushy brow. "Got it?"

Matt steeled himself. He couldn't show fear. Not now. But Walter was right. He deserved a lot of respect. Besides, he was as cool as ice. How many nonmilitary guys could set up a break-in like this? "I got it. I'll stop acting like a jerk."

"Good." Walter handed him the penlight. "Still got the layout memorized?"

"Better than my own barracks. I put the map in my pocket, just in case." Matt rose to his knees, stuffed the penlight into his pocket, and extended his hand. "Let's have the chip."

Walter laid the chip in his palm. "You're more like your dad than you know."

"I hope that means my dad's cool."

"He's cool, that's for sure, and he can also breathe fire. Imagine if you had that ability."

"That would be amazing." Matt pushed the wafer between two molars, a tight fit. "I could use a weapon like that."

"Speaking of weapons ..." Walter shed his coat and shoulder belt and extended the belt with the Glock dangling in the holster. "I assume you know how to use one."

Matt stood and reached for it tentatively. "Well, yeah. It's part of our training."

"It has armor-piercing rounds, so ..." Walter grinned. "Be careful."

As he strapped it on under his jacket, Matt glanced up. "Do you have a weapon?"

"Another one just like it in my backpack, but I'm not worried about anyone climbing all the way up here." Walter reached into his pack, withdrew a set of headphones with a built-in microphone, and slid it over his head. "Can you hear me?" he whispered into the mike.

As the scratchy voice vibrated in his tooth, Matt rubbed his tongue across it. "Yeah. Can you adjust this thing? It feels like an electrical buzz."

"Sorry. No can do." Walter pulled a radio box from his backpack and set it on the ground. Stooping next to it, he extended a telescoping antenna and flipped on a power switch. As the radio emitted a low hum, he stripped a Velcro-attached remote control unit from the box and began pushing buttons.

"What are you doing?"

"Signaling Yereq. Letting him know we'll be ready in two minutes." Walter rose and, staying low, attached the rope to a hefty tree trunk before feeding the line to the edge of the cliff. "This isn't by the book, but I assume you're no rookie at rappelling. We won't have a backup anchor."

"Not a problem." Matt took the rope and slid it through a figure-eight hook and attached it to his harness. "I'm set."

"Do you have your ascenders for coming back?"

Matt touched the clips hanging from his belt. "Check."

"Pocketknife?"

"Check again. Right pants pocket."

"It's sharp as a razor, so be careful."

"I can handle it. Anything else?"

"Just this." Walter shoved a hand into his pants pocket and withdrew something in his fist. As he slowly uncurled his fingers, a shining gem came into view, about the size of a Ping-Pong ball, oblong instead of round. In spite of the lack of light, it glittered, as if shining with a light of its own.

"What's that?"

"It's called a candlestone." Walter held it closer to Matt's eyes. "Do you feel anything?"

"No." Matt crossed his eyes to see it clearly. "What's it supposed to feel like?"

"That depends. Do you feel any pain at all? Weakness?"

Matt shook his head. "No. Nothing."

"Perfect." Walter stuffed the gem back into his pocket and used a carabiner to attach heavy-duty wire cutters to Matt's harness. "Now I know what your second dragon trait is."

"Really? Something about me not getting cold easily?"

"Nope." Walter slid a memory drive into Matt's shirt pocket. "Bring back the files, and I'll tell you."

Lauren dove for the volleyball and smacked it with her fist just before it hit the gym floor. As she slid across the varnished wood, the ball flew higher than the net, reaching the top of its arc at the perfect spot. Brandy had already leaped and cocked her lanky body into position. With a whip of her arm, she spiked the ball, making it slap the opposing team's floor.

Lauren pumped a fist. *Yes! Victory!* Before she could scramble to her feet, Micaela grabbed her wrist and jerked her upright. While the rest of the team mobbed Brandy, Micaela hugged Lauren and

97

whispered, "Let her have her celebration. Everyone knows who made that dig."

Nodding, Lauren pulled back. "Thanks."

After the opposing teams exchanged handshakes, Lauren walked up to Brandy and extended her hand. "Great spike. You really put that one away."

While the other girls chanted the team's victory cheer, Brandy locked thumbs with Lauren. "That dig was impossible … and perfect. You're the best libero we've ever had."

Lauren blinked. A sincere compliment? She smiled and nodded. "Thanks."

As she walked toward the sideline with Micaela, her back tingled, as it always did when her emotions surged. Like an electrical impulse, the sensation traveled up her spine until it reached her ears with a whispered, "Freak!"

Lauren wheeled around. Brandy averted her eyes and began talking to a reporter while her sycophants hovered close. Still, Brandy kept glancing Lauren's way every few seconds.

The tingling continued, sending the buzzing conversation into her ears.

"So, Brandy, now that you've led your team to the regional championship, tell us how it feels to be going to state."

Brandy's blonde ponytail bobbed as she spoke in her annoying singsong, the cadence she reserved for people who couldn't see through to her malice. "It's really cool, you know, like, it's a dream come true. Even though I'm the one who gets her spikes replayed on TV, we're all a team. You know, all for one and one for all …"

As Lauren turned again toward the side, she hummed a tune, her usual way to drown out the noise. This weird ability to hear things no one else could had gotten out of control, and the last thing she wanted to do was to listen in on Brandy's idol-wannabe chatter.

"What's bugging you?" Micaela asked. "Irritated by Miss Superstar?"

"That's part of it."

Micaela set a fist on her hip. "Don't let her get to you. She makes the girls in the blonde jokes look like geniuses."

Lauren noted Micaela's hair, as dark as chocolate and trimmed short for the tournament. Since their hair color matched, Micaela's love of telling jokes about dumb blondes never strained their friendship. "Brandy's a pain sometimes, but ..." Lauren shook her head. "Never mind."

"Spill it. What else is wrong?"

"Well ..." Lauren touched her ear. "The sounds I told you about. They're back."

"Oh. That. I asked Mr. Early about it, and he said—"

Lauren clenched her fists. "You did what?"

"I asked Mr. Early. I thought you wanted to know what might be causing it, and since he's a physics teacher, maybe—"

"He's a physics teacher who has a blog for a mouth. No wonder Brandy called me a freak."

"She did?" Micaela glanced back at Brandy. "And you think Mr. Early told her about your rabbit ears?"

"How else would you explain it?"

Micaela patted Lauren's arm. "Lauren, I love you like a sister, but there're lots of other reasons Brandy thinks you're a freak."

Lauren's cheeks flushed hot. "Like what?"

"Besides the way you dress, walk, and talk?" Micaela lowered her voice to a whisper. "How about when it's dark? You sometimes—" She made a shushing sound. "Coach is coming. We'll talk later."

While Coach Schmitt delivered her postgame talk, Lauren looked down at her sweaty uniform. Her sleeveless jersey, royal blue with white trim, differed from her teammates' white with blue trim, but only because she played the libero position. Although her black shorts were the same as everyone else's, she had pulled her socks all the way up to her kneepads, hoping to cover as much skin as possible. The darkness issue was getting worse. Just yesterday Brandy posted something on her Internet social wall about her glow-in-the-dark volleyball teammate. If she noticed something that strange, why couldn't Lauren see it herself?

"That was a great dig, Hunt."

Shaking herself out of her trance, Lauren smiled at Coach. Tall and lean, sporting short red hair, and probably wishing she was back in her teens instead of her forties, she looked like the stereotypical volleyball retiree.

"Thanks. It was a wild stab. I guess I got lucky."

While the other players dispersed, Micaela hovered nearby. Coach Schmitt took a step closer to Lauren, her brow wrinkled. "Don't look, but there is a strange man standing near the gym's main exit. Before the game, he asked a lot of questions about you, and I think he's waiting to talk to you."

Lauren kept her stare on Coach's face. "What does he look like?"

"Have you ever seen zombie movies?"

"A couple."

"He's their mutant prince. Just look for a pale man dressed in black pants and long-sleeved shirt. He's so thin, he looks like a coat hanger draped in black."

"A mutant in black. I think I got the picture."

Micaela tugged on Lauren's shirt. "Do you want me to get him off your trail?"

"Sure. Maybe you can find out what he wants."

"Just be careful," Coach said. "When I hear the state tournament details and know how many chaperones we'll need, I'll call your parents."

"That'd be great." Lauren pondered Coach's words. Even though the adoption went through a while ago, *parents* still sounded misplaced. Memories of her birth parents remained implanted in her mind's most sacred refuge, though, since she was so young when they died, the memories were likely generated from cherished photos that proved their love. If not for a tragic car crash, they would still be together. Her super-secure car seat had apparently kept her alive, indirectly contributing to making her an orphan.

Coach touched Lauren's arm and let her hand linger. "I'm sorry to hear about your mother. Please tell her she's in my prayers."

"Thanks." Lauren looked down at the team's wolf logo painted on the gym floor. "I'll do that."

Coach lifted Lauren's chin with a finger. "Hey! Don't be so glum. We won, and we're going to state."

"I know. It's just all the stuff with my mother."

"Well, try to buck up for her." Coach gestured with her eyes. "I saw her come in during the first game. You might want to try to find her. I don't see the zombie prince anymore."

Lauren scanned the gym. While her other teammates filed toward the locker room, Micaela trotted across the gym floor and blended in with the crowd. Apparently most fans had stayed around waiting for players and friends, or maybe they wanted to hear the announcement of the door prize winners. It seemed that giving away coupons for free ice cream helped fill the stands, at least with a couple of hundred spectators. Many students stood about either chatting or zoning out while listening to their digital music players, some with old-fashioned, wired earbuds and others with infrared connections.

Finally, a line of people parted, giving way to a wheelchair. Mom rolled toward her, working the controls with a thin hand while using the other to straighten her brunette wig. Although it looked fairly realistic, she never seemed quite comfortable with it. When the chemo stole her hair, it signaled a downward spiral that also robbed her mobility. Dad, wearing a white shirt and red tie, followed a few steps behind. His thick glasses with a built-in computer micro-screen made him look like the stereotypical geek. His face displayed his usual concern. He had always been a timid and kind sort who took good care of Mom.

"Talk to you soon." Coach compressed Lauren's arm and hurried to the locker room.

Putting on a smile, Lauren hustled toward her mother. "Mom! You came!" She stopped in front of the chair and looked at her mother's gaunt face. In the gym's bright lights, she seemed paler than usual. "I thought you were too sick."

"I was." She reached for Dad. He hurried to catch up and took her hand. "Your father picked me up right after work. He thought it might be my last chance to see you play."

"*This* year," Dad chimed in. "In case your team lost." He scratched the back of his balding head, just as he always did when he was nervous, which was pretty much all the time. "If she's feeling good enough, we'll come to state."

Lauren patted her mother's hand. "Did you enjoy it?"

"I did!" Smiling, she punched the air weakly. "I saw that dig. You were wonderful!"

"Thanks." Tears welled in Lauren's eyes. It felt so good to hear her get pumped up about something. "I'm glad you came."

Dad jingled the keys in his pocket. "Need a ride home?"

Lauren shook her head. "Micaela's counting on me riding with her. We're practicing for *A Christmas Carol*, and we need to recite."

"I remember," Dad said. "The all-female version."

Lauren grinned. "Esmeralda Scrooge and Barbara Cratchit need their practice."

"Well, stay away from ghosts." He peered over the wheelchair. "Ready to go?"

"In a minute." Mom gestured with a curled finger. "Come closer."

Lauren slid up to the wheelchair and leaned over. "What is it?"

Mom kissed her cheek. "I just needed to do that. With my prognosis, you never know when you're going to get another chance."

Tears now spilling over, Lauren returned the kiss. "Thank you."

"Don't stay out too late. There's something I want to talk to you about tonight, and you know how tired I get."

"Sure, Mom. What is it?"

"It's about why we moved to Flagstaff. I know it was hard for you to leave your friends in Nashville, but there was a good reason I never told you. It's a long story that involves an old friend of mine from England. He's dead now, and I want to make sure I tell you before I join him in Heaven."

"Okay, but you're going to be all right. I know you are."

She patted Lauren's hand. "Keep telling me that. I need to hear it."

Lauren looked at the tender touch. It felt odd, almost like a final good-bye gesture. Mom seemed sure that she was going to die soon, much sooner than the doctors thought.

"I love you," Mom said as she reached for the controls. "Remember that."

"I'll remember. And I love you, too." She backed away a step. "I'll see you when I get home."

As Mom wheeled around, a new voice broke in. "Ms. Hunt, may I have a few minutes of your time?"

Lauren turned. The reporter who had interviewed Brandy now stood at her side, a digital recorder in hand.

"Uh … Sure. I have a minute."

He pushed the recorder close. "Your team captain suggested that I ask you a question."

"Brandy suggested it?" She narrowed her eyes at him. "What's the question?"

Flipping a page in a small spiral notebook, the reporter began reading. "Now that you're going to state, are you ready to show everyone what you're made of?"

Lauren looked at the page. "Were those her exact words?"

"Well, yeah. I assume she meant, you know, grit, determination, hustle. Everyone noticed that great dig. You're probably

the second-best player on the team now, so you're really stepping up …"

Lauren tuned out the reporter and scanned the gym again.
Brandy stood at the locker tunnel access with three other teammates, all four sucking down extra large sodas. When they saw her
looking, they burst out laughing and sauntered into the tunnel.

Fresh tingles rode up Lauren's back, and buzzing whispers followed, including Brandy's voice. "Oh, she knew exactly what I
meant. She's a freak, but she's not stupid."

As a new wave of heat surged through Lauren's body, more
conversations traveled up her spine, too jumbled to decipher. It
seemed that everyone in the gym stood next to her and shouted
into her ears.

"Ms. Hunt?" The reporter tapped her shoulder. "Ms. Hunt,
would you like to make a statement?"

His voice melded with the others. Lauren's skin crawled with
stinging pulses, each pinprick feeling like the reception of another
distant sound.

The PA announcer boomed. "The winners of tonight's ice
cream promotion are ticket holders forty-nine, twenty-seven, and
nineteen. Come to the concession stand—"

Loud static interrupted. All across the gym, people covered
their ears. The reporter slung his digital recorder to the floor and
shook his hand, grimacing. A string of profanity in the reporter's
voice pierced her mind, though his lips stayed closed.

The lights darkened. Gasps shot through the gym. As the
bulbs above flickered dimly, the gasps turned to moans.

Keeping her head low, Lauren eased toward her gym bag.
These lamps always took a long time to come back on. Since she
was able to see well in the dark, this would be a perfect opportunity to sneak past the zombies' mutant prince. Whoever he was,
he probably thought she would spend some time in the locker
room before leaving.

After snatching up her bag, she unzipped it, dug out her phone, and threw the bag strap over her shoulder. Texting as she walked, she glanced between her thumbs and the floor in front of her. Although some people funneling toward the exit bumped into each other, she had no problem weaving past them.

"Weird stuff going on," she typed. "Seen the mutant?"

After a few seconds, a beep sounded—Micaela's answer. "Lost track of him. C U at my car. Usual space."

"Got it." Lauren closed her phone and slid it into her bag.

Once outside, she stopped and scanned the walkway to the parking lot. At least fifty people filed toward their cars, many putting on jackets. Lauren glanced at her jersey and bare arms. The air had definitely chilled, maybe close to freezing.

She reached back and stripped off her ponytail holder, letting her hair drop to her shoulders. That helped. At least her neck would stay warm. She could get her sweats from the bag later if she had to.

To the right of the line of people, a solitary figure stood in the grass courtyard next to the school's marquee. Outdoor flood lamps mounted at the corners of the building cast shafts of light, but the glow stopped just before striking the motionless form.

Another beep sounded. She fumbled in her bag for her phone, nearly dropping it as she pulled it out. She lifted it close to her face and read the message. "If you want to live, do not go to Micaela's car. I planted a bomb inside. Proceed to the rear of the school. Say nothing and contact no one, or your friend is dead."

Lauren gulped. Was that the mutant standing out there? Did he send this message? What should she do now? Maybe pretend to obey and text Micaela to scat? Yes, that might work. She nodded at the dark figure and reversed course. As soon as the corner of the building blocked the stranger's view, she leaned against the wall.

Breathing heavily, she propped her elbows and began texting. Her heart thumped, making her jumble the letters, forcing her to retype. "Don't start your car! Get out of it now! Call the police!"

A few seconds later, the phone beeped. The message read, "You have made a poor decision. You will see the results in a moment."

Lauren dropped the phone. It thudded against her shoe and toppled to the concrete. Gasping for breath, she looked both ways. Toward the back of the school, all was dark. Toward the front, several people waited for rides at the edge of the pick-up lane.

An explosion shook the ground. A plume of fire and smoke shot into the sky, lighting up the parking lot. Lauren dropped to her knees, spilling her bag. Micaela's car!

CHAPTER

Voices

Her hands shaking, Lauren groped for her phone. *No! It can't be! Not Micaela! She had to be all right. She had to have gotten the message and jumped out in time.*

Finally, she grabbed the phone and punched 911, but a beep interrupted. She read the text, barely visible through a blur of tears. "You have ten seconds to arrive at the back parking lot. Otherwise, your parents will suffer Micaela's fate. If you could see her burning body, you would not delay."

As shouts and cries erupted from the parking lot, Lauren scooped her sweats and change of clothes into her bag, then jumped up and ran toward the rear of the school. When she arrived at the lot, a stretch limousine sat alone in the front row, its engine running.

A distant siren wailed, and another called from a different direction. A new text beeped. "Wait for the emergency vehicles to arrive, then get in the car and drive north on Route 180 out of Flagstaff."

The approaching sirens drifted in on a cold breeze, raising a chill. She set her phone and gym bag on the hood and pulled out her sweatpants. As she put them on, she tried to look through the closest backseat window on the driver's side, but the tinted glass blocked her view. A peek through the windshield revealed nothing in the front seat. As big as this vehicle was, someone could be hiding in the back.

She pulled the front latch slowly, opened the door, and leaned over the driver's headrest. In the spacious rear compartment, luxurious leather seats, enough to accommodate at least eight people, surrounded a central chessboard table with chess pieces standing at their starting positions, several of them over half a foot tall.

Setting her hand on the headrest, she pulled in for a closer look. White pieces on the left side of the table and black on the right, the chessmen appeared to be inspired by an odd mixture of fairy tales. The kings and queens looked thin and frail, like rulers of a besieged realm. The bishops were ravens perched on tree stumps, while the knights were Don Quixote–style men riding sag-backed horses, and the rooks resembled the ruins of castle turrets with gaps in the ragged brickwork. Finally, the pawns looked like peasant children carrying buckets and scrub brushes.

A fire engine roared by and passed out of sight in front of the school. An ambulance and a police car followed close behind. Lauren grabbed her bag and phone and set them in the front passenger's seat, making sure to prop the phone at an easy reading angle. She closed the door and studied the dashboard. She had driven Dad's old convertible several times. This limo probably wasn't much different. The gear lever was mounted on the steering wheel in the same place, and the brake and gas pedals matched. With a nod, she whispered, "Don't panic. You can do this."

Her hands shaking, she grasped the wheel and shifted into reverse. The car lurched backwards. She slammed the brake pedal, whipping her body with the momentum. The chess pieces stayed in place as if riveted to the table.

She slapped the steering wheel and buried her face in her hands. Tears flowed. No! She couldn't do this! Micaela was dead. Her best friend. Her only friend. How could she go on like nothing happened?

Another beep sounded. Lauren peeked between her fingers and read the text. "I give you five seconds to mourn. If you do not continue following my instructions, you will weep at your parents' graves."

Lauren lowered her hands. A shadow passed over the car, momentarily blocking the moon. Ducking her head, she shifted to drive and sent the limo over the curb, onto the sidewalk, then back down to level pavement. Again, the chess pieces remained steady.

As the car's bouncing eased, she looked out the windshield for the huge bird that must have flown low overhead, but nothing came into sight. It had to be something big, something quiet, maybe an owl. No airplane could have flown that low without making a huge racket.

After she turned onto the school's long access road, the phone beeped again. She read the message, her thumb on the scroll button. "You will proceed to Route 180 until you receive further instructions from me."

Lauren slowed at a yield sign, turned onto the county road leading to the highway, and accelerated to the speed limit. She again glanced at the moonlit sky. This mutant creature, whoever he was, must be able to see her every move. How could she do anything but follow his instructions?

She reached into her bag and withdrew her wallet. After flipping it open, she thumbed to the photo of herself with her new parents. Posing in front of the Orpheum Theatre, she stood between Mom and Dad. She and Mom had dressed up country style for a bluegrass concert, while Dad wore his usual long-sleeved shirt and tie. He wouldn't be caught dead in flannel and overalls.

New tears trickled down her cheeks. What would they think when she didn't show up tonight? After hearing about Micaela's

109

death, they would worry themselves sick. Well, at least Mom would. Dad might grumble a few I-told-you-so's about letting their daughter play sports, but it would just be a cover-up for what really bothered him. After Mom settled his ranting, he would probably go to his study and cry. He did that a lot lately, ever since Mom's most recent cancer report.

Lauren wiped the tears away. Mom and Dad weren't perfect, but they were all she had. And it wasn't so bad that she was really a replacement for the daughter they lost to a drunk driver. They were kind and always willing to talk, sometimes late into the night, and the only thing they ever argued about was Dad's habit of drinking too much diet soda, and they never raised their voices.

And now? Now they wouldn't have any more talks. With a murderous mutant sending her to who-knows-where, she might never see Mom and Dad again. She would return to being an orphan. Micaela would never be Barbara Cratchit. It seemed that every time something good came along in her life, something terrible happened to destroy it.

After driving on Route 180 for what seemed like an hour, the shadow returned, drifting overhead. Lauren bent down to look up through the windshield, but a sudden bump sounded from the rear. She glanced back. A panel of lights in the ceiling illuminated the compartment, still empty and quiet. One of the white pawns had moved two spaces forward and sat perfectly still at the center of its new square.

She whipped her head toward the front. The tingling sensation zipped up and down her back, worse than ever. Sucking in quick, shallow breaths, she whispered to herself, "This has to be the most vivid nightmare in history. I'll wake up soon, right? Whenever you figure out that a dream is really a dream, that means you're about to wake up."

"It's not a dream, Lauren."

A jolt ripped through her body, locking her fingers around the steering wheel. Her throat clamped shut. Even the scream that pushed up from her chest couldn't get out.

The phone beeped again. The text read, "If you want to see me, turn around."

Shaking her head hard, she squeaked, "I don't think so. I ... I have to drive."

"Come now, Lauren." The voice carried a smooth tone, emanating from the backseat instead of from her skin. Every word seemed spiced with a hum, almost as if sung. "If you are trying to tell me that you are too diligent to avert your eyes, I will have to disbelieve you. I saw you trying to find me when I flew over."

She swallowed. "Flew over?"

"Yes. I am an angel."

Holding her breath, she adjusted the rearview mirror until a dark form appeared in the reflection. Humanlike, he leaned over the chessboard. A pair of wings stretched out behind him, taking up much of the seating space in the rear before folding in and vanishing.

"This is an intriguing game," he said as he touched one of the ravens. "I heard that an old friend of mine used to play it, so I have been learning the moves."

Lauren churned inside. This so-called angel killed Micaela! And now he calmly sat in the back, chatting about chess as if nothing ever happened. Swallowing again, she managed to loosen her throat. "How ... how could an angel kill a girl? That's murder!"

The creature looked at the mirror. His stare locked on hers. Pale and narrow, his face gave away no signs of gender, and his hair, jet black with tight curls, looked unearthly.

"Are you a religious girl?" he asked, his telltale hum continuing long after the last word.

Lauren broke away from the stare and looked at the road. "I go to church with my parents. At least we used to go until my mother got sick."

"Oh, yes, the cancer. I heard about that. What a pity." A clinking sound rose from the back, as if the creature had knocked two chess pieces together. "I asked, because I wondered if you ever read the Bible. It is filled with stories of angels killing people, even innocent souls, in order to bring about an intended purpose. You might remember the story about an angel killing thousands because King David numbered the people. They did nothing at all to deserve that fate, yet the angel killed them just the same."

Lauren drew a mental image of her church's youth group leader, an ex–football player who knew a lot about the Bible. He told the story of King David one time, but the details now seemed sketchy. "That sounds familiar."

"Then why are you surprised that I would send Micaela's soul to God? Because of your stubborn refusal to obey me, I had to carry out my promise in order to get you to acquiesce."

A sick feeling burned in Lauren's stomach. Knowingly or not, she had a role in her best friend's death, and now she was trapped. "Acquiesce? To what? Where are you taking me?"

"Actually, you are taking me. I have not bothered to learn how to drive, so this seemed to be the best idea. It was a simple matter to persuade the limousine owner to leave the vehicle at the school. Apparently he loves his wife dearly."

She glared at the angel through the mirror. "Then why didn't you get *him* to drive you? Why did you have to kidnap me and kill Micaela?"

"I needed you, not just a driver." He pointed at a sign indicating an upcoming junction. "Turn left and continue until I tell you to stop."

Lauren guided the limo onto a dirt road, so dark the edges were almost invisible. Fortunately, no headlights loomed in the distance, so maybe she could drive near the middle.

As pebbles crunched under the tires, she studied her surroundings. A lack of streetlights allowed her to see well into the moonlit fields and rolling hills, but no buildings stood anywhere in sight. This lonely stretch of road seemed to be a perfect place for a murder, or worse.

As she continued driving, she glanced between the road and the mirror. The mutant moved the black pieces on his side of the board, and the white pieces moved on their own in response. Humming as he whispered, he seemed to be communicating with an imaginary opponent. With fear and anxiety once again raising her antenna, his words amplified in her ears.

"Your spies were correct about her. She has the traits we are looking for."

A new voice entered her mind, this one feminine and quiet. "A blood sample will prove who she is. Once we test her abilities, we will soon learn if she can retrieve what you covet."

Lauren kept her face slack. No need to let the mutant know she was listening to the conversation. But what could it all mean? She was driving a stretch limo out in the middle of nowhere, while an angel played chess with an invisible woman in the back. The situation was crazier than any nightmare.

"In the meantime," the mutant continued, "I will keep the other two until they can be tested. They might yet prove useful."

"Yes. My son and I will help you with that."

"I hope so. I paid a great price for your freedom."

She laughed softly. "A great price? Hardly. Elam won't know what to do with it. He doesn't even realize who resides there."

"Perhaps. In any case, your son has already demonstrated his technical expertise. I hope you can prove your worth as well. The art of deception is not so easily measured."

A white Don Quixote knight rose by itself and settled two rows forward and one square to the side. "I will prove my worth, but we must quell the rattling sabers of war. Ever since Elam and Sapphira closed and locked the portal, our abilities have been … well … limited. We cannot be restored until they reopen it."

"It is a simple matter." The mutant advanced his own knight. "Everything is falling into place. Soon, they will gladly open a portal."

The white king castled with a rook. "With all the hatred toward dragons?" the woman asked. "The leaders of the religious rabble have incited so much fear, the politicians are all too ready to please the masses. The treaty is fragile, but it's the only reason there is peace now. If Earth's warning systems detect a portal opening, missiles will fly."

The mutant slid a raven-topped bishop toward the middle of the table and captured a white pawn. The little peasant boy and his scrub brush vanished without a trace. "You underestimate Queen Sapphira and the dragons. While it is difficult to create a new portal, with the proper incentive, they will do it, and the powers here will never know it exists. I think my plan will provide the incentive Second Eden requires. They will invade with a small but powerful force, so you will need more men and equipment than are currently working at the compound."

"We have called for reinforcements, but they won't come unless an invasion is actually underway. In fact, with all the false alarms, they are talking about removing the men and tanks we have there now. After all, the lure has been there for fifteen years."

"Are you saying that you will be unable to defend the facility?" he asked.

"Of course not. My son's defenses will keep the invaders at bay until reinforcements arrive."

"I hope so. It would be a shame if your body were to taste flames only moments after your restoration. In any case, my plan looks far beyond the goal of opening a portal."

The white queen rose into the air and twirled as it hovered, first in one direction, then in the other. "As does mine. After you find your prize, I trust that you will keep your promise."

"Fear not. If I find the prize, I will be quite pleased to reward you. The song hunter will be yours. I trust that you will use her more expeditiously than you did Shachar."

The woman's tone grew agitated. "I had only one scale. Just one. I drained every drop of restoration it had. It was Morgan who wasted her supply. Every time she felt her precious beauty being drained, she wrapped herself in a cocoon and drank from the vial until she finally ran out. If I had access to as many scales as she did, I wouldn't be in this predicament now."

"Your anger is understandable. I was unaware of your lack of supply. This time, you will have abundance, skin instead of scales."

"Excellent." Her voice settled. "But even if the little darling is able to find what you seek, will you be able to keep it?"

"There are ways to secure it. I am not worried." The mutant glanced at the mirror and smiled. "Seeing that our driver has already noticed your ghostly antics," he said in a louder voice, "you might as well show yourself."

Lauren kept her stare on the mirror. In the seat opposite the mutant, a woman materialized, the white queen spinning between her thumb and finger. Wearing a red dress, cloak, and hood, she bore smooth skin and bright eyes, making her appear to be in her twenties or thirties.

115

The right front tire slid off the road. Lauren jerked it back. Her hands trembling, she slowed the limo to a crawl. "Who … who are you?"

"I am Semiramis, and this angel is Tamiel." The woman lowered her hood. Her auburn hair shone under the ceiling lights. "Do not be frightened. We have no intention of harming you. If you cooperate with us, all will be well."

Like a geyser, Lauren's emotions erupted. "All will be well? Like for Micaela? Like for my parents if I don't do whatever this mutant angel tells me to do? He's a murderer! A devil!" As tears flowed, her body shook violently, and her voice rattled. "Don't tell me all will be well! It's not well! My best friend is dead!"

Semiramis glanced at Tamiel before continuing. "You sent your friend a message before the explosion. Perhaps she escaped."

Lauren stabbed a finger at the mirror. "He texted something about Micaela's burning body."

"She was in the flaming car," Tamiel said. "I did not stay to verify her death or survival. A possibility exists that someone rescued her."

Lauren punched the radio's power button and tuned through a bunch of static-filled channels until she found a news station. A slow-talking man droned through the speakers, rattling off current events. Apparently war tensions had renewed. Yesterday, the King of Second Eden sent an ambassador from Earth home without comment. The temporary opening of the portal had already put every military power in the world on high alert, but the story the ambassador told when he returned to the UN made the situation worse. He claimed that he saw Queen Sapphira wearing a battle uniform while riding a dragon in what appeared to be fighting maneuvers.

Tamiel advanced his bishop. "Just as I thought. The anthrozils are already planning for a rescue. Our timing is perfect."

The newsreader took a breath and continued. "In local news, authorities are trying to determine the cause of a car explosion that killed a female high school student near Flagstaff. The name of the victim and her school are being withheld until next of kin are notified."

Lauren slammed the brakes, slapped the car into park, and threw the door open. She leaped out and sprinted as fast as she could, following the road in the glow of the headlights. Sobbing as she ran, she stumbled on a stone but caught herself and hurried on.

As a new cluster of lights shone ahead, she slowed to a jog. Maybe they were buildings—a home or a store of some kind. She had to get to them, find other people. Yes, that was it. If she could get around other people, maybe she'd be safe. Ghosts didn't like crowds, right? And that angel always stayed aloof, didn't he? But would anyone believe her crazy story?

8

CHAPTER

PRISONER

Lauren ran on and on, leaving behind the headlights' glow. It was so cold. Her bare arms grew numb. Frigid, dry air assaulted her eyes and cheeks. Why hadn't she put on the sweatshirt when she had the chance?

A cloud passed in front of the moon. All lay dark except for the lights ahead. As she drew closer, the road shifted from dirt and pebbles to pavement, and the scene grew clear. On the other side of a tall chain-link fence, a well-lit compound stretched out beyond her view. With concrete one-story buildings, neatly manicured lawns, and fences topped with razor wire, it looked like a jail or a military correctional facility.

She passed a sign—Caution. Enter on Green Light Only—and slowed to a stop several feet from an entry gate with a drop-down bar. Gasping and pressing a hand against her stomach, she crouched and dry heaved, having nothing inside to vomit. A uniformed man with a pistol in a hip holster walked from a guardhouse. "Miss? Are you all right?"

Shaking her head as she caught her breath, she pointed back toward the limo. "Two people … a man and a woman … kidnapped me. … I escaped … from the car. They're chasing me."

The guard pulled a flashlight from his belt and shone it down the road. After shifting the beam from side to side several times, he slid it back in place. "Whoever they are, they must have high-tailed it."

Lauren read the guard's name tag—Private M. Tate. The military facility guess was probably on target. "I wouldn't count on it," she said, still gasping for breath.

Tate snapped a phone from a belt clip, held it to his ear, and pushed a button on the side.

When it beeped, the sound seemed to pinch something in Lauren's back, worse than a bee sting. Both the cold and the mystery prompted a new shiver.

"Yeah, I have a girl here at the gate, maybe sixteen years old." He looked at her with raised eyebrows.

"Yes. Sixteen." Lauren rubbed heat into her arms as she tried to hide the pain. It seemed that every word he spoke into the radio stung her skin.

"She said she was kidnapped, but she escaped. There's no sign of anyone else around."

Loud static buzzed from the earpiece. Tate jerked it away and stared at it. The lights around the guardhouse flickered, as did other lights in the compound. When a sizzling noise and smoke erupted from the phone, he slung it to the pavement.

"Short circuit," he said as he shook a wounded finger. "We're probably on generator power now. But it doesn't make sense that my phone would react to an electrical surge."

The lights steadied, though they stayed dimmer than before. The entire facility looked like a dreary school under a twilight sky.

Lauren's pain eased. "Weird."

Tate set a hand on her back and guided her around the drop-down arm and into a shadowed area. As he pulled a stool from the guardhouse, he stared at her. "Are you … glowing?"

She glanced at her bare forearm. As always, the glow was invisible to her own eyes. "Too much sunlight, maybe?"

"Could be. I've heard that certain herbs can cause it, too." He grabbed a jacket off the stool and gestured for her to sit. "I can't leave my post, so you'll have to wait here until the patrol officer comes by. He'll know where to take you." He draped the jacket over her shoulders. "That should help."

Lauren sat on the stool and, sliding her arms through the fleece-lined sleeves, gave him a nod and a halfhearted smile. He was trying to be nice, but she couldn't trust him yet. Although she had escaped, the crisis was far from over.

She pushed her hand into one of the jacket's pockets and found wadded material inside. She pulled it halfway out—a baseball-style cap with gray and light green splotches, similar to caps she had seen in photos of army soldiers.

119

After stuffing it back into the pocket, she gritted her teeth to keep them from chattering. She had to call and warn her parents, but her phone lay on the front seat in the limo, and Tate's phone sat on the road in three pieces. That murdering mutant probably had cronies he could call, so he might already be arranging her parents' deaths.

"How long till the patrol officer comes by?" she asked.

Tate glanced at his watch. "About fifteen minutes, but he's not always on time. He's new, so he sometimes explores a bit."

She looked into the compound, following the various walkways leading to darkness-shrouded buildings. "Where do you think he'll take me?"

"Colonel Baxter's office," he said, pointing. "It's hard to see now, but it's under that yellow light. He's working late tonight, so you're in luck."

She followed the guard's finger, scanning a wide walkway until it stopped at a slant-roofed, one-story building. "I think I see it."

"I don't know why it's still so dark. They hauled in a bunch of new generators just last week. They must not be online yet."

"Why so many?"

Tate chuckled. "If I told you, I'd have to kill you."

"Very funny." As Lauren gauged the distance to the Colonel's office, a shadow of a winged creature glided across the walkway before disappearing over the office roof.

Tate's mouth dropped open. "What in blue blazes?"

Lauren slid off the stool and kept her head low. "He's here."

"Who's here?"

"One of the kidnappers."

Tate's eyes darted nervously. "Nothing to be worried about. Probably just a big owl."

"An owl?" Lauren gave him an incredulous stare. "Do you really believe that?"

A new shadow appeared. Lauren and Tate turned toward the road. Now dressed in military camouflage fatigues and cap, Semiramis marched toward them with a confident stride. "Private Tate," she said, eyeing his name tag, "this girl escaped this morning. I was bringing her here, but she bolted from the car just before we arrived."

Lauren leaned close to Tate and whispered, "She's lying. She's one of the kidnappers."

"I didn't hear about any escape," Tate said. "That news gets around fast."

"She's a special case. Everything's been hush-hush about her."

"And you didn't cuff her?" Tate asked. "That doesn't make sense."

"I see you've never worked with juveniles." Semiramis glared at Lauren and sharpened her tone. "The little liar promised she wouldn't need them, so I gave her a break, but it looks like she can't be trusted."

"I know what you mean. My stepdaughter lies all the time."

Lauren stared at Tate. It seemed that his entire countenance had suddenly changed, as if this woman had cast some kind of spell on him.

"Do you have cuffs I could borrow?" Semiramis asked.

"Coming right up."

As Tate stepped toward the guardhouse, Lauren grabbed his arm. "No! She's a kidnapper!" She pointed at Semiramis. "Think about it. Why didn't she drive the rest of the way? Why aren't I dressed in a striped jumpsuit? I'm wearing a volleyball uniform, for crying out loud!"

Tate gave Semiramis a skeptical tilt of his head. "Where is your car?"

"First of all," Semiramis said, setting a hand on her hip, "when I stopped to get this brat to settle down, she jerked out the keys, grabbed my cuffs, and threw them all into a cow pasture. Of course, I didn't think she'd head straight for the base, so I searched around a while before hoofing it here. Second, she is playing a crafty game with the jumpsuit business. She knows the minimum security inmates wear orange instead of stripes, but she's trying to fool you into thinking she's never been here before. She got the volleyball uniform from her girlfriend, thinking she could pose as a jock."

121

Lauren clenched her fists. "It's all a lie. She and this winged—" She bit her lip. Telling the whole truth would just make things worse. If only she could get to someone with an official list of prisoners before Tate handed her over, maybe she could prove her story.

Semiramis laughed. "Did she tell you a tale about a winged creature? She's been singing that wild story ever since she tripped on acid a few hours ago. She got high with her druggie friends as soon as she broke out. That's the kind of garbage we're dealing with."

"She didn't mention any winged creature." Tate withdrew a set of handcuffs from the guardhouse and reached for Lauren's wrist. "But we did see—"

"No!" Lauren jerked her arm away. "Listen! You have to believe me! Do I even *look* like a druggie?" She pointed at the Colonel's office. "Can't you just check it out before you hand me over to her? My name is Lauren Hunt. I live in Flagstaff. My parents' names are Fiona and Gaston Hunt. I go to school at—"

"I'm sorry, Lauren, or whatever your real name is." He pushed the jacket sleeve up and snapped a cuff around her wrist. "But those stripes on her uniform mean I have to do what she says, and I couldn't call to check even if I wanted to."

"Someone has to." Lauren jumped away and sprinted toward Colonel Baxter's office, the handcuffs jingling at her side.

"Catch her!" Semiramis called.

As Lauren continued running, Tate's voice faded behind her. "I can't leave my post. Don't worry. There's no place for her to go."

Lauren leaped up the three steps to the office entrance, twisted the knob, and flung the door open. Heaving deep breaths, she looked inside the dimly lit rectangular room. At the left side, a man in a military uniform sat behind a desk, looking at an open laptop computer. Its glow washed over his face and drew scrolling lines of characters from cheek to cheek.

At the right-hand wall, a woman dressed in an orange jumpsuit sat in a hardback chair, her body erect and her hands on her knees as if ready to jump at the first hint of a command. She glanced Lauren's way but said nothing, though her eyes widened and her brow creased deeply. With closely cropped dark hair, thin face, and pale skin, she gave the appearance of a concentration camp survivor.

Then, as if formed from the darkness itself, Tamiel emerged from a shadow behind the man at the desk. Dressed completely in black, including thin gloves that appeared to be a selection from a women's department store, he looked as ghoulish as ever. "Here she is, Colonel Baxter," he said as he pointed at the screen and nodded toward Lauren. "Now that she has joined us, feel free to verify her identity."

Lauren spun in place and scanned the jail yard. From the direction of the front gate, a big guard strode toward her. She couldn't escape in that direction, and any other direction would lead her into the unknown.

When she swiveled back, the Colonel looked up, squinted at Lauren for a moment, and nodded. "I can see the resemblance."

As the Colonel rose from his seat, Lauren backed down the steps. "No," she said, shivering again. "This can't be. I'm Lauren Hunt. I have never been a prisoner here."

The Colonel, a thin, lanky man wearing beige khakis and a camo shirt, walked slowly toward her, a hand raised. "I know you're scared, but when I take you to your—"

She tightened her fists at her side and shouted, "I'm not supposed to be here!"

"Lauren," Tamiel said, his voice as smooth as silk as he followed the Colonel, "I realize that your friend's death has caused you a tremendous amount of grief, but there is no need to deny reality. We know who you really are."

"Who I really am?" Setting her cuffed hand on her hip, Lauren pointed at Tamiel. "Speaking of who you really are, what did you do with your wings, you mutant zombie freak?"

Tamiel and the Colonel, now standing together on the top step, glanced at each other. "Drugs," Tamiel said, shaking his head sadly. "It is tragic how kids these days try to drown their sorrows by poisoning their brains."

"Ain't that the truth." The Colonel stepped to the next stair, his hand again extended. "We'll get you into the infirmary, and you'll be yourself in no time."

The woman dressed in orange sneaked up behind them and waved her arms, her face wild with alarm, apparently signaling for Lauren to run.

123

Lauren spun again and took off, but she slammed into the big guard. He wrapped a pair of tree-trunk arms around her body. She squirmed and thrashed, but his arms felt like immovable pinchers.

"I have her, Colonel," the soldier said, his voice deep and calm.

The Colonel joined them on the walkway. "Take her to the Healers. They'll detox her."

Semiramis stepped out from behind the big soldier. "Will you allow me to escort her?"

"Are you sure?" the Colonel asked. "She's already proven she's a runner."

Tamiel walked down the steps and stopped at the bottom, keeping his distance, while the female prisoner stayed at the office doorway, now watching stoically. "I think it is a good idea," Tamiel said. "A woman's touch is best for a frightened girl and will ease the transition back to sanity. I vouch for the Major's abilities."

"Very well." The Colonel nodded at the big guard. "Release her, but wait here a moment. I have something in my safe to give her, something that belonged to her mother. The Healers will want to see her with it." Using sign language, the Colonel relayed a message to the female prisoner. She nodded and ran back into the office.

The guard let Lauren go and brushed his hands across her upper arms. "I apologize if I hurt you, Miss. I tried to be as gentle as a sheep."

She looked up at him. With short gray hair standing upright on his balding head, and crow's-feet radiating from his eyes to his temples, he appeared to be in his sixties, and his kind smile made him look more like a grandfather than a prison guard. With a quick glance, she read his name tag—Sergeant D. Hoskins. "I think you mean *as a lamb*."

"Yes, yes, of course." He shifted nervously. "I apologize again."

Lauren studied his eyes. He seemed so sincere, so kind, even if awkward. "I'm not hurt. Thank you for being so concerned."

Tamiel gestured toward the office door. "Shall we return to our research, Colonel Baxter?" He glanced inside before looking at the Colonel again. "Alone this time? I want to show you the possible traits of a male anthrozil we're looking for. I cannot afford anyone knowing who our suspects are."

"Portia is deaf," the Colonel said. "She won't hear our conversation."

"Pardon my frankness, Colonel. I realize that you are unaccustomed to the late hours, but when it comes to anthrozils we have not yet apprehended, complete privacy is more important than having a coffee fetcher on hand."

"She's more than a coffee fetcher. She knows the computer system better than I do, so I keep her at hand whenever I'm here. She's sort of like an idiot savant, kind of simple-minded about everything else, so we protect her from the general population. She has her own room here in the minimum security section."

125

"Is that so?" Tamiel eyed the Colonel carefully. "What was her crime?"

"She killed her husband. He was abusive, so the DA reduced to voluntary manslaughter."

"Voluntary? No self-defense claims?"

The Colonel shook his head. "The public defender let her plead guilty. I guess he didn't care to push the case. Couldn't be bothered, I suppose."

"Very interesting." Tamiel looked into the office again. "Be that as it may, I prefer privacy. I want nothing left to chance. If the anthrozil we're looking for is like his father, we have to be very careful at every step of the process."

"If you insist."

Portia returned, her fingers rolled into a fist. She hurried down the stairs and, grabbing Lauren's closed cuff, examined it, as if checking to make sure it was fastened. She pushed something into Lauren's hand and gave her a long stare before breaking away.

Then, leaping into a jog, she followed the paved walk deeper into the prison facility and blended into the shadows.

After Tamiel and the Colonel reentered the office and closed the door, Hoskins marched away, leaving Lauren alone with Semiramis. Lauren opened her hand. A gold ring with a mounted red gem sat in her palm.

The ghostly woman watched Hoskins, apparently waiting for him to get out of earshot before moving or speaking. Finally, she turned and stared into Lauren's eyes. Her irises altered in color from green to blue and back again—eerie, haunting.

Lauren resisted another shiver. She couldn't let this ghost win any mind games.

"That's a rubellite," Semiramis said, nodding at the ring in Lauren's hand. "A very special gem. It is said that dragons use them as a symbol of power, and since dragons who become humans lose their draconic nature, the gem turns white when they wear such a ring."

Lauren studied the red stone. Glittering in the bare light, it appeared to be nothing more than the fake rubies she had seen in cheap costume jewelry. "How could it have belonged to my mother? I've never seen it before in my life."

"You will soon learn much more about many things." Semiramis kept her focus on Lauren's hands. "Can I trust you? Or should I fasten the second cuff?"

"You can trust me." Lauren lifted her arm, letting the handcuffs dangle. "Can you take this one off?"

"I prefer to leave it. You never know when I might have to attach you to something to keep you from escaping."

Lauren let her arm flap against her side, jangling the cuffs. "I'm in a jail yard. I don't think escaping is possible."

"If you maintain that realistic outlook, you'll stay out of trouble."

Lauren caught a glimpse of a man with a rifle standing in an observation tower near the border of the jail yard. Resisting seemed

126

useless. There was no way to escape, at least not yet. For now, she just had to survive.

She stuffed the ring into her sweatpants pocket and breathed out a quiet, "If you say so."

As she and Semiramis walked side by side on the concrete path, dim lamps atop tall poles gave light to the buildings far ahead. Rectangular and aligned in rows, they looked like barracks from a war movie, though cleaner and more modern. The dark narrow spaces between them might allow one person to walk without brushing the sides, but probably not two. The path divided the barracks into two sections, left and right, and a tall fence blocked the way at the far end. Since Portia was nowhere in sight, she must have already entered one of these living quarters.

Between Lauren and the barracks, a rectangle of lush green sod interrupted the concrete. Beyond the rectangle's left edge lay a field striped for sports, not nearly as green.

As Lauren walked across the sod, moist and mushy under her feet, Semiramis spoke in a low tone. "I am told that this is the minimum security section. I have to take you to a political prisoner in maximum security. It's very important that I see the two of you together."

Lauren glanced at her captor's military boots. Although she walked with a normal gait, she never quite touched the ground. Maybe she really was a ghost. "Since when do we have political prisoners in this country? We're supposed to have freedom of speech."

"Freedom of speech?" Semiramis laughed. "Your country allows freedom until it feels threatened. In case you haven't heard, a war is brewing with Second Eden. Anyone with dragon sympathies is immediately suspect, especially anthrozils, so people with dragon characteristics are detained using a nonlegal pretext."

They crossed the far edge of the sod and proceeded on the paved path. "You might have heard," Semiramis continued, "that

127

some government officials are calling for all anthrozils to be eliminated. Supposedly, anthrozils aren't human, so killing them for the benefit of society is the best option. Until that policy is settled, we have taken some anthrozils into protective custody."

Lauren let the words tumble around. *Protective custody.* That excuse was as lame as a one-legged penguin. The entire story was a crock, an excuse to imprison anyone they wanted—just claim someone has strange characteristics, slap the anthrozil label on her, and she can go to jail without a trial. For now, she would have to play along. Arguing with fanatical conspiracy theorists wouldn't do any good anyway.

As they passed between the two sets of barracks, Lauren's tingling sensation returned, again stinging the skin on her back. Sounds poured into her ears—a quiet sigh from the barracks, a radio playing a country song, and Semiramis's voice, though her lips didn't move to speak. Her words echoed slightly, as if confined in an empty room.

Tamiel thinks he has me trapped, but we shall see about that. After my son tests this girl, we will know if she is a Listener or has all of Shachar's traits. Then, as long as she is in our control, we have the ultimate bargaining leverage, assuming, of course, she survives the tests. There must be a way to assure that Tamiel keeps his end of the bargain. I cannot let her escape.

Lauren concealed a tight swallow. A Listener? What could that be? And who was Shachar? Obviously the story about her freakish abilities had gotten out, and now they planned to use her as a lab rat.

Without moving her head, she glanced from side to side. Running would only delay the inevitable, unless somehow she could find someone who would listen, someone in command who would sympathize with her plight. And Semiramis, being a ghost, might be able to fly faster than an escaping girl could run.

Lauren studied Semiramis's boots again. Since she never touched the ground, and since she summoned that big guard to grab her, and since she didn't attach the second handcuff, maybe this ghost wasn't physical at all. Maybe she wouldn't be able to stop anyone from doing anything. Yet, something moved those chess pieces. The facts weren't exactly adding up.

A crackle sounded in the distance. The lights darkened. Seconds later, sirens blared. Lauren jumped away from the walk and ran into a gap between two barracks. Guided by moonlight, she hurried into the darker recesses, holding the handcuffs to keep them quiet. Finally, she stopped and looked back. Semiramis was nowhere in sight, but being a ghost, she could be invisible, maybe even standing next to her.

Lauren leaned against a wall and took in a deep breath. Her heart thumped wildly. A rollicking clamor drummed in her ears, the barking of dogs now combining with the sirens. Both likely signaled a warning to the prisoners. Anyone caught outside their rooms or cells or whatever they lived in could be in big trouble.

She swallowed through a lump. There was no place to go. Since Semiramis knew where she went, she had to keep moving, get as far away from this area as possible.

Jogging slowly to avoid crashing into a wall, she zigzagged among the barracks until she came out into the open near the side of a road. A tall chain-link fence stood between her and the road's nearer edge, but it had no razor wire on top, probably because it was an interior barrier separating sections of the prison.

A pair of buildings stood on the opposite side of the road. Two stories high and made of brick, they seemed out of place, more like an old-fashioned hotel than a prison. Yet, the two military jeeps parked next to each other in the middle of the road provided a stark reminder that this wasn't a lodging where residents could check out anytime they pleased.

Lauren studied the details. Dark bars crisscrossed the windows. Attached to the wall next to each entry, a tiny LED flashed at the center of a dark square panel. That area had to be the maximum security section. It would be the last place anyone would think to look for her, but how could she possibly get in? And once in, where would she go?

Narrowing her eyes, she looked at an alley separating the buildings. It seemed to exit into a field behind the complex. Maybe there would be a tree to climb or some other place to hide until she could figure out what to do, but how could she get over the fence without being noticed, especially since she glowed in the dark?

She scanned her body. The jacket covered her arms, but her face was still bare, probably enough skin showing to stand out like a human firefly, especially while climbing a fence. And no matter how quiet she tried to be, the combination of shifting fence links and clinking handcuffs would alert anyone within earshot.

A short distance to her left, a guard carrying a rifle got out of a jeep and set a flashlight beam on the road directly in front of her. From her right, another guard approached, walking slowly with a leashed German shepherd at his side. This guard, hefty and balding, looked a lot like Hoskins, but it was hard to tell for sure.

Trembling, Lauren took a step back. That dog would be the first to notice her, whether by sight, smell, or sound. Her back tingled again, but she didn't need a reminder that fear coursed through her body.

Something grabbed her jacket and pulled her deeper into the shadows. She jerked to free herself, but whatever held her wouldn't let go. As she whipped around, a small hand clamped over her mouth and forced her to a crouch.

"Shhhhh!" Her captor's long shush sounded like a leaking tire, growing quieter as she uncovered Lauren's mouth.

Lauren stared through the darkness and located a dim face. "Portia?" she whispered.

Portia set a finger over her lips, again signaling for silence. As they both stooped low, the dog handler joined the first guard at his jeep, and the two began chatting. The shepherd lay on the road, its ears erect.

Portia laid a hand on Lauren's cheek, her eyes wide.

"Yes," Lauren said in the lowest tone possible, "my skin glows."

Using her hands, Portia began a long string of rapid gestures. Lauren pushed her hands down, shaking her head. "I don't know sign language." She then rolled her eyes. "What am I doing? You're deaf. You can't hear me."

Portia spoke slowly and carefully. "I read lips." In spite of her efforts, her words came out slightly warped.

"Even when it's this dark?"

Portia nodded. "I know much. Not an idiot."

Lauren cringed. This poor woman probably read Colonel Baxter's lips when he made the remark about her being an idiot savant. It must have hurt her feelings. Yet, hadn't she already gone back into the office when he said it? Maybe not. Either way, he might have said it in her presence at other times.

131

As the two locked stares, Lauren's skin continued to tingle, and a soft voice rose to her ears, echoing in the same way Semiramis's unspoken words had. *How do I get Lauren to believe I'm not an idiot, that I just can't speak well? It's too much to try to force into words. And if I stop pretending to be a prisoner, my whole cover could be blown.*

Lauren resisted the urge to blurt out the revelation. Obviously Portia had reasons for keeping her secrets. Besides, revealing her own newfound ability to hear thoughts might cause trouble. "I believe you're not an idiot," Lauren whispered, forming her words carefully as she helped Portia read her lips. "Why did you check my cuff?"

"To see if … I have key."

"And you don't?"

Portia shook her head. "Different kind."

"Well, maybe you could help me hide. Do you know how to get across the fence? I don't think they'll look for me there."

"Wait." Portia pointed at the road. "Watch."

The handler led the dog to the fence's gate about a stone's throw to Lauren's left. He paused there and turned toward the other soldier.

When the guard at the gate spoke, his words began in a soft voice, but her tingles amplified the sound until it seemed that he stood right next to her. "It's locked as tight as a drummer."

Lauren couldn't resist smiling. That was Hoskins, all right.

"It's the power outage," the other guard said as he leaned back against a jeep. "The security system is on a dedicated generator, and the interior gates revert to a default code. It's in the manual."

"I haven't read it all yet. It's only been a week."

"I'm coming." The guard walked across the road and punched numbers into a pad. "You'd better read the manual before your next shift."

132

The shepherd's ears perked up, and he let out a rumbling growl. Hoskins tightened his grip on the leash and looked around. "He smells something."

Lauren sniffed the back of her hand. Nothing obvious. But she hadn't showered since the game. Maybe she reeked and couldn't tell.

Hoskins jerked a phone to his ear. "Yes? ... Which door? ... I'll check into it."

"Whatcha got?" the other guard asked.

"Someone accessed the research wing's rear door—rather unexpected this time of night."

"Need backup?"

Hoskins patted the shepherd's head. "I have backup, but I wouldn't mind the human variety."

The other guard shrugged. "Sure." He led the way to the nearer building's front door, held his wrist close to the panel, and disappeared inside. Hoskins glanced back. As he reeled in the leash to keep the dog close, moonlight illuminated his look of concern.

Seconds later, he entered the building, and the door closed behind him.

Portia pulled on Lauren's sleeve. "Come!"

The two ran to the gate. Portia touched a numeric keypad mounted inside a box hanging on a vertical pole next to the locking mechanism.

Lauren mouthed her words carefully. "I heard him say it defaulted to a power-outage code, something that's in their manual."

Portia nodded. "I know … that code."

As Portia punched in the numbers, Lauren took note of the sequence—five, seven, four, one, three.

Portia swung the gate open. "Go," she said, gesturing with an arm. "I must … stay here."

After Lauren passed through, she spun and mouthed, "Thank you."

Smiling, Portia closed the gate, then dashed away along the path. Lauren watched her for a moment. What was she? An under-cover agent of some kind? And why was she helping a girl she couldn't possibly know anything about?

Lauren shrugged. No time to figure it out. She ran across the road and into the alley. When she reached the far end, she leaned out and looked both ways. To her left, a hooded figure skulked toward her, staying close to the building's rear wall. As he drew closer, moonlight illuminated his features. With a strong chin, clean-shaven face, and short, dark hair, he appeared to be about her age, though his bent posture made his height hard to deter-mine—maybe five foot ten. Why would a teenager be sneaking around in the maximum security area of a prison?

She backed into the alley and stepped on something hard and irregular. She picked up the two-handled object and drew it close to her eyes. Wire cutters? Who would leave wire cutters lying around here?

9

CHAPTER

BREAKING IN

M att detached and dropped the rappelling harness. After flicking on his penlight and raising his hood, he hustled toward the prison, wire cutters in hand. With the building's power out, no exterior floodlights could expose his presence, but the penlight, as weak as it was, probably stood out like a beacon. And since everyone would be on high alert, he had to find the rear entrance to the research wing in a hurry and wait in the shadow of the alcove until the power returned. Only then would he be able to test the bracelet's password.

He ran over a grassy field for at least a hundred yards until he reached a chain-link fence. Above, at least six feet over his head, razor wire ran along the top. He began snipping the links, starting at waist level and working his way down. The blades seemed sharp, but the links proved to be rugged, forcing him to prop the handles between his forearms and squeeze them together. With each snip, a metallic ping sounded, swallowed by the surrounding racket. All he needed was a gap big enough to squeeze through, something that might avoid notice until the next scheduled power outage.

After a final clip at the bottom, he pushed his body through the opening and continued his dash. The penlight now off, he stopped at an alley that divided the twin two-story buildings. According to the map, the rear door lay about a hundred feet to the right of the alley. It would be easy to step off the distance.

He looked through the alley to the open area at the far end. A soldier leading a German shepherd walked by on an access road, but they didn't seem to notice him. Beyond where they walked and behind a fence, a female wearing sweats and a jacket stood in the shadows cast by the barracks. Judging from her size and shape, she appeared to be a young woman, maybe a teenager. Normally the distance and darkness would keep him from picking up any details at all, but her face and hands seemed to glow. If she was trying to hide from the guard, she wouldn't last long.

He shook his head. No time to worry about her. He laid the clippers in the alley, then, bending low, scurried to the right. After thirty steps, the wall to the left gave way to a short corridor that ended at a metal door. To the right of the door, a black square panel no bigger than his hand hung on the brick wall. A tiny red LED blinked steadily at its center.

With the roof of this corridor hiding the moon, a shadow veiled the lettering on the security panel. He turned on the penlight and read the words. *Research Wing. Invalid Entry Attempts Will Alert Security Officer.*

Matt studied the panel. Apparently the LED was battery powered, but the computer that read the password couldn't be running unless the system had its own generator somewhere.

He nodded at his own idea. The security system probably *was* powered separately from the rest of the facility. Otherwise, moving from room to room or building to building would be a nightmare during an outage.

He whispered, "Walter. I'm in position. Can you hear me?"

"Not very well." Static cut through Walter's voice. "I assume you can't speak up."

"Not really. Listen. Any idea if the security system works when the power's out? Maybe I can try to get in before what's-his-name restores it. Then I could sneak around in the dark."

"I suppose trying it won't hurt. If it isn't operational, you probably won't alert anyone."

"Okay," Matt said. "I'll keep you up-to-date."

He set the bracelet against the LED. A click sounded, then a faint hum. When he grabbed the handle and pulled, the door opened, silencing the noise.

Holding the door, he probed the dark interior with his penlight. It appeared to be a hallway leading left and right. Nothing stirred. Yet, a sense of danger pricked his mind. Something was wrong. Maybe the power outage wasn't enough to keep a guard from noticing a suspicious access. After all, who would enter through the rear door at this time of night? Of course, he should have thought of that possibility earlier, and Walter counted on his danger-sensing talents to keep him out of trouble, so he didn't mention it.

137

He backed out, set the penlight on the threshold against the jamb, and let the door swing up to it. Good. It stayed ajar. Maybe if the danger settled, he could return, but for now, his inner alarm kept getting stronger.

"Walter, I think someone's coming."

"The baseball feeling?"

"Yeah. A fastball."

"You'd better abort. Get back to the rope. We'll have to come up with another plan."

"On my way." Hugging the wall again, Matt tiptoed toward the alley. No use leaving the wire cutters there and risking someone tracing them back to Walter. He slowly unzipped his jacket. Quick access to the gun might be necessary.

When he reached the opening, he searched the ground for the cutters. Leaving the penlight at the door felt pretty stupid. Now the cutters might be impossible to find.

"Looking for something?"

Matt jumped back. The glowing girl stood in front of him holding the cutters, as if brandishing a weapon. A chain and loose handcuff dangled from her wrist.

"Listen," she whispered, "I don't know who you are or why you're here, but my guess is that you cut the fence to get in. If you'll show me the hole you made, I won't call the guard. Deal?"

Matt grabbed the cutters and matched her low tone. "Since you're trying to escape, I doubt that you'll tell the guard anything, no matter what I do."

As he turned, she pinched his jacket sleeve. "Let me come with you. I'll follow behind as quiet as a mouse."

"And let a convict go free? This is the maximum security area. What did you do? Murder a classmate?"

She clutched the prison insignia on her jacket, making her cuffs rattle. "Does this look like a jailbird's jumpsuit? I'm trapped here." Her whispered voice cracked. "These people think I'm something I'm not, so they want to take me to the Healers and do experiments on me."

Matt looked toward the rear access door. The danger sense had decreased. Maybe he could take a second to deal with this girl. "How'd you manage to slice off one of your cuffs? These cutters barely made it through the fence."

"I didn't cut it. They just didn't fasten it."

"Lift your arm," he said as he opened the cutters.

The girl complied. Matt slid one of the cutting blades under the cuff and clamped down on the handles, but they wouldn't bite through.

"We'll have to get those off later." Touching his jaw, he continued in a whisper. "Walter?"

138

The girl squinted. "Walter?" She opened her jacket, revealing a sports jersey covering her athletic female form. "Do I look like a Walter?"

"I'm here," Walter said through the tooth chip, "but whoever you're talking to isn't coming in very well. Is she female?"

Matt nodded. "Definitely. I think—"

"Definitely?" She whipped the jacket closed again, her face hardening.

"Not you." Matt pointed at his mouth. "I'm talking into a radio."

Her eyes widened, and an embarrassed smile emerged, but she stayed quiet.

"She wants to come with me," Matt continued. "She's half handcuffed, but she claims she isn't a prisoner and that they want to do experiments on her. Considering her appearance, I kind of believe her."

"Her appearance?"

"Yeah, the way she's dressed and the fact that she … well … glows in the dark."

139

"Glows in the dark?" Walter sighed. "Bring her. I'll sort it out when you get here."

"The sense of danger isn't so bad right now. Should I try to break into the lab again?"

"Definitely, but you'd better get the girl over here first. I asked Yereq to make a lot of noise to get the guards off your back, so whoever was tracking you probably headed for the other side of the complex. The next diversion will keep them there, so the timing might be perfect. When you get back to the prison, the coast should be clear."

"What kind of diversion?"

"A fiery one. Let's just say the lights won't be back on anytime soon. They'll be on generator power for a while. Once he's finished, he'll go back to guard the portal to Second Eden, so this will be your last chance to get the job done."

SONG OF THE OVULUM

"Got it." Ducking low, Matt motioned for the girl to follow and hurried toward the fence. When they reached the opening, he pulled the links back. "You first."

She dropped to hands and knees and crawled to the other side, then pulled the links in the opposite direction while he scooted through. He scrambled to his feet and, still holding the cutters, waved for her to follow again. As they hustled, she caught up and ran at his side, clutching the loose cuff in her hand.

Matt noted her form, visible in the dim light. Her stride was strong and effortless, proving that the sports uniform was more than just a gimmick. As her hair bobbed, touching her shoulders with each step, its dark shade prompted a memory. He was looking for data on a girl about her age, but, lacking blonde hair, she wasn't a likely candidate. Even if her hair darkened over the years, the chances that this girl was Karen Bannister were pretty low. Still, there had to be a reason behind her claims that the Healers wanted to do experiments on her. Could she really be an anthrozil … or maybe something even weirder?

"We're approaching the rope," Matt said, raising his voice above a whisper.

She looked at him. "Rope? What rope?"

"I was talking into the radio again."

"Oh …" She stretched out the word. "It's kind of hard to tell. Sometimes I can hear whispers from far away, but it's only when I get a tingling sensation on my back. I'm not feeling it right now."

"Okay, I'll store that bit of trivia for later use."

"Sorry." As she refocused on the ground in front of them, her head drooped a notch. "I was just trying to explain."

"I can hear her now," Walter said. "Must be because you're farther from the sirens."

Matt didn't bother answering either of them. Using the transmitter had gotten him in enough trouble with this girl, and talking directly to her hadn't been much better. He had already said enough stupid things to make her hate him. This girl wasn't like Darcy at all. She deserved better treatment.

Cringing, he mentally shook his head. *Trivia?* What was he thinking?

He stopped at the base of a cliff, dropped the cutters, and grabbed the dangling rope. "Walter, we're here. I doubt she knows how to use the ascenders. Do you think you can pull ..." He gave her an apologetic look. "What's your name?"

"Lauren Hunt." Her brow, not quite as radiant as before, creased deeply. "Listen. Do you have a phone? Or does Walter? Someone has to call my parents. The kidnapper said he would kill them if I didn't cooperate."

"You have parents?"

"Yes." Lauren tilted her head. "Why wouldn't I?"

"I'll explain later." Matt patted his pants pocket. "Walter wouldn't let me bring my phone. He was worried it might be traceable. But he has a secure one."

"She can use it when she gets up here," Walter said. "If I call her parents, they'll think I'm some kind of prankster."

Lauren nodded, her face still pensive. "I can hear Walter now."

"Just to prepare myself," Walter said, "how big is she?"

"About five foot six." Matt looked her over. "How much do you weigh?"

"One twenty-five."

"Did you catch that, Walter?"

"Got it. I think I can handle that much. And you say she glows in the dark?"

"Yeah, it's really ... well ..." He tried to focus away from Lauren, but her expectant eyes made her impossible to avoid. "Unique."

"Is she your age?" Walter asked.

Lauren stepped closer and spoke toward Matt's mouth. "I'm sixteen."

"There you go." Matt stored that piece of data away, more evidence that Lauren matched his supposed sister's description, but since she wasn't an orphan, the similarities were likely just coincidences. "I'll give you another shout when she's ready." He picked up the rappelling harness and handed it to her. "Ever done rope climbing?"

"Lots of times in gym class. How far to the top?"

"Too far. And it's dangerous, so we have the harness, and Walter will pull." A sense of dread stung Matt's gut, the worst ever. "Walter! Another fastball!"

Sudden darkness enveloped them. A shadow drifted across the ground, then disappeared.

"The kidnapper's here!" Lauren grabbed the harness and wrapped the belt around her waist. "Hurry!"

"Wait! You have to put the straps around your thighs."

Gunshots rang out high above. Seconds later, the rope flew upward, jerking Lauren off the ground. As the line ripped through the harness's hook, she bobbed, dangling above Matt's head. Finally, the line jerked away and disappeared, and she dropped into his arms. A man shouted from the top of the cliff, but the voice died away, as if smothered by a blanket.

Lauren unbuckled the harness. Her lips moved, but no sound came out.

"Did you say something?" Matt asked. Although the words registered in his mind, they didn't reach his ears.

She nodded and continued speaking, but, again, nothing came out.

He pressed a finger against the flap of his ear, trying to alleviate pressure. "Walter! Can you hear me? What's going on up there?"

Dead silence stifled every sound. The sense of danger spiked again. He reached into his jacket and withdrew the Glock, but with no one around, he felt stupid aiming it at shadows.

A brilliant light flashed over the prison, and a billowing plume of orange and black smoke shot into the sky. The ground shook, nearly knocking them off their feet. A fire roared and crackled in the distance.

Matt touched an ear. His hearing had returned.

Lauren let the harness fall to her ankles. "Now what?"

"I don't know. Walter said the only way out of here is straight up. No one told me what to do if something like this happened."

"Why did you come here in the first place?"

"To find my mother and get her and Walter's wife out. They're being tortured in there."

"Your mother is being tortured? And you were about to leave her behind?" Her accusing eyes sparkled in the midst of her glow. "How could you do that? She's your mother!"

"No. I was going back. I was just trying to get you out first."

"Oh." Her expression softened. "Sorry."

"No problem." A new sensation prodded his nerves, another fastball ready to smack him between the eyes. "I can't wait around here," he said as he slid the gun into its holster. "Are you with me?"

She glanced around. "Do I have any choice?"

"Probably not. Let's hope the guards are distracted by the fire." He jerked off his gloves and handed them to her. "Wear these. We have to keep you from glowing." He shed his jacket. "This has a hood. It should help. And it's thicker, too."

"Won't you be cold?"

Matt waved a hand. "I don't get cold easily. Besides, your jacket will make me look more like a guard."

"I get it." Lauren slid her arms out of her sleeves, a clumsy procedure with the dangling cuffs. "Your voice is probably deep enough to fool someone, but your face looks too young."

"Not much I can do about that." As they put the jackets on, Matt looked at her toned arms. The sleeveless jersey accentuated her radiant skin. She hadn't bothered to explain the glow, but asking

143

might delay them further. Danger still lurked. Although no longer a fastball, it felt like an approaching shadow, a predator crouching, ready to pounce.

"Got it," she said as she zipped the jacket.

After removing the guard's name tag from his new jacket and putting it into a pocket, he raised Lauren's hood and pulled it over her eyes. "Keep your head low and follow me."

Trying to tune out howling sirens, barking dogs, and frantic shouts in the direction of the fire, Matt hustled with Lauren to the fence. After crawling through, they jogged hunchbacked to the building and stooped at the corner next to the alley. Although smoke filled the air, making breathing difficult, it added a helpful gray veil.

Matt looked around the corner. At the alley's far end, prisoners filed along the road. Since the fire raged in a different structure, their evacuation was probably just a precaution. A guard stood watching them, his back toward the alley.

As he glanced between the guard and Lauren, Matt checked his danger sense. Everything seemed normal. Maybe the other guards were preoccupied with the fire and protecting the prisoners. Lauren looked at him from the shadow of the hood, her face glowing and expectant.

"Hear anything important?" he whispered.

She shook her head.

"Then let's go." He led her to the rear entry door, pulled it open, and scooped up the penlight. After stepping inside, he allowed the door to settle with a quiet click. "Now to find the Healers' Room."

As they padded ahead, he guided the light around the dark hallway. Closed metal doors ran along both sides, each one with a square, barred window. Matt peeked through one of the dirty panes. Inside, a pair of unmade beds lined the far wall, and a toilet sat against the adjacent wall. "Empty," he whispered.

"They probably evacuated everyone," Lauren said. "Your mother must be outside with the other prisoners."

"From what I heard, that's not likely."

"Why?"

"According to Walter, she has dragon wings. She's a huge escape risk, for obvious reasons. They'll probably keep her inside as long as possible. We're not to the room where we think she's supposed to be."

"I think I've heard about her," Lauren said. "My mother mentioned seeing someone like that on TV a while back."

"Yeah. There aren't many like her around." He checked his danger sense again. Still no trouble. "The story I've always heard is that my mother was a drug addict who left me in a bassinet at a church, and I went through the foster home circuit until I transferred to a military academy. Then Walter shows up out of the blue and says Billy and Bonnie Bannister are my parents."

"So, Walter thinks you're an anthrozil."

145

"Right. Supposedly, I'm part dragon, and I have a dragon's ability to sense danger."

"Then we might have a bigger problem than I thought."

He shone the penlight on her face, careful to keep it out of her eyes. "What?"

"The reason they kidnapped me. They think I'm an anthrozil, too."

"Why is that a problem?"

She set a finger on his chest. "They know you're here now. That shadow we saw? That was Tamiel, the kidnapper. I know this sounds crazy, but he claims to be an angel, and he has wings. I saw them myself. I heard him say he was looking for another anthrozil, a male, and he seemed nervous that his traits might be like his father's."

"Yeah. Supposedly my father can breathe fire."

"I heard about him, too. Anyway, Tamiel must have had a reason to attack your friend."

"You mean Walter?"

She nodded. "Did Walter have any evidence with him that you're an anthrozil?"

"Maybe." Matt held out an empty palm. "He had this gem he called a candlestone, and he acted like it was important, something about telling whether or not I have another dragon trait. If this Tamiel character knows what the gem is, then maybe he can make the connection."

"I think we should assume he already has."

"If Tamiel can fly," Matt said, "and he took out Walter, then why didn't he stop us on the way to the prison?"

"Maybe he wanted you to come in so he wouldn't have to face you alone. Remember, he was worried that you might be able to breathe fire. But once you're inside with a bunch of guards around ..." She clasped her hands together. "They've got you."

"If they know I'm here, why haven't they closed in on me already? The fire outside?"

"Probably." She tapped her chin with a gloved finger. "No matter what Tamiel said to the Colonel, the prisoners are still going to be his first priority. The guards might not be a problem for now, but you can bet Tamiel and Semiramis won't be far away."

"Semiramis?"

"The other kidnapper. She's posing as an officer here."

"Well, even though I can't breathe fire, I don't mind if they think I can. After I get Mrs. Bannister out, I'm supposed to try to get Walter's wife, too. Walter hoped Mrs. Bannister could help me get past security and find their cell, so if they think I can breathe fire, I might be able to use that to our advantage."

"The fear factor. Good idea." Lauren looked down the hall both ways. "Do you sense any danger?"

He shook his head. "If someone is waiting to pounce on me in the lab, I think I might be able to feel it by now. It's only a few doors away."

"Maybe they're holding back. Maybe they want you to find your mother first."

"Why would they do that?"

"She's the bait. You're the catch. Once you're together, they can threaten her and force you to give up. A hostage can neutralize a powerful weapon, even fire breathing."

He gazed at her glowing face. It seemed that she possessed such a powerful inner character, light spilled out through her pores. She was definitely smart, strong, and passionate. Maybe this was a good time to make up for his stupid comments. "It's great having you around. I'm not used to girls with so much ... well ..." He searched for the right word. Picking the wrong one might mess up everything. "Spirit, I guess."

She slid her hand into his and hooked their thumbs. "I'll take that as a compliment, but I'm really hoping for something else."

"Something else?" Matt studied her face—raised brow, sparkling eyes, slightly pursed lips. She looked like a love-struck kid from a Disney cartoon, but that visage didn't match her moxie. She was obviously more mature than that.

Clearing his throat, he prepared the question he almost didn't want to ask. "What are you hoping for?"

"I'm hoping you'll tell me your name."

CHAPTER

VALOR

Joran opened his eyes. White light flooded his vision. As he lay on his back, his head throbbed, and his limbs ached. One hand touched cloth and metal, and the other touched skin.

He turned his head to his right. His fingers curled around his sonic rod as well as a handful of someone's clothing, but the person lay so close, he couldn't see who it was. Selah, maybe? If so, he must have grabbed her tunic during a nightmare, but she seemed undisturbed.

Letting go of the tunic but keeping the rod, he turned to the opposite side. His other hand lay over a wrist, delicate and feminine. Selah?

He propped himself on an elbow to get a closer look. It *was* Selah! She lay on her back, still clutching her sonic rod, her eyes closed as her chest rose and fell in an even rhythm.

Joran climbed to his feet. He stood on what appeared to be nothing at all, as if he floated in empty air, yet his weight still pressed down on a foundation. This invisible floor had to have some substance.

The person on his right also lay on his back, but an arm covered his face. Still, he seemed vaguely familiar, like a person one meets only in a dream.

"Hello," Joran tried to say, but although his mouth formed the word, and his lungs pushed out the air, no sound emerged, at least none he could hear. Like Selah, this person breathed easily, noiselessly.

Joran stood perfectly still and listened. How strange! Even in the quietest places, the sound of his own heartbeat always registered. But now? Nothing. Nothing at all. He laid a hand over his heart. It thumped, as usual, but the rhythm seemed faster than normal, as if he had just battled a Watcher.

A Watcher? The word sparked an image—a winged creature, smaller than the other demons, mysterious, and … silent.

A flood of memories surged through his mind. Tamiel, the Silent One, stole the purity ovulum, but Joran grabbed his tunic and …

150

He looked at his hand, flexing his fingers around the sonic rod as he imagined dragging that creature into the powerful suction that pulled Selah toward the ovulum. It was a desperate attempt to keep Tamiel from stealing the ovulum, and it worked. He had done it.

Somehow the three of them had traveled into the egg. Father had said each ovulum held a refuge, and since the purity ovulum was crystal clear, it made sense that they would be in the midst of perfect clarity, a world of invisible realities, including a transparent floor that registered white in his eyes.

Turning back to Selah, he lowered himself to his knees. Maybe he was the only one who couldn't hear in this place. He had to be as quiet as possible and not waken Tamiel.

He nudged her shoulder. She blinked, then stared at him. Her mouth formed words, but no sound came out. Her brow bent, and she lifted a hand to her ear.

Joran read her lips as she tried to say, "I can't hear."

He helped her to her feet and nodded toward Tamiel. She covered her mouth as if gasping, but again, silence reigned. Gesturing toward her back, she mouthed, "Where are his wings?"

Joran shrugged. Since Tamiel was able to alter his form to that of a young woman, hiding his wings was probably a simple matter.

Taking Selah's hand, Joran began walking. Maybe Tamiel could hear, and maybe he couldn't. In either case, it would be better to stay as far away from him as possible.

Under their feet, the ground didn't seem to move at all. Yet, Tamiel drifted away like a raft on a slow current, getting smaller and smaller. Ahead, only whiteness appeared, but not the opaque whiteness of pearls or chalk. The background was perfect clarity, an infinite expanse of blended light.

Joran searched for a visual anchor. It felt unnerving to have no point of reference, nothing by which to judge space or movement. It seemed that he might topple over at any moment or fall into an invisible chasm. His reflexes signaled warning after warning, and constantly ignoring them dizzied his mind.

For some reason, his skin felt clean and fresh, no trace of pain from the burns on his back. If they had slept long enough for the burns to heal, why would he feel as though he had just bathed? Wouldn't his skin be oily and smell of dirt and sweat?

After what seemed like several minutes, a smudge appeared to the left, slightly off-white and slowly growing. It couldn't be Tamiel. If they had managed to walk in a reasonably straight line, he lay somewhere behind them, now no longer visible in the expanse. If someone else lurked, who could tell if he or she had evil intent? Except for a few members of their immediate family, most people at home were corrupt and hate-filled, so this place might have residents of the same ilk.

Soon, the smudge took on color and shape, a vague blue rectangle that grew taller as they drew closer. With every step, it seemed

151

that they might have arrived, but whenever Joran reached out a hand, he couldn't quite touch the blueness. It just kept growing.

Finally, the sides of the rectangle extended toward them, and the whiteness faded to blue. Each step raised a company of sounds—swishing clothes, a pair of heartbeats, and two out-of-synch respirations.

Joran stopped and turned toward Selah. A wash of blue light coated her face, making her look sickly, but her bright eyes reflected excitement, even joy.

"Can you hear?" He smiled before she could reply. His own voice never sounded so good.

"Yes." She set a hand against her chest. "Whew! That was torture. I have never been so confused in all my life."

"I felt the same way. What I can't figure out is why being inside the purity ovulum would cause loss of sound."

"Maybe because Tamiel's there." Selah lifted her sonic rod. "He knows these won't do us any good while he's using his power of silence."

Joran glanced at his own rod. "Or maybe the purity ovulum's song has some properties we don't understand."

"That could be." Selah's eyes darted all around. "What do you think this blue light means?"

"I'm not sure." Joran looked back the way they had come. A rectangle of white stood erect like an open door. It didn't make any sense to go back. Nothing was out there except Tamiel, and facing him in an unknown land might be deadly. Maybe they should press on and see where this corridor would lead them. If it led into the blue ovulum, then they would be in a refuge that his father had in his possession. They had no way to know what became of the purity ovulum after they entered. Since it probably vanished, no one would be able to find it.

A new voice floated through the blue air. "Excuse me."

A girl wearing a knee-length dress tied at the waist walked through the white doorway and into the blueness. With long white

152

hair and a white aura, she presented a stark contrast against the darker background.

"Who are you?" Joran asked.

She came within a few steps and halted, a bright smile on her face. "I'm so glad you understand my language. Since the fall of the Tower of Babel, many people lost the ability to speak it." She dipped her knee. "I am Acacia."

Joran bowed his head. "Pleased to meet you, Acacia. I am Joran, and this is my sister, Selah."

Each girl offered a generous smile.

"What is the Tower of Babel?" Selah asked.

"Oh!" Acacia covered her mouth. "I assumed too much. It's a story for the ages, but I haven't the time to relate it now." Lowering her hand, she continued. "I can tell you that its effects on communication are unpredictable. Some people will understand you, and some won't."

Joran glanced again at the white doorway. "Why did you hail us?"

153

"I saw you walk in, so I followed. Other than my sisters, I haven't seen anyone else in the white room, so I was curious and wanted to learn who you are and why you are here."

Joran studied her face. Even in this world of blue, her eyes seemed bluer—sparkling, penetrating. She displayed no hint of the corruption he had feared. "We were drawn in by a powerful wind. I heard a voice within the wind, so I think maybe Elohim wanted to rescue Selah from the flood. She dragged me in with her, and I pulled a demon in behind me."

"A demon?" Acacia's brow wrinkled. "Why would you do such a thing?"

Joran cupped a hand. "He held the great purity ovulum, and I didn't want him to keep it. The only choice I had was to bring him in with us."

"Very interesting." Acacia swiveled toward the doorway. "Where is he now?"

"We left him back there. He's either asleep or unconscious. We were in the same state a few moments ago but were fortunate enough to wake up before he did."

"I'm confused," Acacia said, blinking. "If you escaped the flood, why are you just now awakening?"

Selah grasped Acacia's wrist gently. "Why is that confusing?"

"I entered this place long after the flood," Acacia said, "and I have been here for centuries."

Joran drew his head back. "Centuries?"

Nodding, Acacia sighed. "That is the way of this world. Perception of time passage is skewed. When one day passes here, perhaps a year has flown by in our home world. In a different colored chamber, a decade might pass or perhaps only an hour. You can never be sure."

"Then how do you know you've been here for centuries?" Selah asked.

154

"In the scarlet chamber where my sisters and I usually stay, we have access to a viewing portal by which we can see events in our home world. Also, a great prophet comes to the chamber on occasion and teaches us, and I hope I can remember all he has said. He told me that when I leave this place, much of what I have seen here will probably be purged from my mind."

"Then he expects you to leave," Joran said. "Did he say when?"

"Not exactly, but he believes our departure will be very soon, so …" She pushed a hand into her tunic's pocket and withdrew it as a fist. Slowly uncurling her fingers, she revealed a gemstone—oval and about the size of a small egg, though flatter than any bird's egg. Hexagonal facets no bigger than an infant's fingernail covered its surface. A thin beam of white light emanated from one of the facets, dim but easy to notice in the sea of blue. Deep within, the core appeared to be black, about a tenth of the size of the gem itself.

"During my explorations in my home world," Acacia continued, "I found this, and I had it in my pocket when I came here.

My teacher said it's called a candlestone and that it absorbs light energy. It became part of a puzzle that helped me create a key that will enable me to escape." With a nod at the gem, she whispered, "Give me light!"

The candlestone emanated a brilliant glow, so bright, Joran had to blink to keep his eyes from stinging. "How did this help you find a way to escape?"

"It was one of the keys. I had to find thirteen, one for me and each of my sisters. You must explore the chambers to find *your* keys."

"Keys?" Joran imagined the keys the Watchers taught some of the merchants to make, but they varied greatly in size and shape. "What do they look like?"

"A key might not be one that fits into a lock. Mine were sources of light—a torch, a lantern, this candlestone, and others that would take too long to describe. Yours will likely be quite different. If you can find my teacher, you may ask him for more information, but I never know when he will appear. Now that I have found my keys, I can use them to go home with my sisters."

"Who are your sisters?" Joran asked. "How did all of you get here?"

Acacia slid the gem back into her pocket, returning the chamber to a dimmer blue. "I have no time to tell you. Since there is a demon here, I must hurry back to my sisters. He is darkness in a place of light. He will surely try to hinder our efforts."

"Is there any way we could come with you?" Selah asked.

Acacia shook her head sadly. "My teacher says the portal will open for exactly thirteen people, and my sisters and I have been chosen to go. I cannot explain more, because that's all I know." She dipped her knee again. "Please excuse me. I don't want to miss my opportunity to go home."

Selah embraced Acacia and whispered into her ear. "May Elohim bless you as you and your sisters return to your loved ones."

Drawing back, Acacia brushed a tear from her eye. "Joran and Selah, you have a long, hard journey ahead of you. I will pray for you both." Then, she turned and ran through the white doorway.

As if taking a rest in a song, Joran and Selah said nothing through a moment of silence.

"Explore," Selah whispered. "It is a word of promise—open-ended, the call of faith."

"If Tamiel awakens, it will be a word of danger."

Selah turned to him and smiled. "Someday I'm going to change that pessimistic spirit of yours."

"It's reality. Haven't you thought about it? If the flood is in the past, Father is dead. Except for Noah and his family, all our relations drowned in Elohim's wrath. The color of mercy is dark, indeed."

Selah took in a dramatic breath. "And yet we continue to breathe. If we were not pulled into this place, we would have drowned with the rest. You think I deserved to be rescued and you deserved to die, and now we both stand here alive. It seems to me that the color of mercy might be too bright for you to behold."

Joran stared at Selah. The blue wash made her look older, filled with wisdom beyond her years. "Okay," he said with a sigh, "I won't argue the point. I suppose we should plan this journey."

"Since Acacia said to explore the chambers, that must mean the ovula are all attached somehow, and we just walked into one."

"Blue for valor," Joran said. "Then if we return to the white world and walk in a different direction, we might find other colors."

She nodded. "That's a reasonable guess."

"Well, then ..." He held out his elbow. "Shall we explore?"

She hooked her arm through his. "Definitely."

They walked together into the blue depths. Soon, the color faded, like fog evaporating in the morning light, and their surroundings clarified.

A massive corridor materialized, so high even a Naphil mounted on a dragon's back could pass through, and a dragon's outstretched wings wouldn't touch the tapestries and framed paintings mounted on the walls.

Halting his march, Joran studied one of the paintings. It depicted a battle between a dragon and a man wearing a metal suit. The man carried a shield, a sword, and a hate-filled scowl, while the dragon, red and rearing on its haunches, poured a stream of fire that splashed against the shield.

Joran touched the painting's ornate wooden frame. A spark of blue jumped from the point of contact, sending a jolt up his arm. He jerked his finger back and shook it. How strange! Could the treasures in this hall be protected by sorcery?

"Joran, look at this." Selah pointed at a metallic suit, similar to the one worn by the man in the painting. It clutched the hilt of a sword with gloved hands. The point of the blade touched the marble stand upon which it stood. "He hasn't moved. I think there's no one inside."

157

"It's just a display of some kind." He tapped the metal arm with a finger, again raising a blue spark. "We'd better not touch anything. I think witchcraft is at work here."

"The floor seems harmless." Selah walked to the center of the corridor and made a slow turn. "I have never seen such a place. It's amazing!"

"A different world. Reality seems warped." Joran took in a long breath. A dank odor hung in the air, like a cave without a second airway. Maybe no one had been here for a very long time. "Do you see anything that might be a key?"

She stopped turning and set her gaze on him. "We're Listeners. My guess is that Elohim would have us use our gifts to find what we're looking for."

"This room looks like a chamber for displaying valuables, but I don't see anything related to music."

Selah walked to an empty, waist-high pedestal standing near the wall. Although dust coated most of the circular, wooden surface, a thin line from one side to the other remained clean. "Something was sitting here recently."

"A scroll?" Joran asked as he approached.

"That makes sense." She leaned over and examined the thin supporting column. "It couldn't have been anything heavy."

Joran blew at the dust. His breath raised a shower of sparks along the surface that twinkled and died out, but the dust didn't move. "It looks like this stand is bewitched as well."

A voice drifted in, a woman speaking in a low tone—agitated, yet concealing her mood with forced congeniality.

Gesturing for Selah to follow, Joran padded toward the source. At the far end of the hall, a door stood ajar. He skulked to the opening and peeked inside. Standing behind him, Selah looked over his shoulder.

A woman dressed in black sat in a large chair at the head of a long table. Lines of upright objects, perhaps a foot tall and made of marble, stood on a board in front of her. She stared at them, her face calm and self-assured. The objects appeared to be game pieces of some sort, two lines of white tokens on one side and two lines of black on the other. She held a lyre in her lap and strummed it with a slow, casual hand. With each note, one of the pieces moved, alternating between black and white. At times, one piece took the square occupied by another, causing the usurped piece to disappear.

Joran focused on the lyre. Although it was the same size and shape as Father's, the frame's wood was far more weathered. Maybe the same craftsman had made them.

After dozens of moves, the woman spoke in an even tone, using an odd language. An echo followed that seemed to translate her words. "The end game approaches, and my black knights have made no progress. It is clear that I will have to provide them with more power."

Between her and Joran, a man wearing a dark suit covered with metallic links sat on a low footstool, fidgeting as he looked at her. He ran his fingers along the hilt of a sword sheathed in a scabbard at his hip. He, too, spoke in the unfamiliar language, and the translation took a half second longer. "Morgan, whatever this power is, I vow to use it judiciously."

Joran studied the lyre. When they spoke, the strings vibrated slightly. Could it be acting as their interpreter?

Morgan frowned. "A vow made in ignorance. It is a dangerous device and difficult to control, so your confidence is unwarranted." Her voice altered to a humming song. "Now that the remaining dragons have become human, locating them will be nearly impossible."

"I would be foolish to disagree. Palin and I have been trying to find them, but they have blended in with the villagers quite well. Perhaps I should disguise myself and choose another name."

"Nonsense. What name could be better than Devin the dragon slayer? It has such a lovely alliterative quality, and it strikes fear in the hearts of those who might wish to hide your prey." Morgan touched a wooden box on the floor with her foot. "Pick this up and look inside."

159

Devin lifted the box, about the size of a camel saddle pack, and set it on the table. He opened a hinged lid and tilted the box toward himself. "It is empty."

"So you think." She plucked an E string, and let it vibrate until its note faded. The game pieces disappeared with the note. "Reach in and remove that which your eyes cannot see."

Devin slid his fingers inside, withdrew something, and held it in his palms. Invisible at first, an egg-shaped object slowly took on a variety of colors until it turned completely black.

Selah squeezed Joran's arm and whispered, "The purity ovulum."

Joran didn't dare answer. Getting discovered here would be the worst possible move. Taking the ovulum to its rightful place was all that mattered, so they had to stay quiet and come up with a plan. Yet, it all seemed like an impossible puzzle. Since they had entered the purity ovulum, how was it now in Devin's hands? If they could somehow take it and escape to the white expanse, would they then be walking within the ovulum they carried?

Morgan plucked each string in succession. As if answering, a wild shriek erupted from the ovulum along with streaks of blue light that shot out in quick, short-lived bursts, angling in every direction. Joran covered his ears. Selah did the same. Yet, Morgan and Devin continued to sit calmly, apparently unable to hear the horrid noise or see the streaks.

As the two at the table continued talking, Joran lowered his hands. He had to listen and learn. Maybe they would provide a clue about a portal key. Fortunately, the wailing egg quieted a bit, allowing their words to come through.

"After the flood," Morgan said, the echo continuing to translate, "I explored the ruins of Shinar and unearthed many relics that I now keep in my museum hall. If this egg had not been coated with mud, I would never have seen it. According to my master, this is one of eight ovula and the greatest of its kind. It can seek out the seven others by detecting songs they sing. Each ovulum has its own color and song, so your purpose will be to locate and collect them all."

"That sounds simple enough, but what will having the entire set gain for our ultimate purpose?"

"In theory, a great deal. You see, the dragons and their allies once used these eggs to hide Noah's ark, so my master believes they are now being used to protect the dragons who have become humans. Once you find the eggs and destroy them, you will lift their veil of protection."

"Exactly what I need, but how will I find the dragons after I destroy the shields? Will the loss of this protection cause them to become more draconic? Grow scales or wings? Or perhaps they will revert completely, making them easy to ferret out."

"Since this is an untested theory, we do not yet know. Try to locate one ovulum, and we will see if destroying it makes a difference. Perhaps it will actually be in the dragon's possession, making your mission an easier one. In any case, it is essential that we kill all seven dragons as soon as possible. When they are vanquished, my master wants the purity ovulum returned to me. And you must be careful with it. Anyone who destroys it will surely die a horrible death."

Devin pulled the ovulum closer. "Locating the first egg will be the greatest challenge. Perhaps it will be easier to find a mongrel human and squeeze the information out of her."

"Her?" Morgan's thin eyebrows arched up. "Do you already have a target in mind?"

"My spies are working on one. Soon after Merlin transformed the dragons into humans, I learned from Gartrand, the last remaining dragon, that his mate was pregnant. Of course, I slew him before anyone knew what I had learned, so his mate, who is now a pregnant human, should be easy to find."

"Ah! An unwed mother. She will not easily hide from the gossipers."

Devin nodded. "She might get married quickly as a ruse, but even then she will have trouble. According to Gartrand, she should be near her delivery time, so a hastily arranged wedding will not be enough to quiet the tongue-waggers."

"Excellent. Supposedly, this ovulum sings a song that calls the others, but it is inaudible to most humans. Perhaps you will be able to see something within the shells that will be a clue to how they are connected."

Devin peered into the ovulum. "I see nothing but blackness in this one."

"Because your heart is black." Morgan began plucking the lyre again, this time playing an eerie melody. "The color of your soul can be a disadvantage."

He set the ovulum on the table. It stopped squealing and quickly vanished from sight. "I still see nothing within it."

"As I expected. My master says that human touch activates its search capabilities, so you will have to find a trusted ally whose heart is not as black as your own."

"Palin has shown signs of mercy on occasion."

"He is serviceable," Morgan said. "When you return to your world, the two of you can work together."

Devin shifted his weight from foot to foot. "This could take a very long time."

"If you are concerned about having enough dragon blood for both of you, then I suggest that you find and slay the beasts. Collect and store as much blood as you can. The candlestone will work with the blood of those who have become human."

Joran glanced back at Selah. Her inquisitive expression proved that she, too, had picked up on the word *candlestone*. Apparently the gem had more powers than Acacia had mentioned.

Morgan strummed the lyre. "It is time for you to go. The moat serpents will sleep as long as I play their lullaby, so make haste. I have much to do."

When Devin lifted the ovulum, it instantly turned black and again emitted a torturous call. He laid it gently in the box and closed the lid, bringing silence back to the room.

Joran grabbed Selah's arm and guided her toward the corridor's side, whispering, "I have to get the ovulum."

"How?" Selah asked, her back against the wall. "We can't create a barrier quickly enough, and we have no other weapons."

Joran looked at the standing suit of armor. "We have a sword."

"He is much bigger and stronger. It would be dangerous to confront him with his choice of weaponry."

"Elohim has given us victory against greater odds."

"But if it's bewitched—"

"I'll soon find out." After handing Selah his sonic rod, Joran hustled to the armor and grasped the end of the hilt. Blue sparks

162

flew everywhere. Scalding heat shot through his body, but he couldn't let go. Shaking violently, he wanted to shout, but the jolt paralyzed his throat.

Selah ran across the corridor, leaped at Joran, and knocked him to the floor. After rolling together, they struggled to their feet, helping each other rise. "Thank you." He rubbed his hands together, trying to settle the tingling sensation as he kept an eye on the door. It seemed that Morgan and Devin hadn't heard the ruckus. "I hope you have a better idea than mine."

"Maybe." Selah gave him his rod. "Morgan said she's keeping serpents asleep with the lyre. If we can use our voices to interfere with her song, maybe the serpents will stop Devin."

"That might work." Joran looked at the path leading back the way they had entered. The hallway's floor transformed into blue light only twenty paces away.

Devin burst into the corridor and marched through, apparently unaware of their presence. As he continued, instead of slowly fading into the field of blue, as soon as his foot stepped in, he disappeared.

163

"How strange!" Selah said. "It's like he didn't see the blue at all."

"No time to figure it out. We have to spoil Morgan's song."

"What shall we sing?"

Joran rolled his eyes upward for a moment. "'Trumpet Call' might work."

"Good idea. I'll start the rhythm." Selah lifted her rod and spoke in a singsong cadence. "Make trumpets sound, and set the pace; Awake the crowds, and start the race."

Nodding with the beat, Joran began singing as he tiptoed closer to the door.

> Awaken souls from slumber's rest;
> The trumpet sounds a battle cry.
> Arise and fight the devil's host;
> Our song will make his minions fly.

Joran began the song again, louder this time. Morgan pushed the door open and walked slowly through the hall, still playing the lyre. With her eyes focused straight ahead, she appeared to take no notice of Joran and Selah or their song.

Looking at Selah, Joran broke the rhythm and let his voice fade away. Selah quieted as well.

Morgan stopped near the empty pedestal and hummed as she continued playing.

"She didn't hear us," Joran said.

Selah tiptoed closer, her brow bent as she shifted to Morgan's side. "She can't see us either."

After a final strum, Morgan looked at the pedestal's surface, scowled for a second, and blew off the dust. The particles lifted in a cloud, making her cough as she waved it away. She then set the lyre on the pedestal and walked back to the meeting chamber.

"We have to catch Devin." Joran made a hard step, but Selah pulled him back.

"Look!" Selah set a hand on the lyre. No blue sparks arose. "Could it be Father's?"

"It looks like Father's, but it's too old."

"But centuries have passed, remember? If Morgan found this and the ovulum in the same area, maybe it is."

Joran examined the frame, searching for any identifying sign. He gave Selah his rod, picked up the lyre, and looked at the bottom. The word *Enoch* had been etched in the wood. "It *is* Father's!"

"It's musical, and it's not bewitched. Could it be our key?"

"I wonder." Looking at the door to the meeting room, Joran plucked a string. The note sounded sweet and clear. "Maybe it's *part* of a key."

"Seven strings, seven ovula," Selah said. "Each string might represent a key."

"Does that mean we have to do something in each ovulum that somehow matches the string progression?"

Selah shrugged. "You played a G. Do we have a song in that key?"

"The first that comes to mind is the one we use to make demons grow weak and feeble."

"Of course. The purity song. They can't stand it."

Joran touched the G string again. "So do I just play it here and see if Morgan comes out? She didn't hear us earlier."

"Blue is for valor," Selah said, clenching a fist. "Let's go in and play it right in her face."

Joran patted her on the back. "I should have guessed you'd say that."

As they strode toward the meeting room, she tapped the rods together, setting the rhythm. The moment Joran stepped inside, he began playing.

Morgan, sitting again at the head of the table, rose from her seat and stared, her eyes so narrow, they almost disappeared. "By what magic does my lyre float into this chamber?" This time, there was no echo. It seemed that she spoke in their language.

As Joran and Selah walked slowly closer, Joran began the song.

When demons see our shining lights,
They flee to shadows' shield.
They cannot bear a holy glow;
No weapons can they wield.

Morgan thrust out her arms. A wave of blackness hurtled toward them, but, although it enveloped them in darkness for a moment, it quickly dissipated. "Who is there?" she bellowed. "Is this one of Merlin's tricks?"

They cast their spells in vain attempts
To smite their greatest fear,
A man who bears a spotless soul,
A man whose heart is clear.

165

Her head lowering like a charging bull, Morgan stormed toward them. Her eyes flashed scarlet, and her skin darkened, wrinkling with each passing second.

Joran jumped out of the way.

Then evil shrivels in its place;
It cannot stand the light.
A holy presence overwhelms,
And demons take their flight.

Morgan raised her hands and enveloped herself in a shroud of darkness. Her casing hardened, and she stood completely still, like the suit of armor in the corridor, yet without discernible limbs or head.

Joran stopped singing. He and Selah approached Morgan but halted well out of her reach.

"Now that's something we haven't seen before," Selah said.

"She realized she was shriveling and protected herself."

Selah took a tentative step closer and squinted at the glossy covering. "I wonder how long she'll stay like that."

"I hope long enough to stop her and Devin from carrying out their plans."

"Then maybe we did what we're supposed to do here," she said, stepping back. "Maybe we can go on to the next ovulum."

Joran looked at the lyre. The G string's color had changed to blue. "I think this is all the proof we need."

"Amazing!" Selah ran her finger along the string. Even her slight touch made it hum a lovely G. "Since this is Father's, I think it's all right to take it. It certainly doesn't belong to Morgan."

Joran grasped the frame with both hands. "If what Acacia said is true, we'll probably need it again."

"Let's go." Selah hurried out the door.

Joran caught up, and the two jogged side by side. As they plunged into the light, their surroundings became awash in many shades of blue before disappearing. Soon, the white doorway came into view, their passage back to the purity ovulum.

Joran pulled Selah's arm, halting her. "Let's stop and plan."

"Okay." Selah smiled at him as she caught her breath. "Plan what?"

"The next color?"

She gazed at the doorway. "I suppose we should enter whatever ovulum we find. If Elohim guides our steps, we will come to the right one."

"Maybe Elohim wants us to use our brains as well. After valor, what would be the next logical progression?"

"Red for humility," Selah said without hesitation. "Someone who succeeds at valor needs to be humble, or else he will become prideful."

Joran gazed at her. Filled with sincerity, she radiated the purity he had sung about. It wasn't his own glow that shriveled Morgan; it had to be hers.

167

He laid a hand on her shoulder. "If not for you, I'd be dead. I would have no valor at all. I don't have a single reason to feel prideful about anything."

"Maybe not," Selah said. "Perhaps the red ovulum will reveal what we need to learn."

"Well, well, well. Here are the two fools I have been looking for."

Joran spun toward the sound. A dark winged figure shadowed the doorway leading to the purity ovulum. *Tamiel!*

11

CHAPTER

TAKING FLIGHT

M y name?" A wash of heat flooded Matt's cheeks. "Oh, yeah. It's Matt. Matt Fletcher. Sorry about that."

"No problem." She shook his hand and smiled. "Nice to meet you, Matt Fletcher."

He returned her firm grip. "My pleasure, Lauren Hunt."

She stared at the dim hall. "So which room is your mother supposed to be in?"

"I'll show you." Matt withdrew the map and unfolded it. Shining the penlight on the page, he traced their route from the entry door to their current position. "There should be another hall to the left, then the room she might be in is third on the right."

"We'd better get going."

Stepping softly, Matt led the way. He shone the penlight on the floor a pace or two in front. After making the turn into the new hallway and passing two doors, the room they sought came into view. A solid steel door barred the way, and a sign on the front read—*Healers and Specimens Only.*

Lauren shuddered. "Specimens? That's a chilling way to put it."

"I know what you mean." Matt spied the security panel to the right of the door. "I wish we could peek inside before I try to open this thing."

"Wait a minute." Lauren tilted her head to the side, apparently listening.

"Are you getting that tingling sensation?"

Nodding, she let out a low "Shhh." After a few seconds, she continued in a whisper. "I hear breathing and a soft tune of some kind. And I think I'm picking up some thoughts."

"Now you're a mind reader?"

"Yeah. Go figure." She closed her eyes. "I keep hearing *Joran* and *Selah* and something about a liar. Does that make any sense to you?"

"Not a bit, but if there's only thinking and no talking, I guess it's safe. I still don't feel any danger." He set the ID bracelet against the reader. As soon as the door buzzed, he pulled it open, revealing a hospital-style ward. At a bank of three windows on the far wall, veiled moonlight filtered through open blinds. A bed sat under each window, and a motionless woman lay on the right-most bed.

170

Matt stepped inside and waited for Lauren to join him before letting the door close. He hurried to the bed and clutched the metal rail at the foot. Leather straps fastened the woman's wrists and ankles to the frame, and a pair of huge wings spread out behind her, each stretching well beyond the side rails.

Matt mouthed a silent *Wow!* while Lauren looked on, her mouth agape. The woman appeared to be in her thirties. Her dark hair covered most of the pillow, though the dimness made the color uncertain. She wore a hospital gown, open in front just enough to reveal one electrode at the top of her sternum and wires leading from underneath the gown to a machine at the bed's left. An IV bag hung from a pole at the bed's right, allowing liquid to slowly drip through a tube leading to her left hand. With the restraints in place, instead of a prisoner or a specimen, she looked like a hostile patient.

"I still hear a tune," Lauren said softly. "I think she's humming."

Matt lifted one of the straps. "Look. It's loose."

"Loose?" Lauren picked up the strap's dangling end. "That's strange. It's wrapped around her wrist, but it isn't fastened. Why would they do that?"

Matt leaned close and whispered, "Mrs. Bannister?"

Her eyes moved under her lids, but she didn't respond.

Lauren stepped over to the IV and read the bag. "It's a sedative. If we're going to wake her up, we'll have to pull the needle."

"Do you know how to do that?"

"My mother's a cancer patient. I've seen her nurse do it plenty of times." Lauren peeled tape away from Mrs. Bannister's hand, pulled out the needle while pressing gauze on the insertion site, and let the tube dangle from the IV pole.

"Any experience with how long it takes to wake up from something like this?"

Lauren offered a light shrug. "Not really. Maybe shake her once in a while?"

"I don't think we can wait very long. I'll have to carry her."

"Carry her?" Lauren scanned his body from top to bottom. "Okay. I guess you probably can."

Warmth again flooded his cheeks. "You're ... uh ... more straightforward than most, aren't you?"

She nodded. "It gets me into trouble sometimes. It was a compliment. I hope you don't mind."

"I don't mind. It's probably better to be direct." He let his gaze wander around the room, finally halting at a laptop computer on a table that abutted the right-hand wall. "Before we go, I need to search their database." He strode toward the table, keeping a wary eye on the door.

171

"What are you looking for?"

"Remember when I asked if you had parents? This is why." He flipped open the laptop and turned it on. "I'm looking for a female anthrozil. She's your age, but she's probably listed as an orphan. Apparently your kidnappers think you're that anthrozil."

"Well, I *was* an orphan, but I've been adopted."

He turned toward her. "Then could you be—"

"No." Lauren's response was as firm as the shake of her head. "My birth parents died in a car accident when I was a baby. I have at least a hundred pics of me with them. They were normal humans—no wings, no fire breathing."

"Digital pics?"

"Yes." She folded her arms over her chest. "What are you saying? That my past has been digitally manufactured?"

"I was wondering if I could see them online." Matt turned back to the computer. He had told the truth, just not the whole truth. If he could get Internet access here, maybe he could tell if the photos had been altered. Obviously exploring that possibility openly would ruffle Lauren's feathers. He had to be discrete. "I was just curious."

"They're online, but they're password-protected. If you get Internet, I'll show you how to see them."

"Sounds good." Matt tilted the screen. The system seemed to be making unsuccessful attempts to access a network, extending the boot-up process. The Internet probably wouldn't be available.

"While you're doing that," Lauren said, "I'll unhitch Mrs. Bannister from the electrodes and get her dressed. I saw a pile of clothes on the next bed."

"Good idea." After giving up its network-connection attempts, the computer displayed a message asking him to place his ID close to the flashing LED at the top of the screen's frame. After he complied, a menu appeared. He chose option number one, a prisoner database.

"She has holes for her wings in her T-shirt and her sweatshirt," Lauren said from behind him. "This could get tricky."

"Do the best you can. If you need help, let me know."

"When she wakes up, are you going to tell her who you are?"

"Not yet. I want solid proof first. No sense getting her hopes up if I'm not really her son."

"That's true." Lauren sighed. "I'll keep my mouth shut, too."

For the next few minutes, Matt alternated between searching for records of any teenagers and for any signs of danger. With the power out, the laptop was running on battery, and the meter indicated that only ten percent of the charge remained.

Three records came up for nineteen-year-olds—two incarcerated for drug offenses and one for armed robbery. He examined each photo. Since one was black, and two were Hispanic, they couldn't be Karen Bannister. The data produced no one else under the age of twenty.

As he listened to Lauren working behind him, he imagined her photo on the screen. If they claimed her as a prisoner here, why didn't she come up in the search?

"Okay," Lauren said, "I think she's ready."

Matt turned. Her wings splayed neatly behind her, Mrs. Bannister lay on the bed dressed in jeans and a white sweatshirt. "Good job."

"Now to get her out of here." Lauren grasped her wrist. "You get the other side, and I'll help you lift her into your arms."

"Wait." Matt nodded at the computer. "Since you're a prisoner here, why aren't you in the database?"

"I told you I was kidnapped. I never was an official prisoner. If they entered me, it probably hasn't updated this computer yet."

"Yeah. I could tell it couldn't connect to the network. It must have been reading its own drive." Matt studied Lauren's face. She certainly resembled Mrs. Bannister. Maybe he had found Karen

173

after all, but now wasn't the time to probe that topic any further. "Okay. Let's get her out of here."

"Ah! There you are, Lauren!" A woman wearing a camouflage uniform approached from the door, gliding effortlessly, as if rolling on wheels. "You are quite the elusive one. It seems that we will have to handcuff you to something after all."

Matt glanced at his holster. With auburn hair and angular features, this woman could pass for an adult version of Darcy. Although the resemblance raised a chill, no twinge of danger joined the sensation, so it didn't make sense to pull his gun. Since her stripes indicated that she was a Major, maybe he could play the role of prison guard and get some information. "I apologize, Major ... um ... I don't see a name tag."

"Semiramis." She nodded toward Lauren. "I have been looking for this escaped prisoner. Where did you find her?"

Matt cleared his throat and straightened his prison-issue jacket. "I found her here. Because of the fire, I was checking all the rooms. When you came in, I was looking her up to see where she belongs."

"Excellent work, but there is no need to search for her cell number. I know where she belongs. If you will follow me, I will show you to her cell."

Matt nodded toward Mrs. Bannister. "Why is this anthrozil here? Everyone is supposed to be outside."

"The evacuation was merely a precaution. The fire is under control." Semiramis's voice was so smooth, it seemed almost haunting. "Since this patient has undergone some exhausting procedures, she is safer here than she would be outside."

"How did you get in without making a sound? I didn't hear a buzz."

"A buzz?" Semiramis looked at the door. "I simply opened it. It seems that the security system for this room is no longer operating. Perhaps the fire has something to do with it."

"Well, I guess that answers my questions, but there's no need for you to lead me. Just tell me her cell number, and I'll take her there."

Semiramis squinted. "Aren't you a bit young for a prison guard?"

Matt glanced at Lauren. If she really was a mind reader, maybe she could hear his call for help. "Well …"

Lauren stepped out from behind him. "That's what I thought when he burst in here and barked orders like a know-it-all rookie—he's just a kid. But when he flashed his badge and gun, I kept my mouth shut. Who am I to argue with those?"

Semiramis leaned closer to Lauren. "Where did you get that sweatshirt? I thought you were wearing a …" Her gaze shifted to Matt. "A prison guard's jacket." As her eyes narrowed further, a knowing smile emerged. "I see."

Matt swallowed hard. The ruse had ended. He drew his gun and pointed it at her. "If you'll just let us leave with this woman, no one will get hurt."

"You've watched too many television dramas." She turned and walked toward the door. "Stay here, or else you will be the one who gets hurt." When she reached the door, she walked right through it and disappeared.

Matt staggered backwards. "Did you see …" His mouth froze.

"Yeah. She's some kind of ghost."

"You say that like you've seen a hundred of them."

"Just her and the winged guy. That's enough to make me believe just about anything."

Matt laid the gun and penlight in her hand. "Let's get out of here." He rushed to the bed, slid his hands under Mrs. Bannister, and hoisted her into his arms. Her wings crumpled a bit, making her wince, but it couldn't be helped. There seemed to be no way to carry her without bending the huge leather canopies.

Grunting as he walked, he spoke through clenched teeth. "Get the door for me."

Lauren leaped in front and pushed it open. As soon as he stepped into the hall, he broke into a jog. "Let's go!"

Leading the way with the penlight, Lauren ran ahead, but after a few seconds, the ceiling lights flickered on.

"Not a good sign," she said.

"Just keep moving." Matt glanced at Mrs. Bannister. She blinked at the bright lights, then stared at him.

"Who are you?" she asked groggily.

"A friend of Walter's. I'm trying to get you out of here."

"Walter's?" She squirmed. "I think I can walk if you'll let me—"

"No! We have to hurry! Just let me carry you."

She settled down and watched quietly, her eyes darting back and forth.

After retracing their steps, they arrived at the entry door. Lauren burst through and held it open while Matt carried Mrs. Bannister outside. Searchlights swept across the prison yard between them and the fence.

Matt paused at the edge of the yard. "They'll spot us for sure."

"And they have guns," Lauren added. "Do you feel any danger?"

"Just a general feeling. Nothing sharp. Let's wait just a minute. Maybe the lights will move."

"Will you put me down now, please?" Mrs. Bannister asked.

"Sure." He tilted her body and let her shoes touch the sidewalk. As he shifted more weight, he kept her steady until she could stand on her own. "There you go."

She wrapped her arms around herself and shivered but said nothing. She still seemed somewhat dazed.

Matt dug the knife out of his pocket, stripped off the jacket, and sliced two holes in the back. "We'll help you put this on."

While Mrs. Bannister pushed her arms through the sleeves, Lauren and Matt guided her wings through the holes. By the time they finished, Mrs. Bannister's eyes looked sharp and clear. "I can carry one of you out of here," she said, "but not both."

Matt and Lauren pointed at each other.

"Take her."

"Take him."

Bonnie gave them a weak smile. "No time to argue. I'll take the girl."

"Good." Matt pushed the knife into Bonnie's jacket pocket. "You might have to cut holes in something else."

As Bonnie wrapped her arms around Lauren from behind, Lauren handed the gun to Matt, then blew him a kiss. "Thank you. After we find Walter, we'll come back for you."

"When I get airborne," Mrs. Bannister said, "you can show me the way." She stretched out her wings, gave them a powerful beat, and leaped into the air. She flew in a haphazard circle for a moment before straightening and zooming upward.

The searchlights followed her. Men shouted in the distance. A gunshot sounded, then another, but no one cried out, and no one fell.

Matt pumped a fist. *Yes! They got away!* He sprinted toward the fence. With the searchlights preoccupied, this might be his only chance.

When he reached the severed links, he dropped to all fours, pushed the flap, and crawled.

"Halt!" someone shouted.

Matt scrambled faster. Just two seconds and he would be through. Another gunshot rang out. Sharp pain sliced through his arm, making him fall flat in the dirt. Blood streamed down to his wrist. Something grabbed his ankle and dragged him backwards. As he clawed with one hand, he shoved the gun into its holster with the other.

"Don't fight me, kid," a man growled. "You can't get away."

Matt let himself go limp. Someone rolled him over and flashed a bright light in his face, blinding him.

177

"What should we do with him?" a second man asked with a gentler voice.

The light shifted away from Matt's eyes, allowing him to see. Semiramis stood nearby, her arms folded as she posed in a cocky stance. "Get him up!"

A huge guard grabbed Matt's uninjured arm and pulled him to his feet. The momentum brought Matt close to the guard's chest, eye to eye with his name tag—D. Hoskins. As the guard held him in place, a handgun brushed Matt's hand, hot to the touch. "Where shall we take him?"

"The lab. We have to bind his wound, and I want an immediate blood test."

A second guard, shorter and thinner, held a rifle in one hand and used the other to slide the gun from Matt's holster, no longer hidden behind a jacket. Matt eyed the rifle's muzzle. A line of smoke rose into the air. "Start walking, kid. If you cooperate, it'll go easier for you."

"Easier than what? One of you already shot me."

"Cut the smart talk, or I'll shoot you again." The guard shoved the gun into his waistband and prodded Matt with the butt of his rifle. "Move."

With blood dripping from his fingers, Matt marched ahead. Through dizzied, blurred vision, he watched the movements around him as if played on an out-of-focus screen. The guard opened the same back door he and Lauren used earlier, and, with the rifle constantly jabbing his back, Matt staggered through the familiar corridors.

When they arrived at the lab, the door buzzed. The guard swung it open. Inside, beds spun in a wild circle. After wobbling in place, he collapsed to the floor.

Strong arms lifted him and rolled him onto one of the dancing beds. As the room continued to spin, Semiramis's face appeared, the only stationary object in the room. "You are a brave

178

one," she said. "And if my suspicions are correct, we will soon learn where that courage comes from."

He couldn't answer. Dizziness overtook his senses, forcing him to close his eyes. At least Lauren was safe, and so was Mrs. Bannister. He had succeeded in his mission. Walter would be proud, if he survived. The gunshots at the cliff might have been him shooting at the kidnapper, but if that were true, why did he pull the rope up? Why didn't he shout and let them know what was going on, or at least whisper through the transmitter? Of course, he might have tried during those few minutes of hearing loss. Either way, something terrible must have happened, and maybe Lauren and Mrs. Bannister would have to face the danger next.

A sharp prick jabbed his arm. Seconds later, his muscles relaxed. He couldn't move at all. But he had to move. He had to get up and help them, because ... because of something. What was it again?

As the faces of his new friends entered his mind, a sense of comfort took over. Maybe Mrs. Bannister was his real mother, and maybe Lauren was his sister. Once Mrs. Bannister revived from the sedative, she took charge and flew right into the lights and gunfire. She was as cool as a cucumber. And was Lauren for real? What would it be like to have a smart, strong, no-nonsense girl for a twin sister? Obviously no one could be as evil as Darcy, but she was the only sibling he had ever had. Who could tell what kind of spirit lived behind Lauren's glowing visage?

The faces blurred. Thoughts fled away. And his mind fell into a swirling blackness.

179

CHAPTER 12

SILENCE IN THE WOODS

Lauren held her breath. Dangling in darkness while getting shot at was bad enough, but having her ribs crushed by a winged woman's powerful arms was even worse.

"I think we're out of range now," Mrs. Bannister called. "Which way?"

"Just go down." Lauren squeezed out her words. "We'll talk there."

As they descended, the pressure eased. Lauren took in a deep breath and looked below. Illuminated by moonlight, the tops of trees drew slowly nearer.

"Get ready for a sudden drop," Mrs. Bannister said. "We're in sight of the ground. I don't want anyone to see us."

After they plunged through a gap, Mrs. Bannister set Lauren down gently on a carpet of fallen leaves. With her wings still flapping gently, she laid a hand on her chest. "Whew! That's the farthest I've flown in years. It's a good thing I kept my wings in shape."

Lauren stared. Yes, it might be impolite, but who wouldn't stare? This woman, fair of face and form, had dragon wings! Seeing them in the bed made them look like a movie costume prop, but witnessing them in flight made them ... well ... amazing!

Smiling, Mrs. Bannister extended her hand. "I'm Bonnie Bannister. What's your name?"

"Lauren Hunt." The two shook hands warmly.

"And who was that young man?"

"Matt Fletcher. I just met him in the prison, so I don't know much about him."

"I remember him saying he's Walter's friend." Mrs. Bannister pivoted, peering into the surrounding dark forest. "Speaking of Walter, where do you think he might be?"

Holding the open handcuff, Lauren pointed to her left. "Matt and I tried to climb a cliff somewhere over there."

"Let's go. You can tell me your story on the way." Mrs. Bannister marched in that direction.

"Tell you my story?" Lauren caught up and strode at her side. "Maybe I shouldn't talk much. You see, when we were ready to climb the rope, a winged shadow flew over, and we heard gunshots. Then the rope got pulled up to this level, so we decided to go back to the prison."

Mrs. Bannister stopped and turned toward Lauren. "This winged shadow, was it a bird?"

"I think it was Tamiel. He's one of the kidnap—"

"Tamiel?" Mrs. Bannister's brow lifted. "Are you sure of that name?"

Lauren nodded. "Have you heard it before?"

"I have." Mrs. Bannister looked at the ground as if deep in thought. "I'll have to think about that one."

"Tamiel called himself an angel, but I think he's some kind of demon." Lauren tried to gauge Mrs. Bannister's reaction, but she seemed unaffected. "Or don't you believe in strange things like that?"

"Trust me. I've seen things a lot stranger." Mrs. Bannister laid a hand on Lauren's back. "Just give me a quick summary. Why were you in the prison? What's up with the handcuffs?"

Lauren raised the dangling cuff. "Tamiel kidnapped me and brought me to the prison. Apparently he thinks I'm an anthrozil, because I can hear beyond all reasonable limits, and because I ..." Feeling a flash of heat in her cheeks, she averted her eyes. "Well, Mrs. Bannister, I kind of glow in the dark."

"Call me Bonnie."

"Okay ... Bonnie."

"I heard a rumor that the Enforcers were looking for a girl with unusual hearing, but no one mentioned a glow." Bonnie leaned closer. "I think I can see it. It's not very bright at all."

"Sometimes it's obvious. Anyway, I think they're hunting for any unusual girl my age, because they're—"

"Trying to find my daughter." Nodding, Bonnie sighed. "I know. I'm sorry about that."

"It's not your fault." Lauren slid her shoe across the fallen leaves. "It must be awful not knowing where she is."

Firming her lips, Bonnie nodded again. "So, what's Matt's story?"

Lauren looked into her expectant eyes. No doubt this poor mother ached to hear some good news, but Matt was right. It would be a shame to get her hopes up without proof. "Like I said, I just met him in the prison. He told me Walter got him to help with the jailbreak, so when we find Walter, he'll probably tell you more."

"We'd better hurry. They know I haven't flown in a while, so they might send out dogs, thinking I couldn't have gotten very far." Bonnie gave Lauren a gentle push. "Since you have radar ears, maybe you should lead the way."

"Right." Lauren jumped ahead, slipping for a moment on the leaves before breaking into a brisk walk. With trees, both large and small, forcing her to travel in a weaving pattern, and thick under-brush making her lift her legs high or push through foliage, she had to slow her pace at times. The image of sniffing dogs on her trail and a demon possibly flying overhead raised prickles of fear, and with them, the tingling sensation.

She glanced back. As Bonnie flapped her wings to push her-self along, she kept up without a problem, deftly dodging trees or lifting herself over the bushes and brambles. Watching her agility was almost too much of a distraction.

After a few minutes, a soft moaning sound reached Lauren's ears. She stopped and lifted a hand. "Did you hear that?"

Bonnie settled next to her and quieted her wings. "No. What was it?"

As the familiar tingle ran up Lauren's spine, the moaning con-tinued, and a series of pain-streaked thoughts seeped in. *Got to get to the headset. Have to call Larry.*

"Moaning." Lauren kept her voice whisper soft. "I think some-one's hurt."

"Can you follow the sound?"

"Maybe. Let me see if I can get my bearings." Lauren listened again. Although the moaning continued, the thoughts ceased. "I heard someone mention the name Larry."

Bonnie's whisper spiked. "Larry is Ashley's supercomputer. That has to be Walter."

"I'll keep tracking him." As she tiptoed, leaves crunched under her feet, masking every other sound, and the tingle grew stronger, bringing new thoughts to her ears. *Give me one last chance, Father; that's my only prayer. I have to find Ashley. I have to get her out of that place.*

She turned to the left. The thoughts grew slightly louder, more prayers fervently calling out the same words. This had to be the right direction.

"Now is when I could use my husband's fire breathing," Mrs. Bannister said. "It's dark under these trees."

"Oh, yeah." Lauren stopped again and withdrew the penlight from her pocket. "I forgot I had this." She flicked the light on and guided it across the forest debris—mostly leaves, cones, and twigs. "Should we risk calling his name? Tamiel might be around."

"I'll call him. He'll recognize my voice. And I can fly you out of here in a heartbeat if Tamiel shows up." Bonnie cupped her hands around her mouth and called out, "Walter? Can you hear me?"

Her voice seemed to die, as if caught in a snowstorm and swept away.

"That's odd," Bonnie said. "It's like we're in a dead zone."

"Something like that happened right after we heard the gun-shots. Matt couldn't hear anything until after an explosion inside the prison."

Bonnie pointed at her. "And you *could* hear?"

Lauren nodded. "But I've always been able to hear things other people can't."

"Then keep tracking. If Walter's in some kind of no-sound bubble, he won't be able to hear us call."

185

Leading with the penlight again, Lauren bypassed a hefty tree and pressed on. The prayers continued radiating through her skin and into her ears, weaker now. Had she turned in the wrong direc-tion, or was Walter getting tired?

A weak call sounded. "Hello? Who's behind that light?" Then a stream of thoughts followed. *I can't even hear my own voice. How is anyone else going to hear me?*

Lauren turned to Bonnie. "He's close."

"What did you say?" Bonnie touched an ear. "I think we're inside that bubble."

Lauren waved for her to follow and trudged onward, search-ing with the light. After a few seconds, the beam passed across a man sitting with his back against a tree. Keeping the light trained on him, she brushed between two prickly bushes and ran across a clearing, dodging scattered equipment, including a backpack, a radio headset, and a box with an extended antenna.

She raced to the man's side, dropped to her knees, and shone the light on his forehead, making sure to keep it out of his eyes. Blinking at her, he smiled. Camouflage paint covered his face, and a baseball cap sat sideways on his disheveled hair.

"It's Walter!" Bonnie flew to his other side and settled on her knees. She knocked a cap from his head and ran her fingers through his hair. "Are you all right?"

Slowly lifting a hand, Walter touched an ear and shook his head.

"I know," Bonnie said. "I can't even hear myself."

With pain twisting his face, he forced out, "Where's Ashley?"

Bonnie leaned close and enunciated carefully. "Did you ask about Ashley?"

He nodded.

Bonnie fluttered her wings, still speaking slowly. "We had to fly away in a hurry, but she was okay when I last saw her."

"That's what I guessed." Walter sighed. "It was a long shot."

Lauren touched her own ear and nodded. "I can hear you," she said, also carefully enunciating. "What happened?"

He gave her a weak smile. "You must be Lauren. I see a glow."

Nodding, she smiled in return.

"Where's Matt?"

"We had to leave him behind." Lauren wanted to add more, but it would be torturous to explain that she had heard gunshots while she and Bonnie were ascending.

"Did Matt tell Bonnie who he is?" Walter asked.

"I'll let you tell her." Lauren glanced at Bonnie. Her confused expression probably meant that she wasn't following the conversation. "What happened to you?"

"I …" Walter cleared his throat. "I was about to pull you up with the rope, and this winged guy dropped in." He smiled at Bonnie. "At first I thought Gabriel had come from Second Eden, but when I got a look at his ugly mug, I knew better."

Lauren nodded. "Go on."

"Anyway, he opened his mouth, and black fog came out." Walter's voice strengthened, though his words sometimes sounded a bit off. "I've seen enough demons to know not to mess around trying to figure out if they came for a quilting bee, so I pulled my gun and shot him a couple of times. I had no idea if bullets could hurt him, but what was I going to do? Negotiate? So I got him in the chest, and he staggered backwards. More black fog spewed from the holes in his body, and it spread around this area and made everything completely silent. Well, at least *I* couldn't hear anything. Then the demon fell, and I pulled up the rope and tied his wrists together. All the while, I was yelling for Matt and Lauren to take their chances in the woods, and I would find them later, but they probably couldn't hear me."

Walter took a deep breath, wincing. "Then he used his wings to get up, and he kicked me. I went flying like a shot out of a cannon, and I slammed against this tree. Now I can't move my legs."

Lauren reached around and touched his back. "Your spine?"

"I hope not." He winced again. "At least I feel pain there. I guess that's a good sign."

Bonnie pulled Walter's hiking boots off and began peeling down his socks. "I picked up some of the conversation. I'll see what I can figure out."

"Legs or no legs ..." Walter reached out a hand. "Help me up. I'll try to find that creep."

"You're not going anywhere," Lauren said, pushing his hand down. "Just show me where he went."

Walter lifted his brow. "Show you where he went?"

She nodded.

He pointed toward a darker area of the woods. "He crawled away slower than a slug. I'm guessing he's still leaking fog somewhere around here. Otherwise, we might be able to hear by now."

"What do we do if we find him?" Lauren asked, still mouthing her words carefully.

187

"Get him to tell us what he's up to." Walter pulled a handgun from an inner pocket. "I think he won't want to ingest any more lead. He seemed allergic."

Lauren looked into the forest, imagining a wounded Tamiel sitting against another tree in a similar pose. Searching around in the dark for a demon wasn't exactly a good idea. How could she figure out where he was without him seeing her first? Might the rope still be attached to him? If so, it didn't seem to be lying around anywhere. Yet, maybe there was another way.

Again clutching the loose handcuff, Lauren set an imaginary phone to her ear. "Do you have a cell phone?"

Nodding, Walter pointed at the equipment in the clearing. "I don't know if it still works. He roughed up my stuff, like he was looking for something, but it might be in my backpack."

Lauren grabbed the gun and scrambled to the pack.

"Wait!" Walter called. "I can't let you go after him. It's too dangerous."

Lauren wanted to reply with, "You don't have a choice," but he wouldn't be able to hear it. Using the penlight, she rummaged through the main compartment, digging through a variety of electronics and packaged granola bars, until her hand brushed across the phone. She jerked it out. Since the demon's number popped up on her own phone so many times, it was branded on her memory. She began punching numbers with her thumb as she walked back to the tree.

Looking at the phone, she waited. Soon, a chime sounded in the darkness. She marched straight for it, the gun extended. After a few steps, she halted and waited for a second chime, but it didn't sound. She raised the phone to her ear and spoke a quiet, "Hello?"

"Miss Hunt." The voice was low, measured. "I suggest that you turn back."

"Why?" She shifted her aim from tree to tree. "Are you scared of a girl?"

188

A low chuckle preceded his reply. "Have you noticed that I never touched you? I have guided you from afar. I chose the limousine in order to keep a significant buffer between us. You see, I think you have a rare dragon trait that I need not describe in detail, but suffice it to say that if we come into physical contact, we both will perish."

She edged closer. "Why should I believe you? I hear demons aren't exactly trustworthy."

"I told you the truth about Micaela. I said she would die if you did not heed my warning. Now, I again issue a warning. Stay away. Take care of your wounded friend and leave."

Lauren boiled inside. This monster killed Micaela. She could shoot him without getting close at all. Maybe she could keep him talking long enough to find him.

"Why can you hear when no one else can?"

"You seem quite capable. We both have a special gift. That is all I will say."

189

She tuned her ears from the phone to the forest. "What will you do when we leave?"

"Do not ask inane questions. I will not reveal my plans to anyone."

Lauren stepped toward the voice, trying to keep her footfalls quiet. "Are my parents all right?"

"You have a phone. I suggest you try to call them."

Lauren halted. She lowered the phone and stared at it. He was right. She could call and check on them, but not from this place. They probably wouldn't be able to hear her. Maybe she could kill Tamiel first and then call.

She returned the phone to her ear and again stalked closer to Tamiel's voice. "That's a good idea. I assume they're alive then."

"I see you, Miss Hunt. Your parents are alive, but if my companions do not hear from me within the hour, you will be an orphan once again."

Lauren lowered the gun. This demon had her trapped. Even if he was lying through his teeth, she couldn't risk it. He had proven his willingness to murder.

She hurried back to Walter and gave him the gun. Bonnie had put his cap, socks, and boots back on and was tying the laces.

"We have to go," Lauren said.

Bonnie squinted at her lips. "Did you say we have to go?"

Lauren nodded.

"He has feeling in his toes. I think we can transport him."

Walter slid the gun into a shoulder holster. "Grab what you can, at least the radio and headset. Matt has a tooth transmitter, so we might be able to contact him."

Nodding again, Lauren rose to her feet. She pointed at Walter, then at Bonnie and used her arms to mimic embracing someone from behind.

"Yes, I can carry Walter," Bonnie said. "I assume you couldn't find the demon."

Lauren stared at her for a moment. It would take too long to explain. "I'll tell you later," she said, not bothering to make sure she understood. She pocketed the phone, hustled to the radio and tucked it and the headset into the pack, then hoisted it onto her back and slid her arms through the straps. Matt needed help. Her parents needed help. And this soundproof bubble was keeping her from doing anything about it.

While Bonnie carried Walter, flapping her wings to lift their feet over obstacles, Lauren followed. Of course, since she never lost her sense of hearing, she wouldn't be able to tell when they left the bubble, but it shouldn't be too far. In fact, Bonnie and Walter already seemed to be talking to each other.

She tried to tune in to their conversation, but no sensation in her spine aided the effort. After nearly a minute, Lauren stopped. "Can either of you hear me?"

Bonnie turned, nearly hovering in place. "We regained our hearing almost right away. I've been telling Walter what you told me about Matt, and he's been telling me which way to go. Since your hearing is so good, I thought you might have been listening."

"It comes and goes." She glanced at Walter. "Did you tell her why you brought Matt here?"

"Not yet," Walter said. "I'll tell her everything I know about him when we get settled."

Lauren lowered the backpack to the ground and dug the phone out of her pocket. "I need to make a call."

Bonnie set Walter down in a sitting position. "Here? Now?"

"I have to check on my parents."

Walter looked up through a large gap in the canopy. "It's all right. If you'll put the radio and headset next to me, I'll call for air support. I think this clearing is big enough. When Matt and I came through, we didn't want to risk chopper noise this close, but we don't have much choice now."

While Bonnie helped Walter set up the equipment, Lauren punched her home number into the phone. It rang several times, but no one answered, not even the message system. After disconnecting, she dialed Dad's mobile phone, but his voice mail immediately picked up. She waited through the message and spoke clearly, as if she were still in the bubble. "Dad. It's Lauren." Her throat tightened, making her voice crack. "Please call this number right away. It's an emergency."

She lowered the phone and stared at the keypad. What was Mom's mobile number? Of course, it was stored in her own phone's memory, but she usually just called the home number. Mom hardly ever carried her mobile phone with her anyway.

As an image of her mother entered her mind, tears welled and trickled to her cheeks. Then, every fear, every heartache, every pain that assaulted her during the past few hours tried to erupt, but she swallowed them down. She couldn't fall apart. Not now. Yet, her body quaked as she fought back sobs.

Bonnie scooted over and rubbed her shoulder. "No answer anywhere?"

"I'm worried … about them." Lauren spoke through rhythmic spasms. "Tamiel said he would … would kill them if I didn't cooperate."

"I'll check with Larry by radio," Walter said. "My transmitter chip flew out when my head banged against the tree." He slid the headset on. "Give me your parents' names."

"Fi … Fiona and Gaston Hunt." Lauren swallowed. "We live in Flagstaff."

"I'm on it." Walter plugged in the headset and flipped a button on the radio. "Larry, can you hear me?"

Lauren sucked back another emerging sob. With her surging emotions, tingles again ran along her back, but her own heaving breaths and the rattle of her loose handcuff drowned out Larry's reply.

Walter rolled his eyes. "Cut the humor. This is serious. I need to know if there are any reports out of Flagstaff about Fiona and Gaston Hunt. … Yes, I know Lois is covering that area, but she's not monitoring this radio. Just get the answer. Ask her, if you have to."

192

Lauren wiped her eyes with her sleeve. Her spasms settled, as did her tingling sensation.

Walter nodded. "Gotcha. Give me a call if you hear anything else." He turned a dial on the radio. "Are you reading our GPS location? … Good. We're ready to be picked up. Tell Jared and Marilyn that one of them can get Merlin later. … Five minutes will be fine." As he turned another dial on the radio, he kept his eyes on his work. "There's a report about a girl named Micaela dying in an explosion, but nothing about Gaston and Fiona Hunt."

Lauren smiled but quickly chided herself for the moment of relief. Breathing out a long sigh, she whispered, "Micaela was my best friend. Tamiel killed her."

"Oh, Lauren! I'm so sorry!" Bonnie kissed her forehead and continued rubbing her shoulder. "We have to get you home right away to check on your parents."

"We'll get an airlift in five minutes. That'll give me time to try to contact Matt." Walter set a hand on one of the earpieces. "Matt, can you hear me?"

Lauren whispered to Bonnie. "Matt has a tooth transmitter. I heard him use it."

Bonnie nodded. "Walter's wife invented it. It's come in handy plenty of times."

"Matt," Walter said into the microphone, "I understand if you can't talk, but if you can hear me, click your teeth together. If you know Morse code, send me a message."

As they waited, a gust of cold wind poured down from above. A blizzard was on its way, and it could begin at any time.

Walter looked at Bonnie and shook his head. "Nothing. They might have discovered his transmitter."

"Or he might be asleep," Bonnie said.

Lauren shivered. She nearly added "Or dead," but it sounded too morbid, too hopeless.

"Well ..." Using both hands, Walter pulled a knee toward his chest. "I'm getting more feeling in my legs. Let's see if I can walk."

Lauren and Bonnie helped him rise. They steadied him for a moment before letting go. When he lifted a leg, the other one buckled. Bonnie caught him and eased him back to a sitting position.

"It looks like you'll be laid up for a little while," she said.

"Me?" Looking up at Bonnie and Lauren, he waved a hand. "I've been stabbed in a lung by freaks from another world and chased by demons in Hades. I'm not about to let a bruised spine stop me."

"Hades?" Lauren gave him a quizzical look. "You mean like ... Hell?"

Walter's grimace changed to a grin. "Close, but I've been there, too."

"So, Hell is a real place? You were actually there?"

193

"Oh, it's real, all right. And scary, too. Scariest place I've ever seen. I still get nightmares. The smells are the most vivid memories—sulfur and burning flesh. The condemned souls were burning in black fire, like flaming buoys bobbing in a dark sea of horror."

Lauren shuddered. "That's a bit too real for me."

"It's scary," Bonnie said, "but Heaven is real, too. I've been there. I was dead for quite a while and spent a short time at the outskirts of the heavenly city. Maybe I'll get a chance to tell you about it."

Lauren stared at them in turn. Their eyes exuded sincerity. Either they were telling the truth, or they were the most self-deceived people on the planet. They really believed they went to those places. If only they had proof. "Did you ... um ... take any pictures?"

"My phone back then didn't have a camera," Walter said. "And Bonnie went to Heaven as a spirit. Kind of tough to drag along a camera when you're disembodied."

"Disembodied," she whispered. How strange it all sounded. Just one day earlier, she would have laughed them off as a couple of wild-eyed crackpots, but seeing a demon and his ghostly accomplice had turned her life upside down. She was ready to believe in leprechauns and werewolves.

She offered a tremulous smile. "Next time you go to Hell, remember to take a camera."

As Walter laughed, Lauren's tingle returned. It seemed strange that it would come back after her emotions had settled. Could it be fear again? The revelations about Hell had shaken her pretty hard.

The wind howled like a moaning ghost, and a low whistle in the trees sounded like an oncoming train. Then, echoing words trickled into her ears. *Poor girl. How could I break her heart? The news can wait. It has to wait.*

Lauren folded her arms over her chest. "What news?"

Walter glanced up at Bonnie before returning his gaze to Lauren. "What do you mean?"

"Larry told you something you didn't tell me, didn't he?"

"Oh. Right. You have super hearing." Folding his hands in his lap, Walter heaved a sigh. "I was hoping to wait. There's no use upsetting you when we're not sure."

"Not sure about what?"

"There was a news report ..." His voice halted, as if every word had to be dragged out. "About an explosion in a Flagstaff home, but they aren't releasing any information about the victims, only that there were two deaths. If Larry gets any updates, he'll let me know."

Lauren pressed her lips together. Her legs quivered. The victims had to be Mom and Dad. With a daughter missing, Dad would be parked by his cell phone, waiting for news. He would have called back by now.

She let out a quiet whisper. "My parents are dead."

Looking at the ground, Walter picked up a twig. Light snow began to fall, a few flakes alighting on his cap. "You're probably right."

Bonnie wrapped her arms around Lauren and pulled her close. "I'm sorry, Lauren. So sorry."

Lauren slumped in Bonnie's grip. As she wept, Bonnie spoke in a soothing tone. "I know how you feel. I know exactly how you feel."

Heat crawled into Lauren's cheeks. "No, you don't! How could you?" She stiffened and tried to push away, but Bonnie held her tight, shushing her. The motherly sound seemed to absorb all her fight. Exhaustion took hold, and every limb felt like rubber.

Bonnie lowered her to the ground, and they sat together, Lauren leaning her head on Bonnie's shoulder. "I do know what it's like, Lauren. On my thirteenth birthday, I watched my own mother die, stabbed by a ruthless dragon slayer. It was on a night

195

much like this, dismal and snowy. After it happened, I ran out into the storm to get away from the slayer, and I lost my way, but God sent helpers to guide me to safety."

"You sound ... like my mother." Lauren's voice quaked terribly, but she couldn't help it. "Mom was religious. Even when she got the news ... the news about the cancer, she never got upset. She just prayed more."

As snow continued to fall, Bonnie raised a wing, shielding them both. "And you, Lauren, are you ... religious?"

"I went to church with her a lot, mostly to be with Micaela in youth group, and I believe in God, if that's what you mean."

"Good ... good. That's important." Bonnie combed her fingers through Lauren's hair, humming the same tune she had hummed while asleep in the Healers' bed, a soothing melody, wordless, yet filled with deep meaning all the same. It communicated comfort, peace, and contentment.

196

Lauren closed her eyes. It felt so good, like being petted while drifting on clouds in a dream. Maybe all of this was just a nightmare. Maybe she would wake up to Mom's call to breakfast, go to school and then volleyball practice, just like always. Micaela would be there, and after practice they would ... they would ...

A new sob broke through. There would be no breakfast call, no volleyball practice. Mom was dead. Micaela was dead. By tomorrow she would be back in a foster home or else in prison if that demon had his way. It was hopeless, completely hopeless.

Bonnie's gentle hum traveled through her fingers and into Lauren's skin, soothing her aching heart. "Do you mind if I tell you a little more about my story?"

"I suppose not." Lauren tensed her jaw. That sounded harsher than she had intended.

"Well, even though my mother died, I got a new mother ... new in a way. Believe it or not, she somehow transformed into a dragon."

"A dragon? Didn't that scare you?"

"Not really. When you've had dragon wings as long as I have, you kind of get used to the idea. I learned at six years old that my mother was once a dragon, so sometimes I imagined her that way. She was a bigger dragon in real life, but it wasn't too much of a shock."

Lauren drew a scene in her mind of a girl hugging a dragon's neck. It seemed strange in one way, showing love to a scaly species that no one trusted, but at the same time, it seemed like the most normal reaction in the world. Maybe all the politicians and religious leaders were wrong. Maybe dragons weren't the instigators of war between Earth and Second Eden. She had figured out long ago that political speeches were often just lengthy lies designed to fool the masses, so maybe all the hype about evil dragons wasn't true at all.

Bonnie shifted her hand to Lauren's shoulder. "Do you mind if I pray?"

197

"No." Lauren sniffed, unable to keep her voice from squeaking. "Go ahead."

The same hum emanated from Bonnie's throat, followed by words that flowed with the melody. "Father of all, you are Jehovah-Shammah, the God who is always with us, no matter where we travel. Nothing can separate us from your love, neither demons, nor fiery explosions, nor prison bars, nor hate-filled guards. Your love is never-ending. Father, please show your love to Lauren. Her life has been gutted by a treacherous demon who seeks to destroy. We have no idea why this enemy of souls has taken such a murderous path, but I trust that you know, and although you have allowed this tragedy to occur, I also trust that you will work good in the wake of evil. You will cause the day after destruction to dawn brighter than the day before.

"And Father …" Bonnie's voice trembled, rising in tenor. "Thank you for rescuing me from that horrible prison. Even though I have been separated from my beloved family for these fifteen long years and suffered daily torture, I never doubted your love and faithfulness. I now see the dawn of my own day beginning to appear. Jehovah-Yasha, the Lord my savior, is mounting his conquering steed and will soon set all the captives free. I beg you to ride onto our battlefield like a dread champion. Rescue Billy, Ashley, and Matt. Let them and Lauren rejoice when they see your mighty hand brush aside those who would torment their souls. And when you do, when you conquer your foes as I have seen you do so many times before, we will rejoice, singing your praises on that day and forevermore."

Bonnie's voice settled into a whisper. "Even in this dark hour I praise you. You never forsook me in other dark places, and I know you won't now. Please allow Lauren to see a glimmer of light in her darkest hour, as well as the Light of the World, Jesus Christ, for only he has the power to expel the demons who would imprison her soul."

She finished with a sighing, "Amen."

Walter echoed. "Amen."

Lauren opened her eyes. Her lips made ready to repeat the echo, but the energy to whisper even a simple word had drained away. Yet, the tingling sensation continued along with a parade of sounds—the wind whistling louder than ever, blending with Walter's labored breathing.

He scooted closer to Bonnie. "I need to tell you something."

"Right." She blinked at him, tears evident. "You said you'd tell me more about Matt."

He nodded. "I brought him here because of his training and his ability to ... " He covered her hand with his own. "To sense danger."

Bonnie folded in her legs, her stare riveted on him. "Go on."

"I don't know if you got a good look at him ..."

She shook her head. "It was dark. I was dizzy. We had to fly out before the guards showed up." She squeezed his hand, her voice cracking. "What are you trying to say?"

"I haven't done a DNA test, but after talking to him, I'm sure he's—"

"Charles?" Bonnie nearly shrieked. "Matt is really Charles?"

"Well, you might have to get used to calling him Matt. He's not too fond of—"

"I'll call him anything he wants!" She flung her arms around him, nearly knocking him down. "Oh, Walter! Thank you for finding him!"

Laughing, he returned the embrace. "You're welcome."

Bonnie jerked back, her face hardening. "But now he's—" With a beat of her wings, she leaped to her feet. "I have to go back! Now!"

"I figured as much," Walter said, "but at least wait for the chopper to land. It should be here any minute."

Lauren aimed an ear toward the sky. The sound of blades whipping the air drifted in from far away. "It's coming."

"We'd better give them room to land," Walter said reaching for Bonnie's hand.

Bonnie and Lauren helped him limp to the side of the clearing where he sat gingerly on a pile of leaves. When the helicopter sounds reached a crescendo, a spotlight pierced the forest from above. Snow swirled through the powerful beam. As the helicopter descended, its blades whipped the trees into a frenzy, creating a swirling vortex of frigid air and sparkling flakes.

Seconds before it landed, a woman jumped out and ran through the spotlight's beam, her arms extended. "Bonnie!" she shouted. "Thank God you're free!"

"Mom Bannister!" Bonnie rushed to meet her.

As the two embraced, Lauren looked past them at the pilot, a man guiding a mounted spotlight. The blinding beam kept his face in shadows. "We have to hurry," the man shouted. "The weather's getting worse, and we're so close to the prison, someone's bound to wonder what's going on."

"Walter's hurt," Bonnie called through the noise. "We'll have to carry him."

The pilot flipped a few switches, slowing the blades and dimming the light. He jumped out and jogged toward them. Bonnie's mother-in-law, dressed in a heavy flight suit, ran with Bonnie to Walter's side.

When the pilot joined the huddle, he extended a hand toward Walter. "Need a boost?"

"He can't walk," Bonnie said, "but he has feeling in his legs."

The pilot hoisted Walter to his feet and pushed a shoulder under his arm. "Can you walk like this? I don't think I can carry you."

Walter grimaced slightly. "This way's fine. I can manage."

"Before you leave." Bonnie pulled Lauren closer. "Mom. Dad. This is Lauren Hunt. We rescued her from the prison. A demon kidnapped her. Lauren, this is my husband's mother and father."

"Marilyn Bannister," she said, extending a gloved hand. "We've had our share of run-ins with demons, so I know what you went through."

Lauren shook her hand. "Pleased to meet you."

"And I'm Jared," the pilot said with a smile. "I'd shake your hand, but mine are filled to the brim with Walter."

Lauren grabbed one of Jared's fingers as it clutched Walter's jacket. "Pleased to meet you, too."

"Let me get Walter aboard. We can talk later." Jared and Walter trudged toward the helicopter.

"I didn't get Lauren's whole story, Mom," Bonnie continued, "but maybe you can while you're flying her out of here."

Marilyn pointed at herself. "*I* can get it?" She furrowed her brow deeply. "I know you too well. What are you planning?"

Bonnie leaned close. "Mom, my son's in there, the young man Walter brought here to get me out."

"He is?" Marilyn glanced at the helicopter. "Walter told me he had a hunch about Matt Fletcher, but he still had to do DNA tests."

Bonnie laid a hand over her heart. "We don't need them. I was out of it when I saw him, but it's coming back to me now. He looks so much like Billy, he has to be Charles. Walter agrees."

"I suppose hearing that a blizzard's coming won't faze you. They're calling for sixty-mile-an-hour winds and two feet of snow."

"Perfect. Maybe it'll knock out the power again. By now everyone knows I escaped, and no one will think I stuck around. I have my wings to protect me. I won't freeze. Besides, Ashley's still in there, too. I couldn't leave her behind."

"Well," Marilyn said, "I know better than to argue with a woman who's trying to rescue her son. If I knew Billy was in there, you couldn't keep me away."

Bonnie nodded at the backpack and radio equipment on the ground. "Just leave Walter's stuff. I can use that to get in touch with you. If I find Billy, I'll let you know."

"Okay." Marilyn set a hand behind Lauren's elbow. "We have to get going before the storm hits."

201

Lauren stepped back. "I want to help Bonnie."

"What?" Marilyn squinted at her. "Are you serious?"

"Yes!" Lauren forced a spark of energy into her voice. "Look, that demon killed my parents and my best friend, so I don't have anyone to go home to. And if Bonnie has the guts to stay here and find Matt and this Ashley person, then I'm going to stay with her. We can look out for each other."

"After all you've been through?" Bonnie asked.

"Definitely. Matt saved my life. I'm not about to abandon him now."

"Well, if you're sure." Bonnie wrapped a wing around Lauren and pulled her close. "I'll be glad for your help."

"If you say so." Marilyn breathed out a long stream of white. "Is there anything else I can do?"

Bonnie gave her an expectant look. "How is my mother doing? Walter said something about a disease striking the original anthrozils."

Marilyn nodded sadly. "It's true. It's a slow, progressive debil-
itation, muscle weakness all over. Jared is the only exception.
Although he is weaker than usual, he has resisted well. One of Sir
Patrick's doctors is studying him, hoping to figure out what's causing it. We sent the rest of them, including your mother, to Second
Eden to keep them safe under your father's care. The last I heard,
your mother can't get out of bed, but her heart is strong."

A wrinkle of concern bent Bonnie's brow. "That sounds like what
happened to Acacia in Second Eden. Mardon was behind her disease."

"We're already on top of that possibility. Mardon and Semiramis have been set free, so Mardon might be up to his old tricks."

"Set free? Why?"

"Let's go!" Jared called from the helicopter. "Larry says we're
about to get blasted by a squall line. Less than three minutes!"

"I'll have to tell you later." After kissing Bonnie and Lauren on
the cheek, Marilyn hustled back to the helicopter and climbed into
the copilot's seat. As the blades began to spin faster, Walter leaned
forward from the backseat and lowered something to the ground.
"You might need this," he shouted. "And be sure to use the tooth
transmitters! They're all on the same frequency. I'm hoping we can
listen in. Tap your jaw twice to toggle them on and off."

The chopper lifted into the sky, again churning the trees in a
cold vortex. After several seconds, it disappeared in the darkness,
and the sound of the whipping blades faded.

"We'd better hurry." Bonnie hustled to the radio and slipped
on the headset. "Larry, can you hear me? … Good. Are you able
to communicate on the tooth transmitter frequency? … Excellent.
I was worried we might be out of range. … Right. I understand
relays. Listen, I'm going to put Lauren Hunt on. Copy her voiceprint and give her communications clearance."

Bonnie pulled off the headset and extended it to Lauren. "Just
talk to him about anything while I look for the tooth transmitters."

"Okay," she said, stretching out the word. "I can do that."

While Bonnie dug through the backpack, Lauren slid the headset on and adjusted the microphone. "Larry? This is Lauren."

"`Lauren Hunt.`" His voice sounded more like a stoic professor's than a computer's. "`I have given you full access to all communications functions. Please speak a few more words. I need to confirm your voice.`"

"Got them," Bonnie said, pinching something in her fingers. "I found a flashlight, too. I'll go see what Walter just left on the ground."

While Bonnie flew across the clearing, Lauren turned her attention back to Larry. "Walter mentioned someone named Lois. Is she another computer?"

"`In a manner of speaking. We were once two separate computers, but Ashley combined us before her incarceration, citing efficiency improvements. We are, if you will, married, joined at the chip, living in welded bliss.`"

Lauren smiled. Even bad puns helped ease the tension. "Well, please tell Lois I said hello, and it's been nice talking to you."

"`My pleasure. Larry and Lois are at Lauren's service. Your voiceprint is confirmed.`"

As Lauren slid off the headset, Bonnie walked slowly toward her, shining the flashlight on herself as she held a strap with a gun and holster dangling at the bottom.

"Ever used one of those?" Lauren asked.

Bonnie handed Lauren the flashlight. "Billy taught me. He wanted to make sure I could defend myself if he wasn't around."

"Good idea. He must really love you."

"He does." Bonnie firmed her trembling lips. "And I love him." She shed the guard's jacket most of the way, letting it dangle at the base of her wings, strapped on the holster, and withdrew the gun. After checking the clip, she slid the gun back into place and donned the jacket again. As a new frigid gust flapped their clothes, she took the flashlight back from Lauren. "Are you ready?"

203

"To break in again? I suppose so. We don't have much choice, do we?"

Bonnie pulled something from her jacket and shone the flashlight on it—a thin wafer that looked like a flat, flexible computer chip. "Wedge this between two molars. It'll be uncomfortable at first, but you'll get used to it." She laid it in Lauren's palm. "I already put mine in."

"All right." Lauren pinched the wafer, inserted it into her mouth, and slid it into a gap near the back. It didn't feel bad at all. Ever since the end of her braces ordeal, her teeth had plenty of room. "I'm ready."

"I hope so. This could be a rough ride." Bonnie picked up the nearly empty backpack, dumped out the snacks and remaining electrical components from the main pocket, and handed it to Lauren. "I might be able to use this later, so please carry it."

"Will do." Lauren wrapped the loose handcuff around it and hugged it close. A sharp pain stung her chest, as if something attached to the pack had scratched her. She pulled it away and looked at the material, but it appeared to be normal. Maybe during their previous flight, Bonnie's squeezing arms had bruised a rib.

After sliding the flashlight and a few of the snacks into her jacket pocket, Bonnie wrapped her arms around Lauren's waist and lifted her into the air. Within seconds, they rose above the trees and into a blustery mix of wind and snow. Gusts battered them. Icy flakes buffeted their faces. With every sudden jolt, pain shot through Lauren's rib cage. The bruises must have been worse than she thought.

Battling sudden drops and knocks to the side, they flew on. Darkness kept Lauren from seeing anything for the first minute, but lights from the prison eventually came into view. The towers' search lamps scanned the grounds in back-and-forth sweeps, and bright floodlights hung from tall poles around the perimeter. Yet, in spite of all the security devices—fences, razor wire, alarm systems, and armed guards, no one likely suspected that a winged woman would drop in on them, especially one who so recently escaped.

They flew over the research building and slowly orbited, staying just above the glow as the wind continued to slash them from side to side. "If I'm going to dodge those lights," Bonnie said directly into Lauren's ear, "I have to time this perfectly. When the right moment comes, I'll drop like a rock, even faster than before."

Still hugging the backpack, Lauren nodded. No need to reply. In her position, she couldn't do anything to help anyway.

One of the beams swept slowly over the building. The moment it passed the roof, Bonnie and Lauren plunged. Lauren held her breath. The dim roof hurtled toward them. Seconds later, they settled down near a roof access, a six-foot-high boxlike structure with a glass-paneled door.

Another beam swept by, but the shed blocked its light. As Bonnie tried to catch her breath in the midst of swirling snow, she shone the flashlight through the glass. The room was small, holding only a concrete pad and steps leading downward. She tried the doorknob, but it wouldn't open.

205

"I don't see any security system here," Bonnie said. "This isn't about to stop us." She withdrew the gun and broke one of the glass panels with the butt. Then, reaching through the hole, she unlocked the door.

Lauren let the backpack dangle. The jabbing pain eased a bit. "I hope no one heard that."

"Not likely." Bonnie opened the door and guided Lauren inside. After closing it behind her, she sat on the top step and gestured with a wing for Lauren to join her. "It's still cold in here. Sit close, and I'll keep us warm until we decide what to do next."

Lauren laid the backpack down and sat hip to hip with her. "Do you have a plan?"

"I'm working on one." Bonnie's wing wrapped completely around Lauren, leaving only her head exposed. "This blizzard is an answer to prayer. I just have to figure out the best way to apply it."

Lauren met Bonnie's gaze. Snowflakes clinging to her hair melted and dripped to her clothes. She looked tired and worn, yet determined.

"We'll rest, for a little while at least." Bonnie withdrew four granola bars from her pocket and handed two to Lauren. "By the time two or three o'clock rolls around, only a few guards will be roaming here and there. If the blizzard doesn't cut out the power, maybe we can find a way to cut it ourselves. The darker it is, the better."

As Bonnie spoke, her words entered Lauren's ears through the air, as well as through a buzz in her jaw. Apparently the transmitters were working.

Bonnie shifted their bodies to the side and leaned against a wall. "Go ahead and eat, and then we'll get a little sleep. We can use snow for water if we need it."

"What if we don't wake up in time?" Lauren tore the wrapping from one of the bars and bit off a chunk. It had a gritty texture—granola, nuts, and honey.

Bonnie unwrapped her own snack. "Can you figure out how to set the alarm on Walter's phone?"

"Most likely," Lauren said, not bothering to swallow first.

"Then set it for two hours from now and put it on vibrate. I'll hold it. I'm sure it'll wake me up." She took a bite, pausing until she swallowed. "Then again, with the vivid dreams I've been having, maybe not. We'll just have to pray for the best."

While Lauren pushed the buttons to set the phone alarm, she asked, "What kind of dreams?"

Bonnie poised the granola bar in front of her mouth. "It's more like watching a movie than a dream, because I'm not in them myself. These two teenagers, Joran and Selah, are offspring of

Methuselah, and the last dream ended with them being confronted by a demon."

"Tamiel?" Lauren took another bite.

Bonnie nodded. "That's why I was so surprised when you told me his name. I had never heard it outside this dream. And every time I dream, the story continues. It takes place a long time ago, and now Tamiel is trapped with the teenagers in an ovulum, a glass egg that's also a refuge, another world people can enter."

"That's really bizarre. How could your dream invent a real name you didn't know before, someone who is really tracking us?"

"I'm not sure, but in the dream, Methuselah said that dragons sometimes dream about what happens in an ovulum, so since I have dragon genetics …"

"The dream is telling you why you're dreaming." Lauren altered to a tone of skepticism. "That's not exactly a reliable source."

207

"Maybe not, but both of us knowing Tamiel's name makes me think there might be something to it. It could be that God is giving us information we'll need."

"Okay," Lauren said, adding a nervous laugh. "I can't argue with that. Maybe you should go to sleep and get Joran and … what was the other name?"

"Selah."

"Get Joran and Selah out of their mess."

Bonnie smiled. "I *was* getting kind of worried about them."

Lauren pushed the phone into Bonnie's hand. "I don't think I'll be able to sleep, though. I feel terrible."

"It's no wonder. I felt the same way when my mother died." Bonnie grasped Lauren's hand and intertwined their fingers. "I had to trudge through the snow to a social worker's office and …"

As Bonnie continued talking, pausing now and then to nibble on her snack, Lauren pushed the last morsel of hers into her mouth, leaned her head against Bonnie's shoulder, and closed her eyes, slowly chewing. Like the honey in the granola, being enfolded by a strong wing while their hands intermeshed was a delicious sensation. Mom was kind and loving, but not really like this. Bonnie was … well … different, special, a natural at coating her with comfort. Still, her birth parents were probably like Bonnie. Their family photos proved that they were kind and caring, taking little Lauren to amusement parks, beaches, and zoos. Although years in the foster care system had tarnished any idea that all parents were perfect, nothing could damage the reputation of the two who had given her life.

Lauren pushed the other granola bar into her pocket and felt for the ring the Colonel had given her. He had said it belonged to her mother, probably thinking Bonnie was her mother. If so, maybe Bonnie could explain why Semiramis thought the gem was so special.

She pulled the ring out and enclosed it in her hand. As soon as Bonnie finished, she would ask.

The story continued, an amazing tale about a white-haired girl named Sapphira who could turn her body into flames. She and Gabriel, a young man with dragon wings, guided Bonnie through a snowstorm.

Lauren let the story come alive in her mind, picturing Bonnie, Sapphira, and Gabriel as they walked through the snow to a social worker's office where a friend and confidante of dragons hid Bonnie in the foster care system so the dragon slayer couldn't find her. After a long journey on a train, she arrived in West Virginia, hoping to find the son of another dragon who had turned human.

Soon, Bonnie's soft words faded, and new images entered Lauren's mind—a boy holding a lyre and a girl clutching two metal rods.

CHAPTER

TRAPPED

Joran took a rod from Selah with his left hand, and, still holding the lyre in his right, locked arms with her. "Who is the fool?" he asked. "The mice in the trap, or the trap setter who gets caught in it himself?"

With his wings spread out behind him, Tamiel stepped closer. "You did not bring that lyre in here with you. Where did you get it?"

"Stop!" Joran shouted as he and Selah lifted their rods. "I am not the child you and Naamah deceived in the past."

Tamiel halted. "You are both still children, and you have not faced the likes of me with your sonic defenses. If you create a sound barrier, I will turn it against you."

"If that's true, why are you warning me?"

"I heard the white-haired girl. I need you both to be healthy so you can get the key."

"So you can steal it from us?" Selah asked. "Like you stole Seraphina's voice?"

Tamiel laughed. "Steal it? My dear girl, I would never take the key without your permission. In your search for it, you might discover a way to use it that I could not learn on my own. Considering the circumstances we find ourselves in, we should formulate a plan that would benefit us all. I have a lot more experience with the legends and prophecies than the two of you have, so you would be wise to listen to me."

Joran leaned sideways and whispered, "I don't believe a word he says."

"Neither do I," Selah whispered in return. "If he didn't fear us, he wouldn't have warned us at all. I say, let's attack first and end the threat now. He's evil and will do nothing but evil."

Joran nodded. "Set the rhythm."

"Do not be foolish," Tamiel said, lifting his hands as if ready to block an attack. "I am not one of the stupid Watchers who so easily fell prey to your arts."

"Beguiling serpent." As Selah scowled at Tamiel, her voice resonated in the hollow chamber. "Remove your mask."

"This is your final warning," Tamiel said in a calm, even tone. "Your aggression will not aid our cause."

"Behold the sunlight." Selah's words bristled with energy. "And breathe your last."

Joran sang out probing notes that matched her beat, but no echo returned. Tamiel stood motionless, his hands still lifted with his palms facing out. Somehow, he had the ability to block and cancel the sounds. Joran had to guess the proper key and tune and hope it worked.

After taking a quick breath, he sang out.

A demon strikes with serpent's fangs
To bite the flesh, injecting wrong;
Now biting back, we sing with light
To break the darkness with our song.

As before, a sound wave emanated from his metallic pole and spread across to Selah's, attaching to it and creating a barrier. The wave repeated Joran's voice, twisted and distorted, as if he were singing while riding a dragon in a storm. Tamiel warped in their view, but his confident pose never altered.

"Time to wrap him up," Selah shouted above the noise. "I'll hold the lyre. We don't have a dragon to burn him, but maybe we can incapacitate him."

"With a concussion note?"

"Exactly."

"Let's try it." Joran shifted the lyre to her grasp, then, holding his rod high, ran around the demon. The vibrating barrier encircled him, wrapping him in a banner of reverberating words, but he remained calm and confident in his stance.

When Joran completed the orbit, he pulled the rod to remove the slack in the wall of sound. As it adhered to Tamiel, his face tightened and paled, and his eyes bulged. Tremors shook his body, making his teeth clack together in the midst of the barrier's continuing song.

211

"I think he's ready." Selah reached toward Joran. "I'll take your rod. You'll need your hands free."

"Can you hold everything?"

Selah pressed the lyre against her chest with her wrist. "I think so."

He gave her the rod and stepped away. Lifting his hands, he took in a deep breath. This would take every ounce of energy he could summon.

"Do it!" Selah shouted.

Joran belted out a high A note, the very top of his vocal range, and held it. Like an arrow from his bow, his voice pierced the wall and slammed into Tamiel's head. An appendage of sound protruded from the wall and followed the note into the demon's ear. Grimacing, the demon teetered but soon recovered his balance.

"He can't last much longer," Selah called. "Keep it up!"

Joran continued holding the note. His lungs burned, and pain throttled his skull. Soon he would run out of air, and since the note degenerated the barrier wall, it would eventually collapse. No demon had ever been able to withstand this kind of onslaught. Since the sound barrier amplified the note, no one within its grasp could stand for long.

Just as Joran stopped to draw a breath, Tamiel thrust out his arms, grasped the thinning wall with both hands, and reeled it in. Selah flew toward him, the rods and lyre still in her grip. When she drew within reach, Tamiel looped the sound barrier around her body, and pulled her into his arms. The echoing song jumbled, and the tune twisted. The wall sounded like a strangling man trying to call for help.

Gasping for breath, Joran leaped at Tamiel, but the demon sidestepped out of the way. Joran fell headlong into a sea of blue, then jumped to his feet and spun back.

Tamiel called above the chaotic noise. "Stay where you are!"

"Let my sister go!" Joran shouted, his voice hoarse.

"Gladly." Tamiel snatched the sonic rods from Selah, set her upright, and spun her in place. Holding the rods over her head, he waved the twisted ribbon of sound and wrapped her in a cocoon of rhythmic noise. As she rotated, she thinned out and shrank in place until only the lyre and her hands remained visible.

Seconds later, everything but the lyre vanished. It turned on one of its supports for a moment, wobbling on the blue floor like a faltering top. Before it could fall, Tamiel scooped it up and looked at the strings. "Ah! She is now encased in the A string. She is in the middle, buffered by three strings on each side, so she should be comfortable." He reached the lyre toward Joran. "I believe this is yours."

His arms trembling, Joran took the lyre and stared at the A string. It vibrated slightly, as if recently played, and a weak voice drifted into his ears. "Joran? What happened?"

"Selah?" He ran his finger along the string. It seemed of normal tension and composition, though it tingled against his skin. "Can you hear me?"

"She likely can hear you," Tamiel said, "but I doubt that she can see you. I have done this in order to make sure you carry out the necessary steps to create a key. When you are finished, bring the lyre back to me, and I will release your sister."

Joran balled a fist. "I ought to—"

"If you try to harm me, I will see to it that she never escapes." Tamiel laid the sonic rods on the floor, spread out his wings, and backed away. "I will be monitoring your progress, so always assume that I am watching your every move."

As the demon retreated toward the white door, Joran picked up the rods and pushed them into his leg pouch. Then, setting his lips close to the A string, he whispered, "Selah?" After a few seconds of silence, he plucked the string. It vibrated, emitting the note, as well as Selah's voice.

"It's such a dark place, blackness all around. Oh, Elohim, I hear Joran, but I cannot seem to speak to him. I ask for a voice so that we can communicate. Let him know where I am so he can …"

As the string settled, her words faded. Joran plucked it again, harder this time.

"I will fear nothing. I will trust in you, my deliverer from the flood, with all my heart. So if there is any way you can let him know that I am unhurt and waiting for another way of escape …"

Again, her voice trailed off into silence.

Joran plucked the string again and again. As the note strengthened with every pluck, a white aura formed around the string. It brightened and expanded until an image appeared between Joran and the strings—Selah on her knees with her hands clasped in prayerful entreaty. Completely white and radiant, her body pulsed with the strength of the note.

"I know you will watch over me, Elohim, so—"

"Selah!"

She shot to her feet and looked around. "Joran?"

"Yes! I'm here!"

Staring at him, her mouth dropped open. "You're so big!"

He continued plucking. "You're trapped inside one of the lyre's strings. If I keep playing it, you appear in front of me. You look like a miniature Selah, bright and silvery, like mist in the moonlight."

"How odd!" She set her hands on her hips. "Where's that wicked serpent who put me in here?"

"Gone. He says he'll show me how to get you out when I complete the key."

"The lazy devil. You do all the plowing, and he'll reap the harvest. And once you complete the key, he'll probably demand that you give it to him in exchange for my freedom from the lyre. We'll be trapped in the ovula forever."

"I don't think I have much choice. I'll have to complete the key and figure out how to get us out later." Still playing the string, Joran sighed. "I'm sorry. I failed."

"You haven't failed." She gazed up at him, her eyes bright and hope filled. "Now you have a chance to try again. You can sing me out of the lyre, and you can prove to yourself that your gifts have been restored."

Joran's heart thumped. Her plea stabbed his soul. Of course he wanted to get her out of the lyre. He desperately wanted to. But how could he do the impossible? She might as well have asked him to flap his arms and fly to her rescue. Still, shouldn't he make the attempt? Even if he failed, he had to let her know that he would try anything.

After clearing his throat, he stopped playing, and Selah slowly disappeared. He fixed his stare on the string. Before the betrayal, he could sing the note at a volume that made the string vibrate and cast out its prisoner. Since then, every effort had failed. The

214

string would vibrate slightly and even glow, but no matter how hard he tried, he couldn't make it do anything else.

He sang the A note, raising the volume a notch every second. Soon the string began to vibrate, and a white aura surrounded it. Selah's image grew out of the glow until it appeared as it had before.

She clapped her hands. "You can do it, Joran! Keep singing!"

His cheeks warming, he continued, but Selah neither grew nor shrank. She stayed semitransparent, an embodiment of radiant mist.

Finally, he stopped and heaved in a breath. Gasping, he crouched and began plucking the string again. "I can't … can't keep it up. … I just don't have the gift anymore."

"I understand." Selah's head drooped. "Thank you for trying."

He gripped the frame tightly. "I'll get you out. I promise. It's my fault you're in there, and I'll do whatever it takes to set you free."

"Don't blame yourself. Using a song to fight Tamiel was my idea." With her hands folded behind her, Selah began pacing slowly in a three-step circuit. "At least we know our songs don't hurt him, but we'll have to figure out what can affect him."

Joran straightened to his full height. "All the Watchers are afraid of dragon fire."

Selah stopped pacing and looked at him. "True, and we also know that dragon fire releases them from the lyre strings, so maybe fire can get me out."

"But fire also destroys them as they exit."

"Except for the one that almost escaped," Selah said. "It took a second dose of fire to kill him."

"Right. No matter how you look at it, it's dangerous. Too little fire won't get you out, and too much could kill you. Besides, we don't have a dragon around here anyway."

Selah shrugged. "So we're stuck with trying to complete the key."

215

"Maybe something will come to light while I'm searching the other ovula."

"Maybe." She walked to the edge of the lyre's base, stooped, and caressed the thumb he braced it with. Although he couldn't feel the touch, watching her loving gesture raised goose bumps up and down his arm. "You can't keep playing the string forever, Joran. Just bring me back when you learn something new or want to talk. I'll be all right. There's nothing here to hurt me, nothing at all." She straightened and gave her shoulders another light shrug. "Except maybe loneliness."

Joran caressed the lyre's frame. "As soon as I find the next ovulum, I'll call you back. We probably couldn't talk inside the purity ovulum anyway."

"True." She lowered herself to a sitting position and smiled, her gaze still locked on him. "I love you, Joran. I'll talk to you soon."

"I love you, too, Selah." As he plucked the string a final time, he clenched his teeth. "I'll get you out of there."

Her image melted away. Wrapping his arms around the lyre, he hugged it against his chest, again caressing the A string. He sucked in a halting breath and added, "Somehow."

216

Matt awoke to darkness, almost complete except for a tiny glimmer floating near the center of his view. He lay on a cold, hard surface, like concrete or tiles. His wrists were tied in front of him, forcing his arms together, but they could still move freely as a unit. The binding material felt like thick rope, damp, as if someone had wetted the knots to allow them to shrink as they dried. At the ends of his bent legs, rope bound his ankles. Both binding points were so tight, his fingers and toes tingled.

As he pushed to sit up, pain ripped through his left forearm. The sudden pangs sparked a barrage of memories—crawling through the prison fence, watching Mrs. Bannister and Lauren lift safely into the night sky, getting shot in the arm, and being dragged back to the prison.

He lifted his arms to his face and felt for his wound with his chin. His sleeve had been rolled up and a bandage wrapped around his forearm. Although it was too dark to be sure, it felt like a tight medical bandage rather than a hastily tied piece of cloth.

Feeling dizzy, he probed with his hands, found a wall, and leaned his head back. Pain again roared through his arm, forcing a low moan.

"Are you all right?" someone called.

Matt stiffened. The masculine voice seemed caring, though weak and tortured. "Uh … not exactly all right."

"When they dragged you in here, it looked like you were in pretty bad shape."

"I think I'm still in bad shape. I got shot in the arm." Matt winced at the throbbing pain. "I've never been shot before."

"I doubt that it's something you can get used to."

"No. I guess not."

"The guard told me to give you an update when you woke up." The man's voice seemed livelier now. "The bullet went all the way through, and there was some damage to the bone, more like a chip than a break, so it doesn't need a cast."

"Good news, bad news, huh?"

"Something like that."

Matt peered through the darkness. The slight glimmer floated above a shadowy outline, a man sitting against the opposite wall. "What's that light I see?"

"It's a candlestone hanging from the ceiling. It keeps me weak. They think darkness will also weaken me, which might be true, but it's nothing compared to the candlestone. It's like an energy leech."

"Are you an anthrozil?"

"Yep. Billy Bannister's my name. What's yours?"

"Matt. Matt Fletcher." He imagined a friendly expression on Mr. Bannister's face, though marred by a slight wince, reflecting his weakness. Still, the mental sketch was vague, incomplete. If Walter was right, then this stranger was his real father and might have some of his own features. And by rights, maybe he should be addressing Mr. Bannister as a son would a father, but having drill sergeants for father figures didn't exactly make that easy. For now, it would be better to probe for information before accepting Walter's wild theories. "So, uh, I've heard quite a bit about you. I go to a military school, and there's always talk about preparing for war against Second Eden."

"Is that so?"

"Yeah. The officers say the higher-ups persecute anthrozils to keep dragons away. The stuff about trying to find the answer to long life is a scam."

"Are they saying that any dragon sighting will result in increased torture for imprisoned anthrozils?"

"Something like that."

"I'm not sure how it could increase."

"I guess sitting all alone in the dark is like torture. At least you're not being stretched on a rack or getting water-boarded."

"As if that would be worse." Mr. Bannister let out a sigh. "How old are you, Matt?"

"Sixteen. Why?"

"Just wondering if you could understand. You're probably mature enough." Mr. Bannister grunted, as if shifting his body to a different position. "Anyway, I got married seventeen years ago to the most wonderful woman ever to set foot on this planet. We had a year of unmatched bliss together, and she gave birth to twins, Charles and Karen. They were the joy springs of our mutual love, and we treasured them as gifts from God. But during their first year of life, the peace between Earth and Second Eden started to crumble. Elam and Sapphira—Second Eden's king and queen—

218

wouldn't agree to join Earth's United Nations or acquiesce to any international laws. In a formal letter to the UN, King Elam stated that Second Eden is separate, unique, and sovereign, and he wouldn't relinquish any power, rule, or authority to anyone."

Matt twisted his good arm, trying to get blood to his numbing fingers. "I read about that. It was received like a slap in the face. The UN was furious."

"I should have guessed you'd be up to speed on your history. What did they teach you about what happened next?"

"The UN president said something offensive about the queen of Second Eden, so the king sent dragons to attack Fort Knox and steal the gold reserves. I saw video of the battle."

Mr. Bannister laughed softly. "I thought that would be your answer. And did you see how much gold the dragons carried away?"

"We ... uh ... I mean, the army repelled them, and the dragons didn't get anything. Not a single bar of gold. But that attack began a cold war that's lasted fifteen years."

Another laugh flowed through Mr. Bannister's reply. "Repelled them. That's comical."

"Why is it comical?"

"Before I answer, let me ask you this. Did you see any photos of Fort Knox after the battle?"

Matt shook his head, though Mr. Bannister likely couldn't see him. "The army ordered a media blackout until about two years ago."

"I see. So that means it took them more than ten years to rebuild the fort. The dragons really devastated that place, didn't they?"

"That's not what I heard. Official reports say there was minimal damage."

"Official reports!" Mr. Bannister huffed. "Well, Matt Fletcher, let me reeducate you. After King Elam refused the UN's demands,

219

he agreed to send Queen Sapphira as an emissary to hear a list of grievances lodged against Second Eden. But Elam made it clear that Sapphira was there to seek a remedy, not to be an ambassador who recognized any UN authority or legitimacy. She would come as an agent of peace between two sovereign entities, not in recognition that Second Eden had any obligation to acquiesce to UN demands."

"I never heard any of this," Matt said. "It's like revisionist history."

"Except that my version is the truth. The media and the educational systems create their own version of history to match an agenda. Anyway, the UN goons kidnapped Sapphira and held her hostage in Fort Knox. They said they would let her go only if Second Eden agreed to abide by international law."

"That's insane! You can't use threats to force someone to a negotiating table. As soon as the threat is over, the party being threatened can just walk away from whatever agreement they made. They would have to hold Sapphira permanently to keep Elam honest."

Mr. Bannister growled under his breath. "Keep Elam honest. As if the UN cared anything about honesty."

"So what happened?"

"Elam understood exactly your point and guessed that they would never give Sapphira back, so he set up an appointment to come to the UN in person to negotiate for her release. Of course, the government sent all kinds of troops to New York to make the UN headquarters secure, thinking Elam might bring a squadron of dragons to ensure his safe return. Well, the morning he was supposed to arrive, the dragons launched an attack on Fort Knox to retrieve Sapphira, catching Earth's forces off guard." Mr. Bannister grunted again, and his voice weakened as he continued. "The dragons weren't trying to get gold. They were seeking a greater treasure, and they succeeded."

"How did the dragons know where to find her?"

"We have computer capabilities that allowed us to search for disruptions in military bases. You see, Sapphira is not a weak little princess. We knew she would cause an unbelievable ruckus, possibly creating an inferno that would require outside help to extinguish. When our computers noticed a fire department dispatch to Fort Knox from every surrounding station, it didn't take much more investigative work to figure out where Sapphira was within the compound. They had to put her in a bunker in the tightest security possible."

"Where they keep the gold?"

"Exactly. So when the dragons attacked, the one video the army released made it look like they were trying to get the gold reserves, so the media had all the proof they needed to turn popular opinion against Second Eden. But they didn't want to scare the people too badly, so they framed the attack as a failure, saying that the dragons came with all their firepower and caused only minimal damage. The fact is that the dragons devastated the fort so completely, they wouldn't let anyone outside the military in to see the remains."

221

"Actually, that makes a lot of sense," Matt said. "I never heard a coherent reason for the media blackout."

"Then, as you might expect, the UN retaliated. They demanded that the US arrest my wife and me as spies, and they took away our children before their first birthday. That didn't make the TV or newspapers, I'll bet."

"Not that I ever heard." Matt gazed at the sparkling candlestone. Floating in the air about ten feet from the floor, it looked like a trapped star. "So, why haven't the dragons come to rescue you and your wife?"

Silence descended, a heavy silence that seemed to darken the room. "I don't know. I have been without communication from the outside for fifteen years. I can pick up information from the guards in puzzle pieces, whenever they care to say anything more than a grunt, and I can guess the reason from what I know about Elam. He is a wise and patient man. He thinks the government would be ready for another dragon attack and not be fooled by a diversion. In fact, this facility is so new, the whole place might be an elaborate setup designed to draw dragons here so they can be exterminated. Elam would probably work in stealth, taking his time to find where we are and hatch a plan to get us out. Since he endured suffering for a lot more years than I have, he might assume that we can endure it as well, that we would gladly do so if it meant preventing war."

"Because Second Eden would lose?"

"Because innocent people would die."

"Oh." A flash of heat warmed Matt's cheeks. Too many stupid remarks would quickly make him look like a fool in the eyes of his potential new father. "Right. That makes sense."

222

Mr. Bannister let out a sigh. "I can endure the weakness and physical pain without too much of a problem. The hardest part is not knowing how my wife is doing. Sometimes I have nightmares that she's suffering worse than I am, and the mental anguish is almost more than I can stand."

"Yeah. I suppose it is." Matt nodded to himself. Mr. Bannister's story rang true. He wasn't an enemy at all. He was a loving husband and father who was a victim of vicious inter-world politics. "You can stop worrying about her."

"What?" Mr. Bannister's voice sharpened, and his chains rattled. "What do you know? Tell me!"

"Bonnie Bannister. Your wife. She's safe. I rescued her from this prison. At least I'm pretty sure I did. I saw her fly away, and she was long gone before they shot me."

"*You* rescued her?"

"Yeah. A guy named Walter found me and—"

"Walter Foley?"

"Right. He found out that I have an ability to know when danger is near, so he thinks I'm an anthrozil like you."

A short pause ensued. Matt again tried unsuccessfully to loosen his wrists.

"And you said you're sixteen years old."

"Yeah." Matt intentionally lowered his voice. Mr. Bannister, even in his weakened state, was about to put it all together. Shouts of "Son! I've missed you so much! Thank you for rescuing your mother!" or other equally awkward comments were sure to come.

Again, silence ruled the jail cell. The room seemed darker than ever, and the pain in Matt's wrists and ankles spiked.

After a few seconds, Mr. Bannister spoke up. "I assume the candlestone is weakening you, then."

Matt breathed a silent sigh. Mr. Bannister was being cool. That was good. "Actually, it doesn't bother me. Walter showed one to me and said it told him about a dragon trait I supposedly have. He promised to tell me, but I didn't get to see him again."

"Healing," Mr. Bannister said. "The candlestone doesn't hurt you because you're constantly healing yourself, and you can heal others, too."

Matt probed for pain in his gunshot wound. It had diminished greatly. "I already knew I healed fast. People think I'm weird." He bent his knees and drew his legs closer. "I suppose I am."

"It's better not to think of your gifts as weird, Son. Think of them as blessings. I'm sure Walter sent you because of your abilities, and if not for them, you probably wouldn't have succeeded."

Matt offered another likely unseen nod. In a way, Mr. Bannister was right. The danger-sensing helped a lot. Yet, could getting shot and then trapped in a prison cell be called successful? Still, something felt oddly comforting. Maybe it was the knowledge that he had rescued two people and set them free from bondage. Maybe that and hearing Mr. Bannister's calm words of consolation, especially *Son.*

223

For the next several minutes, Matt related the rest of the prison-break tale, including meeting Lauren and finding Mrs. Bannister in the Healers' Room. That upset Mr. Bannister quite a bit, because it meant Mrs. Bannister had been subjected to intrusive experiments, something she would find particularly torturous.

"Well, she's safe now, Mr. Bannister, so ..." He let his sentence die. The formality sounded awkward. "I guess we both know you're my father, so what should I ... you know ... call you?"

"What would you be comfortable with?"

Matt mouthed the word *Dad*, letting it out in the barest whisper. It sounded all right. He could get used to it. "Is *Dad* okay?"

"I would consider it ..." A tremor sneaked into his voice. "An honor."

Matt let himself smile. This man, his father, was no drill sergeant and no smarmy mama's boy. "Okay ... *Dad*. What are we going to do to get out of here?" He winced. *Dad* still didn't sound natural. Maybe he could say it for his father's sake but mentally call him *Billy*, at least for a while.

"Are the knots pretty tight?"

"Yeah. They're cutting off my circulation."

"You have teeth. You could eventually gnaw your way out. Then you can get that cursed candlestone and hide it somewhere."

"The guards must have known about that possibility," Matt said. "Why would they put me in here with you?"

"They probably assume you're weakened by it, too. And they have another candlestone. They never come in here without flashing it at me."

"Another one? Not exactly a rare gem, I guess."

"There were a bunch of them in a river in Second Eden. Elam closed down tourist diving, but probably not before some collectors picked up a few."

"Pretty bad oversight for a king."

Billy laughed. "I'm glad you're not afraid to tell it like it is. We'll get along fine."

"Seriously, didn't he consider that someone might steal them?"

"I was the one who found them in the first place. To this day I don't remember if I told him. So if it's anyone's fault, it's probably mine."

"Well, I guess I'd better start working on these knots." Matt tried to pull his wrists apart, but the rope held him fast. He lifted his hands toward his mouth, and as he pictured himself biting into the knots, a memory flashed into his mind. The tooth transmitter!

Pushing his tongue back to his molars, he felt for its presence. Yes, it was still there. But could Walter hear him? The transmission might be poor between this cell and wherever Walter was now. And who could tell what condition he might be in?"

"Dad? Do you think it's safe to raise my voice? Walter had me put a tooth transmitter in my mouth, so maybe—"

"Yes! Go for it! We're in a bunker, and it's almost soundproof. The guards hardly ever come by at night."

"Here goes." Matt took in a deep breath and shouted, "Walter! It's Matt! Can you hear me?"

CHAPTER

In Disguise

L auren woke with a start. Someone shouted. It was too real to
be a dream. A sweeping searchlight flashed by, illuminating
the rooftop shed. As it retreated, the room dimmed but not
enough to leave them in darkness.

She gave Bonnie a gentle nudge, whispering, "Did you hear a
shout?"

"Huh? What?" Bonnie leaned forward, yawning. "A shout?
No, I don't think so."

Lauren's tooth buzzed. "Lauren?" a male voice said. "Is that you?"

Bonnie angled her head. "I heard that."

"It's Matt!" Lauren massaged her jaw, once again lifting her
handcuffs and making the loose one jingle. "Where are you?"

"I'm in a prison cell," Matt said. "Where are you?"

"I'd better not say. Someone might be picking up the transmissions."

Bonnie clasped her hands, biting a thumb. Lauren smiled at
her. She seemed ready to jump out of her skin as she waited for
the right time to talk to her son.

"That's cool," Matt said, "but if the guards are listening, they'll probably barge in here. We'll know pretty soon."

Bonnie touched her jaw. "Larry, can you hear me?"

"Quite well." Larry's smooth, casual voice came through loud and clear. "I assume you are at a high elevation."

"I'm not saying, at least not yet. I've been out of the loop for a long time, so I need some information. Are you still using a secure frequency for the tooth transmitters?"

"It is an obscure channel, and I can assure you that even if someone were to tune in to your frequency, he would not be able to understand the communication. The transmitter digitizes your voice, scrambles it with a unique algorithm, and the receiving side decodes it. All should be quite secure."

"Great, Larry. Thanks. Keep listening in."

"I will for a short time. It will be Lois's turn in exactly two minutes."

"That's fine." Bonnie nodded at Lauren. "Sounds like it's secure. Go ahead."

Lauren pushed one of her ears closed, hoping to aid her hearing. "Matt, I'm on the roof of the research wing. Bonnie flew me here. We're going to try to find you and get you out."

"So Mrs. Bannister is with you right now?" Matt asked.

"Yes." Lauren scooted hip to hip with Bonnie. "We couldn't get much closer together."

"Right, Dad. She's with Lauren."

"Dad?" Lauren looked at Bonnie. "Matt, what are you talking about?"

"I'm with Billy Bannister. He's my father."

Bonnie laid a hand on her chest. "My ... my husband is here?"

"Alive and well. ... Not perfect, but he's still got a fire in his belly. ... Wait a minute. No. He says he doesn't have a fire in his belly, but he said his heart is on fire for Bonnie Bannister."

New tears trickled down Bonnie's cheeks. "Oh, my dear Billy! Please tell him I love him, and we'll get you both out as soon as we can!"

"She says she loves you," Matt said, "and she and Lauren will get you out as soon as they can."

"Matt ..." Bonnie wiped the tears, but two more quickly replaced them. Her smile was so broad, a dimple appeared on each cheek. "Thank you for rescuing me. I'm so proud that you're my son."

"Sure ... uh ... Mom. ... Is it okay if I call you that?"

"Okay? Okay? Of course it's okay!" Bonnie buried her face in her hands. "Oh, dear God in Heaven! You are eternally gracious and faithful! Thank you, O my Father, for watching over my husband and son all these years! And now you have brought my son back as my rescuer! Praise your holy name!"

After a brief silence, Matt continued. "That's all very cool, Mom, but now Dad and I are on the receiving end of the rescue business, so I guess we'd better come up with a plan."

"Yes, yes. That's right. Of course."

Lauren looked up at the door's glass panel. Snow blew in through the broken pane, and a curtain of flakes descended outside, lit up from time to time by searchlights. "Blizzard's hitting hard," she said. "But the power's still on."

Bonnie lifted the cell phone and read the display. "It's five before three a.m. This is a good time to try to sneak into the building. Do you have any idea how to guide us to your cell?"

Matt relayed the question and after a few uh-huh's, he replied. "Dad says he gets to go to a big shower room twice a week, so big it looks like it was designed to hose off a dragon. That room is three doors down a cavernous hallway. There aren't any windows anywhere, so we're probably below ground level. If you have a diagram of the facility, you can look for a lower corridor that has plumbing in a big room."

"Larry?" Bonnie said. "Did you get that?"

"This is Lois," a female purred. "I will examine the schematic. One moment, please."

229

Lauren looked at the bare bulb hanging on the wall. It flickered, then dimmed before returning to its normal brightness. Could that be a sign of stress on the power grid, or maybe snow and ice on the lines?

"I have located two possibilities with equal potential," Lois said, "and based on recent GPS data from your transmitters, I have also located your current position on the rooftop. Since the weather report for that facility shows heavy snowfall, I assume you are inside the roof-access shelter."

Bonnie nodded. "Yes. That's perfect, Lois. Good job."

"I can guide you to one of the two locations. I assume the closer one would be preferable."

"Is it in the maximum security area?" Lauren asked.

"Both are in maximum security. The minimum security area has no underground cells."

Bonnie raised a finger. "Lois, do you have an electrical schematic?"

"I have electrical drawings, as well as all communication wiring for cable, satellite, and computer networks."

"Perfect. Is there a way for us to get to a circuit box and shut down the power here?"

"Affirmative. My programming instructs me to warn you of the high security risk. Since I have no information about guard patrols, I cannot judge where they will be at any given moment. I do know, however, that there is a break room near the circuit box access door, so your danger level could be beyond acceptable limits."

"At this point," Bonnie said, "there is no risk too high. We'll be better off in the dark, so lead us to the circuit box first."

"Very well." Lois's cadence altered to the rote monotone of a tour guide. "Descend the stairway to its lowest landing.

230

Be advised that you will pass two other landings with access to corridors, so your descent might be noticed. At the lowest landing, the corridor to the right leads to a break room and a maintenance access room, both on the left side of the corridor. It is possible that guards will congregate at the break room, but it is highly unlikely that anyone will be in the maintenance room. This is where you will find air-conditioning and heating ducts, as well as the circuit breakers. When you arrive at the bottom of the stairwell, let me know, and I will provide further directions."

Bonnie unwrapped Lauren and drew her wings in tightly. "Your backpack, please."

Lauren picked it up. The pain returned, this time radiating up her arm and into her shoulder. She tried to ignore it, but a sudden throb made her wince.

"Is something wrong?" Bonnie asked as she withdrew the pocketknife from her jacket.

"I think the flying bruised my ribs. I'm getting stabbing pains."

"Sorry. The wind made me squeeze you pretty hard." When Bonnie took the backpack, her brow wrinkled. "Now *I'm* feeling a stab."

"Well, your arms are probably tired from—"

"That's not it." Bonnie unzipped one of the backpack's outer pockets and looked inside. "No wonder!"

Lauren peered in. Underneath snuffbox-sized tins, a glimmering gem sat at the bottom of the pocket. "What is it?"

"A candlestone. It's like Kryptonite to dragonkind."

As Lauren studied the sparkling facets, the stabs in her ribs returned. Of course her own pain resulted from internal bruises, not from the candlestone, but why would they flare up now? Might she be an anthrozil after all?

She mentally shook her head. It would be stupid to get caught up in all this dragon talk. Her birth parents were normal humans. Her memories couldn't be a lie. Besides, her strange gifts weren't draconic, nothing like wings, fire breathing, or danger-sensing. Maybe the candlestone affected other kinds of people. "I guess we'd better throw it outside."

Her eyes narrowing, Bonnie zipped up the pocket. "I might be able to use it."

"How?"

"I'm still working on a plan."

"But if it causes you pain, and it stays in the backpack, it'll—"

"Hurt. I know. But I'll do anything … *anything* … to rescue my husband and son." Bonnie used the knife to slice two gashes in the backpack. "Can you help me get it on? It's faster that way."

"Sure." Lauren helped Bonnie push her wings into the holes. With the agility of arms and hands, her wings grasped the backpack from the inside and pushed themselves into place. Finally, after a great deal of shifting around, the backpack bulged as if ready to explode, but it hid the wings beautifully.

232

Bonnie winced. "It's been quite a few years since I've done this, and my backpack then was bigger."

"With all the moving around, it looks like you have ten squirming puppies in there."

"I keep shifting them to get comfortable. They'll be still in a minute." Bonnie extended the knife to Lauren. "Now cut my hair. This is sharp enough."

Lauren lifted the knife from Bonnie's palm. "Why?"

"I'm pretty well known around here. I need to alter my appearance as much as possible." Bonnie withdrew a cap and a name tag from her jacket pocket. "And I found these."

"Right. I noticed the cap earlier. But a cap and a haircut aren't going to hide you very well."

Bonnie fastened the name tag to the jacket. "Did you see those tins in the backpack? I think they were some kind of makeup Walter used on his face."

"I saw them. What are you thinking? Are you going to change to another race?"

"Just a birthmark on my cheek. That should be distracting enough."

After taking off her gloves and laying them on the floor, Lauren unzipped the backpack pocket and rummaged for brown makeup. As she jostled the tins, her fingers touched the candlestone, the contact stinging her as if she had brushed across a prickly nettle. Nausea churned as well, a slow, simmering boil. Finally, she pulled out a tin and popped open the lid. "I'll do the makeup job, but I think you should just push your hair under the cap. That should be good enough."

"I'll let you be the judge." Bonnie slid the cap over her head and pushed her hair up inside. After taking a few seconds to adjust it, she touched the brim of the cap. "How do I look?"

Lauren eyed her closely. "It's kind of lumpy. Let me fix it after I paint on your birthmark."

For the next few minutes, Lauren worked on Bonnie's left cheek, creating a thumb-sized splotch of dark brown. She used a bit of black makeup from a different tin to create tiny lines that looked like dark fuzz. When she finished adjusting Bonnie's hair, Lauren studied her new look. Her hair still protruded a bit at the back of the too-large cap, but the smudge on her cheek looked natural. "The mark definitely draws attention away from your eyes, and your grimace makes you look kind of mean. If I didn't know it was you, I'd be fooled."

"That's exactly what I wanted to hear." Bonnie slid the knife back into her pocket, straightened the cap, and shone the flashlight down the stairway. "Follow me."

As they descended, a light from below grew brighter. Bonnie flicked the flashlight off and slowed her pace while letting out a low *Shhh*. A door with a glass panel came into view. On the opposite side, flickering lights illuminated gray floor tiles, but nothing moved, not even a shadow.

Bonnie hurried to the landing and turned a one-eighty to descend another flight. Lauren followed, keeping her stare trained on the still-shifting backpack. Every second with this strange but amazing woman seemed like a fairy tale, a dangerous chase through a dream. It was scary … and wonderful.

The next landing led to a bare wall and a new set of stairs going down the opposite way. Bonnie continued, this time not slowing when they reached another glass-paneled door. After turning twice more, they descended into a darker stairwell. Bonnie turned the flashlight on and sent its beam into the depths. Dust particles swirled through the shaft of light, agitated by their approach.

"Wow!" Bonnie whispered. "This goes way down. Were they preparing for a nuclear war?"

"Is that question for me?" Lois asked.

Bonnie descended once again, this time at a slower pace. Lauren stayed three steps behind, giving Bonnie's backpack plenty of room.

"Sure," Bonnie said. "Do you have an answer?"

"The schematic notes indicate that this facility was designed to house captured dragons. The prevailing belief is that dragons lose power if subjected to darkness for a long period of time."

"They're right. That's what my father did to my mother when she was a dragon."

Lauren slowed further. This fairy tale had a sharp edge. Walking in darkness with the daughter of a dragon wasn't exactly comforting.

After nearly a minute, Bonnie stopped at a solid metal door. Grasping the knob, she turned it slowly. "Unlocked," she whispered. "Lois, we're here."

"As I instructed earlier, when you enter the corridor, turn right. You will pass the break room on your left, and the next door on your left will be the maintenance room. There are no indications as to whether or not it has a lock."

"Got it, Lois. Thank you." Bonnie pulled the door open and peered into the corridor. Lauren drew as close as possible behind her and looked over her shoulder. Even now, Bonnie hummed the same tune, exuding a quiet confidence. Ahead, bright fluorescent lights illuminated a hallway. With concrete floors and bare plaster walls, it looked like a bomb shelter from an apocalypse movie. Yet, the corridor was wide enough for six people to walk side by side, and the ceiling wasn't even in sight.

Bonnie clipped the flashlight to her belt. "Give me your loose handcuff."

Lauren lifted her arm, letting the cuff dangle. The sight brought back a memory, Portia checking the fastened cuff just before giving her the ring. But where was it now? "I must have dropped it."

"Dropped what?"

"The Colonel gave me a ring. It has a red gem in it. He said—"

"A rubellite?"

"Right. I suppose you know all about it. I was going to show it to you, but I guess I fell asleep with it in my hand. It's probably still upstairs. I think I left my gloves up there, too."

Bonnie showed Lauren her bare fingers. "They took my rubellite and my wedding ring. They're so superstitious, they thought I might be able to use them to escape. I suppose they analyzed it to death and decided it was harmless. They probably gave the rubellite to you to see if it changed color. They're ignorant about its real properties."

"What properties?"

"If we have time later, we'll go back up there and find it, and I'll tell you all about them." Bonnie pushed the open cuff around Lauren's wrist and left it unfastened. "If we're stopped, we're going to pose as guard and prisoner."

"Sounds good." Lauren glanced at the backpack again. "So, what if someone asks you what you're carrying?"

"I'll think of something." Bonnie strode into the corridor and, turning right, guided Lauren to the front. "Just stay a step or two in front of me."

When they reached the break room, Lauren sneaked a peak inside. A heavyset man with a dark mustache sat at a round table, eating a thick sandwich partially wrapped in paper. Lauren breezed by, her hands in front of her, the cuffs in full view.

"Hey!" the man called. "The cells are the other way!"

Pulling Lauren to a stop, Bonnie halted a few steps past the door. "Sorry. I've never been down here before."

"No problem. Want me to show you?"

"Sure. I'll be right there." Bonnie altered to a whisper. "I'm going for broke. Get ready for a bit of pushing around."

"Let's do it," Lauren said. "I'm not fragile."

"Get the candlestone for me."

236

Lauren unzipped the backpack's pouch and dug out the gem. It felt like fire against her skin, and the nausea returned. After juggling it like a hot potato, she thrust it into Bonnie's hand.

Clenching her teeth, Bonnie returned to the break room and, grasping Lauren by the arm, shoved her in front of the doorway. "This anthrozil is too dangerous for a normal cell. She's supposed to go next to Bannister's. It's empty, right?"

The guard chuckled. "As if we had any dragons down here. Bannister is the only fire-breather around."

"Then lead the way."

"Sure." The guard wolfed down the rest of his sandwich and slid back from the table. He grabbed a tall cup with a protruding straw and spoke while chewing. "What makes her dangerous?"

"They didn't tell me her dragon traits." Bonnie's words seemed tortured as they came out in halting phrases. "I have a candlestone, though. … It's keeping her in check."

Lauren spied the guard's name tag—Private L. Anderson—then noted the goofy little-boy expression on his pudgy face. He seemed fooled so far.

Anderson wiped his mouth with his sleeve. "Let me see it. They tell me they come in different colors and shapes."

"Yeah. Sure." Bonnie uncurled her fingers, revealing the gem. Light flowed into one of the facets and emerged again from another, making it glimmer. As Bonnie's brow furrowed, she bit her lip, apparently battling the effects.

A sudden pain stabbed Lauren's gut. Holding her cuffed hands against her abdomen, she doubled over, gasping. It felt like claws digging into her stomach.

Bonnie closed her hand around the gem and turned toward Anderson. "So you see, this girl is easily controlled."

The pain eased. Heaving in shallow breaths, Lauren straightened and scowled. "If you bring that thing out one more time, I'll—"

"You'll what?" Bonnie set her fist directly in front of Lauren's eyes. "I'll make you crawl to your cell before I let you use any of your devilish powers on me."

"Woo hoo!" Anderson called. "That's telling her! You'll fit in just fine here."

Bonnie stuffed the candlestone into her pocket. "Great. Now if you'll—"

"By the way, what're you carrying in that backpack?"

Bonnie smiled and gave him a sly wink. "Dragon wings, of course."

Anderson laughed. "That's a good one!"

"Well, she needs stuff for her bed and toilet. I couldn't have my hands full in case I had to deal with her."

Anderson reached for the backpack. "Here. Let me help you with—"

"No need." Bonnie swung away. "Let's just get her locked up. I'll feel a lot better when she's behind bars."

"Yeah. You're as jumpy as a cat on coals." Anderson leaned closer, squinting at her jacket. "Private Tate?"

Bonnie touched her name tag. "Is there a problem?"

"Not at all. I just wanted to know who I'll be working with. We have another Tate at the front gate, so—"

"Oh, I'm not being assigned here. I'm just transporting this girl, because I'm experienced with dealing with anthrozils."

"Too bad. I could get used to seeing your pretty face in this hole." Anderson walked slowly down the hall, pressing buttons on his bracelet as he spoke. "The cells down here have individual codes, so if you ever come back, you'll have to program your access key. The one next to Bannister is four, eight, seven, two, two."

"Four, eight, seven, two, two," Bonnie repeated. "Got it."

As they turned a corner and proceeded down another high, wide corridor, the lights on the ceiling flickered wildly. "How do the locks work if the power goes out?" Bonnie asked.

Anderson jangled a ring of keys hanging from his belt. "The security system disengages, and a regular key can unlock them. I was just thinking about that a little while ago. This blizzard might knock out the power."

He stopped in front of a huge metal door, at least twice his height and three times his width. He set his bracelet next to a reader at the right. A buzz and click followed. Using both hands, he grasped a metal handle and pulled the door, grunting as he slid it to the right until it disappeared into a pocket in the wall.

A double door stood in the way, also metal, almost as large and apparently just as impenetrable. "This one always needs a key," Anderson said as he lifted the ring. He pushed a different key into a lock next to a horizontal lever on the right-hand door. After a click sounded, he shoved the lever down and pulled the massive plate of steel open. "Supposedly, if a dragon rammed against this inner door, it would just be blocked by the outer one. I kind of wish we'd get a chance to test it. I've seen the dragons on the training videos but never in real life."

Bonnie shoved Lauren inside and followed her into the cell. "I'll get her set up." She turned and looked back at Anderson. "Do the doors lock automatically?"

"Yep. Just close them and wait for the click." Anderson pulled a radio from his belt and gave her a friendly smile. "I'm going on patrol, but I don't have much floor to cover, so if you need me, I'll be back here soon." He strode down the corridor, away from the break room.

Bonnie tiptoed to the door and peeked around it. Spinning back, she gestured for Lauren to follow. The two jogged on the balls of their feet, retracing the way they had come. Lauren glanced behind her. The open cell door blocked part of the hall, but the guard was nowhere in sight.

They careened around the corner, passed the break room, and stopped at the maintenance door. Bonnie grabbed the knob, but it wouldn't budge. "Locked!"

Lauren let out a quiet groan. "What now?"

"I have to get the keys." Bonnie began sliding the backpack straps down her arms. "Help me get this off."

While Lauren pulled the material, she whispered, "Why are you doing this?"

239

"My wings are cramping. We'll have to go for the direct approach from now on."

"Direct approach? When you told him you had dragon wings, I nearly had a heart attack. How more direct can you get?"

"You might find out very soon." Bonnie pulled the candlestone from her pocket and rolled it down the corridor. It ricocheted off the left side, then the far wall, before tumbling into the right-hand corridor leading to the cells. "That helps."

With a final shake, the backpack fell to the ground. Her wings spread out fully in the spacious corridor. The ceiling lights shone through the honey-colored membrane, highlighting the support structure and vein network running throughout.

"Wow!" Lauren whispered. "This is the first time I've seen them in the light."

"Let's hope I can use them to get us out of here." Bonnie folded her wings in. "The guard had a radio, so he might be checking to see if we're legit."

"I don't know," Lauren said. "He wasn't exactly Mr. Observant, but the name tag might have tipped the scales."

"Not having one at all might have been worse." Bonnie took Lauren's hand in a thumb-locking shake. "Things might get a little rough from here on out. Are you ready for it?"

Lauren gazed into Bonnie's fiery eyes. This woman looked like she could whip that guard with one wing tied behind her back. "I'm ready!"

"Let's go." Bonnie withdrew the gun from her shoulder holster and led the way toward the corner at the end of the hall, this time at a slow, skulking pace.

A clopping sound reached Lauren's ears—shoes on a hard floor. A voice followed. "The name tag said Tate. Don't we have another Tate here? ... That's what I thought."

"The guard's coming," she whispered.

240

Bonnie halted and spread out her wings. While Lauren stood on tiptoes to see over them, Anderson's voice continued in a whisper, intermixed with more footsteps, slower and quieter now.

"She had a hairy birthmark on her cheek. It sounds worse than it is. She's really quite a looker. ... No, she wasn't on patrol. When I find her, I'll call you back and tell you more." He peeked around the corner, his gun drawn. When he saw Bonnie, he scowled. "Thought you could get away with it, didn't you?"

DISCOVERED

With a beat of her wings, Bonnie flew at Anderson, partially blocking Lauren's view. A gunshot sounded. Bonnie jerked back, and her gun clanked on the floor.

Anderson leaped from behind the corner. Bonnie surged ahead again, slammed into him, and knocked him against the far wall. In a flurry of wings and fists, the two fought wildly, both still standing.

Lauren sprinted toward the fray, pausing to pick up the fallen gun. She pointed it at Anderson but couldn't get a clear shot.

With both hands firmly clenching Anderson's gun hand, Bonnie kept the barrel pointed toward the ceiling, while Anderson punched her in the pelvis. As the violent stalemate continued, blood dripped from Bonnie's tight fingers.

Lauren leaped at Anderson and slammed the gun against his head. He set a foot in her stomach and shoved her away, making her slide on her bottom. She jumped up, rushed in again. Pressing the gun barrel into his stomach, she fired.

Anderson doubled over and toppled to the floor. Bonnie snatched his gun and flew backwards, dragging Lauren with her.

Lauren dropped her gun. "I … I shot him."

A sad frown darkened Bonnie's face. "I'm not sure what to do with him. If I try to get help, we'll never escape."

Lauren's legs wobbled. Tremors rode up her limbs, shaking her whole body. "Do you think he'll die?"

Bonnie drew close and felt Anderson's neck. "His heart is strong. I guess it depends on if you hit any vital organs, but even if not, he might bleed to death if we don't get him to a doctor."

"What about you?" Lauren asked, pointing at Bonnie's bloody hand.

"I hardly noticed." Bonnie pushed back her sleeve, revealing a stream of blood from her elbow to her wrist.

Lauren opened Bonnie's jacket and pulled back her sweatshirt's neckband. Blood soaked her T-shirt. "Oh, no!"

As Bonnie looked at the blood, her face turned chalky white. Drawing back the sticky shirt, Lauren stared at a gaping wound just below Bonnie's clavicle.

Bonnie tipped to the side. Lauren caught her and helped her down to the floor.

"Lauren?" A male voice buzzed in her tooth. "Can you hear me?"

Lauren's throat squeezed so tight, she could barely talk. "Matt?"

"Yeah. I've been listening in. My father says I might be able to help the guard you shot. You can get the access key from him. Bring him to us."

"It's not just the guard. Bonnie's been shot, too. It looks bad."

Matt repeated the message, apparently to his father.

"Quick!" Matt shouted. "Get her over here!"

Lauren pushed her arms under Bonnie's body and lifted with her legs. At last her thousands of squats would come in handy. She straightened and began to waddle down the hall, grunting as she talked. "I'm on my way."

"Do you have the key?"

"Oh, yeah. The key." She laid Bonnie down within a few steps of the open cell door and hurried back to Anderson. As she drew near, the lights blacked out. Lauren froze in place. Seeing in a poorly lit gym wasn't hard, but seeing in complete darkness was impossible. Somewhere in the distance, a whistle sounded, probably an alarm. She could go back to Bonnie and see if she had the flashlight, but if she didn't, it would be a waste of time.

Touching the wall to her right, she pressed onward. "Matt, the lights went out. I guess they don't have generator power on the lower level."

"Maybe they reserve it for other places," Matt said. "Just get the key. We'll work it out."

Lauren made her way to the guard and brushed her hand along his face, then down his chest and stomach. Her fingers dipped into warm, sticky liquid. She cringed but kept her hands moving. Finally, she found his belt, grasped the key ring, and, pushing a release button, jerked the ring away. "Got it!"

"Good! Now hurry!"

Lauren scrambled up and, again brushing her fingers along the wall, hustled back. With complete darkness veiling her path, she had to guess where Bonnie lay. Ten more steps? Five more steps? She slowed her pace, bent low, and swept a hand just above the floor. A familiar melody reached her ears—Bonnie's song. Even while unconscious she hummed the peaceful tune. At least that meant she was still alive. Now following the sound, Lauren continued sweeping with her hand. After a few seconds, her fingers touched a leathery membrane—a wing.

She scurried around Bonnie and felt the opposite wall for the cell door. After passing the one Anderson opened for her, she found another and groped for the handle. "I'm here." The keys jingled in her trembling hands. "Now I have to find the lock."

"Dad says it's to the right of the door," Matt said. "About waist high."

"I saw one at another cell." Lauren ran her fingers across cold metal until she found the edge of a protruding box. She flipped open the cover, pushed a key in, and turned it easily. A click sounded. "I think I got it!"

"Now slide the door to the right."

Lauren felt her way back to the handle at the far left, grasped it with both hands, and pulled. The door budged, but just barely. "It's heavier than I thought!"

"You have to open it! Give it all you've got!"

She set her foot on the jamb and pulled back as hard as she could. Letting out a low squeal, the door slowly inched its way to the right. After moving it a foot or so, she could no longer brace herself. She shifted to the other side, set her hands on the handle, and heaved her body into it, pushing with every ounce of energy she could muster.

244

The huge door squealed again and continued its slow progress. Lauren grunted. Her arms and legs ached. What could be wrong? If that guard could handle this door so easily, why was she having so much trouble?

A glimmer flashed in her eye. Several steps away, something glittered on the floor. The candlestone Bonnie rolled? She staggered to it and picked it up. It again stung her palm like an electrical shock, and the stomach stabs returned. She heaved it toward the guard and watched the light tumble until it stopped at the hall's end.

As the pain faded, she pressed a hand against her stomach. That was better, much better.

With a quick spin, she hurried back to the door and shoved it easily to the side. After pulling the key from the first lock, she felt for the lock on the inner door. "I'm almost there, Matt. I'm just worried someone's going to show up."

"Dad says he's the only prisoner down here, so there's just one guard on patrol at night. A janitor sometimes comes by, but he probably won't with the power out."

"But the guard here radioed about us. When they don't hear from him, they're bound to send someone." Her hand brushed across a hole. After trying two keys that didn't work, she inserted a third and turned the lock, then pushed down the lever and swung open the door, revealing more darkness. New pangs shot through her stomach, forcing her to bend over. "Is there a candlestone in here?"

"It's hanging from the ceiling almost right in front of you." This time, Matt's voice came from within the cell as well as through the transmitter. He sat somewhere to the right.

"I thought you might be at the door," Lauren said.

"I'm kind of tied up at the moment. I can't get the knots loose." Another voice sounded from her left. "How is Bonnie?"

"Mr. Bannister?" Lauren called. "Is that you?"

"Yes." Pain streaked his voice. "Is my wife badly hurt?"

"It's pretty bad. I'll bring her as soon as I can, and I'll try to get the candlestone out of here." Lauren spotted the glimmering jewel hovering above. She walked in and reached for it, but missed. Darkness made its height hard to judge. More pain knifed through her stomach. Her legs weakened, feeling like they were melting from the inside out. She leaped and missed again.

"I … can't jump. … I feel so … so weak."

"Untie me," Matt said. "I'll get it."

Lauren stumbled toward him. "Keep talking."

"I'm here, sitting on the floor with my back against the wall." She followed his voice as he continued.

"I'm going to stand, but I can't move toward you. One end of this rope is tied to some kind of bracket—"

She bumped into him and grabbed an arm. At least it felt like an arm. "Here you are." She felt for his wrists and found the rope.

245

Digging in with her nails, she clawed at the knots, but they wouldn't budge.

"Do you still have my pocketknife?" Matt asked.

"Bonnie does. I'll get it."

As Lauren walked toward the cell door, she wobbled back and forth, the pain getting worse by the second. When she reached the corridor, she hurried to Bonnie and groped for the flashlight. After finding it on her belt, she jerked it from its clip, flipped it on, and dug into Bonnie's pocket. She slid the knife out and pushed it into her own pocket.

As she ran back into the cell, the candlestone sucked her energy dry. She slipped and fell on her side. The flashlight tumbled from her hands, cracked on the floor, and blinked off.

Calls of "Are you all right?" came from both sides of the dark room.

"Not really." Pushing against the floor, she climbed to all fours and crawled toward Matt. "I have the knife. I'll be there in a second."

"You can do it," Matt said. "I'm stretching out as far as I can."

Swiping the air in front of her with one hand, she pulled along with the other, pushing desperately with her aching legs. Dread filled her mind. Bonnie might be bleeding to death, and here she was crawling like a turtle with a broken shell.

Finally, her fingers struck flesh. Matt grabbed her wrist and pulled her the rest of the way. "Where's the knife?" he asked.

Weakness washed through her limbs. Even her lips became flaccid. "In my ... my pocket." She reached in and pulled the knife out, but it slipped from her fingers and fell to the floor with a click.

"Got it," Matt said. "Now if I can just open it and cut through. This blade should be sharp enough, but there are a lot of knots."

"Can you crawl back to Bonnie?" Mr. Bannister asked. "It sounds like it might take a little while for Matt to get loose. The longer you stay in here, the worse off you'll be."

Lauren shifted back to all fours and struggled toward the door. "Why is … is it affecting me? … I'm not an anthrozil. One of the kidnappers … called me a … a Listener. … I don't have dragon traits."

"We'll figure it out," Mr. Bannister said. "Let's just get Bonnie and the guard in here."

Continuing her slow crawl, Lauren felt her way into the corridor. When her strength returned, she rose to her feet and walked in a weaving line toward Bonnie.

As she settled at Bonnie's side, a wave of sympathy raised a new tingling sensation across her back. Her tooth felt like someone had plugged her into an electrical outlet, drilling a painful shock into her jaw. Noises filled her ears—a heartbeat, labored breathing, gurgling. Bonnie was alive, but the signs of blood in her lungs sounded awful, and her humming had dwindled to almost nothing.

"Bonnie," Lauren whispered, "can you hear me?"

No response traveled through the air, but the odd echoes of unspoken thought rode her spine up to her ears. *I can't talk. I can't move. Please, God, help me.*

247

Pain still throbbing in her jaw, Lauren ran her fingers through Bonnie's hair. "Help is coming. Just hang on. Your son will be here in a minute."

My son? Charles? You found him?

"I found Matt, yes. I gave him the knife. He's cutting himself loose."

Oh. Matt. I remember now.

"Yes, he—"

"I'm coming!" Matt called from the doorway.

"Over here."

A glimmer of light approached, as did the sound of jingling keys. As he drew nearer, the stabbing pains returned. Lauren forced out a whimpering, "Why did you bring that thing?"

"It's the only light I had until I saw your glow. I'll put it in my pocket." The light disappeared. "Are you okay?"

"I will be … I think."

"I'll carry her to the cell. Go check on the guard. I grabbed the keys from the lock. I'll hang on to them." A warm hand touched her cheek. "I just want you to know that you're the most amazing girl I've ever met." Then, a jingle sounded. Matt let out a brief grunt, and Bonnie's body slid away from Lauren's hands. His footsteps squeaked for a moment before fading.

Lauren touched her cheek. As her strength began returning, heat radiated across her skin. Amazing? How could she be amazing? She couldn't even cut Matt's rope.

Holding the dangling handcuff close to her body, she got up and jogged toward the guard. Total darkness made her feel as if she were running in a nightmare, chased by invisible horrors all around. Yet, these horrors were real, death and imprisonment lurked only steps away.

As the tingling and jaw pain eased, she slowed. The turn in the corridor had to be close. Tripping over Anderson's body would be another bad move. She felt along the wall again, trying to imagine where the guard lay. New pains dug into her stomach. The other candlestone had to be close, but at least the pain meant she was nearing the end of the hall.

A familiar glimmer appeared at the corner of her eye. As she inched toward it, her foot dragged on something. She dropped to her knees and felt the object, probably Anderson's leg. Probing toward his torso, she sucked in quick breaths. Pain stormed through her body. Nausea boiled, creating an urge to heave. With every move, the handcuff chain jingled, sounding like an echoing alarm.

After finding Anderson's neck, she felt for a pulse. Nothing. She set her ear next to his mouth. No breathing.

Her heart thumped. Heat rushed into her cheeks, and nausea finally took over. Still on her knees, she dry heaved three times before ending with a series of spasmodic coughs.

"I killed him," she whispered, her voice barely more than a rasping squeak. "I killed this poor man."

The candlestone glittered on the floor, now pulsing like a strobe. She lunged for it, snatched it up, and threw it toward the break room as hard as she could. The sparkle skittered along the tiles, easing to a stop near the stairway door.

Another light appeared down the hall, far past the open cells, a flashlight beam waving from side to side.

"Lonnie? It's Pete. Are you here?"

Lauren stiffened.

"You haven't radioed in a while, so I thought—" The beam landed on the open cell door. "What the—"

Trying to keep the cuffs silent, Lauren swept her hands along the floor. The gun she dropped had to be around somewhere.

A door slammed shut, then another, sounding like twin gunshots echoing through the hall. The new guard's agitated voice followed. "This is Sergeant Miller. Someone unlocked and opened Bannister's cell. He's still chained in there, and the boy's still there, too. When I flashed my light inside, I caught a glimpse of the winged woman."

Lauren's fingers nudged the gun. She picked it up slowly, again keeping as quiet as possible.

"Yeah, she's locked up with them," Miller continued. "She was on the floor, and the boy was trying to help her. I'm guessing she got shot while flying away, and she came back to get her husband."

Lauren rose to her feet and tiptoed through the hallway leading to the stairwell door. Where should she hide? The break room? The roof access?

Miller's voice grew louder. "No sign of Anderson. I'm going to check the break room."

That settled it. She would escape up the stairs. As she skulked, the candlestone glittered in her view. Yet again, pain shot through

her body. Still, the gem's presence helped. The tiny light illuminated the stairway door's outline and knob.

The guard's clopping footsteps drew closer. Behind her, the
flashlight beam struck the adjacent hall's end and drifted lower.

Lauren scooped up the candlestone and grasped the knob.
Miller would find Anderson at any second. If she timed this just
right …

"Lonnie!" A flurry of rustling, jingling, and flying obscenities
followed. In the midst of the noise, she opened the door and slid
through the gap. As she allowed it to silently close, the gem
gnawed at her palm. Pain streaked from her hand to her spine to
every extremity, but she couldn't drop the stone. It was the only
light she had.

No longer bothering to silence the cuffs, she held the candlestone in front of her and staggered up the stairs. Again her legs
ached, turning to mushy sticks of butter, but she had to get past
the first floor immediately. Other guards and medical staff could
show up and barrel down the steps at any second. Of course, they
might choose instead to come down the same access Miller used,
but who could know? She just had to hurry.

When she finally passed the first floor, she struggled up ten
more steps, stuffed the candlestone into her pocket, and sat on a
stair. That helped. Although it seemed to drill a hole in her thigh,
the energy drain eased, and her stomach settled.

She took in long, deep breaths. Just a few more seconds and
she could climb the rest of the way. From her vantage point, the
door to the first floor stood below, a light in its window panel
making it easy to see. Obviously a generator powered that level.

A man burst through the door and bustled down the stairs,
barking into a radio. "On my way! The gurney is waiting for the
elevator. I'm taking the stairs."

After several seconds, the door below slammed. The sudden
noise brought back the tingles and the pain. Her ears picked up a

250

chaotic blend of voices, too many to understand. The sounds made sense, but why the pain? Electrical disturbances had occurred around her before—the lights at the gym and Tate's phone. Could the transmitter be short-circuiting? Might she, herself, be some kind of catalyst for electrical malfunctions?

Rising slowly, she continued her march up the stairs. She could take her time now. It sounded like Anderson hadn't mentioned Bonnie's pretend prisoner, so they would probably think Bonnie was the only culprit. Since they had her in custody, why search anywhere else?

After passing the second floor, Lauren stopped and whispered, "Matt, can you hear me?"

No one answered.

"Okay. If you can't talk right now, that's fine. Just let me know when you can." As she climbed within a few steps of the roof-access door, the window in the door below provided light to her path. A dusting of snow coated the top two stairs, and swirling flakes poured in through the broken window above.

Cold air spilled down the stairwell, bringing a chill. Her teeth chattering, she climbed the rest of the way to the top, her shoes crunching broken glass under the thin layer of snow. Crouching, she peered over the lower edge of the door's window and looked outside. A single searchlight waved back and forth across the rooftops, revealing a blanket of snow covering each one, probably at least ten inches thick. Apparently, they didn't want to drain the generator, so they left the other searchlights off.

She withdrew the candlestone and tried to open the door, but it was locked. Why would a guard do that? With the window broken, locking the door wouldn't stop anyone from coming in, and she could easily unlock it and get out.

She tossed the candlestone through the jagged hole in the pane and resumed her crouch. Hugging herself tightly, she shivered hard. It was so cold! So lonely! What should she do now? As her teeth continued to chatter, she imagined the scene on the lowest level—guards interrogating Matt and his parents and accusing Bonnie of murdering Anderson, if she survived her own wounds. Obviously Matt wouldn't reveal Bonnie's accomplice, but someone was bound to come back up to the rooftop eventually.

She closed her eyes. The dimness became darkness, and the events of the past few nightmarish hours flashed across her mind— Micaela's car exploding; her phone's beep followed by a demon's murderous message; Tamiel's evil glare as the chess pieces moved by themselves; the harrowing escape in the arms of a winged woman; and finally, the news that her adoptive parents had most likely been killed.

An image of her house came into view. Fire erupted through every window, breaking glass and spewing flaming tongues. Her mother's scream pierced her thoughts, an agonizing cry to God for help as she sat burning in her wheelchair.

Lauren buried her face in her hands. She couldn't take this! Everything wonderful in her life had been ripped away, destroyed, annihilated! Why would God allow all this horror?

Sniffling, she wiped a tear with a finger. Of course, she wasn't very religious, so maybe God just let bad things happen to people like her. But what about Mom and Micaela? It just wasn't right! If God were really out there, he wouldn't let good people suffer so much.

As the thoughts filtered through, another image came to mind—Bonnie as she prayed in the midst of the forest. Her skin continued tingling, and the words replayed, as if spoken by Bonnie herself, somehow sitting next to her with a wing enfolding her.

Even though I have been separated from my beloved family for these fifteen long years and suffered daily torture, I never doubted your love and faithfulness. I now see the dawn of my own day beginning to appear. Jehovah-Yasha, the Lord my savior, is mounting his conquering steed and will soon set all the captives free. I beg you to ride onto our battlefield like a dread champion. Rescue Billy, Ashley, and Matt. Let them and Lauren rejoice when they see your mighty hand brush aside those who would torment their souls. And when you do, when you conquer your foes as I have seen you do so many times before, we will rejoice, singing your praises on that day and forevermore.

Lauren sighed. Such amazing faith! How could anyone hang on for so long? Bonnie lost her husband and her children, and she went without news of them for fifteen years! Incredible!

Firming her lips, she nodded. She had to get through this. If Bonnie could endure so much suffering, she could endure her own small portion. What choice did she have anyway? Surrender? Give in to the demon who killed her parents and Micaela?

She clenched a fist. Never! She couldn't let that foul beast win, no matter what.

With her fingers rolled into a tight ball, a memory stirred, the rubellite ring she had dropped somewhere nearby. She got up and, using the dim light from outside, searched the stairs where she and Bonnie had slept, then every step on the flight all the way to the landing. The ring was nowhere in sight, and neither were her gloves.

After returning to her former spot, she sat again. Someone must have picked them up, and that same person probably locked the door. At least, then, whoever found it likely considered this area clear of intruders and escapees. Maybe it was the safest place to wait.

As her mind settled, the tingling sensation died away, as did the pain in her jaw. A sense of coldness filtered down to her bones. She shivered harder than ever, and her teeth chattered uncontrollably.

A feminine voice buzzed in her tooth. "I have been instructed by Walter to inform you of an emergency status."

Lauren touched her cheek. "Lois?"

"I am also here," Larry said. "We will work together to help you prepare. Please tell us where you are. Your transmitter is not accessing the GPS satellites."

253

"I'm back at the roof-access door." Lauren forced her voice into a more even keel. "Bonnie's been shot, and she's in a cell with her husband and Matt at the lowest level. I got away, and I don't think the guards know I'm here."

Larry continued. "I will summon the helicopter to alert its pilot and passengers. Lois will examine the facility's schematic to determine the best access for a potential rescue. Since Code Red status has been initiated, everything humanly and dragonly possible will be done to complete the task."

"What's a Code—"

"Examination underway," Lois said. "I will prepare a detailed plan in moments."

"Great, but what's a—"

Larry's voice broke through again. "Jared, Marilyn, and Walter have provided the security keys necessary to complete the Code Red launch. I am contacting Second Eden to obtain their planned schedule."

"Second Eden?" Lauren imagined a flurry of communications zipping from helicopter to computer to the mysterious world everyone talked about but few people had actually seen. "How is Second Eden involved?"

"Code Red requires no further interaction with you," Lois said. "I have your location on my map, so if you move from that point, it is imperative that you let me know."

"Wait a minute!" Lauren hissed. "If you want me to participate in this Code Red thing, you'd better tell me what's going on!"

While Lauren continued a bone-rattling shiver, silence ensued. Finally, Larry spoke up. "Walter has authorized a higher security clearance for you, so I will provide the information. Red is the color of a male dragon's scales, making Code Red an appropriate moniker for a rescue plan led by the king of all dragons. For your reference, a female has tawny scales."

"My analysis," Lois said, "indicates that Lauren's location is unsuitable for dragon entry. There is a wider door at the front of the research wing that compares favorably with Makaidos's size. A dragon is able, however, to land on the roof where Lauren is. Since she can provide the intelligence necessary to find and rescue the prisoners, one of the dragons should pick her up as the operation begins."

"Here?" Lauren tapped the snow-covered floor with a finger, her voice spiking. "Right here? You're sending a dragon to this spot?"

"Not just *a* dragon," Larry said. "The *king* of the dragons, Makaidos. We will soon learn how many dragons will accompany him and who their riders will be."

Lauren repeated the name in a trembling whisper. "Makaidos."

255

"Your rescue is at hand," Larry continued. "King Makaidos successfully penetrated Fort Knox, and this facility is not as heavily fortified."

"But why? Why did you decide to launch Code Red after fifteen years of letting Bonnie and the others rot in prison?"

A new voice broke in. "Lauren, this is Walter. I'm patched into your channel now. Listen, we're going to let Larry and Lois do their thing, and I'm going to talk you through what's about to happen."

"Okay. That's fine. But did you hear my question?"

"The fifteen-year question?"

"Right. Why now?"

"Because of you."

"Me? What are you talking about?"

"I secretly got a DNA sample from you, just a strand of hair, and checked you out. You are an anthrozil. In fact, you are Billy and Bonnie's daughter, Karen."

Lauren bit her lip. Although the news was no shock, it still hurt. It meant that every cherished photo was a lie. Her memories were nothing more than a dream. Of course, whoever fabricated her history did so to protect her, and the revelation meant that her real birth parents were Billy and Bonnie Bannister, which was great, but that didn't lessen the pain. "Okay," she said, sniffling. "I can deal with that. So, Matt's my brother."

"Twin brother to be exact."

"One puzzle piece is missing. The last time I saw my adoptive mother, she wanted to tell me why we moved to Flagstaff, something about a friend from England. Do you have any idea what she meant?"

"The friend was probably Sir Patrick, a guy who knew the foster-care systems inside and out. He had friends trying to find you. I guess one of them succeeded and adopted you. Maybe she moved you to this area so you could be closer to your real mother. She hid your identity from everyone, including me. Since I've been posing as an agent for the Enforcers, she didn't know who to trust."

"She was getting ready to tell me, because she thought she was going to die soon, and ..." Her throat tightened. "And I guess she was right."

"Yeah." Walter's tone became melancholy. "I guess she was."

Lauren swallowed, forcing a steady voice. "But none of this explains why you're doing this Code Red thing after all this time."

"We have a spy in that prison named Sir Winston Barlow, and he told us the reason you were kidnapped. You have a dragon trait that hasn't been seen since the days of Shachar, the first dragoness. Sir Barlow didn't know what that trait was, but when I told King Elam about your ability to hear anything and your glow-in-the-dark skin, he told Makaidos. All of a sudden, they hit the Code Red button."

"Okay, so I have special traits. Why would hearing and glowing make them take such a risk?"

"I don't know yet. Elam said he would give me the details later. Must be huge, though. They never tried to rescue Billy, Bonnie, and Ashley before, because they think this place is a setup to lure the dragons into a trap."

"I wouldn't doubt it. I heard talk about tanks and reinforcements, so they're expecting some kind of invasion." Lauren let out a deep sigh. "I just don't get why anything about me is so important."

"Trust me. I understand. I don't have any dragon traits, but you wouldn't believe what I've been involved in. I've seen stuff that would make Medusa turn to stone."

"Okay, I get the point. But what do I do while I'm waiting?"

"You're safe where you are, right?"

"I think so. They don't have any reason to come looking for me. And I have a gun." She almost added that she had killed a guard, but what good would that do?

"Get some sleep. You'll need the energy."

Lauren shivered again. Sleep? In this weather? With a near riot taking place a couple of floors below? "I can try." She walked down to a dry stair and sat with her head against the wall. It was still cold, but bearable. "How will I know when to wake up?"

"Don't worry. We'll take care of that. Meeting a dragon face-to-face is a wake-up call you'll never forget."

"Okay. I suppose that's something to look forward to."

She closed her eyes. With total exhaustion setting in, it felt good to rest. She could probably sleep in spite of all that was going on.

Soon, a field of pure white formed in her mind—silence, perfect peace.

257

16

CHAPTER

THE SLAYER'S TRIUMPH

Carrying the lyre, Joran ran across the white expanse. Just as silent as before, it seemed like an endless field of chalk that absorbed every sound, even his pounding footsteps and the slapping of the two sonic rods against his leg within his trousers pouch. Somewhere out there, a door to another ovulum lay ready for him to enter and explore ... he hoped.

To his left stood a barrier of white, a curved boundary that prevented anyone from going in that direction. Apparently that was the purity ovulum's inner shell, so if he followed the perimeter, he wouldn't miss an access to another ovulum.

Every few seconds, he reached out with his left hand and touched the boundary. It was so smooth and silky, it barely felt like anything at all. The fanciful stories about the mysterious eggs certainly filled him with wonder, but nothing could have prepared him for this journey through nothingness.

Soon, a hazy orange mist rose in the distance. Unlike the static blue doorway, this entry changed from a ragged square to a pulsing circle to a vertical ellipse to a number of amorphous shapes, each shift coming with a geyser of flaming tongues that shot a dozen feet out into the whiteness before vanishing.

Joran stopped beside the new passage. Now it looked like an undulating, flaming blanket as it hovered just above the white floor. He set a hand close to the fire. No heat radiated at all.

Turning, he looked back. Somewhere in the distance, Tamiel probably lurked, the only one who could get Selah out of the lyre. Every moment he paused was another moment she remained trapped in that place of darkness. He had to go on.

He tucked the lyre under his tunic and leaped through the blaze. For a few seconds, he floated in a sea of orange, tumbling and twisting. Then, as if spewed from a dragon's snout, he flew in a wash of flames, burst out into cold air, and landed on a carpet of lush, damp grass.

Protecting the lyre with his arms, he rolled to a stop. Several steps away, a woman with dark, braided hair sat against a tree, holding an orange ovulum in her hands. It hummed a lovely melody, a hymn his father once sang when he and Selah were much younger.

She cocked her head. "Are you hurt?"

Joran rose to his feet and pulled out the lyre. "I don't think so."

"You …" The woman tapped her chin. "You appeared from nothing." She gave him a broad smile. "Yes, *appeared* is the word."

"I suppose I did." He glanced around. The thick grass spread out as far as the eye could see. A few trees towered in the midst of the meadow, most of them in full summer leaf. Behind him, a rocky path wound down a slope into a river valley far away, and a humble cottage of stone and mortar sat about fifty paces to his right. "My name is Joran," he said, bowing.

The woman rose and offered a clumsy bend of the knee, nearly dropping the ovulum in the process. Her face reddened, a stark contrast to her lily-white dress. "My name is Soren—" She covered her lips with her hand. "I mean, Tamara."

260

"I'm glad to meet you, Tamara." Joran studied her closely. Her skirt reached just below her knees, exposing bare legs and feet, not fitting for this cool, damp day. Her silky, see-through sleeves ended between her elbows and wrists, and her abdomen protruded in pregnancy, making the skirt hike slightly higher in front. Maybe the burden of carrying a child kept her warm.

She glanced at the ovulum and gasped, as if forgetting she held it in her hands. She quickly slid it into a leather bag on the ground and sat cross-legged next to it. "I hope you don't mind if I sit. I tire easily."

"By all means. Rest." Morgan's instructions to Devin raced through Joran's mind. The woman was likely a former dragon, and she held one of the seven ovula as a device to protect herself. Yet, why could Tamara see him when Morgan could not? "Tamara, I'm not sure why I'm here or how I got here, but I need to warn you about something. I know you used to be a dragon, and someone is hunting for you. He intends to kill you."

"Oh, yes! Devin." Her voice sounded more like that of a young girl than a mother-to-be. "I know about him. He is in England, and he will not likely … um … travel here to Wales."

"Wales?" Joran eyed her again. Apparently he stood in a region he knew nothing about. Judging from the summertime foliage combined with the cool temperature, this place wasn't anywhere near home. "What do you call this language we're speaking?"

She glanced around, her smile wilting. "Is this a … a joke? Will someone jump out and laugh at me if I give the wrong answer?"

"No, it's not a joke. I'm a stranger here, so I thought you might have a word for it that I'm not familiar with."

"I see." Her eyes kept darting, and her expression remained skeptical. "I am a poor … um … talker. So sometimes people make fun of me."

Joran raised a hand. "I promise I won't."

"We are talking English. I was … um … surprised when I could understand you. Although we are all … Britons … most people here speak with strange sounds I do not understand."

"Then why did you come here?"

"Legossi said she and I had to be apart … to stay away from Devin. She brought me here and said she would return to help me make … weapons, because she thinks the ovulum is not enough to keep us safe. But she stayed with me long enough to teach me how to …" Confused for a moment, she looked away, then turned back and gestured with her hands, as if stitching something with thread and needle.

"To sew?"

Letting out a relieved sigh, she smiled. "Yes, I sew."

Joran nodded. "Making and repairing clothes is an honorable profession."

She dipped her head and looked at her intertwining fingers. "I know," she said in a dreary tone.

"Is something wrong? Don't you like to sew?"

She lifted her head, a hint of alarm in her voice. "Oh, I like to sew. I love making things, especially beautiful dresses. It is just that I had a … a …" Her words trailed away.

"You had a different dream?" Joran asked. "You wanted to pursue something closer to your heart?"

She nodded, her head down again.

He sat in front of her and touched her hand. "What is your dream, Tamara?"

She looked up, tears glistening. "You will laugh at me."

"No, I won't. I promise."

"Well …" She smoothed out her dress, watching her nervous fingers while she spoke. "Many dragons tell stories, and I always wanted to tell stories, but my … talking is … is crippled. I can think fast in my head, but the words … stall before they get to my lips. When my mother told stories, I sometimes … acted them out. It was so much fun, and Mother said I was good at it."

"I see. I'm sure that made her storytelling more entertaining for others."

A thin smile emerged. "Yes. Other dragons came to watch."

"That must have been a lot of fun."

"It was, and that is why I wanted to continue, but dragons have no acting ..." She gave him an expectant look. "Tradition?"

Joran nodded. "Tradition is a good word, if you mean dragons prefer oral storytelling over dramatic reenactments. When I was around dragons, I never saw them act out a story."

"Yes, that is what I mean. But now that I am human ..." She again seemed at a loss for words.

"You want to be a performer, an actor."

"Yes, but that is not a ... an honorable profession. And no woman is ever permitted. It is a dream that cannot come to pass." As she turned away again, a tear dripped to her cheek. "And my talking is getting ... worse, I think. Maybe soon I will not be able to talk at all."

"I see what you mean." Joran took in a deep breath. What could he say? The same was true in his own time. Drama players were usually scoundrels, and no woman would be caught dead performing on a stage. It just wasn't done. And Tamara? Since she could barely speak a complete sentence, how could she possibly recite lines in a play? And if her speech problems were getting worse, her handicap would keep her dream from ever coming true. It was better for her to dream about her next clothing creation. Still, who was he to smother her aspirations?

"Here's what I think, Tamara. Sometimes it looks like everything is going to crash all around, as if Elohim isn't paying any attention to you. Then, he does something so surprising, you never would have guessed it, and everything changes. Maybe you'll get a chance to act. You just have to wait for the opportunity and be ready to grab it when it comes. Don't let anyone convince you that you can't do it."

Tamara's eyes misted. "I will remember that. Thank you for having ... confidence in me."

"You're welcome." Joran fidgeted. Since he wasn't sure how much confidence he really had in her, it would be best to change the subject. "Where is your husband?"

Tamara set a hand on her protruding stomach. A slight pout exposed her bottom lip. "He is dead. Devin killed him after the ..." She looked upward, again searching for a word.

"Transformation?"

"Yes. He did not become human, because he did not believe." She tilted her head. "If you know about me, why did you not know this?"

"I apologize. My knowledge is limited to what I have been told, which isn't much." He nodded toward the bag. "I do know that the ovulum you carry for protection might be the very object that leads to the destruction of the other dragons. Supposedly, each ovulum sings a song, and Devin has one that can detect the others, but he doesn't know how to use it yet, so he has to find one former dragon to test it. He's looking for you in particular, because he knows you're pregnant, so you should be easier to find than the others."

Tamara lifted the bag to her ear. "I hear no song."

"No," Joran said, waving a hand. "You don't understand. It's inaudible to most humans. Only a Listener like me can hear it."

"A Listener?" Shaking her head, Tamara heaved another sigh and rubbed her belly. "I wish I could ask more questions, but speaking is hard. If only a ... a gentleman would take me as his wife, then I would be ... protected. I would have someone to speak for me, and my daughter would have a father. As long as I live alone, people will ..." Again she searched for a word.

"Gossip?"

She nodded gratefully. "As you said, since Devin knows that I am with ... youngling, it will not take long for him ... to find me. Yet, few are the men who would do such a *kindness*, to take a widow such as I into his arms. As long as I am alone, I am ... in danger."

Tamara's words pierced Joran's heart like a dagger. This poor woman really did need a husband, and her emphasis on *kindness* plunged the dagger even deeper. The orange ovulum represented kindness, so somehow he had to play the role of protector, at least for as long as he could. "You call your baby your daughter. How do you know the gender?"

She set the ovulum bag at her side. "When the time gets close, we dragons can tell. Before I changed, I knew."

"So when you changed, I suppose she changed, too. You couldn't carry a baby dragon inside."

"I do not think I could." Tamara blinked, as if confused. "I am worried about her. When I sing to her now, she no longer … responds as she did. She stays so still, so quiet."

Joran gazed at her abdomen. He had seen many pregnant women before. Some babies kicked and rolled so violently anyone could detect the lumps and protrusions. This one, indeed, showed no signs of life. Yet, a faint heartbeat reached his ears, thrumming more quickly than Tamara's. Her baby was alive, but Tamara needed more proof than the word of a stranger.

Strumming the lyre, Joran forced an energetic tone. "Maybe if we sing together, she'll perk up."

"Are you a … a minstrel?"

"In a manner of speaking." He brushed away a few stones from the grass and slid closer to her. "As a Listener, I am able to hear sounds in the wind that others cannot, and I am able to reproduce them with my voice—the joy of springtime, the gloom of decay, even the rage of thunder. My voice might quicken her spirit."

Tamara clapped her hands. "There is a song she used to love. I could … teach it to you."

"By all means." Joran plucked the F-sharp string next to the blue G. "I will echo each line you sing."

Her smile brimming, Tamara continued caressing her abdomen as she sang. "When younglings play so hard all day."

Recognizing the key, Joran nodded and strummed the lyre as he repeated the words. "When younglings play so hard all day."

Tamara's eyes widened again. "How lovely! Your voice is like a … like an angel's."

"Thank you." He strummed the strings again. Every time he touched the A, the white aura formed, but it didn't have enough time to expand and summon Selah. "Let's start again, shall we?"

"Very well."

This time, Tamara sang without pausing, and Joran echoed each line, sometimes altering to a descant, challenging the limits of his tenor range.

266

> When younglings play so hard all day,
> They need to rest in mother's care.
> Regain the light your play has spent;
> My bed of gems I now will share.
>
> So leave your eyes as open doors
> To gather truth, to gather light,
> For truth and light will call as one,
> "Rebuke the false and scatter night."
>
> And now I call to you in song;
> Regenerate within my womb.
> Above all gems you are to me,
> I call you from your hidden room.

When they finished, Tamara looked at her abdomen, her face brightening like a rising sun. "She is moving! I think she is dancing!"

As Joran watched her belly shift, warmth flooded his skin. "That's wonderful, Tamara. I'm glad I could help."

She gazed at him, her smile trembling. "I pray that my daughter can become a Listener. Such a gift is … is richer than gold, and you have used it to bless us. For that I am forever thankful."

Joran laid a hand on his chest. "A mother's prayer is always from the heart. I'm sure Elohim has heard your request."

"I hope so." Her head dipped low. "No matter how bad things get … Elohim is always good."

Joran, too, let his head sag. Except for Selah, everyone he knew was now dead, and she was trapped in a string. Yet, he himself, an unworthy recipient of blessings, lived on. Was this really justice? "I trust that your words are true, Tamara. I hope everything works out all right."

She leaned forward and patted his knee, her smile returning. "Let me tell you something Merlin said."

"Merlin? I have heard that name before. Who is he?"

"If you know about my ovulum, and you have heard of Devin, why are you so … unfamiliar with the great prophet?"

"It would take too long to explain. Please, tell me what the prophet said."

She glanced around, then, looking him in the eye, she lowered her voice. "Shachar was the first … dragoness, and she was able to find any … ovulum."

267

He nodded. "I know about Shachar's gift."

"Good, but maybe you do not know that … another will be born with the same gift, a female who will … hear the song of the ovulum in her scales … and find it no matter where it might be."

Joran listened again to the song of the orange ovulum. Although he and Selah could hear such songs, they had never tried to track one. Since the sound was so light, so nebulous, it would be a difficult task. "Are all seven ovula accounted for?"

Tamara shook her head. "I have one, as do … five others. We know not where the missing one is. And no one has seen the great … purity ovulum since the flood."

"I see. So the prophesied tracker will be needed, especially for the purity ovulum."

"Joran?" Tamara turned her head from side to side, as if looking for someone. "Where did you go?"

"I'm here, still sitting in front of you."

"Joran?" Her voice took on a plaintive tone. "You went away so quickly. Are you … are you really an angel?"

He reached forward and touched her knee, but his hand passed right through.

"Greetings!"

Joran turned toward the new voice. A man wearing a hooded gray cloak strode up the path. Following him, a shorter, stockier man pushed a cart, straining against the two handles as the wheels rolled over rocks and through divots. Filled with clothing, dark bottles, scrolls, and various pieces of furniture, it looked ready to topple at any moment, but the man kept it in check.

Eyeing the lead man closely, Joran plucked the lyre's A string multiple times in rapid succession. Selah appeared as radiant mist, lying curled on her side.

"Selah!" he whisper-shouted. "You need to see this!"

She pushed to a sitting position, bracing with one hand. "What is it?"

He turned the lyre toward the merchant. "Does he look like Devin to you?"

Selah rose to her feet, blinking. "In a way, but his hood shadows his eyes, and a scruffy beard conceals his face. If he were to speak, I would know."

"That's what I was thinking. He said one word, but he seemed to be altering his voice."

The merchant stopped next to Tamara and helped her to her feet while the other man wheeled the cart within reach. "The villagers told me you will soon deliver your child. I have just what a young mother needs."

The merchant's gravelly voice penetrated Joran's mind. Although he tried to disguise it, he couldn't fool a Listener.

"He is Devin," Selah said. "There's no doubt about it."

"So his helper is probably Palin." Joran set the lyre upright against a stone.

"You have no weapons!" she called as she faded.

"I have to do something to stop him." He charged ahead and halted within reach of Devin, his fist raised to attack. "Leave this woman alone!"

Devin pulled a small white blanket from the top of a pile of clothing. He spoke again, but now his words seemed nothing more than gibberish.

"I said …" Joran jumped in front of Devin and yelled into his face. "Leave her alone!"

Devin never flinched. In fact, he seemed not to notice at all.

Joran retrieved the lyre and held it while Devin continued his salesman's pitch. "Cold winds will be here soon. Your baby will need this for comfort."

Smiling, Tamara waved a hand. "It would be good for warmth, but I have no silver or gold."

269

"As is true for many in this region. But we can barter." Devin set his gaze on the leather bag on the ground. "Do you have something you are willing to trade? I see a bag."

Joran backed away, passing through Tamara as he gaped at the scene. This deceiver had found his prey. The clucking gossipers had scattered their dirt far and wide.

Tamara glanced at the bag. "It holds nothing of … of value."

"Perhaps not, but the bag itself has some value." Devin stepped past her, picked up the bag, and slid out the ovulum. "Ah! What is this?"

"It is a … an heirloom," Tamara said, reaching for the ovulum. "I cannot trade it."

Devin looked into the orange glass. "I have seen such heirlooms before. In fact, I have one of my own."

Palin retrieved a box from the cart and, opening its lid, brought it to Devin.

"Remove it," Devin said to Palin, "and tell me what you see."

Palin set the box on the ground and lifted the purity ovulum. As he straightened, he gazed into its graying glass shell. "Nothing. It's too cloudy."

"Just as before." Devin smiled at Tamara. "Would you like to see this one? It changes colors, and it will tell you how pure your heart is."

Joran fumed. This devil's deceit knew no bounds! But what could he do to stop him?

"I am not … interested. I let God … judge how pure I am." She reached for her ovulum. "If you will please—"

Devin pulled it away. "You're right, of course. God is the only judge of a person's heart, but surely you can understand that my partner and I cannot see what God can see. We have made a vow that if we find anyone with a pure heart, he or she can choose anything from our cart for free. If you will just try it, I will give you the blanket no matter what color the ovulum turns."

"Run!" Joran shouted. "It's a trap! Forget your ovulum, and just run and scream for help!"

Tamara looked at the cart, then at the blanket. With every moment's hesitation, Devin's smile grew wider. Palin carried the ever-darkening purity ovulum closer and settled behind her, blocking any escape.

Finally, she shook her head and whispered, "I trust God."

"Then trust God to spare your life." Devin drew a sword from underneath his cloak and pressed the point against Tamara's abdomen. "If you don't do what I ask, the blanket will become your baby's shroud."

She turned to run but bumped into Palin. He grabbed her arm and held her in place while balancing the ovulum in his other hand. "I suggest that you do what he says."

Trembling violently, Tamara cupped her hands. "If … if I must."

Palin set the ovulum in her palms and regripped her arm, helping her keep the egg steady. The shell faded to light gray, then to white, then to crystal clear until it became completely invisible.

"So she *is* pure of heart," Palin said. "She must not be who we thought she was after all. I wonder where she got the orange ovulum."

"Don't be a fool, Palin. How many unmarried, pregnant women do you think we will find with an ovulum in their possession?"

"My liege, the reason we slay dragons—"

"The reason we slay dragons is to rid the world of the species. Even if this woman is nobler than the others, the offspring she whelps won't be."

"You are right, my liege." Palin bowed his head. "As always."

Joran kicked at a stone, but his sandal passed through it. Disgusting sycophant!

Devin shifted the orange ovulum closer. "Now, Palin, tell me what you see."

271

As Palin peered into the invisible egg, he slowly loosened his fingers from around Tamara's wrist. "I see the colors of the rainbow, like bubbles of light. The orange bubble is much larger than the others, and it swells and deflates like a beating heart."

"So when we get close to another egg," Devin said, "a different color will enlarge."

Palin nodded. "That stands to reason, but we will need someone with a pure heart or else we won't be able to see the colors. Maybe we should take her with us and—"

Tamara broke free and ran toward her cottage, still carrying the purity ovulum. Seconds later, the cottage door slammed shut behind her.

"I'll get her." Devin handed the orange ovulum to Palin and marched after Tamara, his sword propped at his shoulder. "Stay here if you're too squeamish. With two victims, I will be able to collect a great deal of blood."

Joran followed. What would Tamara do with the purity ovulum? Destroy it? Hide it? As he walked, he looked at the strings. Selah's image had disappeared, and the C string had turned orange. For some reason, his task here was finished, and he had already collected the second part of the key.

He stopped and plucked the A string rapidly. Selah took shape again. "Devin's going to kill Tamara and her baby. I'm like a ghost here. There's nothing I can do."

Devin threw the door open and disappeared inside. An orange hue coated the scene, and the cottage grew fuzzy, as if veiled by tears. Tamara screamed, but her cry ended abruptly.

Joran closed his eyes. Poor Tamara! She was such a sweet, lovely woman! Her naïve simplicity had dressed her in innocence, but inexperience had kept her from shrewdly defending herself. And her baby, too, must have perished by Devin's sword. Tamara had wrapped that child in so many dreams, even hoping she would become a Listener, and now every dream had been dashed to pieces.

Opening his eyes, he backed away. Somehow he had to get out of this place and warn other dragons about—

He tripped on something and fell backwards. When he rocked to a sitting position, he looked ahead. A flaming orange circle floated in front of him, surrounded by an infinite expanse of white. The geyser of flames spewed, washing over him with warmth, more like a hot breeze than a dragon's fire.

Lifting the lyre, he stared at it. Selah had disappeared again, and the C string was still bright orange. Yet, now the frame was no longer weathered and worn. With smooth, polished wood, it looked newer than he had ever seen it. How could he possibly have earned these changes? He had failed to stop Tamara's murder and failed to secure either ovulum.

Pushing against the floor, he rose slowly. What could he do but search for the next color? Although his kindness hadn't helped

272

Tamara, he couldn't allow that fact to keep him from rescuing Selah.

He touched the white barrier on his left and broke into a steady run. What color might be next? The violet of generosity? The green of diligence?

Joran sighed deeply. If it turned out to be the yellow of patience, he would surely fail.

273

17

HEALING TOUCH

Matt knelt at Bonnie's side. Ever since the guard slammed the doors, shutting off the beam from his patrol flashlight, the prison cell had been completely dark. Although he couldn't see his mother's wound, her labored breathing made her desperate situation obvious. He had already stripped off her jacket and sweatshirt, and now a T-shirt remained, wet and sticking to her chest.

"Dad! What should we do?"

"Do you have the candlestone?" Billy asked, still chained to the wall.

"Right here." Matt withdrew it and displayed it between his thumb and finger. A thin beam of light emanated from one of its facets.

"And the knife?"

Matt touched his pocket and felt the knife's outline. "Got it."

"Cut me and apply some blood to the candlestone. I'm not sure it will work to use her own blood."

Matt shuddered. The thought of slicing someone raised a chill. "I might be able to squeeze some blood from my bullet wound."

"Then use that. A healer's blood is even better."

Matt pulled out the knife and sawed through the bandage. "Just drip blood over it?"

"Right. Make sure you cover as much as you can."

As he pushed the gem against his arm, blood oozed from the wound and passed across the beam of light, sparkling as it flowed over the surface. The bullet hole was smaller than he expected, apparently another sign of his healing gift. After a few seconds, he turned the gem until blood covered the other half. "Now what?"

"Tear her shirt open and set the candlestone on her chest near the wound."

Matt obeyed, glad now for the darkness as he cut through the T-shirt. He felt for the spot, touching her shoulder before sliding his fingers through the blood. He set the gem in place, holding it there to keep her heaving chest from rolling it off. "Got it."

"Now we need an energy source."

"Okay. What do we use?"

"Cover the stone with your hand."

Matt cupped his hand over it. "It's covered."

Billy inhaled and exhaled several times. "I can feel my strength coming back already."

"You mean fire breathing?"

"Exactly. Move her as close to me as you can."

"Wait! The keys!"

"To the cell?"

"The key to your chains is probably on the same ring."

"I thought you just had the key to the door," Billy said, "not the whole ring."

"Sorry. I didn't tell you everything. I'm not thinking straight."

"It's okay, Son. Just give me the key ring. I know what the key looks like. I can probably feel for it."

Matt grabbed the candlestone, jumped up, and pushed the key ring into Billy's hand. After a few metal-on-metal clicks, the sound of dropping chains rang through the cell.

"Let's go," Billy said.

After finding his way back to Bonnie, Matt set the gem on her chest and again cupped his hand over it. "So how do we do this?"

"I'm building up some strength. In a few seconds, you'll move your hand, and I'll blow fire on the candlestone. That should activate its healing power."

"Am I supposed to do anything else?"

"When Ashley healed people, her touch cauterized wounds. She used that gift to save Walter's life and the life of a girl named Listener."

"Great. So how do I do it?"

Billy touched Matt's hand. "While I apply heat, I want you to feel for the bullet hole, push your finger in as far as you can, and swab the inside. If the hole is big, you might need more than one finger. If there's an exit wound on her back, we'll have to do the same there."

"I don't think there's an exit wound. I didn't feel any blood back there when I took her sweatshirt off."

"Then you might find the bullet inside. If so, try to pull it out."

Matt shuddered again. Now he had to be a surgeon without light or instruments, and his mother's life was at stake. But he had to stay calm and do this. If Billy could be so cool with his wife in danger, so could he.

"The fire might get real close and burn like crazy," Billy continued, "but you have to do it. If this works, you should feel everything sealing as you slowly pull out."

Matt sucked in a breath. "Okay. Ready when you are."

"Let's do it."

Matt uncovered the candlestone, releasing a haze of red-tinted light. Billy blew a thin stream of fire directly at the stone. Like orange phosphorescence, the fire splashed outward in short arcs that sparkled and disappeared.

The fire lit up her shoulder and a sea of blood around the gem. While the jet of flames continued, Matt touched the wounded area,

277

probed for a hole, and found it less than an inch from the candle-stone. Cringing, he pushed his index finger inside, then inserted his middle finger. Bonnie twitched and let out a low moan.

Billy took a breath. "Keep going. It's all right." He resumed the stream of fire.

Matt stared at Billy for a moment. With firelight illuminating his face, his features became clear for the first time—dark hair down to his collar and over his ears, choppy, as if scissors-cut without a mirror; a similar beard, trim in places, but uneven; and bright eyes set under a creased, determined brow.

Pushing his fingers deeper, Matt touched something hard, likely a bone. Something sharp pricked his skin, maybe a splinter in the bone. Blood oozed around his fingers. It seemed that the cavity inside was bigger than the exterior hole. The bullet had done quite a bit of damage.

278

The arcs of fire spilled across his hand, scalding his skin, but that didn't matter. He had to keep working; ignore the pain. A tingling sensation ran along his arm from his shoulder to his elbow to his hand, growing stronger with each passing second. It radiated down his fingers and seemed to flow from the tips.

He swabbed around, imagining his fingers applying a healing salve to everything he touched. One fingertip brushed across something that moved. He pinched it between his fingers and began drawing it out. "I think I have the bullet."

Billy didn't answer. He just took a quick breath and continued blowing fire.

After withdrawing the bullet, Matt pushed his fingers back inside and continued the massage. The hole felt like it was closing in. "I think it's working."

Billy took another breath. "Keep it up, Son. You're doing great." Again he poured on the fire, but the stream seemed much weaker than before. The candlestone was probably sapping his energy.

Matt pulled out slowly, swabbing along the way. Centimeter by centimeter, the hole collapsed behind his fingertips. When he finally withdrew them, he rubbed along the external wound until it sealed. "Got it!"

The flames ceased. Breathing heavily, Billy coughed through his words. "Take the candlestone and hide it somewhere."

Matt scooped it up and buried it under the pile of chains. "How's that?"

"Perfect." Another burst of flame coated the end of a rope in Billy's hand. It caught fire and burned steadily, casting a dim glow. "Hold this."

Matt took the rope. The flame dwindled but still provided enough light to see by. Billy closed Bonnie's shirt, pushed a wing to one side, and pulled her into his arms. "Bonnie," he said softly. "You should be able to wake up now."

Her lips trembled for a moment, then moved more freely. "Billy?"

279

"Let's see if you can stand." The two rose together, and Billy steadied her. "How do you feel?"

Bonnie jerked away and stared at him. "Billy!"

"In the flesh." He held out his arms. "We're finally together."

With a beat of her wings, she flew into his arms and pressed her head against his chest. "Oh, Billy! I missed you so much! Tell me this isn't a dream. Tell me right now!"

"It's not a dream. You're awake, and I'm awake. We're still in prison, but I feel freer than a bird."

With tears flowing, they rubbed noses, then kissed tenderly.

Matt smiled. This reunion was cool, very cool.

Billy turned Bonnie around and nodded toward Matt. "And our son used his healing powers to save you ... his *dragon* healing powers."

Again beating her wings, Bonnie flew to Matt and embraced him. "Thank you for healing me. I'm so proud of you!"

He dropped the rope, wrapped his arms around her shoulders, and patted her on the back. The hug felt warm and good. "You're welcome. I'm glad I could do it." He let a smile break through. Actually, healing her was the most awesome thing he had ever done in his life. And to be able to do it for his long-lost mother? Doubly awesome.

Billy picked up the rope and relit it with a quick burst of flames. "Maybe you should get that wet shirt off and put the sweatshirt and jacket back on."

"You're right." Bonnie pinched the neckband and peeled it away from her shoulder. "It's a mess."

Billy laid an arm around Matt and walked him toward the opposite wall. "While your mother's getting dressed, I want to tell you something about her. You might have been wondering how I could stay so calm when my wife had been shot and lay bleeding to death."

"It did cross my mind."

"I once carried her dead body through the seventh circle of Hades, and she carried mine through a portal that spanned two other realms. We have both seen the wonders of Heaven and lived to tell about them. She has even been burned in the flames of the gatekeeper to the abyss and transformed into an Oracle of Fire. Being an Oracle makes her bold and fearless, though she can't create fire like other Oracles can, but that's a long story." Billy compressed Matt's shoulder. "The bottom line is, after all we've been through, don't be surprised if we do things that would make most people curl up and suck their thumbs. We're not afraid to die."

Matt nodded. He ached to hear the story details, but the summary would have to do for now. "I get it. Thanks."

"I'm decent," Bonnie called.

Billy and Matt turned. In the glow of the rope, Bonnie spread out her wings and arms. "Good as new!"

"What's that on your face?" Billy asked.

Bonnie rubbed her cheek, smearing a black smudge. "A fake birthmark. I was trying to disguise myself. I also pushed my hair under a cap, but I guess it fell off somewhere."

A clank sounded. Billy handed Bonnie the rope and tiptoed to the door. "If anyone comes in," he whispered, "he'll get a face full of fire. They don't know I'm loose from my chains."

Matt eased closer to the door, also whispering, "I sense some danger, but it's not intense, kind of low-key."

"You're sensing potential danger. Someone out there doesn't intend to attack us, but he wants to do something that could eventually do us harm. It's hard to tell the difference sometimes, but you'll learn. That means I probably won't need fire, but I have to be ready."

A grinding noise floated through the air, probably the outer door sliding. Then, keys jangled near the center of the inner door. It opened a crack, then closed again with a click.

Matt lunged, but Billy grabbed his sleeve and pulled him back. "Don't sweat it. It's too late."

The sliding noise returned, followed by a thud, another click, and a shout. "I put a camera with a microphone in there. Don't try to obstruct it, or it'll blow you to bits."

A light appeared on the floor. A golf ball–sized sphere emitted tiny beams, maybe a dozen or more, like a diamond with a laser on each facet. The beams passed across their bodies and lit up the cell, but they seemed to do no harm.

"What is it?" Bonnie asked.

Matt bent over, scooped up the sphere, and displayed it in his palm. "A spy device. The army calls it an eye bomb. You can't turn it off, and it's indestructible. I saw a steamroller drive over one. Didn't faze it."

"So they're watching us remotely." Billy took it and brought it close to his face, making his eyes sparkle. "They didn't put a camera in my cell before, because they always kept it dark in here. Now they want to see what they're up against before they storm the room."

Matt nodded. "That's my guess."

"What did the guard mean when he warned us not to obstruct it?" Bonnie asked.

"That's where the bomb part comes in. If most of the eyes get blocked, it sets off an alarm and blows up in fifteen seconds, but if the camera view clears up in time, it won't explode."

Billy let it roll around on his palm. "Was he telling the truth about how big of a punch it packs?"

"It packs enough of a blast to kill everyone in this cell."

"Then we'll make them squint." Billy set it in a far corner. As he walked back, the eye bomb followed at his heels.

"Remote control," Matt said. "The one I saw didn't do that, but I heard a new model was coming out."

Billy rolled his eyes. "Perfect. A puppy that'll bite you if you don't do what it wants."

"And it has a microphone, so we should assume it can pick up anything we say." Matt turned his back to the eye bomb and concentrated on the transmitter between his molars. No sound came through. Should he risk a whisper?

"I have an idea," Bonnie said. She and Billy joined Matt, forming a line with Bonnie at the center, all three blocking the eye's view. Bonnie spread out her wings and filled the gaps between their bodies. She withdrew a mobile phone from her pocket and pointed at the reception indicator.

Matt nodded. It was low, but maybe not too low.

The eye bomb rolled to their side, so they shifted, putting it behind them again, continuing that motion every time the bomb tried to get to a better viewing position.

Bonnie set the phone to silent mode, then, using her thumbs, typed out a text message addressed to Walter. "Billy, Bonnie, and Matt locked in cell together. Expecting a storm of guards soon."

She sent the message. After a few seconds, a reply came through. "Code Red. Six hours."

Billy and Bonnie looked at each other, both mouthing *Code Red* at the same time.

Matt lifted his eyebrows, hoping to signal his desire to learn what *Code Red* means.

Her thumbs working the keypad again, Bonnie typed out, "Dragons will come to free us." She then erased the message and typed, "We need to let Lauren know before they find her."

Matt nodded. As he reached for the phone to type a response, a new voice broke in from behind them. "Dragons are on the way, I see. And if you fear us finding Lauren, that means she must still be here. That's useful information."

"What?" Matt spun and looked at the eye bomb. "I didn't know this model had speakers."

Bonnie pushed the phone into her pocket. "And X-ray vision."

"That's not the eye bomb," Billy said as he scanned the cell. "I could never forget that voice." As his eyes narrowed, he called out, "Where are you, Semiramis?"

"Ah! Billy Bannister!" The sultry feminine voice seemed to come out of nowhere. "I am so glad to hear that you haven't forgotten me."

Billy stepped toward the door. "Show yourself."

"I will show myself as you remember me." A woman wearing a red dress and hooded cloak appeared two paces in front of Billy. Bathed by the light of dozens of white lasers, she appeared to be a hologram, semitransparent and hovering in place. She spread out her arms and smiled. "As you can see, I have once again defeated death."

"Defeated death?" Billy smirked. "You're a ghost. You're dead and don't know it."

Lowering her hood and revealing long auburn locks, she took a step closer, solidifying as she moved. "Who is really dead, Billy

Bannister? The woman who walks freely in a spiritual state, or the man who has been locked up in prison for fifteen years without hope of release? We have you exactly where we want you, and you will be more comfortable now that your wife is here. I hope you never say that I haven't been kind to a lonely prisoner."

As Semiramis drifted nearly nose to nose with Billy, he stood his ground, unflinching. "The last time I listened to your viper's tongue, we nearly lost everything. Just speak your mind and leave."

Semiramis let out a humming laugh. "The warrior speaks bravely, as always. A real hero. But will any courage remain when his dragon friends fly here only to meet their doom?"

"As if the prison guards here could repel them," Billy said. "The ones I have met can conquer a hero sandwich, but that's about it."

"I know you are wiser than that, Billy. Since Elam has withheld rescue for this long, you must realize that he knows the danger. Surely someone with his character would not forsake his imprisoned friends without cause." She looked away with feigned concern. "Or would he?"

Billy shook his head, laughing under his breath. "You sound like the villain in a bad horror flick. Do you get sadistic pleasure out of this taunting?"

"I do. Very much so." She turned toward him again, her smile as sinister as ever. "Yet, there is more than mere pleasure that motivates me. I am here to distract you from using your mobile phone while my allies set up a mechanism to jam it. It should be ready by now, so when I leave, you will not be able to contact your dragon friends. They need not know that we will be prepared to repel their attack. This was one of our reasons for bringing Lauren here in the first place. She was the bait for catching dragons."

Bonnie gave Semiramis a quizzical look. "Why was Lauren the bait and not Billy or me?"

"Now I must keep some secrets, mustn't I?" Semiramis glided to the door and turned back. "It's sad that those who call themselves alive know less than those who are supposedly dead." She faded to semitransparency. "In six hours, we will snag our prey. We will be ready." She backed through the door and disappeared.

Bonnie typed out a message on the phone, whispering the words. "Walter, they know you're coming. Be prepared." After she sent it, she clicked a few more keys and shook her head. "It didn't go through. No signal at all."

Matt grabbed the eye bomb and slung it at the door. It ricocheted at an angle, and bounced along the floor a few times before rolling to a stop. Like a persistent cockroach, it crawled toward them, its lasers again filling the room.

Setting a fist on her hip, Bonnie scowled at the door. "How did that witch get away from Second Eden? Didn't Elam lock her up with her pathetic excuse for a son?"

Billy gave the eye bomb a swift kick, sending it back toward the corner. "Obviously there's a lot going on we don't know about."

When the eye bomb returned, Matt nudged it with his shoe. If only they could speak freely without this robotic spy broadcasting every word.

Bonnie reached for Matt and pulled him close. She kissed him on the cheek and whispered at the same time, muffling her voice. "Lauren's tooth transmitter."

Drawing back, she looked at him. The lasers cast white beams across her hair and face. Tears sparkled in her eyes, accentuating her blue irises.

"I love you, too," he said softly. The words rang true, expressing a growing love for his newfound mother, but they were also the only words he could think to say. Obviously he couldn't talk about Lauren. They had to communicate without letting the eavesdroppers know.

Bonnie eased over to Billy and gave him a whispering kiss. Matt scooped up the eye bomb and shouted to drown out her message. "Dragons are coming! You think you're ready, but you'd better be shaking in your boots. You're all expendable frontline troops who'll die in the first wave. The officers don't care squat about you. Consider that when you think about the spouses and kids who will cry when you don't come home from work tomorrow!"

Billy took the eye bomb from Matt. "Everyone huddle."

As they gathered together, Billy concealed the bomb in his hands. "Bonnie, tell him."

The bomb began to whistle like an old-fashioned coffeepot. "We have fifteen seconds," Matt said.

"No problem." Bonnie typed out a message on the phone and showed it to Matt.

It read, "Walter spoke in code."

Matt nodded. "Got it."

She typed again. "Hours divided by three."

Again, Matt nodded. That meant the dragons would arrive in two hours, not six.

Billy set the eye bomb on the floor and rolled it away. As the whistling faded, the bomb made a wide arc and headed toward them again.

"Since we have no way to contact anyone," Matt said, "maybe we should take turns yelling … to … uh … annoy our eavesdroppers."

Bonnie pinched Matt's sleeve and pulled him closer. "Jamming could block anything. No use giving away information."

As he looked again into her gleaming eyes, Matt parsed her words. Apparently she thought yelling would tip off the guards that they were trying to communicate with Lauren. No one in his right mind would think their shouts could penetrate these walls, and if the guards were jamming a phone frequency, that might hinder the tooth transmitter as well.

Billy crouched near the eye bomb and looked directly at it. "Listen up, whoever is spying on our conversations. Like Matt said, you should be afraid, very afraid. The dragons will come with a fury that you have never seen before. Ask yourselves why the video files for the dragon attack on Fort Knox show only the initial wave. Why weren't the media ever allowed to visit the complex afterward? I'll tell you why. Because even with all the firepower they had at Fort Knox, the dragons annihilated every building, every weapon, and every soldier who dared oppose them. The carnage was unbelievable. But there is still hope for you. If you become our allies and fight alongside the dragons, we will spare your lives. Of course if you've already faced and conquered a squadron of dagger-toothed, scaly-backed, winged infernos storming at you while blasting white-hot balls of flame, you have nothing to worry about. Otherwise, you'll just have to take your chances."

THE RED WALL

Joran stood in front of two statues—a girl to the left and a boy to the right. Each carried a basin with a towel draped over an arm, servants ready to wash someone's feet. Carved out of fine-grained hardwood and as tall as his waist, their colors provided a stark contrast to the white backdrop. The girl emanated a violet glow, while the boy blushed indigo, and their eyes radiated yellow. A thin wooden pole stretched across the one-pace gap between them, ending at their shoulders where they held it in place with a hand. A lamb carved from red cherry wood hung under the pole, recently slaughtered and now carried by these smiling children who likely hoped to serve their guests a fine meal.

Reaching out, Joran touched the pole. It felt tingly, the way the air sizzled when a dragon shot a stream of flames nearby. As if reacting to the tingle, the lyre tucked under his arm vibrated, though it made no sound in this realm of silence.

As he rubbed the pole's smooth wood, drops of red fell from the lamb to the white floor. The rate of dripping increased until the lamb and the space beneath transformed into a curtain of red, undulating and shimmering, like a sea of sparkling blood churning in the sunlight.

Keeping his finger on the pole, Joran studied the sight. This time four colors showed themselves. Maybe this was a gateway leading to four different ovula.

He slid his sandal from his foot and pushed it through the red curtain. When he lifted his finger, the curtain slowly faded away, revealing nothing but white on the other side. His sandal was gone.

Looking back the way he had come, Joran searched the vast whiteness for any sign of Tamiel. Nothing appeared, not even the orange or blue gateways he had passed through earlier.

Joran touched the pole again, and the flow of red returned. Clutching the lyre close to his chest, he lowered himself to his knees, ducked his head, and scooted through the curtain. Warm liquid soaked his tunic, as if real blood poured down from the pole. The sensation was soothing, healing, satisfying, better than the hot sulfur springs in Enoch's pool.

290

Still on his knees, Joran felt his tunic—dry, no trace of blood. He looked back. The pole was gone. Only a field of yellowed grass lay all around, apparently endless. At the point where the pole should have been, a line of red fire burned atop the grass, though it didn't consume the blades. The dimensions of the flames matched the gateway, the same height as the pole, the same width as the gap between the two statues, and barely any depth at all. Using an index finger, he touched the fire. Although it stung with prickly heat, it didn't melt his skin.

His sandal lay next to the fire, cool and unscorched. After putting it back on, he looked in the direction he had been crawling. The grass field ended abruptly at a line where the yellow met a wall of red. Above, without sun or moon, a dismal crimson sky stretched across the heavens, somehow providing normal light without a reddish tint.

He stood and plucked the lyre's A string until Selah's image formed. She sat cross-legged, floating in place.

"Selah," he called. "We're in a new ovulum."

She rose to her feet. "Which one?"

"I crawled through a gateway that had four colors—red, yellow, violet, and indigo."

She set her hands on her hips and looked down at the grass. "It looks like yellow here and red far away. You might be able to walk from one ovulum right into the other."

"Could be." Joran continued plucking the string. "I'll explore and see what I can find."

Selah turned her gaze toward him. "Have you seen Tamiel?"

"No, but I don't think I would see him or hear him even if I wanted to. I'm just assuming he's always around."

"Good idea." As she looked at his playing hand, she extended her own hand toward it. "You'd better stop. Otherwise, you won't be able to get anything done."

"I'll bring you back if something important happens." When he rested his hand, Selah slowly disappeared. Tucking the lyre under his arm, he shuffled toward the wall of red. What was there to do but march onward? Understanding this puzzling path apparently wasn't a prerequisite for completing it.

As his sandaled feet brushed the grass, violet and indigo plants waded to each side, as if hurrying to get out of the way. He paused and stooped next to one of the ten-inch-high stalks. Since it had only a pod-like bud on top and no blossom, it was impossible to identify. Maybe it wasn't yet time for it to bloom.

He studied the indigo pod—a thumb-sized oval with eyelets and a thin mouth. Two leaflets, one growing from each side of the main stalk, drew in and covered its face. The entire plant trembled, as if frightened.

Three other plants edged closer but stayed out of reach, their eyelets wide.

291

"Don't be scared," Joran said softly. "I won't hurt you." He reached to pet one, but it dodged his touch, shivering harder.

Withdrawing his hand, Joran scanned the sea of purple. At least a hundred similar plants had gathered around, each one looking on with curiosity-filled eyes. They pushed through the dirt with two leg-like stalks, as if walking, and as they brushed past the yellow blades, the soil sealed behind them, leaving the grass undisturbed.

"Who are you?" Joran called out.

A few tilted their pods to the side, while others blinked, as if not understanding. One of the smallest plants caught his attention. With wider eyes than most, it stared at him as if mesmerized. Like a whispering wind, soft voices rose from among them and brushed against his face, cooling his skin. "Who are you?" they said, the sound like rustling leaves as they echoed his question.

"I am Joran, son of Methuselah. I have come here searching for a way of escape from the ovula."

The plants began to lift their side stalks, and the voices grew into a bustling breeze that brushed back Joran's hair. "Take us with you. Please. Take us with you."

As the plaintive call repeated again and again, Joran waved his hand. "Wait. Calm down. You haven't told me who you are yet."

While most quieted, one of the taller ones, a plant with slightly yellowed stalks, edged closer and spoke in a breezy, feminine voice. Her words came out in frightened whispers, as if someone might crush her at any moment. "I have chosen the name Mendallah. We are spawns from the lower realms. We were growing, learning, hoping someday to uproot and walk among the sons of men, but when our keeper thought us too weak for his purpose, he threw us into a fire. Then we awoke here in this field of yellow, neither growing nor bearing fruit. We have been here for countless years, knowing there is more to our lives than wondering what our creator wishes to do with us. We have been waiting endless days for his will to be revealed, watching events in the outside world and learning the various languages in order to prepare for the day of our rescue."

292

Mendallah bowed her head-like pod. "If you, kind sir, will help us, we will be most thankful."

"But how?" Joran asked. "If I uproot you, you'll die."

Mendallah's hair-thin lips turned upward. "You can scoop up soil and put us into pots. Even if it takes a long time to collect enough pots to transport us, we are willing to wait."

"*You're* willing to wait?" Joran looked into Mendallah's tiny eyes. Although they were little more than slits, they seemed filled with passion. Of course, doing as she asked was probably impossible. Where would he find pots? How would he haul the plants out? And what would he do with them? Reroot them and see what they would become?

"I'll tell you what I can do," Joran said. "When I find the key to get out of here, I will see if there is a way to take you with me, but for now, I have to leave and do what I came here to do."

The voices built up again, creating a swirling wind. "No! Do not leave without us! It has been so long, so terribly long!"

293

"Patience!" Joran shouted. As the word left his lips, it created a breeze of its own and brushed the plants back, silencing them and briefly turning their stalks as yellow as the grass.

When they reverted to their original colors, they closed in on him and lifted their voices in a rush of rustling words. "Take us! Take us!"

"You're hopeless!" Joran rose and strode toward the red horizon, dodging the plants.

They continued shouting, "We cannot stay here! Do not leave us behind!"

As their voices faded behind him, the sound of his own words echoed in his mind. *You're hopeless!* The words stung. They were true, of course, but what good had he done by reminding them of their desperate state? At least he could walk from place to place and try to get out. They could do nothing but wade in the soil, hoping that a deity-like being would come along and collect them one by one and take them to a better place, though they had no idea what that better place might be like. Yet, any new place had to be better than this field of yellow.

Joran halted. Yellow meant patience. These poor souls, whoever they were, had practiced patience for a long time, but they certainly hadn't perfected it. Maybe if he could inject some positive vision into their miserable lives, they could gain some hope. It was the least he could do … and maybe the most he could do.

He turned and looked at the sea of indigo and purple faces staring back at him. He knelt and strummed the lyre's four highest strings, A through D, and began a song Father taught him long ago.

> My journey takes a thousand steps
> To gain the wisdom I must learn;
> I dance in light, through darkest nights,
> While you shed tears till I return

294

> So sing this song to bide the time;
> A sprout must grow from root to stalk,
> And truth reminds the earthbound minds,
> To dance, you first must learn to walk.

As he played and repeated the words, Selah appeared in front of the strings. Like a swaying mist, she danced along, her arms and legs moving in flawless beauty. The plants stood motionless, their little mouths agape.

When Joran reached the final note, he stretched it out in a hum and continued plucking the A string. Selah finished her dance with an elegant twirl and spread out her arms as if expressing the joy of mobility.

The plants waded closer. They crowded around quietly, their side stalks pressed together in front as if in prayer or worship. The smallest plant, however, stayed back and continued staring, tiny specks of blue sparkling in its eyes.

Joran dubbed that plant Zohar, because of its brightness. For some reason it seemed more intelligent than the others. "Now," he said as he continued playing Selah's string, "here is what you have to do. I want each of you to push together a pile of dirt, enough to fill a pot."

"Joran," Selah said with a tone of warning. "Are you sure they can do this?"

"Of course they can. It'll take some effort, but they're capable."

"Okay." Her tone shifted to one of skepticism. "If you're sure."

"When your pile is finished," he continued, "stand next to it and wait. When I return with the key, I will take those who have completed their task."

While the other plants cheered, Mendallah bowed her head and spoke in her rustling voice. "We are able to gather soil, though it is toilsome. They cry for joy now, but will this joy last?"

"Maybe they need a little more incentive." Still plucking the string, Joran swept his gaze across the animated plants. "Tell them that those who aren't ready when I return will be in big trouble, because I will set the field ablaze, and those I leave behind will burn."

"Joran!" Selah cried.

"What?"

She folded her arms in front and looked away. "I'll tell you later."

Joran rose and scanned the plants. "If you don't want to burn, be ready." He pivoted and walked toward the red horizon again, the breeze from their voices flapping his tunic as he continued playing the A. When he passed out of earshot, he looked at Selah. "What are you so upset about?"

She moved her hands to her hips. "Why did you threaten those poor little plants?"

"I'm just doing what Elohim did, except with fire instead of water."

"And exactly how do you plan to start a fire? I don't see any flint around here."

295

"There are other ways. I'll find something."

"I hope not." Selah's frown deepened. "Even if you could start a fire, who are we to judge who is worthy and who is not?"

"Someone has to. There's no way I can take them all, so the ones who get the job done are probably the most worthy. The rest live pathetic, worthless lives anyway."

"Joran?" She blinked at him. "Are you really my brother? Are you really the warrior who hunts demons to rid the world of evil?"

"What do you mean?"

"You're supposed to be an instrument of Elohim, not Elohim himself. You can't make such judgments. Besides, what did *we* have to do to prove ourselves and escape the flood? Nothing!"

"I have no idea why I escaped, but you had faith, and you proved it by your righteousness. Noah proved his faith by working a hundred years building an ark. I'm just asking them to prove theirs."

"Joran, you're treading on dangerous ground. Elohim decided to flood the world because the people were evil, not to goad them into becoming righteous."

"Maybe, but I don't have much choice. I have to make a decision. For all I know, they might be evil, so I have to give them a test to see what kind of plants they are."

Keeping her hands on her hips, Selah gave him a long, hard stare. "And what kind of plant were you, Joran, when Elohim rescued you?"

Joran focused on the red wall, now drawing closer. What could he say? Elohim hadn't given him what he deserved.

"Help them first," Selah continued. "Even an evil heart can be conquered by love."

As her words dug into his mind, they gouged a painful divot. She had talked about love and faith so many times, practically memorizing Father's nightly lessons, and it all sounded so good, so wonderful. Who wouldn't fall down and worship a loving deity

296

who obliterated every horrible deed a person had ever done? Who wouldn't want a fresh start, free from a haunting past?

Yet, Elohim didn't work that way. He threatened everyone with destruction if they didn't do what he demanded, and untold thousands drowned in his watery retribution. Such was the love of Elohim.

"Do you mind if I stop playing your string for a while? My fingers are getting tired."

"It's all right, Joran. I understand." Selah lowered herself and sat cross-legged. "You have a lot to think about."

Still walking, he held the lyre's frame with both hands and watched her disappear, then, looking through the strings, he gazed at the red wall in the distance, now much closer. A man knelt in front of the wall, his hands folded, as if in prayer.

Joran slowed his pace. Might he be Tamiel?

"Come, stranger," the man called, "and I will show you events that very few people witnessed. And fewer have survived to tell the tales."

297

Joran hurried to join him. "I am—"

"I know who you are." The man rose to his feet, turned, and smiled. Dried tear tracks smudged his cheeks. "Joran, the Listener."

Joran looked him over. In his thirties and dressed in unusual garb that covered his arms, legs, and feet, he didn't seem familiar. "How do you know me?"

"I am an old friend of yours. You do not recognize me, of course, because I have changed a great deal. Yet, I am surprised that you have not changed. Millennia have passed, and you have not aged at all."

Joran studied his sincere face. The only way he could have been a friend would be if he somehow rode in the ark, but he certainly didn't look like any of Noah's sons. "What is your name?"

"Timothy, but you know me by another name."

"And that name is ..." Joran prodded.

"I will show you who I am in a moment." Timothy reached out and laid a palm on the red wall. Pushing to his right, he slid the redness out of the way, as if drawing a curtain open.

Behind the curtain lay a water-laden field with Noah's ark in the middle. Droplets poured from the sky, and low clouds swirled. Two dragons, one red and one tawny, stood on the deck and looked down upon the growing flood.

Joran took a step closer and touched the wall. It seemed that power emanated from the surface, passing through his arm and into the lyre. Selah, still sitting cross-legged, appeared again in front of the strings.

"Joran?" She rose to her feet. "I didn't hear the A note."

"I didn't play it. I don't know why you appeared."

Selah stared at the wall. "I know those dragons. Makaidos and Thigocia."

"Correct," Timothy said. "Now watch quietly. Listen and learn."

Joran stood at the man's side. Even though he no longer touched the wall, Selah's image stayed intact, apparently energized by the radiance emanating from the scene. It had started out as a two-dimensional painting, but now it looked so deep, so real, it seemed that if he were to jump, he might splash into the rising water. A moist breeze blew across his face, and sounds from the ark reached his ears.

"I cannot leave my father!" Makaidos shouted as he beat his wings, apparently getting ready to fly from the ark's deck.

"We must go!" Thigocia bit his tail and pulled him down.

Makaidos jerked his tail away. "Don't make me fight you!"

Scarlet light flashed on all sides. A pulsing ball of fire descended from the clouds, egg-shaped, like a huge ovulum. Fingers of flame sprouted from the egg and pierced the ground, giving birth to geysers of muddy water. Thunder rumbled, and torrents of rain veiled the ark, leaving only flailing arms visible as people fought to keep their heads above the raging waters.

Another red dragon, as large as Makaidos, floundered in the surge. Red beams emanated from his eyes and pierced the black clouds above. "To you, Maker of All," he shouted, "I commit my spirit!"

Joran reached out. "Arramos!"

A few seconds later, Arramos submerged, along with dozens of humans who could no longer fight the current. The ark floated atop the waves and drifted into the distance, becoming a tiny craft in the midst of the stormy swells.

As a damp breeze continued to brush Joran's face, he stood and stared, barely able to speak above a whisper. "Arramos told me he wasn't going on the ark, so I knew he drowned, but seeing it happen right before my eyes makes it … well …"

"Personal?" Timothy asked. "Trust me, I understand better than you can imagine."

Joran touched the wall again. So many bodies lay underneath that sea, including his father and most of his family. Dragons, too, went to a watery grave. Shachar, the dragon who was supposed to find the purity ovulum, was no more. "So it fell into Morgan's hands."

"I assume you're referring to the purity ovulum," Timothy said. "You are grieving the fact that Shachar perished in the waters."

"Yes. How did you guess?"

"I have watched many events through this wall, so I know what your father hoped Shachar would do after the flood. Yet, that plan failed, and the flood washed the ovulum into the sediment until the day that evil sorceress collected it for her own use."

"Why would Elohim allow that to happen?" Joran asked. "If he wanted Noah's descendants to have the ovulum, why didn't he prevent someone like Morgan from getting it?"

"The fact that there is such a demoness as Morgan is proof that Elohim allows much evil to occur, but we can rest assured that his ultimate purpose will never be thwarted. Good will come. You will see."

Heat surged into Joran's cheeks. "Good will come? How can you say that? I saw a vile murderer hunt down and kill a dragon who had turned into a human—a sweet, innocent, pregnant woman who had no way to protect herself."

"Yes, I know. She was Tamara, who used to be Sorentine. I watched the murder, including your attempts to warn her. I shouted at this wall like a madman, but it was useless."

Joran brushed a foot across the yellow grass. The look in Tamara's eyes—so frightened, so hopeless—still haunted him. She trusted in Elohim to protect her, to keep her and her precious little one safe, but the slayer's blade slashed them both. So much for protection. He sighed and looked again at Timothy. "You never told me your other name."

Smiling, he gestured with a thumb toward his back. "You and your sister rode on me, and we battled demons together, though I was one of your later and more inexperienced mounts."

"Makaidos? Did you get transformed with Sorentine?"

"Not with her, but I was transformed." Timothy turned toward the wall and gazed at the ark as it bobbed on the undulating waves. "After the flood, I became king of the dragons, and Thigocia was my queen. We watched over our growing brood for centuries until I was killed by the very monster who ended Tamara's life. My spirit traveled to a place called Dragons' Rest, where I appeared in the human form you see now. There, I took the name Timothy and established a community. Many years later, I was transported to this ovulum, which is now being carried by Elam, son of Shem. He has been assigned to watch over Hannah, the former Thigocia."

Joran focused on the ark. Its up-and-down ride was appropriate. With a flood of strange information pouring in, it seemed that his mind was treading water in a storm. He had to process thousands of years of history in a matter of moments, and witnessing the flood's devastation while standing next to his former dragon

300

mount in human form didn't help matters. The entire world had lost all semblance of sanity.

Timothy touched the wall. "This viewing partition also showed me how you, your sister, and Tamiel were absorbed into the purity ovulum, but I was unable to see what became of you after that. Apparently it doesn't display activities inside the ovula."

Joran showed him the lyre and Selah's image. "Tamiel trapped Selah in a string. He won't release her until I go into all seven ovula and do something that will give the strings color. From what I have been able to figure out, once the strings have taken on the colors, the lyre will become a key that will allow us to get out. Tamiel said he would release Selah when I give him the key."

"That is quite a dilemma," Timothy said as he stroked his chin. "You are being forced to create the device by which a demon will be loosed to again terrorize the world. That is not a burden I would want on my shoulders."

Joran spread out an arm. "What choice do I have?"

"We always have a choice." Timothy laid his palm on the wall again. "Let me show you something else."

301

As if brushing dust off the wall, he moved his hand rapidly, shifting the flood scene to the left. A new scene replaced it, but it flew by too quickly for Joran to figure out what it was. A blur of colors raced past until Timothy's hand rested again and brought the rolling scenes to a halt.

A white-haired girl stood next to a table, clutching the edge of her work smock. A man with an oval-shaped head and short brown hair stood beside her. He waved an arm over the table and said, "Here is where it all begins."

Small glass jars covered the surface, each one carrying a semi-transparent egg suspended in clear liquid. A tiny creature floated at the center of each egg, its spindly limbs stroking as if trying to swim.

"This is where we plant the garden, Mara," the man said. "I experiment with different combinations of eggs and seeds to find

which ones make the strongest embryos. I sometimes even com-
bine two seeds into one to make them stronger."

Joran hovered a finger over the wall. Again the scene appeared
to be three-dimensional, as if he could walk into the room and
look over Mara's shoulder. Even from his stance only two paces
away, Mara's heartbeat sounded loud and clear as she took in rapid,
shallow breaths.

Mara stared at one of the jars. "Where do you get the seeds
and eggs?"

"That lesson can wait until later," the man said. "For now, I
want you to see the beginning and the end."

She looked up at him. "The end?"

He lifted a jar and held it in front of her eyes. "Do you see
anything unusual about this one?"

Joran stepped so close the tip of his nose touched the wall. The
tiny creature looked like a miniature version of the plants in the
yellow field.

"It's smaller," Mara said, "and it's not swimming as hard as the
others."

"Exactly." The man opened a door on his right. As flames shot
up from within, he dumped the embryo into the fire, then
slammed the door shut.

Mara gaped at the door, her blue eyes sparkling with tears.

Timothy pressed both palms on the wall, and the scene froze.
"That is enough."

As Joran stepped back, he rubbed his eyes. "What did I see?"

"An event from long ago in another realm. The girl you saw,
however, is still alive. Her name then was Mara, but now it is Sapphira Adi. She is what is called an Oracle of Fire and is able to
make things ignite in flames by command, even herself, though
her flames do not harm her. She can also open portals to other
realms by spinning her fire into a cyclone. She was once one of
those embryos. Many grew to be giants, while only Sapphira and

one other girl became Oracles." Timothy nodded toward the wall. "Have you guessed the truth about the discarded embryos?"

"Are they related somehow to the plants in the field of yellow grass?"

"Related is an inadequate term. They are one and the same."

"How did they survive the fire? And how did they get here?"

"They perished, and their spirits were transported here, replanted in the ineffective soil."

Joran looked back at the plants. A few had wandered close enough to watch the wall from a safe distance. "Ineffective?"

"Yes. They sprouted but never grew beyond the stage of infancy. I have no doubt that they could all become giants, unless, of course, one might be an infant Oracle. The scientist you saw is named Mardon, a fool who believed that these precious lives were worthless, fit only to be thrown into the fire. He hoped to replicate Mara as well as a budding giant named Yereq, but since the genetic codes he created did not match the prototypes exactly, and since they showed poor performance in their formative stages, he assumed they were nothing more than failed experiments. Although he had great knowledge, he viewed the world through a narrow tunnel, unable to perceive the potential of those who did not match his preconceived criteria. What he believed to be crippled could be nothing else. As I said, we always have a choice, but our choices depend on the breadth of our vision."

303

Joran took in the words, carefully tracking the meaning of each one. They rang true. Too many people refused to believe that someone who appeared to lack talents or skills could ever blossom into something more … like Tamara, a tongue-tied actor … like Makaidos, a young and inexperienced dragon back in his demon-battling days. "So are you saying that Mardon was too blind to notice the value of those he threw away?"

"That is exactly what I am saying." Timothy shook his head sadly. "The fools of this age are no better than those who hurled mocking insults at Noah as he built the ark. They hear but do not understand. They listen but never learn."

"So the flood didn't destroy sin. It didn't stop rebellion. Nothing good came of it."

"Nothing good?" Timothy laid a hand on the wall. "Do not let Mardon's tunnel vision blind you to the fullness of the landscape. Step up to a higher plane and look again." He pushed Mara and Mardon to the left, and myriad scenes again ran across the wall. As they rolled by, Timothy continued. "Just as Elohim gave the world another chance in your day, he still gives opportunities to others who were condemned by those who thought them beyond repair. He offers resurrection, a new life."

Timothy laid a hand on the wall again, stopping the moving scenes. A building with an inner courtyard appeared. At one boundary of the courtyard, twenty or more people gathered in front of a series of seven steps that led to a row of ivory columns. A man sat on the sixth step, speaking to the gathering.

304

As Joran leaned closer, the wall seemed to swallow his body and absorb him into the scene. Still holding the lyre, he stood in the courtyard, now within a few steps of the back row of the crowd. From his right, a cacophony reached his ears—feet shuffling, men shouting, a woman grunting as if in pain.

From the same direction, several men in long robes appeared from around a column, two holding a woman's arms as they dragged her across the courtyard. She squirmed but to no avail. With her head low, her face stayed out of sight.

As the men threw her down in the center of the court, a few paces in front of the stairs, the speaker on the sixth step rose and walked down to level ground. The men, perhaps ten in all, surrounded the woman and faced the speaker. One pointed a finger at her. "Teacher, this woman was caught in adultery, in the very act. The Law of Moses commanded us to stone such women. What do you say?"

While Joran and the others drew closer, the teacher stooped and began writing on the ground with a finger, as if he hadn't heard the accusation at all.

"Teacher?" the man said, his expression stern behind a thick, dark beard. "Did you hear me? She is an adulteress. What do you say we should do? Stone her?"

Joran took another step closer, hoping to see the woman better. Young, petite, and wearing a tattered brown dress, she kept her head low. Long shadows from surrounding columns shaded her face, as did her dark hair. With scratches and dirt covering her ankles and bare feet, she appeared to have been dragged quite a distance. Whoever these accusers might be, they were determined to see justice done, and they looked up to this teacher as a judge. Obviously an adulteress deserved whatever harsh judgment he declared.

The accusers each picked up a stone, as did those who had been listening to the teacher. The woman raised her head and stared straight at Joran, her eyes wide and wet.

305

Joran felt his mouth drop open. Naamah! How could that be? She died in the flood!

"Teacher?" the head accuser said again. "Will you render judgment according to the Law of Moses?"

Joran scooped up a stone and held it tightly. At last he could take revenge on the murderess who stole his sister's voice … and her life.

The teacher straightened and faced the accusers. "He who is without sin among you, let him be the first to cast a stone." Then, he stooped again and wrote on the ground.

The accusers stared at each other, apparently dumbstruck. One man with a deeply creased face and white hair dropped his stone and walked slowly toward the columns. Another of similar age joined him. Soon, they all filed away one by one, including those who had been listening to the teacher, ending with a young man about Joran's age.

Still holding the lyre, Joran looked at his stone, then at Naamah. The others had no idea that she was a murderess. Should he shout the truth? Maybe the teacher would change his mind and alter his cryptic statement. If only those who had never sinned could pass judgment, corruption would flood the world. Adultery and murder demanded punishment.

He glared at her and spoke with a growl. "You helped a demon kill my sister, and you stole her voice. Now you'll finally get what's coming to you." He drew his arm back and slung the stone at her, but it vanished as soon as it left his hand. The motion cast him away from the courtyard, and he flew backwards until he stood again with Timothy in front of the wall.

His heart pounding, Joran heaved for breath. "What happened?"

Timothy let out a shushing sound. "Keep watching."

As the teacher rose again, Naamah looked at him, tears streaming. "Woman," the teacher said, "where are they? Did no one condemn you?"

She squeaked in reply. "No one, Lord."

"Neither do I condemn you. Go and sin no more." As the teacher walked away, the woman kept her gaze fixed on him until his shadow passed out of sight. Then, she drooped her head and wept, letting her hair touch the ground with each spasmodic sob.

Joran's throat narrowed. "When did this happen?"

"Almost two thousand years ago," Timothy replied.

Joran glanced at Selah's image. She watched with rapt attention. There was no doubt that she recognized the evil prostitute.

On the viewing wall, Naamah picked up one of the stones and held it close to her chest. Looking at the dirt, her lips moved, as if she were reading what the teacher wrote there. As she rose to her feet, a man walked by, then another, neither bothering to glance at her.

Naamah looked up, her eyes still brimming with tears as she clutched the stone and sang in a lovely contralto.

How can a man of flesh and bone
Embrace my heart and soften stone?
For I am she who woos men's hearts,
And none resist my vocal arts.

Weeping, she lifted the stone in her open palm.

Yet now 'tis I who trembles here
As conquered, broken, shedding tears,
Deserving stones and ruptured flesh,
Instead he offers life afresh.

This man of mercy knows my mind,
Commands me leave my sin behind;
But how can scarlet change to white
When evil steals my will to fight?

307

She looked at the ground, touching the writing with a toe.

These words remind of sin's great cost
To sheep that choose to wander lost;
Yet other costs weigh down my wrists,
The price I'd pay should I resist.

Gazing at the sky again, she sang on.

In chains I lie each night in bed
As one who wishes she were dead;
Now torn apart, I must decide,
Because to follow is to die.

When she finished, she dropped the stone and hurried away,
leaving the courtyard empty.

Joran stared, sweating and shivering at the same time. The melody was rapturous! How could a vile woman produce such a song? Hearing the perfection of Seraphina's voice emanating from this wicked vessel was like seeing a flower bloom from manure. It was so ... so wrong!

"Joran," Selah said, her voice cracking with emotion. "We have to remember that tune. It is glorious!"

"But ..." Joran pointed at the wall, barely able to speak. "But it's Naamah! Some kind of devilry has brought her back to life! We can't trust anything she sings."

"Maybe not, but that doesn't make the melody any less beautiful. I still want to remember it."

"If you are able to remember it." Timothy hummed the melody's first few notes. "I call it the mercy song, and I have heard it replayed in Naamah's life and also in the lives of others who are gifted enough to hear and sing the song of the ovulum."

308

"The mercy song is the same as the song of the ovulum?" Joran asked.

"Of the purity ovulum, yes. During the moment a soul receives mercy, she is able to hear the melody, and it stirs up passions, inciting her to sing the words that flow from her heart. Then, moments later, she hears it no more, and she remembers it no more." Timothy nodded at Joran. "Go ahead. Try to sing it. You will see."

Joran again looked at the courtyard, still empty. As he pictured Naamah, the words returned to his mind, but try as he might, he couldn't resurrect the melody. "Selah, do you remember it?"

She crossed her arms over her chest, tapping her foot. "No, Joran. It's so frustrating!"

Timothy gave them a knowing smile. "The song is like the wind, invisible, yet able to fill a sail. It tickles the skin on your back, a hint of a tune, three notes, but the rest slips away. You know it is within you. You know it has changed you. You know it more surely than you know that the sun shines in the sky. It is unspeakable glory. It is the full expression of God's mercy. Even if you cannot sing it, you feel it. You feel it with all your heart. And there is one way to hear it again. Whenever you offer the mercy that you have so graciously been granted, the song will be renewed and implanted in another. So, as long as we give mercy, we will be granted its cleansing flow and enjoy again the song of life."

Joran boiled inside. "Naamah deserves no mercy. Her own words gave away her double mindedness. I'm sure if you kept watching her life, you'd find that she went back to her harlotries."

"Does that matter?" Timothy asked. "Who are we to cast stones at one who hopes for mercy? I grant you that forgiveness and reconciliation require something more than a penitent posture, but mercy should not be withheld from anyone. Forsake vengeance and any desire to punish. Leave retribution in the hands of God, for bitterness is a stone that strikes only the one who hurls it."

Joran looked at the stones, so close and so real, it seemed that he could reach out and pick one up again. Although Naamah deserved to be pummeled with stones, the words of her protector were powerful enough to disarm her accusers. "Who was the man who spoke to her?"

"Jesus of Nazareth, the Son of God, the great ark who delivers us from the flood of this age. He is the one who writes the mercy song on every believing heart. Just as the sins of each supplicant are different, so the words change from person to person, but the tune is always the same. The words infuse the song with captivating beauty, which explains why you were so taken by it. Although you have heard the melody before from the ovulum, hearing it expressed in its fullness captured your hearts."

"Do you know how Naamah survived the flood? She looks like she hasn't aged at all."

"She married Ham and went aboard the ark. Although I was there in my dragon form, I was unaware at that time of her crimes against your family, so I could not warn Noah of her treachery. I am, however, an eyewitness that she was a good wife, and when her baby was born, she cared for him faithfully. Then, through the sorcery of her villainous sister, Morgan, she became a wraith-like creature who does not age. For all I know, she is still alive to this day."

Joran let a growl invade his whisper. "And she still sings with my sister's voice."

"My old friend," Timothy said, clasping Joran's shoulder, "if you keep holding tightly to bitterness, you will find that you are strangling yourself."

Joran averted his eyes. It was easy for Timothy to preach about releasing bitterness. He wasn't there when Naamah conspired with Tamiel to murder Seraphina.

"And this was the point I was hoping to make from the beginning," Timothy continued. "You always have a choice. You are free to listen to Tamiel and believe that the options he has set before you are the only ones available, or you can step up to a higher plane and broaden your vision. Just as there is more to the purple plants than your eyes can see, and just as there is more to Naamah than the wickedness that your own heart projects, there are more options than those that darkness sets before you. Open the eyes of faith, and let God show you a brighter, broader perspective. As long as you reject hope, as long as you refuse to believe in something better than what you can see with your eyes, you will never be able to unlock the mystery of true liberty. A heart that cannot give mercy is a far more confining prison than is a glass egg."

Joran returned his gaze to Timothy. He longed to take those powerful words and make them real within, but they seemed elusive, ineffective, much like the yellow soil that imprisoned the plants.

"In any case," Timothy continued, laying a hand over his heart. "I believe mercy will someday be made manifest in me, and I will be able to walk through this wall and rejoin my dear Hannah."

"How long have you been waiting?" Selah asked.

"Centuries. But I would be a fool to complain. I am content."

"Why would Elohim wait so long to set you free?"

"Has it been so long? I neither hunger nor thirst here, and I never tire, so years seem inconsequential. When the time is right, I will be able to leave."

"I see," Selah said. "The ark carries us to new life, safe from the floodwaters, and we wait for the new land to appear. Such is the love of Elohim."

Joran flinched. Selah's words bit hard. Only moments ago he had mentally spoken that sentiment—Such is the love of Elohim—as a sarcastic slap, but now …

Letting out a sigh, he looked again at the courtyard as it filled with people, some likely as enslaved to their passions as Naamah was, and others carrying the song of mercy in their bosoms. The flood was finally beginning to make sense. Without punishment, there can be no justice. Without justice, there can be no mercy. Without mercy, there can be no hope. And hope is the heartbeat of both the forgiver and the forgiven.

Still, how could anyone believe Naamah was truly contrite? He would have to see it to believe it.

A splash sounded. Seven colors splattered the wall and spread out, repainting the scene—a woman with frightened eyes standing outside a small cottage with an open window on one wall.

Joran glanced at Timothy. "Do you know who she is?"

"Hannah!" Timothy reached toward the wall. "My wife!"

311

19

CHAPTER

A Hidden Dragon

Lauren blinked her eyes open, again shivering. The dream was so real! With all the colors and textures, the facial expressions, and the sorrows, it seemed like reality had played in her sleeping mind. Why would she be dreaming about Joran and Selah, the same people Bonnie mentioned? Besides that, how long had she been asleep? The dream seemed to last for hours.

Touching her cheek, she whispered. "Larry? Lois?"

"I am here," Larry said. "How may I help you?"

"I dozed off. I'm wondering how much longer till the dragons come."

"I cannot give you an estimate. The weather conditions are too variable. I suggest that you go back to sleep. I am able to send a vibration signal that should awaken you when the dragons approach."

"Thanks." Lauren closed her eyes. Joran's plight called her back to slumber. She had to see what would happen to Timothy and his wife and how Joran would get Selah out of the lyre … if only the dream would continue.

As sleep closed in, one of the dream events came to mind, the woman with the stones lying around her. It was a familiar Bible story, one Micaela had memorized about a woman caught in adultery, a woman who found mercy in the words of Jesus. And that song! It was so tragic, yet so beautiful, a blend of sorrow and joy.

"Jesus," she whispered, "let me finish the dream. Show me what I need to know."

After heaving a long sigh, she drifted off to sleep.

Barlow descended a narrow stairway, making sure each foot touched down with the utmost silence. Portia was deaf, so noise wouldn't make her turn to see who followed her, but there were so many odd circumstances surrounding this woman, it didn't make sense to take a chance. Her ability to read lips seemed too remarkable to be real, especially considering her lack of understanding regarding simple concepts. Yet, the Colonel's label for her could explain everything. She might really be an idiot savant. If not, she was an actress of extraordinary skill.

Barlow chuckled to himself. Portia was "a tough act to follow," a delightful application of an idiom.

At the bottom of the stairs, Portia, with her back toward Barlow, aimed her flashlight at a door's security pad and punched a series of keys. Her orange jumpsuit made her easy to see, even in the dimness. When a buzz sounded, she pulled the door open and hurried through.

Barlow hustled down and caught the door before it closed. Ahead, the flashlight's beam illuminated a dark tunnel. The beam shifted as Portia walked, alternately shining on the paneled walls at each side.

Pushing a hand into his pocket, Barlow felt for something to keep the door from latching, perhaps a penny. His finger brushed across the rubellite ring he had found at the roof-access door in the research building, but no coins. No matter. There had to be a way out.

After letting the door close quietly, he tiptoed after her. He glanced at the plaster ceiling just above his head. Since they had descended through a secret door in the Colonel's office, they should now be heading toward the walkway leading to the barracks. Soon they would approach the area underneath the mysterious plot of greenery that interrupted the walkway. The sod there had obviously been laid down recently, a mystery he had hoped to solve. Earlier, pulling up one of the squares had revealed a shallow layer of dirt and a metal floor underneath. Now, it seemed, he would learn what lay even farther below.

Portia stopped at another door and again typed on a security keypad. A door slid to the left, revealing a dim chamber with flashing lights on control panels at the far end and on both sides. Other than swivel seats in front of the panels, the room appeared to be empty.

Breaking into a jog, Barlow hurried to catch up. His shoes squeaked, but that didn't matter. Supposedly, she wouldn't be able to hear the noise.

The flashlight beam swung around and struck Barlow's face. "Who is there?"

Barlow ducked under the beam and rushed ahead. He grabbed Portia's wrist, pried the flashlight from her hand, and aimed the light at his mouth. "I am Sergeant Daniel Hoskins. What are you doing here?"

She trembled. "I … I work … for the Colonel. … I check the guns."

"Guns?" Barlow pulled her into the chamber and set her gently on one of the chairs. The door slid closed, and fluorescent lamps on the walls flickered to life. As he hooked the flashlight to his belt, he read the labels under the various dials, slider bars, and display screens—*Intensity, Angle, Degradation, Coverage*, among others. The controls seemed to be divided into eight stations with repeated labels. A headset/microphone combination lay at each station along with a black electrode-covered glove. "What is this place?" Barlow asked, making sure Portia could see his lips.

She opened her mouth, straining, as if trying to speak a difficult word. "Ex … Excali …"

"Excalibur? The famed sword of King Arthur?"

She nodded. "Guns shoot … like sword."

"How do you know about Excalibur's abilities?"

Again straining to speak, she forced out, "Colonel told me."

Barlow pointed at the panel. "Do these stations control weapons that create a disintegrating beam?"

"And more." She waved a hand over her head. "Um … umbrella."

"A photo umbrella," he said, nodding. "Excalibur can do that. It creates a shield overhead and all around, like a dome of light energy."

As she nodded in return, Barlow studied her face. She seemed familiar somehow, like someone he had met long ago. Yet, since she was so pallid and haggard, if she had been in full health when he met her, it would be difficult to match the images. And she didn't show any signs of recognizing him. Maybe they were two ships passing by a knight. "Why did you come here at this hour?"

316

"I show you." She pressed a button on one of the right-hand control panels. A thin computer monitor rose from the surface, displaying a graphic representation of a cannon-like object. She put the closest glove on her right hand, and as she moved her fingers, the cannon's barrel shifted up and down and side to side.

With each movement, a quiet hum emanated from above. Barlow looked up. A drop-panel ceiling blocked his view, but no doubt a real gun sat up there, guided by Portia's hand. As his eyes shifted, he imagined seven other guns positioned in a rectangle. Apparently, a mechanism existed whereby they could rise above the ground and shoot, either to obliterate an enemy or to create a shielding dome. Such a battery of weapons would be a devastating arsenal against a dragon invasion.

"I understand the operation," Barlow said. "Continue your explanation."

Portia slid the headset on and spoke into the microphone, her voice strained, as usual. "Set to … manual … alert."

A message flashed under the cannon graphic—Command Not Recognized.

Portia smacked her palm on the control panel. Her face straining, she spoke again. "Set to … manual alert."

Again, the error message flashed.

Barlow pondered the command. Apparently this weapons system could defend the facility automatically, and the eight stations proved that it could be operated manually as well. Since no one manned the stations, they had set it to automatic mode, confident their equipment could hold off a surprise attack until the gun operators arrived. Now Portia wanted to shift it to manual to make the facility more vulnerable.

"Is there any other way to switch the mode?"

Portia shook her head. "Voice command. … Colonel must do. I wanted … to try."

"Ah! I see. Voice recognition. Are there any other options? Sabotage, maybe?"

She touched the panel with a finger. "Cannot break."

"It's indestructible?"

"Not in … indes …"

"It's not indestructible. I understand."

She splayed her fingers, folded them in, then splayed them again. "Alarms."

"So you want to destroy it, but you can't because of an alarm system."

She nodded vigorously.

"Why do you want to destroy it?"

"Pro … protect … dragons."

Barlow pointed at her. "You're a dragon sympathizer?"

317

She aimed her own finger back at him. "So are you … Ssss … Sir Barlow."

He glanced at his "Hoskins" name tag, now a useless façade. "How have we met?"

"Not telling." Portia rose from the chair and began gathering the gloves. "Help me."

Barlow collected four gloves, while Portia piled the other four into her arms. As they stood together at the door, Barlow looked her in the eye. "I understand your plan, Miss. Although you were unable to delay the activation of the weapons, at least now the operators won't be able to move the guns around when they arrive, but what I do not yet understand is your motivation."

She shook her head. "Secret."

Barlow kept his stare locked on her. How could he just let her go? Without full knowledge of her person and purpose, he had no way of knowing whether or not his own identity might be exposed. Still, she specifically mentioned protecting dragons, and she had a familiar look about her, so maybe …

He set his gloves on the closest panel and dug the rubellite ring out of his pocket.

When she saw it, her eyes grew wide, and she dropped her gloves.

Barlow grabbed her wrist and slid the ring over her pinky. The gem's red color drained away until it turned pearly white. As he looked again into her eyes, they sparkled with tears. "Now I understand," he said in a soothing tone. "We will finish here and go our separate ways."

Portia nodded, a tear trickling down her cheek. She slid the ring off and pushed it back into his hand, curling his fingers around it.

He gave her a smile. There was no need to find out which former dragon she was. They were one in purpose, and that was all that mattered. They were birds of a feather flocking to gather the anthrozils and take them to safety.

318

Timothy gaped at the image on the wall. "I have not seen this before. It must be new, maybe happening at this moment."

In the image, Devin vaulted out through the window, and Palin followed. As Devin straightened, he faltered for a moment, clutching his leg.

"He's hurt!" Someone shouted as a hand reached out and grabbed Hannah's elbow. "Run!"

Devin and Palin stalked toward the foreground, each wielding a sword. Hannah's voice came through again but too garbled to understand.

Then, as if materializing out of nowhere, a white-haired man appeared in front of the wall, facing Joran and Timothy and blocking their view.

Timothy's mouth dropped open. "Enoch!"

"Yes," Enoch said calmly. "Timothy, you will eject from here in a cloud of gas that will temporarily disable the dark knights and place you safely next to Hannah. But since the effects from the gas will not last long, you must flee with all haste. Tell Elam that his next assignment is to find Valcor. He lives in Glastonbury, England, under the name Patrick Nathanson. Elam will learn how he must aid Patrick as faithfully as he aided Thigocia. Lock this command in your mind, for you will quickly forget much of what you experienced within this ovulum."

Devin's sword sliced through the viewing wall, cutting off the top half.

Enoch grabbed Joran's arm and pulled him away from Timothy. "It is time!"

Red mist spun around Timothy, lifted him into the air, and sent him flying through the breach.

"Your turn," Enoch said to Joran, a hint of a smile on his face.

Joran squinted at him. Could this man really be his grandfather? "Am I leaving now?"

"Perhaps not permanently. We shall see."

319

More mist erupted from the floor. It swirled around Joran and carried him away. Blinded by the redness, he twirled and flew upward, holding the lyre close to his chest. Selah had disappeared. At least she was safe in the string.

Soon, he began to descend, and the swirling eased. After a few seconds, his feet touched ground, and the mist evaporated. In the distance, Timothy, Hannah, and a young man climbed a low fence, then ran across a grassy field toward a trio of horses.

The sound of coughing made Joran turn. Devin and Palin knelt nearby, both retching with violent spasms.

Joran grabbed Devin's sword and set the point against his throat. "Give me the ovulum."

After coughing several more times, Devin nodded toward Joran's feet. "Are you blind? It's right there. But it's no good for protecting dragonkind. I destroyed it."

Joran glanced down. An ovulum lay in two halves in a pool of red liquid. "Not this one. I want the ovulum you used to find it."

"I have no idea what you're talking about."

Joran pushed the blade, pricking Devin's skin, making him wince. Blood oozed around the point and streamed behind his shirt. "I know what you did to Tamara," Joran growled, "and if you don't give me the ovulum, I will not hesitate to separate your head from your body."

"Let's say that I have it. How do I know you'll let me go if I give it to you?"

"You'll just have to trust me." Joran gave the blade a slight twist, drawing more blood. "Give it to me now."

Moving only his eyes, Devin looked at Palin. "It has served its purpose."

"As you wish, my liege." Palin reached into a pouch attached to his belt and withdrew an ovulum. Gray mist fogged the inside, darkening as he held the egg in his palms.

Joran nodded at the ground near the broken ovulum. "Set it there."

Palin rolled it gently out of his hands. As soon as it settled on the grass, the fog began to clear.

"How did you look into it?" Joran asked. "Neither of you has the purity of a rat."

Devin sneered. "There are nunneries aplenty, and the novices are easily duped. Once we found the mongrel's hideout, we sent a pretty little novice home on a donkey."

Keeping his sword pointed at Devin, Joran stooped, set the lyre on his knee, and felt for the invisible purity ovulum. When he found it, he slid his palm underneath and lifted. As before, the glass became cloudy.

"Are we free to go?" Devin asked with a sarcastic bite.

Hugging the lyre and ovulum close, Joran backed away and looked beyond the fence at the field. The trio mingled with the horses, apparently making ready to ride them away. "Go," he said, waving the sword. "If you so much as look back, I will relieve you of your eyes."

Palin jumped to his feet and ran toward the fence and horses. As blood streamed down his neck, Devin rose more slowly, his evil eye trained on Joran. With a sudden leap, he lunged and jerked the sword away. He swiped the blade, but Joran ducked just before it could slice his neck.

Then, instead of attacking again, Devin ran after Palin. "I am coming! Don't let them get away!"

"It seems that dragon killing carries a greater weight than does revenge."

Joran spun toward the voice. Enoch held the broken ovulum, one half in each hand. "I assume you have wondered about the multiple colors in the field of yellow grass."

"I have." Joran turned back to the horses and riders. Timothy and Hannah rode away safely, but it seemed that Palin had thrown a dagger and wounded the third escapee, likely Elam. Still, Elam's horse broke into a gallop with Elam safely mounted.

"When entering this red ovulum," Enoch said, "you actually passed through three others. They belonged to dragons the slayer has already killed. I assume they are stored together somewhere, because when they were apart, the grass in the field you traversed was not yellow, and the plants were fewer, all violet. After the deaths of those dragons, the three virtues merged." He nodded at the lyre. "It seems, however, that you have not completed all four parts of the key."

Joran shifted the purity ovulum to his other hand and looked at the lyre. Only one new color had appeared. The string with the highest note had turned red. Yes, he had been humbled and shamed, his bitterness exposed, giving the D string its blush, but there was still much to do. "I know why."

"Yes, I have also deduced the reason."

"So now I have to figure out *how* to show mercy to the plants."

"To the plants?" Enoch bent his brow. "Is that what you think?"

Joran nodded. "Shouldn't I show mercy to them? They begged me to take them with me. Shouldn't I do everything I can to help them?"

"Of course. We should be merciful to every humiliated soul in God's creation." Enoch's face slackened. "What do you think you should do?"

"Go back to them. But is it even possible? The red ovulum is broken."

"It is possible. I can arrange it."

"Okay, but where am I going to get so many pots?"

"There is no need to worry about pots. When you return, wisdom will guide you. Eventually you will be shown how to give mercy even to creatures you deem to be the lowliest." Enoch swiped a sandaled foot across the ground. "Why do you think the grass was yellow in that field and the plants never grew to maturity?"

Joran kicked the turf with the toe of his sandal. "It has to be the soil. Nothing can grow if it feeds on futility."

Enoch smiled. "My son has taught you well. I hope some of the plants will understand and go with you. It is essential that you take at least one. In fact, the more, the better."

Joran looked Enoch over. Dressed in a tunic, belt, and sandals suitable for the days of old, this man really was his grandfather. "So the legend is true. You lived within the ovulum all these years."

"I did, but time is short. I will have to explain everything when we meet again. For now, you must continue your journey."

"So after I gather all the plants, how do I get Selah out of the lyre?"

"The only way is to complete the final steps in constructing your key, and even then, freeing her will be a difficult task."

Joran gripped the lyre tightly. "It doesn't matter. I would fight the devil himself to rescue her."

"As you should. You and she must be reunited." Enoch displayed the two halves of the ovulum, the open ends facing up. "It is strange how common this piece of glass seems to be when it has been cleaved in two. It is impotent, worthless, ready to be cast away into a junk pile. Yet ..." He fit the two pieces together. "When its parts are rejoined, they become a unit, a powerful tool for God to use for his glory. That is why Tamiel wants you and Selah to be separated. Apart, you are no more useful than two halves of a broken egg, but together ..." He held the restored ovulum over his head. Red light emanated down and around his arm, expanding until it enveloped his body as well as Joran's. "Together, you will be a greater force than before, because now you will be sharpened blades forged by the one who told Naamah to go and sin no more."

Joran basked in the restored ovulum's glow. Already his mind felt different, more alive, less afraid. Maybe he could finally leave his past behind and be the warrior he was meant to be. "I think I understand."

"Excellent." As Enoch lowered the ovulum, the surrounding light faded, but the egg itself still glowed red. "The path to freedom will be fraught with great risk, and you will have to learn the details as they emerge, but I can tell you one important fact. The dragon you once knew as Arramos has changed. The devil himself now inhabits his body, and the spirit of the true Arramos has gone to a place called Second Eden. He is a human named Abraham who shepherds the people there."

Joran lifted the purity ovulum. "Why is it still cloudy when I carry it?"

"Your journey is not yet complete. Some virtues remain to be gathered."

Joran pressed his lips together. If only virtues could really be gathered like fruit from a tree. It seemed that some came at great cost. "Should I take it with me?"

"No, you cannot enter something you carry any more than a dog can eat itself." Still holding the red ovulum, Enoch extended his empty hand. "You must give it to me."

324

Joran rolled it onto his grandfather's weathered palm. Although it turned invisible, a tiny red light sparkled within, apparently signaling its closeness to the other ovulum. At the same time, the red egg's light began to fade. "What will you do with them?"

"I have a secret purpose for the red ovulum, and I will begin a search for the discarded ones. I have a good idea where each one is from watching that vile dragon slayer kill his victims. Unfortunately, the green ovulum has fallen into the hands of the enemy of souls, so when you enter it, you should assume that you will encounter evil."

Joran nodded. Even after all he and Selah had been through, it seemed that their journey had just begun.

"In the meantime," Enoch continued, "I will have to transfer the purity ovulum's song to another vessel."

"Another vessel? Will it still be protected by a curse?"

"It will be my goal to ensure that the one who destroys it will be destroyed. A more urgent objective will be to find a vessel with greater mobility. That way, even I will not know where it is at any given moment."

"If it's mobile, will anyone be able to find it?"

Enoch offered a gentle smile. "God will raise up another Shachar who will be able to hear the song in her scales and locate it when it is needed. She will be in human form, so she will be quite vulnerable, because Tamiel has known about the Shachar prophecy for a long time. Yet, he also knows what else the prophecy says. Since this human Shachar will have scales that absorb sound and energy, and since Tamiel is the Silent One who can create a shell of silence, if they should touch one another, they would create a clash of powers that would be fatal to both. So Tamiel would have to use extraordinary skill and deception to get her to do his will from a distance."

"Did Tamiel escape when the red ovulum split in half?"

Enoch shook his head. "I would have seen him. You should assume that he will continue to stalk you as you try to complete the key." He held out the red ovulum in his palm. "Now play the strings that do not yet have color, and you will be taken back in."

Joran strummed the lyre, taking care to skip the D, C, and G strings. He managed to create a melody, but without Selah's guidance, it sounded less than beautiful.

As he played, light glimmered within the purity ovulum, a spark of green, then yellow, then indigo and violet. They grew larger with each note, as if the egg were drawing toward him.

Soon, he stood once again in the field of yellow grass. A few tiny mounds of soil had been pushed together at various spots, but no plants stood or waded anywhere.

"Hello!" Joran called.

Mendallah's head popped up through a pile of soil. She blinked away granules and smiled weakly. "I am here," she said in her breezy voice.

Joran stepped closer and knelt. "Mendallah, what happened?"

"Most tried to gather soil, but it is hard work. They gave up."

"Where did they go?"

"They fled the promised fire. They are hiding." Mendallah wiggled higher and pulled her side stalks from the soil. "I fear that I have gathered only a small pile. I grew tired."

"Then why did you come up when I called?"

Mendallah bowed her pod. "To beg for mercy."

"Granted." Joran reached out a hand. "Is it safe to uproot you? If you're the only one who is coming with me, I can try to fit you in my pocket."

"And will you take my soil?"

"No. The soil will have to stay. You'll just have to trust me to find new soil as soon as possible."

"When will you burn the grass?"

Sighing, Joran shook his head. "That was a stupid threat. I'm not going to burn anything."

Several more plant heads popped up, then dozens. Cheers followed—shouts of "No fire!" and "Safety!" and "No work!" breezed across the grass.

As they burrowed upward, exposing their stalks, Joran looked at Mendallah. Her face took on a morose expression.

"What's wrong?" he asked.

"The others will refuse to come with us. They are motivated only by fear, and they will fear being uprooted."

"Don't they fear staying in this place and never growing?"

Mendallah shook her pod. "Not so much. They want to leave, but they are unwilling to risk their lives to do so."

"I can still make the offer. I'll take as many as are brave enough to come."

"How many pockets do you have?"

Joran smiled. "Since I'm not carrying soil, I can bundle you up. It might be uncomfortable, but it should work. First, we'll go to a place that's all white and completely silent. Then we'll search for a land of green. Maybe we'll find fertile soil there."

Mendallah pulled up on one of her supporting stalks, partially exposing a root. "It is very painful to uproot."

"I can believe that, but it's the only way to get out of here."

"I trust you. You are strong, and I am weak."

Joran cupped his hands around his mouth and called out. "Earlier you all asked me to take you with me. Now here's your chance. I don't have any pots, so I will have to uproot you and carry you without soil. Those who agree, come to me, and we will leave this place immediately."

The cheers suddenly silenced. The plants stared at him, their eyes and mouths as wide as the tiny slits allowed. While most seemed frozen in place, several waded backwards. Whispers of "No soil?" and "Unearth our roots?" flowed from pod to pod.

"If you stay here," Joran shouted above their breezy words, "you can't grow. This soil will never provide what you need to mature. Come with me, and I will take you to a place where you will become …" He searched for a word. What would they become?

As if echoing his thoughts, several called out, "Become what?"

"I don't know. Something different. Something new. Maybe a man, maybe a woman, but certainly something more useful than you are now."

More plants backed away.

"Trust me," Joran continued. "It will be worth the risk and pain of uprooting."

Like a stampede, dozens of plants turned and rushed through the grass as if blown by a storm. They huddled in the distance, crying out in a jumble of fearful laments. One small plant, however, stayed—Zohar. Trembling, Zohar reached out a side stalk. "I will come."

"Good," Joran said. "Do you have a name?"

Zohar shook its pod. "Not a real name. They call me Wilt, because I am so weak."

"It is true," Mendallah said. "It is an unkind name, but he is weaker than most of the male plants."

"That doesn't matter even a little bit." He gave "Wilt" a brief head bow. "May I call you Zohar? It means radiance."

"Yes," Zohar replied, copying Joran's head bow. "I am honored."

Joran wrapped his fingers around Mendallah. "Are you ready?"

Mendallah closed her eyes. "Take me from this fetid soil, good master, and set me free. It is better to suffer and die than to be rooted in this valley of death."

Joran pulled. As Mendallah rose from the ground, two long roots, thick and black, emerged. They appeared to be legs with the last inch angled like a foot. He set Mendallah on her "feet" and tried to steady her legs, but her entire structure collapsed in a heap of stalks and roots.

"Are you all right?" Joran asked.

Mendallah didn't answer. With her eyelets closed and indigo draining from her pod, she appeared to be dying.

Joran fell back to his seat. What had he done? Instead of helping the poor plant, he had brought her to death's door.

"Take *me* now," Zohar called.

Joran pointed at Mendallah. "Didn't you see what happened?"

"She has been set free from this corrupted soil. Perhaps she will recover." He reached his stalk farther. "Take *me* now."

"Okay, I'll—" A crackle sounded, and the smell of smoke drifted by. Joran looked to his rear. Less than thirty paces away, a waist-high wall of flames raced toward them, running parallel with the red viewing wall. Plants fled in front of it. Some started behind Joran and waded past, like humans would through water, trudging while pumping their side stalks furiously. Tongues of orange devoured every blade of grass in the fire's path. One flaming tongue shot out and engulfed a fleeing plant. It screamed but quickly fell silent as its spindly stalks vanished in puffs of gray smoke.

As a wave of heat rushed over Joran, he grabbed Zohar by his side stem and ripped him out. He laid Zohar and Mendallah on the lyre, and, hugging it to his chest, ran parallel to the viewing wall. Behind him, more cries arose, the dying shrieks of wayward plants.

Joran looked over his shoulder. The fire raged closer, growing taller as it closed the gap. The wall to his left pulsed red, like a warning flag signaling danger. Ahead, yellow grass went on and on with no shelter in sight.

Heat scalded Joran's back. He pumped his legs harder. His muscles cramped. His lungs ached. Finally, he toppled forward. The lyre flew to his side and, as he slid in the grass, it fell behind him. With a quick twist, he lunged for it, now within inches of the fire, but as he jerked it away, the two plants fell off. The fire engulfed them and burned onward, blocking them from view. Mendallah and Zohar were gone.

329

CHAPTER

A Hand of Mercy

Joran leaped to his feet and, ducking his head and pulling the
lyre close, reversed course and ran through the fiery wall. Once
on the other side, he scanned his body. The flames singed his
sleeves but nothing more.

Near his feet, Mendallah and Zohar lay on green grass. Fire
had caught their leaflets and crawled across their stalks. Joran set
the lyre down and batted at the licking orange tongues, but his
waving hands just fanned the flames, making them flash bigger
and brighter.

Yet, instead of dwindling in the fire, the plants began to grow.
As both stretched, their indigo and violet skin transformed into
flesh tones, Mendallah's much darker than Zohar's. Their leaves
altered from plant material to cloth and wrapped around them in
knee-length tunics. Mendallah grew long, stiff hair and took on
the body shape and facial features of a human woman.

Soon, the flames died away. Mendallah opened her eyes and
climbed to her feet. With sepia skin and muscular frame, she tow-

ered over Joran like one of the Nephilim. Zohar also rose. No taller
than Selah, his pale complexion and sparkling blue eyes matched
Seraphina's, and his hair, collar-length and as white as chalk, resembled the hair of the girl who watched the embryonic plants as Mardon threw them into the fire. He seemed to be about Selah's age,
perhaps a year or two older.

Mendallah wrapped her arms around Joran, lifted him off his
feet, and twirled in place, laughing with a bellowing howl. As the
spinning continued, Zohar clapped his hands and shouted in a
strange language.

Finally, Mendallah set Joran down. Dizzy but smiling, Joran
picked up the lyre and looked at the strings. From left to right,
they carried all but one color of the spectrum—a violet E, an
indigo F-sharp, a blue G, a yellow B, an orange C, and a red D.
Only the middle string, the A note, lacked color.

Joran raised and lowered his feet in the green grass. Except for
the red wall to the left, and the marching fire now well in front,
the verdant meadow spread out as far as the eye could see.

Strumming the A, he summoned Selah and showed her the
two rescued plants. After introductory bows among the new
acquaintances, and a quick explanation of recent events, Joran
looked at Mendallah and Zohar in turn and studied their faces.
Zohar's skin carried the fairness of Seraphina's, perhaps even paler.
His nose seemed as small as a child's, and his eyes shone so blue,
they looked like the sky on the clearest of days. Mendallah's nose
flared, and as her full lips stretched into a smile, a breeze tossed
her wild, wiry hair. They both bore the aspect of people who possessed great knowledge and wisdom. These two had been close
enough to Timothy's viewing wall to watch and listen to all the
events portrayed there day after day. It was no wonder they could
understand so much and speak so well.

Joran smiled at his two traveling companions. "With the grass
so green now, I'm wondering if we're already in the green ovulum."

"It could be," Mendallah said, her voice deep and melodic. "Shall we explore?"

Zohar pointed at the flames, still moving ahead, perhaps fifty paces away. "May I suggest that we follow the fire?"

"Agreed." Still playing Selah's string, Joran walked parallel to the red viewing wall on his left, while Mendallah lumbered at one side and Zohar stepped lightly at the other. The wall changed from red to a full-color scene, moving at their pace and allowing them to watch the action as it unfolded. It related the story of Second Eden and its founder, Abraham, the former Arramos. It told of a Second Eden resident named Angel, her adopted daughter Listener, and a usurper's attempt to gain control of the realm and force Angel to become his wife. Abraham turned into a wall of fire that encircled the usurper's territory and cut him off, and Angel joined Abraham in the flames, strengthening the protective barrier.

Joran glanced ahead. The flames continued burning, still advancing at the same pace. It seemed that hours passed, perhaps days. In this world of skewed perspectives, who could tell? How long had he and Selah been here now? Thousands of years? And, like Timothy, they had eaten no food, drunk no water, and slept not at all. All bodily needs seemed dormant, and only needs of the mind and heart stayed active. Not only that, ever since this newest journey began, he had plucked the A string almost continually without tiring. This place never ceased to grow more puzzling.

333

Soon, the wall of fire stopped, as if waiting. When Joran, Mendallah, and Zohar drew close, words emanated from the flames. "You have arrived at a new portal, a gateway to the purity ovulum." The voice sounded like a blend of two, both male and female. "Yet, you are unprepared for the next step in your journey."

Joran straightened himself, squaring his shoulders. "What do I need to do to prepare?"

"You must watch one last event on the wall, a story involving Elam and his two traveling companions. One is a horse named

Dikaios, and you will recognize the other. We do not expect you to fully understand the significance of this story immediately. It will take some time to digest."

Joran turned toward the wall. "That sounds easy enough."

"So you say." The flames drew back a few paces. "When the scene fades, come close to us again."

On the wall, a young man appeared, reclining on his back in a meadow of green grass and red flowers. Beyond him, a horse lay on its side, apparently asleep as well.

Joran stepped closer, reciting their names—Elam and Dikaios. He had seen Elam before, but not this close.

To the right, a small woman crawled toward Elam on hands and knees. Her chest heaved, as if she were gasping for breath. She wore an oversized cloak, its hood back, exposing her dark hair and hungry eyes. As she drew near, she opened her mouth wide, exposing a pair of fangs.

334

Joran gulped. Naamah! He wanted to shout a warning, but, of course, it would do no good. It seemed that Naamah had ignored the command to sin no more, and now she was ready to plunder another innocent soul.

Laying a hand softly on Elam's chest, she set her mouth close to his neck, ready to bite. Then, she paused, an odd expression on her face. Concern? Remorse? She was difficult to read. Finally, she drew her mouth away.

Elam's eyes opened. He jumped to his feet and stepped back, shouting, "What do you think you're doing?"

Dikaios leaped up. "What? What did she do?"

Joran gasped. A talking horse? Could this be real?

Naamah straightened, her cheeks flushed scarlet. "I ... I was trying to get close to you. I woke up all alone, and I was scared, so I wanted ..." She covered her face with her hands and wept.

"She was after your life's blood!" Dikaios yelled. "She was using her harlotries to seduce you so she could steal your eternal life for herself!"

Elam glared at her. "Naamah? Is that true?"

Staying on her knees and clasping her hands, she shuffled toward him. "No, Elam! Please believe me. I just wanted to be close to you. You're the only one who ever showed me any mercy." She grabbed his ankles and bowed low. "I confess that I thought about stealing your life while you slept, but I didn't do it. Even as my lips drew near to your throat, I changed my mind and decided just to rest at your side." She wiped his sandaled feet with her hair. "Please forgive me!"

Dikaios wagged his head. "The only reason she didn't steal your life is because you awakened before she could strike! She has used your goodness against you, Elam. She gained your trust only to get close enough to drain your life. She is the worst of harlots! She is a deceiver! A betrayer!"

Elam stepped back, pulling free from Naamah's grasp. "What should I do?"

"The harlot must die. If you let her live, she will only seek your life again. She is insatiable and can never change." Dikaios kicked a stone near Elam's foot. "You must do away with her. Stone the wretch and cast her into the eternal fire."

Elam picked up the fist-sized stone. As he tightened his grip around it, he glared again at Naamah. "You have been a deceiver all your life. You tortured both Sapphira and me and lots of other laborers in your slave pit. Give me one good reason why I shouldn't do what Dikaios says!"

"No, Elam!" Naamah raised her folded hands. "You must believe me! The angel said a man would cover me and offer me life. Other men came by, but they did the opposite. They talked of Jesus, but it wasn't the Jesus I knew. It wasn't the Jesus I met in Palestine. He offered me freedom from Morgan's spell, but I refused. He was kind and gentle, not like those fools. They mistreated me and counted me as nothing but a harlot, a worthless harlot."

Her eyes grew wide, and she gasped for breath. "But you … you covered me, so I knew you were the one who had life. All I

335

had to do was somehow get it, but I thought when I came to the mountain face I would be unable to make the drawing change, and you would send me away. So, in my vain imaginings, I wondered if I could take the blessing before you learned of my inability to serve you. But I didn't do it, I …" She lowered her hands and gazed at him. As tears dripped down her chin, she curled into a trembling ball. "I *am* still a foolish harlot. Do to me what you must. Even for thinking about betraying you, I deserve worse than stoning."

Dikaios nudged Elam's arm. "She has finally spoken the truth. Take back your cloak, which she has defiled with her filthy body, and cast her into the Lake of Fire. One stone well-aimed will take care of this witch once and for all!"

As Naamah trembled, a melody poured from her lips—lamenting, forlorn, and plaintive.

336

O who will wash the stains I bear
The harlot's mark of sin I wear?
Exposed and shorn of all I prized,
And now I beg for mercy's eyes.

O Jesus, look upon my strife
And spare this foolish harlot's life.
I bow, surrender, pour my tears;
Forgive my sins and draw me near.

She finished with a whisper. "However many moments you allow me to live, Jesus, I will go and sin no more." Then she covered her head with her hands.

Joran looked at Elam for any sign of change. Since he didn't have a Listener's ears, he likely didn't hear Naamah's final whisper. And he probably had no idea that she had sung the same tune after Jesus showed her mercy. No matter how beautiful the melody, no matter how many tears she shed, she didn't deserve to be believed.

Dikaios snorted. "Her words have proven vain, Elam! She cannot be trusted. Take your vengeance now!"

While Naamah shivered, Elam stood in front of her, glancing between the stone and the horse. Finally, as her tremors heightened, Elam dropped the stone and laid a hand on her back. "You asked me to forgive you, Naamah. Who am I to refuse?"

She looked up at him, wet strands of hair plastered to her dirty face. "Do you mean, you …?"

"I forgive you. That's really the only life I have to offer … yours."

Reaching out with trembling fingers, she took his hand and rose to her feet. When he released her, she stared at her palm, now smeared with blood. Her mouth opened, but she didn't speak.

Elam kicked the stone away. "You don't have to say anything. You don't have to do anything at all." He nodded at Dikaios. "If you will lead the way, good horse, I will follow. What Naamah does is up to her."

As Dikaios plodded away, Elam marched behind him, glancing back at Naamah every few seconds. She continued staring at her hand, and as the distance between them widened, the entire scene drew back to show their shrinking forms in the seemingly endless meadow.

Elam walked up a gently rising slope. When he reached the top, he and Dikaios halted. Still facing away from Naamah, Elam raised a fist and stared at it for a long moment. Then, turning slowly, he opened his hand and extended it toward Naamah.

She leaped up and ran toward him, her bare legs and feet kicking up the cloak's hem. As she narrowed the gap, the viewing wall brought the scene closer again, as if Joran and company were riding on a dragon and zooming toward them.

When she reached the slope's summit, she dropped to her knees. She grabbed his hand and kissed his palm, crying, "You won't regret this, Elam. I promise, you won't regret your mercy."

337

He raised her to her feet and looked into her eyes. "To be wanted and not lusted for. To be loved and not pitied. To be asked and not commanded." After passing his fingers over her tangled hair, he slipped his hand into hers and touched their palms together. "Is that right?"

Her cheeks flushed, and a shy smile emerged. Her white teeth dazzled, now void of fangs. "And to be believed, even after all my lies."

As the two walked on, now hand in hand, the wall faded to red, then to white.

Joran backed away a step. Elam believed her! Even after she was ready to bite him with those devilish fangs, he still believed her!

"A beautiful sight to behold," Mendallah said. "I am thankful that someone believed in me enough to take my hand."

Zohar nodded. "I agree. If not for Joran's faith in what two feeble plants could become, we would have burned in the fire. Elam demonstrated the same kind of love and mercy."

"But ..." Joran pointed at the wall. "Didn't you see what Naamah was about to do?"

Mendallah smiled. "I saw. With such a flood of mercy overwhelming her, I doubt she will do it again."

Joran glanced between Mendallah and Zohar. Both had seemed helpless and worthless, but neither was as wicked as Naamah. Neither had conspired to kill his sister and steal her voice. Neither had threatened to bite the neck of a sleeping companion. It just wasn't the same. Still, Elam showed mercy when he was her intended victim. Why would he do that? She would probably just try again later.

He looked at Selah. With tears in her eyes, she looked back at him, saying nothing. She needed no words. Obviously she agreed with Mendallah and Zohar.

"Let's go." Joran strode toward the wall of fire, now several paces away. When he arrived with Mendallah and Zohar, he took in a deep breath and spoke to the flames. "What do I do now?"

The wall replied with the same blend of voices. "Did you understand the revelations provided by the wall?"

"Not all of them. Naamah mentioned changing a drawing and something about an angel."

"These were earlier events that are not crucial. You saw everything you needed to see."

Joran nodded. "I think I understood. My companions helped me."

"Very well. Now the three of you must jump through the fire to enter the purity ovulum."

Joran looked around at the field of green. "Where are we now?"

"You are on a path that would eventually lead to the green ovulum, but in order to understand the ultimate purpose of your journeys, you must first return to the land of white."

"What will happen in Second Eden?"

"Those who wish to overthrow the residents of Second Eden will be released, but these foul usurpers are merely fodder for the enemy who uses them for his evil designs. Your real enemy is gathering a much greater horde of trained warriors, and he plans to destroy the people of Second Eden. After that, he hopes to launch an assault on a portal leading to Heaven itself. It will be up to you and Selah and your two companions to cripple his forces."

As Joran continued plucking the string, he looked at Selah, Mendallah, and Zohar in turn. Although Mendallah was huge, she probably wouldn't be able to defeat more than five or six warriors at a time. "How can the four of us stop such a horde?"

"Simply follow the path set before you," the voices said. "Walk with faith and courage. Be willing to do whatever it takes to fulfill your calling, even if it means death." The voices lowered to a whisper. "Come closer, Joran."

Joran stepped within inches of the flames, warming his ear and cheek.

339

"The two whom you rescued from the yellow grass have been chosen to help you in the last ovulum. They cannot, however, travel to your world with you. When you complete the key, leave them in the green ovulum. They will be preserved there until God has need of them. Do not worry about their fate. They have learned patience and will be content."

"I understand." As Joran stepped back, he glanced at his former-plant companions. Both gave him hopeful looks, obviously ready to jump at his command. It would be a shame to have to leave them behind.

The voices in the flames continued, now loud enough for all to hear. "It is essential that you jump through now, for our flames will not harm you. Other flames can do you harm, so from this time forward, you must be wise in discerning those that heal from those that hurt."

"What about you?" Joran asked. "Will you let us know who you are?"

"You will learn all you need to know very soon. Go now."

Joran stopped playing the string. As soon as Selah disappeared, he nodded at Mendallah and Zohar. "Are you ready?"

Zohar clenched a fist. "I am."

"We will leap at your side," Mendallah said.

"Then let's go." Joran jumped through the flames. For a moment, a flash of orange blinded him, but when his feet touched solid ground, the orange faded away. He stood between Mendallah and Zohar in an expanse of pure white. Even the area behind him displayed no hint of the wall of fire.

He reached out but felt only empty air. Without the purity ovulum's shell to guide their way, walking in a straight line would be nearly impossible. Yet, what choice did they have but to try?

Joran opened his mouth to say, "Follow me," but no sound came out. He touched each of his companions and nodded in the direction he thought they had been traveling. Then, trying to show confidence in his gait, he marched into the whiteness.

Mendallah and Zohar caught up and walked with him, one on each side, both with smiles that exuded enthusiasm. It felt good to have these fellow travelers, two souls who had suffered for so long, not only through their fiery deaths in Mardon's domain, but also through countless years of hopeless stagnation. Now they had something to live for besides bare survival.

After what seemed like an hour, a line of green came into view, but not a small gateway this time. The line stretched from left to right as far as the eye could see, as if the purity ovulum's distant boundaries had melted away.

As they drew closer, the line deepened, expanding into a field of what looked like green grass. Even the sky directly above the boundary line altered from white to green, extending down to the far horizon.

"I wonder," Joran whispered.

Zohar turned toward him. "I heard you."

"So did I," Mendallah said.

341

Joran stopped at the edge of the grass and looked back into the whiteness. A high wall of flames crawled toward them, now crackling, as if devouring the silencing effect. Although there was no fuel for the flames to consume, they marched on, so tall there seemed to be no apex. The flames had a familiar color and consistency, more like dragon fire than flames that burned grass or wood.

He touched the lyre's A string. Dragon fire had often been a tool to release someone's spirit from a lyre. Maybe this was a gift from Elohim that could set Selah free. "This fire might be useful."

"Remember the warning," Mendallah said. "We cannot be sure that this flame will not harm us."

Joran kept his gaze on the fire. "I remember. We'll go in a minute."

High above, a flying man shot from the flames and zoomed past the boundary of white and green, smoke trailing from his wings. After a few seconds, he became a dark speck against the green sky.

"When the rats flee," Joran said, "you know the fire will burn."

"Shall we run into the field?" Mendallah asked.

"You two can go ahead. Now that we have sound, I want my sister to see this." Joran played the A string, again generating Selah's image. She paced back and forth, her head tilted downward. "Selah," Joran called. "Take a look!"

She stopped and gaped at the fire, now only twenty paces away. "What is it?"

"Could it be dragon fire?"

She took a step closer and leaned forward. "It certainly looks like it."

"Should I see if it will burn you out of the string? I can pull you away as soon as you're free."

Before Selah could answer, someone called from above. "Bonnie Silver!" The voice was low and growling, more like a dragon's than a human's. "Why must you be set aflame?"

342

Joran held the lyre close to the inferno. It drew so near, heat scalded his fingers, but he had to try. With Tamiel now in the green ovulum, this might be his only chance to set Selah free without the demon's interference.

Embedded in the wall of flames, the shape of a young woman appeared, as if she, herself, were on fire. At least a hundred feet tall, she lifted her head, stretching to breathe, her face twisting in pain. She called out, her voice tortured, punctuated with spasms. "My … my name … is Silver. All dross … is purged … and my body … is a living … illustration."

As the flames drew even closer, Joran pulled the lyre back. What could this vision mean? This young woman's pain, her passion, her resolve seemed to flow from her body, creating the fire, the heat, and the song—the song of the ovulum. "Dross is purged," he whispered. "That's what purity means."

Finally, the flames leaped toward them. Mendallah grabbed Joran and Zohar and jumped over the boundary between white and green and tumbled across the grass before rolling to a stop.

Joran looked back. No whiteness or fire met his eyes, nothing but green grass and a green sky. "The purity ovulum. It's gone."

"What does its absence mean?" Zohar asked.

Joran sat up and held the lyre in his lap. "I don't know. Enoch said he would hide the song in a mobile vessel, but why would the original vessel have to be destroyed?"

"Did the woman in the fire destroy it?"

"I think she was a victim. I heard another voice before she spoke. That was probably the torturer."

Zohar rose and brushed grass from his tunic. "Do you think it was Tamiel?"

Joran shook his head. "It sounded draconic, not demonic. Besides, Tamiel flew out of the flames right before I heard the voice."

"Well," Mendallah said as she climbed to her feet and helped Joran to his, "I assume we should explore this place."

"I think we have no choice." Joran plucked the lyre's A string again. "I'd better let Selah know we're all safe."

343

As always, the string sang out its lovely note, and a white aura expanded into Selah's form. Smiling, she turned as she looked at Joran, Mendallah, and Zohar. "I see we're all here, wherever here is."

Joran angled the lyre toward the sky. "This has to be the green ovulum. We'll soon have the key."

"Diligence," Selah said. "That should be easy for you. You never miss a detail."

"Details, sure. But diligence also means patience. I'm not always good at that."

"Mendallah and I know all about patience." Zohar thumped his chest with a fist. "I pledge my heart, my body, and my soul to the effort. No matter what it takes, we will get your sister out of that lyre."

Mendallah copied Zohar's chest thump. "I, too, will do whatever is necessary to rescue the maiden. You have my sacred vow."

As Joran continued plucking the string, he smiled and nodded at each in turn. "Thank you, my friends."

"Before you send me back to the string," Selah said, "remember that you can summon me with your voice. You might need me when your hands are busy."

"I'll remember."

"Call me if you need a song." Selah set her hands on her hips. "I'll be waiting."

"I will." Joran stopped playing, sending her image into oblivion. Clutching the lyre close, he scanned the field. Far in the distance, something moved. "You have a height advantage," Joran said to Mendallah. "Tell me what you see."

Mendallah set a hand above her brow. "A creature with wings. Perhaps a dragon. His back is toward us, so he cannot see us, but there are many humans beyond him who are looking this way. Still, we are likely too far for them to notice."

"A dragon is good news. Let's get closer."

"We must take care," Zohar said. "I have seen many evil dragons on Timothy's wall. We do not know this one's character."

Mendallah nodded. "He is right. We should approach with stealth."

"How are we going to approach with stealth? You're nine feet tall, and he has hair as white as pearls."

Mendallah lowered herself to her belly. "We can crawl. I am accustomed to being close to the dirt."

Zohar dropped down at her side. "Come, Joran. If the humans are focusing on the dragon, they might not notice our approach."

Joran joined them. Reaching around, he laid the lyre on his back and began to pull forward. "Let's go."

After crawling for several minutes, Mendallah lifted her head. "It is a dragon, to be sure. I have seen this one on the wall. He is dangerous, indeed."

The dragon stood about a hundred paces in front of them, still facing away. Tamiel stood next to him, facing in the same direc-

344

tion. Beyond those two, a horde of people looked on as the dragon's audience, roaring with approval every time he paused. At one side of the crowd, odd-looking metallic devices loomed taller than the people, some with long protrusions on top and others with birdlike wings, though stiff and always spread out.

"I see tanks and airplanes," Zohar whispered.

"Tanks?" Joran squinted at him. "Airplanes?"

"They are dread fighting machines that can kill with great skill and speed, and these appear even larger and sleeker than the ones I saw on Timothy's wall. Airplanes are metallic birds that fly through the air, and tanks shoot hard projectiles from those long cylinders. Such projectiles would put a hole through a dragon. If these men are enemies, they will overwhelm us."

"The carts with large wheels are chariots," Mendallah said. "The newer war instruments are closer to us, and the older ones are farther away."

Joran grabbed the lyre from his back and listened to the dragon's deep voice.

"Since Hades and Second Eden are now joined, you have the opportunity to leave the realm to which you have been condemned. You will march through Second Eden and assault the gates of Heaven itself. There you will satisfy your desire for revenge against the wrathful deity and his angelic host."

"Arramos," a man on a black horse at the front of the crowd shouted. "What kind of defenses will we encounter?"

Arramos laughed with a draconic roar. "The pitiful defenses in Second Eden consist of a small cadre of dragons and simpleton villagers. You will squash them like bugs."

"What about the angels in Heaven? They will not take kindly to a rude knock upon their door."

The dragon paused for a moment, giving Joran a chance to study the soldiers. The man atop the horse, wearing a suit of black metal rings, spoke with a voice that matched Devin's perfectly. Also clad in black armor, the men around him carried metallic weapons with protrusions similar to those on the tanks, and the bearers aimed them at an upward angle. Far behind them, other men carried shields, wooden spears, and bows.

"When you successfully take control of the portal to Heaven," Arramos said, "I will call a host of forsaken angels into battle. Between us and your weaponry, our opponents will not be able to withstand the onslaught. They are vulnerable. I know this from personal experience. You will see."

Devin bowed his head. "Very well. I agreed to allow myself to be pulled into this place, but the waiting is getting tiresome. How and when do we leave?"

"Semiramis, my servant in Second Eden, is holding this refuge in her hands, and she uses her arts to watch and listen for my signal. Since Second Eden's wall of fire is gone, all should be ready. Soon, she will break the ovulum, and you will all be cast into Second Eden in a cyclone of green mist. When everyone has assembled there, you will mount your attack.

"I aligned you so that the first wave will consist of the more primitive warriors. That way the residents of Second Eden will think they are the only force we can muster. If we sent the modern weapons first, they might flee into their wilderness, and we would never find them. It is essential that we snuff out every life there."

"Agreed." Devin guided the horse around, faced the other humans, and shouted, "Make ready!" The troops, arrayed in a rectangle of columns and rows, turned to face the green horizon, and Devin galloped to the front of the lines. About halfway between the closest and farthest row, a gap separated the two divisions—primitive and modern. From Joran's perspective, the war machines lined the left side of the modern division—seven tanks and three airplanes.

Joran gaped at the horde. Could he possibly corral them all? Maybe a more realistic goal would be to try to capture only the more modern troops. To do that he would have to carry a sound barrier to the left of the machines while running toward the horizon, turn right and run through the gap between the two divisions, cutting off the primitive troops, then run back on the right side and complete the circuit.

Arramos extended his neck, raising his head high and looking at the distant horizon. "Semiramis? We are assembled. You may open the ovulum whenever you are prepared for our arrival."

A feminine voice rumbled from the sky. "Soon, my master. All will be ready very soon."

Joran stood and waved for Zohar and Mendallah to join him. "No one's looking this way," he whispered. "We have to stop them."

"Stop such an army?" Mendallah asked. "How?"

"Diligence." Joran withdrew the rods from his pouch. "Zohar, you look like what Timothy called an Oracle of Fire. Supposedly, people like you can make things burst into flames."

"I have seen Sapphira do that," Zohar said. "I will try."

"Your first target will be Tamiel and then anyone else who tries to stop us."

Zohar laid a hand over his chest. "I will do what I can."

"Take the lyre and one of these rods," Joran said, handing them to him. "When I lift my rod with my left hand, you lift yours with your right. We're going to make the biggest trapping net ever. You'll be my anchor at the closer corner on the left side of the troops' rectangle. Do you understand?"

Zohar nodded. "Perfectly."

"Great." Joran grasped Mendallah's arm. "I will sing at a concussive level to keep the soldiers from retaliating, but it will affect only those on the opposite side of my sound barrier. If we get any resistance, I'm counting on you for brute strength."

She laid her hand over his. "My strength is yours to command."

A loud crack sounded. The ground shook violently, tossing them back to the grass. A jagged crack ripped across the horizon

347

directly in front of them, running parallel to the front row of troops. Rays of normal sunlight spilled through the widening breach and onto the field.

As Joran and his companions scrambled back to their feet, green mist spewed from cracks in the ground and crawled along the grass, raising a low hiss.

"The transporting mist!" Joran called. "Let's go!" He ran toward the army, stopped a few paces behind Arramos, and, locking elbows with Zohar, lifted a rod. Zohar did the same, holding the lyre in his left hand and the rod in his right. Mendallah lumbered past and stood in front of them, setting her feet and spreading her arms like a shield.

Touching the lyre, Joran sang out an A note, mimicking Selah's string. The lyre vibrated, and Selah appeared. She sang a warbling melody of notes, and Joran shifted to the lyre's other six notes, switching among them as he followed her rhythm. If this plan succeeded, he didn't want anyone absorbed into Selah's string with her. The song poured out like honey, spreading along the ground and eating away at the mist.

Tamiel whirled toward them. "Here they are, my master. Shall I create a silence barrier?"

"Let it be so," Arramos growled as he bobbed his head. "Then I will torch them."

21

CHAPTER

FORGIVENESS

Matt leaned back against the wall, sitting with his knees propped up. Bonnie sat to his left with a wing around his shoulder, while Billy paced the floor in front of them, stroking his chin. The eye bomb rocked from side to side a foot or so in front of Matt. He had long ago grown tired of kicking it across the cell, so he just let it roll wherever it pleased.

Still projecting dozens of laser beams, it provided plenty of light, but it also had grown far more ornery, preventing them from talking about anything important. Whenever anyone tried to type something into the phone or whisper in someone's ear, the eye bomb let out its warning squeal, as if ready to detonate. Using encrypted speech had become too difficult, since the guards could probably figure out anything simple.

Still, one option remained, a slow option, but it worked, and while they sat close, Bonnie and Matt used it to full advantage.

Bonnie tapped Matt's shoulder, using Morse code.

As Matt read the combinations of short taps, long taps, and pauses, he pieced the words together. *How does this sound?*

Bonnie hummed a tune with her teeth clenched, making a buzzing melody. Her transmitter sent it to his own tooth, amplifying the buzz. He nodded. With Lauren's sensitive ears, maybe she could pick up the noise even with the jamming. If so, she might tune her ears to listen to a coded message ... if she understood Morse code.

"Dad," Matt said. "Take a break. Have a seat next to Mom."

Billy stopped pacing. "Just trying to limber up my legs. I sat in chains most of the time for fifteen years."

"Trust me. You need the rest."

"I'll take your word for it."

When Billy settled next to Bonnie, she wrapped a wing around him and began silently communicating their new idea. Matt buzzed "Happy Birthday to You" through his teeth, the first tune that popped into his head. After humming it twice, he clicked a coded message with his teeth. *Danger. They know you are here.*

After he finished, Bonnie took a turn, though she changed the tune to "Amazing Grace" before repeating the message.

Matt nodded. He knew the song. It certainly fit better than his choice. They would need all the grace they could get.

Billy prayed out loud, asking for rescue and giving a pretext for their hums. Even if their captors heard the songs, they probably wouldn't suspect anything.

Now all they could do was settle back and continue casting their transmissions into the sky, hoping someone would hear.

Zohar pointed at Tamiel and shouted, "Ignite!" Flames erupted on Tamiel's clothes. He slapped at them, but they continued to spread. He dropped to the ground and rolled in the grass, but every time the flames began to die, Zohar repeated his command, reigniting the fire.

As Joran held his note at a concussive level, a sound barrier stretched between the rods. This one didn't need to be designed for a specific demon's song. It just had to be powerful, and it had to thicken soon.

The soldiers dropped their weapons, clapped their hands over their ears, and closed their eyes tightly. Staggering, they bumped into each other, some dropping to their knees. Arramos blasted Mendallah with a fireball. Swinging her arm, the giant batted it away. Then, with a run and lunge, she leaped at the dragon, grabbed his neck, and wrestled him to the ground.

In the distance, the transporting mist rose into the middle of the primitive division and engulfed them and Devin in a green fog. The mist swirled and carried them out through the breach in the wall. All the while, Mendallah and Arramos continued to wrestle, both roaring, punching, and biting.

Joran stopped his song long enough to shout, "Let's go!" then took a breath and ran around the corner and along the left side of the rectangle, singing again with the rod held high. The barrier stretched almost to the breaking point, but when Zohar followed, the tension eased. Zohar stopped at the rectangle's closer left corner and stood with his feet set firmly and his rod high. Selah floated in front of the lyre, singing with all her might.

As Joran ran on, the distance between his rod and Zohar's lengthened, and the barrier thickened, allowing it to stretch safely. Since the barrier reached from the ground to the top of Joran's rod, it was over six feet high, plenty of height to corral everyone … he hoped.

The troops farthest away had already disappeared, and those remaining continued their pain-filled lurching, most with their eyes still closed. As Joran ran past the war machines, sparks jumped from the metal, creating a storm of arcing light. When he reached the far left corner of the rectangle, he turned right and dashed along the former gap between the troop divisions, following a path parallel to the fractured green shell. The swirling mist adhered to the sound barrier, making it shimmer with a reflective green coat.

351

After rounding the horde's far right corner, he ran away from the crack in the horizon and back toward where he had started. At the original closer right-hand corner, Arramos stood with a claw on Mendallah's back, pinning her to the ground. She struggled underneath, but with blood splotching her tunic and a broken arm flailing, she was obviously beaten. Tamiel stood next to Arramos, his clothing torn and scorched, and his face sooty, apparently too far from Zohar to catch fire again.

Arramos lifted his claw from Mendallah and shuffled closer to the troops. "Silence the singers!" he shouted in Joran's native language.

Tamiel followed, and opening his mouth, spewed a cloud of black fog that spread toward the wall of sound.

Joran never slowed. He circled around Arramos and Tamiel, hemming them in with the troops while leaving Mendallah, now lying motionless, on the outside. The dark fog drifted into the wall. Tiny holes appeared in the green fabric, and they quickly grew as the wall continued stretching.

His voice faltering, Joran churned his legs. If only he could get to Zohar before the barrier snapped, they could shrivel the troops or at least disarm them.

All across the mass of soldiers, sparks began to fly from the metal in their clothing. Many writhed in pain. Yet, their cries carried no sound. Fire arced everywhere, dissipating the green mist. Soldiers began falling in silence, their clothes aflame.

When he reached Zohar at the corner, Joran locked arms with him again. Selah, now on her knees, sang on, her body wobbling. She couldn't hold out much longer.

With holes still widening, the wall of sound closed in on the soldiers, pushing Tamiel and Arramos in. Tamiel's silencing mist had dispersed, and murmurs began to break through.

Wherever the sound barrier touched a war machine, its metal skin fizzled and dissolved into gray gas, leaving nothing behind.

The soldiers nearest the wall dwindled into scrawny, withered effigies. Their flesh sizzling and popping, the wall absorbed them, and the new energy ran in both directions, sealing holes along the way. Soon, the entire wall had healed.

Arramos beat his wings and flew up in a tight spiral. Then, with fire shooting from his nostrils, he dove toward Joran and Zohar.

"Raise the barrier!" Joran shouted.

He and Zohar lifted their rods high, touching them together to complete their shield. The flames splashed against it and arced over the top, but a few tongues snaked through and struck the singers. One plunged into Joran's tunic and set it on fire. Another knifed through the lyre's strings and jabbed Zohar, instantly covering him in a mantle of undulating flames, but he didn't cry out. He just held the lyre away from his body as tiny firelets danced across the strings. Selah collapsed, and the A string reabsorbed her image.

Joran batted flames from his tunic, sucked in another breath, and called out, "I'm reeling it in while it lasts!" He twirled his rod, making the sound wrap around it. As the wall tightened, more soldiers vanished. Plumes of gray gas flew upward, veiling the shrinking mob.

Arramos rose back into the air and zoomed toward the ovulum's breach, calling back, "Tamiel! Let these perish! We will conquer Second Eden with what we have!" Then, instead of flying out, he just disappeared.

Tamiel lifted off the ground and flew toward Joran, pointing a finger. "The mists that transport the ovulum refugees have been spent, so you will stay here forever!" He flew out of the ovulum, but, unlike Arramos, he didn't vanish. When he reached the outside, he called, "Semiramis! It is finished! Seal the ovulum!"

Like teeth closing around its prey, the upper and lower edges of the breach drew together until they clamped shut with a loud

353

click. Green light spread across the area, darkening the field. The sound barrier reeled into the rods and flowed into the lyre, still gripped tightly within Zohar's fiery hands.

As the vapor dissipated, grass came into view, now littered with shards of wood stripped from the soldiers' weapons.

Joran gasped for breath. His head and lungs ached. Blackness pulsed in his vision, painting dark shadows spreading out from the center. Only the flames coating Zohar and the glowing lyre stayed visible. With his blue eyes sparkling, Zohar smiled. "We did it."

"Yes." Joran coughed through heavy spasms, bracing his hands on his knees. Finally, he caught his breath again and looked at Zohar. "Yes, we did."

"I see Mendallah. She is alive. Her progress is slow, but she is coming this way."

Joran coughed once more. "I need to see if Selah's all right."

Zohar raised the lyre. Every string glowed so brightly, it seemed to be alight with the fire streaming from his fingers. Multicolored radiance rippled back and forth across the strings and played each note in rapid succession. The sounds emanated without pattern or rhythm, just runs of notes from low to high and back to low again, each one pouring out its spectral color, all seven, from red to violet, now in place.

"Pure energy." Joran set his hand close to the strings. They radiated warmth, tingling with greater intensity as his fingertips drew nearer. Unlike captured demons, the soldiers died before being absorbed. He probably didn't have to worry about dozens of prisoners in the lyre.

He touched the A string, now as green as the surrounding grass, and plucked it. "Selah? Are you in there?"

As if drawn by the vibration, light flowed from Zohar's hands and covered the string. The usual white aura formed around it, and it expanded and drifted to the front of the lyre. This time, the colors from all the strings blended with the white and painted Selah in rich color. She lay curled, as if asleep or unconscious. The exhausting singing battle likely knocked her out.

"Selah?" Joran called. "Are you all right?"

Her hand twitched, and her brow knitted, but the rest of her body lay slack.

"She is a daughter of music," Zohar said. "Perhaps you can awaken her with a song."

"There is a song …" Tears filling his eyes, Joran swallowed. "There is a song my older sister used to sing to me that was designed to bind our hearts as one, but I can't sing it again. It's just too painful."

Zohar tilted his head. "Painful? From what I have seen, you fear nothing."

"Fear nothing," Joran said, laughing under his breath. "If only you knew what I have done. I fear ghosts that haunt my dreams."

Zohar bent his brow. "If you are referring to the time you betrayed your older sister, I saw it with my own eyes."

Mendallah arrived, holding her broken forearm in front. "We both saw. Timothy's wall tells no lies. We have learned a great deal listening to the teachers there."

"And you still followed me?" Joran asked. "You risked your lives to help me?"

"Of course." Zohar extinguished his flames. "Who am I to take account of your past deeds when you have obviously forsaken them? To hold sins against a repentant soul is to block the river of mercy, the stream of life that flows to us when it is freely bestowed from us. When we pour out mercy to others, we refresh our own reservoir."

Mendallah knelt and looked Joran in the eye. "Your past is but a memory. Those who love you have erased its blotches. We see what is true now—light and love—not the darkness of days gone by."

Joran absorbed the giant's soft-spoken words, so rich, so filled with grace. She had indeed learned much from Timothy's wall.

Was this the same message the teacher uttered to Naamah when he said, "Neither do I condemn you?"

Relighting a single finger with a pulsing glow, Zohar pointed at Joran. "If you have received mercy, can you not find it within yourself to extend mercy to others, including yourself? Or will you continue to inflict stripes on your back and the backs of others?"

Joran laid a hand over his chest. The words pierced his heart, as if lancing a festering abscess. Drowning in his own guilt, he had tearfully begged for mercy's flow and found only a begrudging trickle from those he had so sorely wounded. Later, his mercy toward Zohar and the other plants had flowed at the same pitiful rate. And even now, his mercy toward Naamah was nonexistent, a dry riverbed, parched and thirsty.

Wrapping his fingers around his throat, he tried to swallow. The river's blockade was all too real, a stranglehold from his own hand.

356

He gazed at Selah. Her peaceful security seemed so beautiful, so perfect. Without memories of heinous sins, she slept undisturbed by nightmares conjured by a wicked past. She didn't feel what he felt. Even trapped within that lyre string, she was freer than he was.

Closing his eyes to hold back the tears, he whispered with a trembling voice, "Selah, it's all my fault. If I hadn't done what I did to Seraphina, none of this would have happened. How can I forgive myself when I don't know that she's forgiven me? How can I forgive Naamah when she has deceived with her words so many times before? How can I trust in the sincerity of a woman who has scorned trust all her life?"

A warm hand touched his cheek, bringing flickering light across his closed eyelids. "I know the answer, Joran."

He sucked in a breath. That voice! His legs wobbling, he straightened and turned around. Naamah stood before him, her face and white dress radiating light that bounced off the green walls, brightening the ovulum's interior. She looked up at him, tears sparkling in her eyes.

Joran heaved shallow breaths. "I thought it might be …"

"Seraphina. I know." Her lips quivering, Naamah kept her gaze fixed on him. "Her voice was restored to her in Heaven, so she was able to carry out this task, but since I also have her voice, God decided it would be better for me to deliver a message from both of us."

"A message?" Joran's mouth dried out. "What message?"

Naamah reached deep into her throat and withdrew a tiny sphere of light, so brilliant, its radiance outshone Zohar's flames. Her own radiance dimmed, and as she held the sphere in her palm, a voice emanated, making it spark with each word.

"Joran, this is Seraphina. I am speaking to you from Heaven. It has been many years since we hunted demons together, and now Naamah and I will help you slay the demon you have allowed to bind your heart."

He set a hand around his throat again. The stranglehold tightened, choking off his air supply.

The sparks continued. "Ever since she arrived in Heaven, Naamah has used my voice to sing glorious praises to God, and she cherishes every second as she tries to give thanks for all the mercy she has received, but now she sees that her stolen gift stands between you and your freedom, so she is willing to become mute for all eternity."

"You mean …" Joran swallowed. He couldn't manage another word.

"Yes, Naamah is giving my voice back to you. If you ingest it, you will be able to sing Selah out of the lyre. Naamah asks for nothing in return, praying that you will find peace when at least one sister is able to sing at your side. That peace will be her solace as she kneels in front of Jesus in silent adoration. To her, your mercy, your forgiveness, is more precious than her song."

357

His hand shaking, Joran pinched the sphere and stared at it. What a priceless treasure! Sacrifice, love, a plea for peace and reconciliation! Naamah offered this gem, this incomparable gift, to a blind, ignorant boy who couldn't see past his own guilt to believe in the repentance of another. There was no greater treasure than this, not the gift itself, but rather the giving ... and the forgiving.

Who was he to deny her sincerity? Who was he to say that a murderess cannot beg for blood to be washed from her hands, that a harlot cannot rend her filthy garments and receive a gown of white? How could he withhold from her the gift that he had received but did not deserve?

Joran let the tears flow. This former harlot, this diminutive warrior for peace, had vanquished his wrath.

"Naamah," he said softly. "Are you saying that this is mine to do with whatever I wish?"

Wiping tears with her knuckles, she nodded.

"And you will gladly agree to do what I ask?"

Again she nodded.

"Then open your mouth."

Her brow shot upward, and her lips formed, "What?" though no sound came out.

Joran touched her chin. "Please, just do as I ask."

Her entire body shaking, Naamah opened her mouth. Joran placed the sphere on her tongue and, pressing a finger under her chin, pushed her mouth closed again. A new glow radiated from her face.

Placing his hands on her cheeks, he kissed her forehead. "I forgive you, Naamah, and I hope you will forgive me for withholding mercy from you. I should have believed you, even after all your lies."

She threw her arms around him and pressed her cheek against his chest. "I forgive you! Oh, dear Joran, I forgive you with all my heart."

358

Joran ran a hand across her shiny dark hair. "Who forgives me? Naamah or Seraphina?"

"Both of us!" It seemed that two voices spoke together. "We both forgive you."

Like a river breaking through a crumbling dam, cooling relief flooded his body, washing away anger. The scalding heat of self-hatred sizzled and evaporated. He kissed the top of Naamah's head, the same head he had hoped to crush not long ago. This harlot had become a heavenly angel, an object of scorn transformed into a vessel of mercy. As he held her, it truly felt as if he embraced an angel—tingling, airy, brimming with warmth and delight.

Naamah's heart thumped in a methodic cadence, more consistent than any heart he had ever heard, as if she had taken Selah's role of setting the rhythm for a song. As with her voices, it seemed that two hearts beat as one. She whispered, her blended voices musical and breathy. "Your trials are not over, Joran. Much time has already passed since the armies left this place, and your tormentor carries this ovulum. Tamiel hopes to use you for his devilish purposes, so you are still quite valuable to him."

359

"I understand," he whispered in return. "What should I do now? Tamiel said the mists are spent."

"He spoke the truth. If you try to leave too early, you will perish. So you must wait for the mists to replenish. From now on, the time here will match the time outside, though you will not age or have need of physical sustenance. Use your captivity wisely. Prepare. Allow Zohar and Mendallah to teach you the history of the world as well as the modern languages. When the right time comes, you will be strong enough to break open the ovulum yourself. Listen for the call of desperation, the cry of one in a prison of her own. When you feel her danger, it will ignite the passion you need to play the key you have collected on the lyre."

Joran looked at the lyre in Zohar's grip. The seven colors shimmered, bright and vibrant. "What song do I play?"

"One that you will compose while you wait. Trust me. It will come to you."

"What about Selah? How do I get her out of the lyre?"

Naamah pulled back and, grasping his shoulders, looked into his eyes. "The flow of mercy has released you. Now release your spirit from the cage you have constructed. Let your real voice out. Allow it to fly as freely as a liberated songbird, and like a songbird, it will spread the joy of deliverance to everyone who hears. Your song can now loosen every bond, unlock every prison, set free any captive. Now you are not merely a Listener; you are a Liberator."

Stepping back, Naamah called out, "Sing now, Joran! Sing with all the passion in your heart!"

The scene in the misty woods roared back into Joran's mind. Those were the same words Seraphina uttered so long ago, the command he ignored, leading to her murder. The nightmare that haunted him for so long was finally coming to an end. This time, he would answer the call.

He looked at the lyre, still glowing in Zohar's hands. Selah slept on, her face pale in the midst of the spectral brilliance. The strings cast colorful stripes across her body as if fashioning a cage of hues ranging from crimson to purple. Reaching out, Joran passed his fingers through her image. He touched the A string and sang out its note. The string vibrated, returning the sound into the air and through his body.

Selah pushed against her invisible floor and rose to her feet. "Joran! You're alive!"

"True, dear sister," he said, tears again brimming. "You have no idea how true it is."

She looked up. "I see we're still in the green ovulum."

"For a while, maybe a long while. We have to stay and learn the modern languages from Zohar and Mendallah." Joran turned to introduce Selah to the resurrected Naamah, but she was gone.

"Selah," he said, turning back to her.

She looked directly at him. A fraction of her usual size and now flush with color, she appeared to be a doll come to life. "Yes, Joran?"

"I want to sing a song for you."

She gave him a tired, weak smile. "Shall I set the beat once I hear the beginning?"

He shook his head. "I know the beat. It matches the rhythm of my sisters' hearts, all three of them."

"Three?"

"You, Seraphina, and Naamah."

She cocked her head. "Naamah?"

"Yes. I'll explain later." While Zohar held the lyre, Joran began humming the tune. With each note, the corresponding lyre string played. Then, as he gazed at Selah, the words came to mind, sung in Seraphina's lilting voice. Of course he would have to alter them for singing to a sister rather than a brother, as well as for the differing circumstances, but that would be easy enough.

After taking a deep breath, he sang.

361

When Mother cried with labor's pangs,
Her torture pierced my lonely heart;
Would she survive to meet the dawn,
Or bid farewell, her soul depart?

O why do blessings come with pain;
The shadows cast with every light?
I prayed for comfort, not a trial,
And not another lonely night.

My heart needs a friend.
Is it you? Is it you?
A friend who will stay
To the bitterest of ends.

Is it you? Is it you?
I prayed for you then, and I pray for you now.
O come to my arms, and with you I vow
To sing out with love, to sing out with cheer,
To sing for an end to this hatred and fear.

Then with the morning's healing rays,
My father sat upon my bed
And he laid a bundle in my arms.
"Your sister needs a name," he said.

"A name?" I asked in disbelief.
"Has mother flown through death's dark door?"
"She has flown," he whispered soft.
"She wants you with her evermore."

362

The lyre pulsed with color, and Selah drifted farther from the
strings. Smiling through her flowing tears, she locked gazes with
Joran, and with every word he sang, she stretched and grew.

Then I saw your eyes so dark and wide,
And I knew what God had done.
He brought the friend for whom I'd prayed.
I whispered, "Selah, now we're one!"

My heart has a friend.
It is you! It is you!
A friend who will stay
To the bitterest of ends.
It is you! It is you!
I prayed for you then, and I pray for you now.
And wrapped in my arms, this is still our vow,
To sing out with love, to sing out with cheer,
To sing for an end to this hatred and fear.

Together we'll rise to the highest of peaks,
Interlacing our hands in the darkest of holes.
As one we will sing of the caretaker's love
And weave sibling hearts into unified souls.

As he breathed out the final note, Selah's feet touched the grass, and she solidified, now standing at her normal height. The lyre's spectral lights faded. Only Zohar's fire remained, covering Selah with a flickering yellow glow.

She leaped into Joran's arms. "You did it! I knew you could!"

"Selah!" he whispered. "You're back!"

"And you're back, too." She kissed his cheek and held him close. "We've both been set free."

Joran pulled away and gripped her arms, still hard and lean. It was so good to hold his flesh-and-blood sister again! Leaning his forehead against hers, he whispered, "You never gave up on me. Thank you for that."

"You're welcome." Grinning, she poked his chest with a finger. "Now we'll test our diligence another way."

"Another way? How?"

"Learning languages, and . . ." She nodded at Mendallah as she supported her broken arm. "Fixing a Naphil instead of slaying one."

363

CHAPTER

A Knight Disguised

A noise pierced Lauren's brain. She blinked her eyes open and touched her jaw. An electrostatic buzz shot stinging pain through her teeth. What could be causing it this time?

She listened. What was that? A song? Yes, someone was humming through the tooth transmitter, but static kept interrupting, making it difficult to tie the melody together.

A clicking noise replaced the hum. It seemed to have cadence, like a code of some kind. Walter had mentioned using Morse code when trying to talk to Matt. Could he be doing that now? If so, it wouldn't do any good. She knew the code for an SOS signal but nothing more.

She looked around. At the stairway's landing below, the window in the door no longer provided light. With the power outage, maybe they had to conserve energy. The generators couldn't last forever.

Lauren lifted away from the wall. A man's voice filtered through and rose to her ears, but it was quiet, distant, and static cut out so much, his words didn't make sense.

365

While looking toward the darkened door, she whispered, "Can anyone hear me?"

More clicks and more static droned through the transmitter.

Picking up the gun, Lauren climbed to her feet. The humming sounded like a woman's voice, so maybe Bonnie was trying to contact her, meaning that the first voice was probably Matt's. Either way, one fact seemed clear—they couldn't communicate freely. If they were trying so hard to disguise the message, apparently they thought delivering it was crucial. It was probably best to stay awake and alert.

She rubbed her thumb along the gun butt's smooth surface. She couldn't hold off everyone on a military base with such a feeble weapon. And killing that other guard was so repulsive she could never do it again. Yet maybe just the threat would keep someone at bay for a little while and give the dragons enough time to show up.

A beam of light appeared through the window on the level below. The door creaked open, and a man holding a flashlight stepped through. He pointed the beam downstairs and waved it from side to side.

Lauren lifted the gun with both hands and aimed it at him. As violently as she was trembling, how convincing could she be?

The beam shifted and struck her directly in the face, blinding her. "Point that light away from me right now!" she shouted.

The beam dropped to the floor. "Lauren Hunt?" The man's voice was deep and carried a kind tone, accented with a British flavor.

"Who wants to know?"

"Miss Hunt, you have no need to fear. I am here to help you."

Her hands dampening, Lauren regripped the gun. "Like I'm supposed to believe that."

"Walter Foley said he told you he has a spy planted here." He shone the beam in his own face. "I am that spy."

Lauren eyed him as closely as the distance would allow. He appeared to be Hoskins, the same man who caught her for Semiramis and then led the German shepherd. But he didn't have a British accent before. Could he have been disguising it? "How can I be sure you're telling the truth?"

"Well, if I weren't the spy, I wouldn't know about me, would I?" The man's expression twisted in confusion. "I hope that made sense. When it comes to words, sometimes I am like a fish out of a water hole."

She lowered the gun but kept it firmly in her grip. This man seemed friendly but not quite polished enough to be a spy. His fractured idioms could make people suspicious. "What's your name?"

"Officially, I am Sergeant Daniel Hoskins, but that's not my real name."

"Okay, so what can you tell me to prove you're on my side? You could be making up the spy thing, or maybe you caught a spy, and you're pretending to be him."

He charged up the stairs. Lauren slipped and fell backwards, smacking her bottom and back on the edge of a step. As her gun went off, the man snatched it out of her hand. He wrapped her up in a powerful arm, lifting her as he held her in a vise grip.

Lauren kicked and squirmed, but it did no good. Hoskins was just too strong.

"Now if you will stop acting like a scared rabbit, I will prove who I am."

Lauren grunted. "What do you mean?"

He set her down and slowly released her. Then, turning the flashlight back on himself, he placed the gun in her hand. "My real name is Winston Barlow. My friends just call me Barlow, or Sir Barlow. And I am at your service."

She stared at the gun, then at the guard's smiling face. Yes, he was Hoskins. Even in the dark, his crow's-feet were evident.

367

"Okay, I'm convinced." She pushed the gun back into his hand. "If you don't mind, Sir Barlow, I would feel a lot more comfortable if you carry it."

"By all means. Better safe than sound."

"You mean, better safe than sorry."

"Yes, of course." He slid the gun behind his waistband, revealing a paunch, but his broad chest and shoulders seemed to minimize it. "Now, speaking of safe, if you'll follow me, I will put you in a safe place. When the dragons arrive, there won't be many safe refuges anywhere."

As he walked down the stairs, Lauren followed. "How long have you been here?" she asked.

"One week. It took years to establish my identity and get transferred here."

"So why did you catch me for Semiramis?"

"I had no choice at the moment, but I was watching over you. Didn't you see me when I was leading the shepherd in front of the research wing?"

"I did."

"I saw you, as well, and I tried to keep the other guard distracted so he wouldn't see your, shall we say, glowing personality."

Lauren touched her cheek. "Thanks. It's something I can't stop."

"As I suspected. In any case, I hoped to keep everyone away from Matt while he broke into the building, but when you attempted an escape, I couldn't hold them off without compromising my identity. Fortunately, I was the one shooting at Bonnie as she and you flew away. The darkness served as a good excuse for my poor aim."

When they reached the main floor, a dim light shone through the door's window. Sir Barlow lifted a key ring from his belt. "I see that you already have handcuffs. Please allow me to fasten the loose one. I have the key and will unlock them at the appropriate time."

Lauren extended her arms, allowing Sir Barlow to cuff her wrists together.

"This will open your cell door," he said, holding up a key, "and you will have it soon, but use it only if necessary."

"If necessary? How will I know?"

"When the dragons attack, your cell will be your refuge, but if the building catches on fire or begins to collapse, I suggest that you leave at once."

"Good advice."

Sir Barlow pushed a mobile phone into her hand. "Hide it well. It could be helpful in the direst circumstances. Act as though you are being watched at all times."

"Okay." Lauren slid it into her pocket.

"And you will have company, so the two of you can decide such matters together."

"Company? Who?"

"You will see. I will make the appropriate introductions when you meet." Sir Barlow withdrew his gun and opened the door. "Walk in front of me and pretend to be upset, angry, furious, whatever will make you appear to be my prisoner. Just follow the hallway to the left and turn when I tell you."

"I can do that."

Bending her face into a scowl, she walked through the door and turned left. A line of at least twenty soldiers passed by, marching in the opposite direction. Holding rifles and wearing anxious expressions, a few glanced at her, but her glare worked to slap their probing eyes away.

When the last soldier passed, she looked over her shoulder. Where might they be going? They seemed worried about something.

As she continued walking, Sir Barlow pulled a radio from his belt. "This is Hoskins," he said, again disguising his accent. "I have apprehended the missing girl. I will take her to a cell for safe-keeping."

369

"Good work," a scratchy voice replied. "Which cell?"

"I am taking her to A fourteen."

"A fourteen? Why?"

"To keep our dragon guests together, of course. It's easier to watch them that way."

"Okay. For now. I'll verify when the power comes back on."

After a series of turns, the hallway grew colder, as if ventilated from the outside. Lauren shivered. This place was frigid! How could anyone stand living in such conditions? Why would they treat prisoners so harshly?

Sir Barlow whispered, "Stop, please, Miss."

Lauren halted next to a prison door. Hallway light shining through the spaces between the bars provided a view of the inside. A woman dressed in jeans and a navy sweatshirt knelt low, her hands folded atop a thin mat and her forehead resting on her hands. From a high window, snowflakes blew in and settled to the concrete floor where they melted in a puddle. A toilet sat against the wall adjacent to the cell door, and a ratty yellow cloth hung from the ceiling by a series of hooks embedded in the plaster. Although drawn to the side now, the cloth was likely used as a privacy shield.

Sir Barlow inserted a key into a lock, turned it, and slid the cell door open.

The woman didn't budge. "What do you want this time?" she said. "Blood, tissue samples, or a vital organ?"

"A look at your face," Sir Barlow said, "is all I ask."

The woman jerked her head up and stared. Her eyes widened, and her lips formed an indistinguishable word.

"Ah! Yes. Thank you. I studied your photograph, and now I have confirmed that Ashley Foley is in this cell, though that bruise alters your appearance somewhat. Now I can proceed with my duty."

Ashley rose slowly to her feet, her lips trembling as she touched a finger-length bruise on her left cheek. She appeared to be ready to cry, but her tone remained sharp. "Who are you? We don't get many male guards around here."

"I am Sergeant Daniel Hoskins. I am not normally assigned to this wing, but because of the weather conditions and other concerns ..." He gave her an almost imperceptible wink. "I will be in the area for the time being."

"So you're bringing me a new roommate?" Ashley looked Lauren over. "Kind of young, isn't she?"

Sir Barlow unlocked the handcuffs and guided Lauren into the cell. "This is Lauren Hunt. I'm sure the two of you can get acquainted on your own."

Ashley raised her voice to a near shout. "What did you goons do with Bonnie?"

Sir Barlow tapped his finger on his temple. "I'm no fool, Mrs. Foley. I heard you can read minds, so I will guard our secrets carefully. My mind is a steel trap."

"Is that so?" Ashley set her hands on her hips. "Someday we'll all get to see who the fools are."

Sir Barlow bowed his head. "I must be going now, so—"

371

Ashley rushed at the cell door, but Sir Barlow caught her and wrapped her in his arms. He pressed Lauren's gun into Ashley's stomach, but Ashley turned the barrel back toward him. "Get that foul weapon away from me. You guards are all the same, bullying us around, and we can't even defend ourselves."

Sir Barlow shoved Ashley and sent her backpedaling until she fell and slid on her bottom. "That should teach you," he said, shaking a finger. "I am not a man to be trifled with."

Lauren rushed to Ashley and helped her to her feet. "Are you all right?" As she spoke the words, her back began to tingle, apparently incited by the drama.

Ashley brushed dust from her jeans, scowling at Sir Barlow. "Trifle is a good word for you."

"And petulant witch is a good word for you." He slammed the door and marched away.

"That's two words!" Ashley shouted as she peeked between the bars. When Sir Barlow was out of sight, she turned and grabbed

Lauren's upper arms. "Listen carefully. There's a camera and microphone in here, so they're listening to every word. They already know I can read minds, so it's not going to raise any alarms when I tell you that you can talk to me by concentrating your thoughts in my direction. Understand?"

After Ashley's lips stopped moving, the tingling sensation brought more words to Lauren's ears. *Please say you understand. You certainly don't look like a dummy.*

"I do understand," Lauren said. "And I'm no dummy."

Ashley's brow shot upward. "Did you just …"

Again thought-words came through. *Read my mind?*

Lauren nodded and directed thoughts of her own. *I think so. I'm kind of new at this. And it doesn't work all the time.*

"Very interesting," Ashley said out loud before reverting to thought-speech. *I read Sir Barlow's mind, and he said the people here think you're an anthrozil. Do you know what that word means?*

As each sound radiated from Lauren's back to her ears, she resisted the urge to shiver. It all felt so weird. *It means I'm part dragon.*

Do you have any other dragon traits?

I didn't know I had any at all. I do know I have great hearing sometimes, and recently my hearing has been picking up thoughts. I also sometimes glow in the dark.

Glow in the dark? Ashley looked her over again. *Okay, I think I can see it.*

This room isn't very dark, and I've been told my glow is pretty dim a lot of the time. I think it gets worse when my emotions are high.

Well, glowing is a new one on me, and mind reading is rare among dragons. In my case, I can't penetrate people's thoughts unless they're careless or they actually want me to know what they're thinking. So it can come in handy, like just now. When Sir Barlow and I tussled, that was an act. He spoke to me in his mind and said you know who he is and that he's on our side.

Yes, he told me. Lauren touched her ear. *For me the mind reading is more like hearing. I get a tingling sensation along my spine, and the sounds and thoughts ride up to my ears.*

Ashley gave her a quizzical look. *Along your spine?*

Lauren nodded.

Interesting. Ashley touched Lauren's back. *I have medical training. Will you let me feel your skin?*

Lauren's tingles spiked. *I … I suppose so.*

Ashley reached under Lauren's collar and felt the upper portion of her spine, pressing deeply and rubbing up and down. After a few seconds, she withdrew and straightened Lauren's jacket. *When was the last time you had a physical?*

Before volleyball started, maybe three months ago.

Did the doctor examine your back?

Just the usual stethoscope routine, you know, breathe deeply and cough.

Ashley tapped her chin. *Very interesting.*

What? What is it?

Brace yourself. Ashley looked into Lauren's eyes. *I think you have scales under your skin.*

Scales? As the word blazed through her mind, a sequence from her dream replayed, Enoch speaking to Joran as they stood outside the red ovulum.

God will raise up another Shachar who will be able to hear its song in her scales and locate it when it is needed. She will be in human form, so she will be quite vulnerable, because Tamiel has known about the Shachar prophecy for a long time.

"Human form," Lauren whispered.

"I heard that in your thoughts," Ashley said out loud. She then added her own thoughts. *I know who Shachar was, the first female dragon on Earth, but I didn't know about an ability to hear a song in her scales. I assume you think you're the one who inherited that ability.*

373

Lauren nodded.

Where did you learn all this?

I know it sounds crazy, but it was in a dream. This guy named Timothy mentioned Shachar, then someone else named Enoch mentioned her.

Timothy? Are you sure?

Yes.

And you've never heard these names before, right?

Right.

Ashley's thoughts mumbled something about hearing the dream's details later. She glanced away for a moment, her brow bending downward. *Could this hearing gift be a recessive trait? Neither of your parents has it.*

Did Sir Barlow tell you who my parents are? Lauren asked.

No, but it wasn't hard to figure out. Ashley grasped Lauren's hand. *Do the Bannisters know?*

I'm not sure. My twin brother is here, too, and they're all together in a cell on the lowest level. They know who he is, but I don't think they've made a connection with me. I told them I couldn't be Karen Bannister, so they might not figure out the truth. One of the guards shot Bonnie, so Billy and Matt are probably too busy to think about me. I don't know how she's doing, but she didn't look good.

Ashley sat heavily on the mat and stared at the floor. For a few seconds, a barrage of words flew from her mind, too many and too fast to register. Finally, she looked up at Lauren. *I have to get to her. I'm a healer.*

"But how?" Lauren whispered.

The reason I tried to run out the door a few seconds ago wasn't to escape. It was so Sir Barlow could plant a key in my pocket. He wanted to give me a gun, too, but I pushed it back. We wouldn't be able to hide it.

So we can leave? Right now?

Sir Barlow told me we're supposed to wait for the dragon attack. Ashley nodded toward a window above Lauren's head. *The guard*

374

who watches through a camera up there would be distracted by the attack, but I think we should try to go now. I need to heal Bonnie.

How are we going to leave without the guard seeing us?

Sir Barlow said you have a phone.

I do.

Ashley nodded toward the privacy curtain separating the cell from the toilet. *Go over there and set it down. If you need to use the toilet, now is a good time. Then come back here.*

Lauren pulled the curtain and stepped behind it. After using the toilet and laying the phone on the floor, she returned. Still sitting on the mat, Ashley looked at her as if projecting more thoughts. Lauren focused her mind on the pathway between her spine and her ears, but nothing came through. The tingling sensation had stopped. She touched her ear and shook her head, hoping to signal her loss of mental hearing.

"I understand." Ashley rose and walked behind the partition.

While she waited, Lauren scanned the room. With so little light available, she couldn't see much, but there wasn't much to be seen. The cell was a freezing, dismal concrete hole.

375

After a few minutes, Ashley emerged and strode to the wall, stopping under the window. She reached up and set the phone next to the camera at a point out of the lens's view.

As she returned to the bed, she stretched her arms and yawned. "We'd better get some sleep."

Lauren gave the phone and camera a furtive glance. "Okay, but I see only one mat."

"Bonnie and I sleep together. It's the only way to stay warm at night." Ashley took her by the arm. "Come on."

Lauren followed Ashley's pull and lay on the mat with her, back to back, her face toward the wall.

"Close your eyes," Ashley whispered.

Lauren complied. With their backs touching, the closeness fueled a sense of comfort and security. Warmth flooded her skin. It felt good to rest with a friend who understood what was going on.

As the combined body heat radiated up her spine, the tingling returned, and with it, Ashley's thoughts. *So I'm hoping you'll let me know when you can hear me again. It's no trouble to ramble on in my head like a mental chatterbox. With all that's going on, there's no way I could sleep—*

I can hear you, Lauren said in her mind.

Perfect. I'm letting the phone record us lying here. I erased the phone's video memory, so I'm hoping there's plenty of room.

Just let me know what to do.

Do you have any acting skills?

Some. I was rehearsing for the lead role in A Christmas Carol.

A girl playing Ebenezer Scrooge? That would take some skills.

Lauren held back a laugh. *Esmeralda Scrooge. It's an all-girl version. The director chose me in the audition, so I guess I can act.*

We'll find out. You're going to complain about getting too warm lying next to me. You'll get up, take off your sweatshirt, and throw it over the camera. Then stay near the window. I'll need a boost.

Will riding my shoulders do?

It should.

Now?

Whenever you're ready.

Let's do it. Lauren climbed over her and stood on the floor, staring at Ashley with her hands on her hips. "What are you, a human radiator? You're too hot."

"Just deal with it and go to sleep," Ashley said, yawning. "It's late."

Lauren stripped her sweatshirt over her head, exposing her bare arms. It was freezing, but shivering could end their charade. "This dump is worse than a cheap motel. Don't you have any place to hang your clothes?"

"This isn't the Hilton, my dear. Just toss it somewhere."

Lauren threw the sweatshirt over the camera.

"Not there!" Ashley barked as she jumped toward the window. *Boost me!*

Lauren crouched, and Ashley straddled her neck, one leg over each shoulder. While Lauren straightened, Ashley called out. "Sorry about that, Ms. Guard. Lauren's new here. I'll get the camera unblocked in just a second."

A muffled feminine voice sounded from under the sweatshirt. "Hurry up. All the other guards are occupied, and I'm in no mood to come down there myself."

"Almost got it." Ashley pulled two wires from the back of the camera and draped the sweatshirt over her shoulder. "Okay. She can't hear or see us now. After I plug the audio feed back into the security camera and the video feed into the phone, you can let me down. Make sure the phone camera sees you putting the sweatshirt back on. Then I'll fix it so that the video recording we made with the phone feeds back to them."

"Their video wire plugs right into the phone?" Lauren asked.

"My husband smuggled in a universal adapter, and I already installed it on their camera. Sir Barlow made sure the phone he gave you is compatible. We were hoping to do something like this, but he couldn't get a phone to me until now." Ashley covered the phone with the sweatshirt and plugged the video wire into the back. Then, after restoring the audio wire to the security camera, she whipped the sweatshirt away. "Got it loose!"

377

Lauren helped Ashley slide down and began putting the sweatshirt on in plain sight of the phone's camera. Standing on tiptoes, Ashley reached up and jiggled the phone. "Can you see us all right?"

"The picture is jumpy," the guard said.

"The sweatshirt probably put its balance out of kilter. Maybe you'd better hit the calibration reset."

"Good idea."

"Knock yourself out. We're going to bed." Ashley nodded at Lauren. *That was literal. The calibration should knock out the transmission for at least five seconds.* She punched a few buttons on the phone, pulled out the jail camera's audio wire, and settled back to her normal height. "If all goes well, she should see a loop of us sleeping peacefully, at least for as long as the battery lasts."

"I didn't notice the battery meter."

"It was fully charged. Sir Barlow knew what he was doing." Ashley pulled a key from her pocket and skulked to the cell door. After peering out to check the corridor, she reached between two bars, pointed the key toward the cell, and unlocked the door.

As she slid it open, she gestured for Lauren to follow. They tip-toed through the corridor leading to the stairwell. *Tell me which way to the place they're keeping Bonnie.*

How about if I go first? I'm beyond being scared of these wannabe Nazis.

Ashley stopped and smiled. *Lauren, you're my kind of girl.*

Thanks. You're pretty cool yourself. She touched her jaw. *I have a tooth transmitter, but the reception's been pretty bad lately. Should I try to contact your husband?*

When we're sure no one can hear us. For now, let's find Bonnie.

378

23

DRAGON WARRIORS

Walter paced back and forth, making a trench in knee-deep snow while wind drove stinging flakes into his cheeks. The dragons were due fifteen minutes earlier. Blizzard conditions must have slowed them down. The new portal from Second Eden lay nearly a hundred miles away in a wilderness area the computers thought undetectable by government monitoring systems. If the storm was this fierce between here and there, who could tell how long it might be before the dragons and their riders arrived?

He stopped and stamped his feet, trying to get circulation back into his toes. Wearing thermal everything under his coat and trousers, most of his body stayed warm, but his extremities had gone numb, probably from a combination of the cold and his recent back injury. Regardless of cold or injury, he had to charge in with the dragons and fight like a crazed warrior. Ashley was waiting, and no amount of pain or suffering could keep him away.

Walter set his lips close to his gloves and blew, making the warmth bounce back to his frozen cheeks. It would be great to have Matt's ability to stay warm. Was that a dragon trait? Could it be that Matt had his father's gift in a mutated way—heat expelled through his skin instead of his mouth? He shook his head. Ashley would be quick to dismiss that idea. The anatomical passages were too different. Of course, the dragons on Second Eden could generate heat through their scales, but Matt descended from Earth dragons, not Second Eden dragons. Could there be a connection between the two families somehow? Could the gene pool on Second Eden be allowing a recessive trait to flourish, while on Earth the trait stayed dormant until now? If the two families were connected, why did the Second Eden dragons lack the intelligence and verbal abilities of their Earth counterparts?

A voice buzzed in his jaw. "Any sign of them?"

"Not yet." Walter stared through the veil of blowing snow. Far in the distance over the flat terrain, a light blinked—Jared's helicopter waiting on the ground. "I can still see you. You might want to shut your lights off."

"I have to keep everything running. If anything ices over, we'll be in trouble. But don't worry. We're in the middle of nowhere. They'll be watching more obvious places to gather."

"Like a ski lodge?"

Jared laughed. "Something like that. I could use a fireplace and a mug of hot cocoa right about now."

"I know what you mean. When the dragons show up, I'm going to get one to toast my toes."

"How much longer are you going to wait? Marilyn's worried about your injury."

Walter kicked at the snow. "Jared Bannister, if Marilyn were locked up in that jail, how long would you wait?"

"Until I was a statue of ice."

"Exactly. So please tell your lovely wife that I—" A gust of wind sent him staggering forward. As he regained his balance, he stared at the sky. The gust was warm, not cold.

A growling voice sounded from behind him. "Turn around, dragon rider."

Walter spun in place. Makaidos sat on his haunches, blowing snuffs of orange-tinged smoke. Red beams shot from his eyes, and his ears twitched in the wind.

"Makaidos!" Walter reached out and stroked the dragon's neck three times, the usual protocol for greeting a dragon warrior. "Where are the others?"

"I found a sheltered refuge in a nearby forest," Makaidos said. "The dragons are warming the humans in preparation for attack. I will take you there and prepare you as well."

"Sounds great." Walter touched his jaw. "Jared, I'm going with Makaidos. I'll let you know when we have someone for you to transport."

Makaidos lowered his head to the ground, making his neck a staircase. After hopping over the shorter spines and dodging the longer ones, Walter settled at the base of Makaidos's neck. "I'm ready!"

381

With a beat of his wings, Makaidos leaped into the air. A gust pushed him down and to the side, but the mighty dragon battled back, flapping again and again until darkness and the shield of flakes blocked any further view of the ground below.

As the bumpy ride continued, Walter talked in spite of his chattering teeth. "Larry and Lois, have you heard from Lauren or Matt lately?"

"We are monitoring Lauren," Larry said. "It seems that a signal-blocking mechanism has been put in place at the prison facility. We are able to hear some of her transmissions, but she does not seem to hear us. Carly thinks she heard Sir Barlow's voice, but I am unable to verify any samples with his voiceprint."

Walter had to shout to hear himself. "If she's with Sir Barlow, that's great news."

"Unless they are both prisoners," Lois said.

Walter scowled. "Who installed a pessimism chip in you?"

"It is not pessimism. I calculated the probability of Sir Barlow's discovery and capture at sixty-three percent, so it is a reasonable assumption. The confidence interval is—"

"Don't give me statistics. I've beaten the odds too many times to think we're living by chance. Have some faith."

"Carly was working on a faith component in our estimate algorithm, but she abandoned the idea. She said something about a deity moving in mysterious ways that could not be measured."

"Exactly. That's the way it should be."

"I asked Lauren to report to me if she relocated," Lois continued, "and she has not done so. We should assume that she is still at the roof-access shelter."

Blinking at the icy crystals, Walter let out a sigh. "Thank you both. Let me know if you hear anything else important."

After a few minutes, Makaidos's eyebeams flicked on and pierced the nearly horizontal sheets of snow. His ruby lasers ran across a field of treetops before stopping at a gap in the foliage. Flying in a ragged circle, Makaidos descended toward the gap, again battling the gusts assaulting his body, first from one side, then from another as he continued orbiting.

Finally, he dropped below the treetop level and landed in a clearing, sliding on a thick blanket of snow. As soon as Walter jumped to the ground, a small blaze appeared at the entrance to a cave.

"Come and get warm!" Sapphira shouted from within the fire. Although covered in orange flames, her bright blue eyes and white hair shone as clear as ever. "Since we were late, I assume we have to launch the attack as soon as possible."

Pushing through the snow, Walter ran to the cave. As he drew closer, the silhouettes of other dragons and humans appeared just inside. Although cold wind knifed through his coat, the thought of blessed heat brushed the pain away.

The moment he arrived, he stripped off his coat and held it aloft. "If one of you kind dragons will dry this for me, I'll stay close to Sapphira and get warm."

"I'll hold it in front of Thigocia," a man said as the coat slipped away from Walter's hand.

Sapphira's flames cast light over the man's face—Elam, King of Second Eden.

Walter embraced him and added a pat on the back of his thick woolen cloak. "It's been a long time," Walter said.

"Too long, my friend."

Walter gazed at Sapphira. As stunning as ever with her bright blue eyes, white hair, and glowing face, he longed to embrace her as well, but her flames allowed only a close bow and a heartfelt, "It's good to see you again."

She smiled and curtsied. "To fight again alongside a warrior such as yourself is a blessing indeed."

"Are we ready?" Walter asked.

"We'd better be." Elam brushed ice crystals from his bushy hair with a gloved hand. "We have been training for a Code Red attack for a month, so when we heard about Lauren's gift, we were able to launch immediately. We are four dragons strong with a seasoned warrior for each back. We had hoped to include Karrick as a fifth dragon, but he was injured in training."

Sapphira slowly shifted a flaming hand from one dragon to the next, moving a flickering circle of light.

When Makaidos flew in and settled, Walter bowed and spoke to each of the other dragons in turn. "Thigocia, it will be an honor to go into battle with the queen of all dragons. Roxil, the fire in your eyes kindles my warrior's heart. And Legossi, it will be a pleasure to once again witness your aerial acrobatics." Walter raised a finger. "By the way, I spoke to Sir Barlow earlier today. He told me to ask you if you ever installed Velcro."

383

Legossi rumbled within, sounding like a purring tiger. "I hope to see that stellar dragon rider when we invade the prison, but if not, tell him that warriors who wear slippery shorts should not ride on shiny scales."

"I'll tell him." Walter counted the four dragons and three humans. "Who is our fourth rider? Valiant? Candle?"

In the light of Sapphira's flames, Elam shook his head. "Although those two wanted to come, birth residents of Second Eden must stay in Second Eden until we're sure we have an untraceable portal. Of course, since Tamara has been missing all these months, Listener begged to join us."

Walter nodded. Listener loved her Earth mother dearly and hoped for a chance to sneak into the Earth realm to find her. "She would've been a great choice. I hear she's a fully trained warrior now."

"She is brilliant," Elam said. "If the new portal proves to be secure, I'll let her come. But we have an excellent fourth warrior who has gone to the prison as a scout to see what kind of defenses they have."

"On foot? In this weather?"

"By wings, though I think the weather will hinder him while in the air more than it would if he were walking. . . ."

"Ah! Gabriel. Perfect." As Walter imagined his dragon-winged brother-in-law flying through the snow, a picture of Ashley shivering in her cell came to mind. Only Gabriel's passion to help her escape rivaled his own, and his willingness to leave his wife, Shiloh, and their children behind in Second Eden during such dangerous times proved his passion. "Which dragon do I have the privilege of riding?"

"That will be my honor." Thigocia lowered her head to the ground. "Go ahead and mount. When Gabriel returns with his report, we will make haste."

After putting on his coat, now dry and toasty, Walter climbed Thigocia's neck stairway while Elam did the same on Makaidos.

384

When both had settled on the dragons' backs, Sapphira lowered her flame, leaving only a white ball of sparks in her palm to guide her way. As she walked up Roxil's neck, a dragon symbol emblazoned on her tunic shimmered. With her ability to call fire to her body to stay warm, she needed only her old battle uniform, the same togs she wore during the victory over the evil armies that tried to break through the portal to Heaven.

As they waited for Gabriel, Walter's thoughts drifted back to that battle. In many ways, the army of Second Eden was badly outnumbered by the invaders—a conglomeration of soldiers from ancient and medieval times. Yet, it could have been much worse. What would have happened if the forces of evil had resurrected modern soldiers with high-tech weapons? How could Elam, Sapphira, and their primitive defenses have countered laser-guided missiles, stealth bombers, and machine guns?

When his mind returned to the present, Walter sighed. If the military compound was preparing for the attack, maybe everyone would learn how a unit of dragons and riders would fare against such weapons. Because of the weather and the need to attack by stealth, they had no way to carry high-tech weapons of their own. They had to rely on flames from dragons and an Oracle of Fire. He patted his coat where his holster lay underneath. *And a handgun with an extra ammo clip.*

"While we're waiting," Elam said. "I have something to show you. Perhaps you can help us unravel a mystery."

Walter nodded. "I'll do what I can."

Elam withdrew a glass egg from a pocket inside his cloak and displayed it in his palm. Sapphira's light made it appear to have a greenish hue, though it was difficult to be sure. "Before I tell you what kind of deal I made to get this, let me assure you that I gained counsel from a reliable source."

"I have no doubt," Walter said. "I wouldn't expect anything less from you."

"You might doubt when you hear the next part. While I was on Earth trying to rescue Sapphira from Fort Knox, a demon named Tamiel offered this to me in exchange for delivering Semiramis and Mardon to him."

"Okay," Walter said, drawing out the word. "Go on."

"Tamiel claimed that two of Methuselah's children are trapped inside, and they would stay there forever unless I agreed to the deal. He said I could take it with me and examine it on one condition—that I give him Semiramis and Mardon if I decided to keep the ovulum or if I found a way to release its captives."

"How convenient for Tamiel that you're so trustworthy."

Elam caressed the top of the glass. "When I returned to Second Eden, I did a lot of research about this ovulum, including interviewing Thigocia. She told me that several of the dragons who became humans carried one of these as a protective device. It was supposed to act as a shield to keep Devin the dragon slayer away. Unfortunately, Devin obtained an ovulum that actually drew him to the dragons. What was supposed to be a protective device actually became a homing device of sorts."

Walter patted Thigocia's neck. "Which dragon carried this one?"

"Yellinia," Thigocia said. "Since she is dead, we could not ask her if it has any special properties, but we did learn much more from another source. I will allow Elam to explain."

"Okay." Walter nodded at Elam. "Continue."

"You might remember the story I told you about the time I found Naamah in the Bridgelands and how she gave her life to save Acacia and me."

"And the world," Walter added.

"Right. Anyway, after she appeared at the wedding ceremony, I thought I would never see her again, but one night while I was praying about what to do, she showed up in my bedroom, whispering, 'Shhh. Don't wake your lovely wife. I have important news.' She looked more like a glowing angel than a human. Anyway, she told me that a boy and girl named Joran and Selah are inside the ovulum, and keeping them out of Tamiel's hands was more valuable than holding Semiramis and Mardon in custody. She reminded me of the day that I decided to believe her repentance, and that I should believe her again, no matter how crazy it seemed to let those two criminals go."

"So you let them go."

Elam nodded. "I sent them through a portal to Earth, and Gabriel secretly followed to see what they would do, but when they crossed over, they became like ghosts, able to turn invisible. Gabriel lost track of them pretty quickly."

"Then we can assume they're here and up to no good."

"Definitely." Elam rubbed the egg with both hands, as if warming it. "Naamah said that breaking the egg wouldn't help, that Joran has to play a special song to get out, something he won't be able to do except in response to turmoil he hears from within the egg. Apparently, he invents tunes that respond to the environment around him, so he won't know the tune until he is in the right place and time. Bottom line, he needs to be involved in a crisis, so Naamah asked me to take the egg the next time I go into battle."

387

"I guess you can't ignore a visitor from Heaven," Walter said. "Kind of a pain keeping it safe, though."

"I know what you mean." Elam slid the ovulum back into his pocket. "If it breaks, it breaks. I can't worry about it too much."

Soon, Gabriel ran into the cave, slinging snow and ice pellets from his wings. Thigocia blew a sparks-filled stream of air over him, melting his cloak's frosty coating. Then, all four dragons took turns providing warming blasts.

"What have you learned?" Elam asked from atop Makaidos.

Gabriel spread out his cloak, allowing the inside to dry. "Sir Barlow and I talked through our tooth transmitters, and he guided me from below. He said he was working on blocking the radar system to make it show an all-clear sky, so let's hope that's in place. He also said there's a gun battery Mardon designed that can shoot Excalibur-like lasers from a ground base. The transmission was garbled, so I couldn't catch everything, but he said something about the guns being immobile. After that, I lost contact. Anyway, I flew over a bunch of stuff that's covered by tarps, and they have two guys who are sweeping snow to keep the tarps clear. Whatever is underneath has long protrusions, like narrow cannon barrels."

"That sounds like a good target," Elam said. "If we knock that out, we're in good shape."

Walter pictured the battle to rescue Sapphira at Fort Knox. The dragons' scales had protected them from a battery of laser cannons. They reported a stinging effect, but they did little harm. If Mardon was able to harness Excalibur, scales wouldn't protect anyone. "Sir Barlow told me yesterday that they have a bunch of tiny candlestones in an ammunition cache, so I'm worried about how they might use those."

388

"Candlestone bullets?" Elam asked. "It sounds like Mardon has been busy."

Walter shivered. Sapphira's warming effect was wearing off. "We can't worry about Mardon now. We'll just have to take one step at a time. Since tarps are covering the laser guns, they probably won't uncover them until right before they think we're going to attack. We can blast them with fire while they're still sweeping snow."

"Exactly." Gabriel flew up to Legossi's back. "So we should direct the first wave at those guns, or whatever they are."

"Instead of going straight for the prisoners?" Sapphira asked. "As soon as they're alerted to our presence, won't Bonnie and the others be in more danger if we delay at all in getting to their cells?"

"Good point." Walter nodded at Gabriel. "Do you think one dragon can take out the lasers?"

"I assume so, but it depends on what those guns really are."

"We'll have to take the risk," Walter said. "You and Legossi will attack them while the rest of us invade the research wing. Thigocia and I will pick up Lauren at the roof access, and the others will crash into the front door. We can create such a firestorm that we'll be gone before they figure out what hit them."

Elam nodded. "If all are in agreement, then let it be so."

"I am," Sapphira said, a shimmer of flames coating her body.

When the dragons echoed her call, their voices resonated in the cave.

Walter lifted a hand. "Now for the final preparation step. Sapphira, please provide a bit more light."

Sapphira spread out her arms. Blue and white flames leapt from her palms, and rippling light filled the cave. Walter looked at each warrior dragon and rider in turn. Without exception, they were much older and more experienced than he, and each one had suffered far more and witnessed more amazing miracles than he could possibly imagine. Yet, they still respected him, a normal human, as an equal. And now, as arranged earlier, he was supposed to dedicate the rescue mission to the Lord and ask for his blessing. Finding the right words without squeaking would be a miracle in itself.

389

"Dragons and humans, because of the weather, I will keep this as brief as possible. There is no need to remind you of God's provision in times of trouble. We have all seen rescues against impossible odds, to the point where we are now ready to launch into the air and fly without fear into the teeth of sophisticated weapons wielded by highly trained soldiers. We are accustomed to seeing God's mighty hand slap his enemies down on our behalf, and we have come to expect the same every time we go into battle. Even tonight I see no fear in any eyes, only steady countenances and peaceful confidence. Yes, faith that God will be with us is good and right, but as we make ready to take wing and hurl fire, allow me to challenge you to examine the fire in your hearts.

"What passion is driving you to risk your lives once again, to plunge yourselves into a hail of deadly resistance, and to expose your underbellies to the sharpened spears of Satan's evil purposes? Is it hatred of his diabolical schemes? Anger at the injustice of captive innocents? Surely these are noble motivations. But let me tell you, my friends, these passions will not be enough. When we face the fury of demonic opposition, hatred will fail. Anger will wither. The only passion that will survive this onslaught is love, love for God and love for those trapped within that prison.

"My beloved Ashley has been tortured in that serpents' pit for fifteen years, and I have wept for her every day. Gabriel and I have prayed for her countless times, so he, too, shares this unquenchable fire to risk everything for her. Now, as if ignited by Sapphira's gift, I call on you to search your hearts for the flaming love that burns within, so that when we stare into the face of death, we will not flag, we will not turn, we will not doubt. Even if we lose some of our comrades, we will continue to press forward until either every innocent captive is liberated or we all rise to Heaven's gate and meet God face-to-face. And when we stand in his presence, we will stand with our heads held high, because we will know that we surrendered our lives to set the captives free, just as the one who will be sitting at the Father's right hand did for us so long ago."

Breathing in the frigid air, Walter lifted his hand. "Now I ask you, Father in Heaven, to go *ahead* of us and prepare the way, for we know not the danger that lies in our path; go *with* us, for we will need strength, courage, and endurance beyond what we will feel as we fly through a cold, dark blizzard into the enemy's lair; and finally, go *behind* us and repair the damage from any errors we might make, turning bad decisions into good results and ruin into rejoicing."

When he finished, he lowered his hand and spoke with a passionate growl. "If you're ready to fight for freedom with me, say *Aye!*"

"Aye!" they all shouted. Streams of hot breath turned into clouds of white vapor, filling the cave.

Grabbing a spine on Thigocia's back, Walter leaned forward and yelled, "Then let's fly!"

Makaidos and Thigocia launched out of the cave together. A barrage of snow assaulted Walter's face, blinding and stinging. He lowered his head and watched the ground as the dragons dipped in and out of tree cover. Since the dragons carried GPS and transmitter chips embedded in their facial scales, Larry and Lois could guide them to the precise location, allowing Walter the freedom to listen to the instructions while scanning the world below for any sign of trouble. Of course, with the dragons' ability to sense danger, they would probably feel it before he could see it.

As they flew through the bitter wind, Walter scrunched low and pushed his hands under his coat, sweater, and shirt. Quite a few miles lay between them and the prison, so staying as warm as possible was essential. He took off his gloves and pressed his fingers against his skin. They were ice cold, even colder than Ashley's toes when she snuggled next to him on frosty nights and he and Ashley playfully fought about who had the colder feet.

Walter sighed. If only he could get her out of that overgrown tin can of a prison, she could put those arctic feet right on his back if she wanted to, and he wouldn't say a word. He wouldn't even flinch.

He slid his gloves on and again grasped one of Thigocia's protruding spines. Dreams could wait. For now, nothing mattered more than getting ready to fight, and he would bring a fight the enemies of God would never forget.

CHAPTER

THE SONG RESTORED

Afte following the hallway through its right-angled turns, Ashley and Lauren arrived at the stairway door. Ashley pulled on Lauren's sleeve, halting her. "Do you hear something?" she whispered. "I'm picking up thoughts somewhere close, but they're garbled."

"Nothing in the hall." Lauren turned the knob, cracked the door open, and listened. As her subdermal scales tingled, a voice came from below.

"Since the anthrozils are locked up," a woman said, "all personnel are now preparing for ground-to-air combat. We have a few hours, so they're going over the procedures. We have three tanks on site and ten more on the way."

Lauren repeated every word in her thoughts to make sure Ashley could "hear" with her.

"We're confident," the woman continued, "that underground munitions haven't been discovered. When they attack the decoy, we'll have enough time to bring the real weapons to the surface. Colonel Baxter is still here, personally seeing to the preparations."

Footsteps sounded on the stairs. In the dim glow cast from the door's window, a woman appeared, holding a cell phone to her ear as she walked up the steps leading to the landing below. In seconds she would turn and climb the next flight and face them. A flashlight beam struck the far wall, and when the woman grasped the railing to turn, Lauren pulled Ashley down below the window and eased the door closed.

She tossed a thought to Ashley. *This will take perfect timing.*

Ashley's brow dipped low. *I'm with you. As soon as she wiggles the knob, we'll give it a shove.*

Footsteps clopped closer. The beam flashed through the window, striking the wall on the other side and shifting from left to right and back again. Her voice returned. "Any reason to check on the two females? Or should I go straight to the roof?"

Lauren looked up at the window. The guard's face was out of view, but she could almost feel her standing near the door. Was she close enough to hit if they shoved the door open?

"That's what I was thinking," the guard continued. "Lauren was parked near the roof for a reason. We picked up some encoded communication, so I'm going to see if she left a clue. Hoskins wouldn't have known what to look for. ... Sure. I'll check on them first. No harm in that."

The doorknob jiggled.

Now! Ashley screamed with her mind.

Each thrusting with a shoulder, they threw the door open, slamming it into the guard. She staggered backwards, and as she hit the railing with her hip, the flashlight and phone flew into the air. Screaming, she flipped over the railing and plummeted headfirst. A clang sounded from below, then another. Finally, a loud thud ended the plunge.

"Catherine?" a scratchy voice called from the phone on the floor. "Are you there?"

Ashley snatched it up. "Sorry," she said, altering her voice to a lower pitch. "I dropped the phone. ... I'm okay. I just slammed a finger against the stair rail. I hope it's not broken. … I'll check, but … After the rooftop, I should also check the munitions to see if—" She frowned. "I know I don't have clearance, but I should at least check the perimeter. … From the rooftop? In a blizzard? … Okay. That will have to do." She pressed the disconnect and used her thumb to scroll through the directory. "It's Stella, Catherine's crony. She said I could check the underground munitions perimeter from the rooftop. That means we can narrow down its location. We should go there first and see what we can see."

Lauren bit her lip hard. "Shouldn't we check on Catherine?"

"She's an Enforcer. If you knew what a vile monster *Catherine* is, you might not be so concerned about her."

"Why did you emphasize her name?"

"Because it's so absurdly inappropriate. It means *purity*."

"Purity," Lauren whispered. *Why does that word seem so important?*

I have no idea. Sighing, Ashley picked up the flashlight and handed it to Lauren. *We'll check on her. If you'll lead the way, I'll keep looking through these numbers. I picked up a tidbit from Catherine's mind earlier today when I intentionally made her furious. She's proud of her connections with the higher-ups, so I'm guessing she'll have an important number programmed in.*

They've been jamming other signals. I guess their phones aren't affected.

We'll soon find out.

Lauren shone the beam on the steps and hurried down. As she descended, Ashley followed, speaking in her mind.

Here's a number for something labeled Headquarters. That could come in handy.

Lauren turned and followed the second flight down. *How did you know they'd believe you were Catherine?*

I practiced imitating her voice. I can do a couple of other guards, too. It irritates them, and that usually makes them slip up when they're trying to keep their minds from leaking information. Ashley let out a quiet "Hmmm." *The signal's worse the lower we go. It was already bad up there, kind of cutting in and out. Maybe the jamming is affecting it after all.*

When they reached the bottom floor, Lauren scanned it with the beam until it ran across Catherine's prostrate body. Although there seemed to be no blood, her head and limbs were cocked at impossible angles.

Ashley set a pair of fingers on Catherine's throat. After a moment, she whispered, "She's dead." She then ran her hand around Catherine's waist and jerked away a set of keys. "These should get us into any door."

Her hands trembling, Lauren knelt and, holding the flashlight under her arm, slid Catherine's ID bracelet off. "We might need this, too."

"Perfect." Ashley pushed the phone into a pocket and, grabbing Catherine's ankles, dragged her body under the stairwell. When she returned, she held something in each hand. "Two weapons," she said, showing them to Lauren, "a gun and a baton. Which one do you want?"

Lauren grasped the baton, a black metal rod about the length of her forearm. "I don't think I have the nerve to shoot anyone."

"Fine. I know from experience that her baton packs a wallop, so keep it handy." Ashley displayed the gun, a long-barreled weapon with a short grip. "It looks almost transparent, and the flashlight beam is being drawn toward it."

Lauren felt a twinge in her gut, similar to candlestone pain, though not as intense. "What does that mean?"

"I have an idea, but I'll explain after I have a chance to look it over." Ashley looked up. "Let's go to the roof and see what we can see."

"Shouldn't we let Matt and the others out first?"

Ashley gave Lauren the key ring. "You do that while I go up and look for the munitions site. Since the signal's better up there,

I can call my husband and let him know what's going on, then I'll call headquarters. With Catherine's voice, I think I can stir up a lot of trouble around here. At least I might be able to delay their reinforcements."

Ashley grasped the railing and vaulted up the steps. Within seconds, she disappeared in the darkness above.

After taking a deep breath, Lauren pushed the keys and bracelet into her pocket. Tucking the baton under her arm, she pointed the flashlight at the door and opened it slowly. With all the lights off, the beam seemed solid, almost like a Star Wars light saber. If only it would cut down opponents in the same way.

Padding on the balls of her feet, she hurried to the end of the hall. She paused at the corner and scanned the area where her victim once lay. A ragged-edged bloodstain smeared the floor, probably a mixture of Bonnie's and the guard's.

Nausea again churned in her stomach. Why did it have to happen this way? Why so much pain and death? As tears crept into her eyes, she tried to blink them away. It seemed that she would never wake up from this nightmare.

The thought repeated in her mind. *Nightmare?* There was something about the dream she needed to remember, something important.

As she walked toward the cell, the flashlight beam again cut through the darkness. The shaft of radiance brought back images from the dream—Zohar's flames, Selah's colorful projection in front of the lyre, and the wall of fire that raced through the purity ovulum and chased Joran and company into the green one. The voices within the flames echoed.

Bonnie Silver! Why must you be set aflame?

My … my name … is Silver. All dross … is purged … and my body … is a living … illustration.

A beautiful melody entered her mind, the same melody Joran heard as he watched the wall of flames draw closer. It was the song of the purity ovulum, the tune only Shachar or gifted Listeners could hear.

Then, Joran's reaction followed. *Dross is purged. That's what purity means.*

Lauren pulled out the bracelet and stared at the name—Catherine. Purity. Like the purity ovulum, this bearer of the purity name was no more. Since, according to Ashley, Catherine belied her name, what would become of her spirit? Did she go to Hell? After hearing Walter talk about Hell like it was a real place—a place he could see, touch, and smell—the idea of someone going there seemed more terrible than ever.

When she reached the cell door, she set the baton on the floor, pointed the light at the security panel, and lifted the bracelet close to it. A new hum drifted into her ear, not a memory, but a real sound in the air—Bonnie's song, the melody she emitted without even realizing it. It sounded exactly like the song in the dream.

398

Lauren felt her mouth drop open. Bonnie was emitting the song of the ovulum! So that's what Enoch meant! He moved the song to a mobile host, a human being!

A voice overpowered the tune. "That's a cool story, Mom," Matt said. "It's amazing all the stuff you and Dad did."

Then Bonnie's voice came through. "I'd tell you more, but there are some stories I don't want our eavesdroppers to hear."

Lauren waved the bracelet in front of the panel. Although the LED flashed, the bracelet didn't unlock the mechanism, no surprise, really, considering the power outage. Setting the ring in front of the beam, Lauren fumbled through the set of five keys. Which one was the right one? It was dark last time, so she would have to guess.

Her fingers quivered. The keys jingled, sounding like rusty chains being slung against the wall. Finally, she pushed a key into the override lock and turned it.

A loud click sounded. She ran to the handle and pulled the door to the side, making it squeal loudly, but it couldn't be helped. It was the only way to get in.

"Someone's opening the cell," Billy said.

"Don't blow fire on me!" Lauren fumbled with the keys again. "It's me! Lauren!"

"Dad," Matt said in an agitated voice, "the eye bomb."

Billy's tone stayed calm. "Too late. They already heard her name."

"Hang on. I just have to find the right key." Guiding her hand with the flashlight, Lauren pushed one into the second door's hole, but it wouldn't turn. "Bonnie, I think I figured out something about you."

A squeal from within pierced the door. Lauren jerked back. "What's that?"

"I'm covering something that's listening in," Matt said. "Just hurry."

"The song of the purity ovulum emanates from you," Lauren continued. "I can hear it."

While she pulled a second key from the ring, Bonnie called back, "I dreamed about that."

"Right. I did, too." Lauren pushed the key in, but it didn't turn. "When you burned, so did the ovulum, and now you're the song's vessel. If Tamiel finds out, he'll come after you."

"Because he doesn't want the world to hear the song."

Lauren lifted a third key. "Something like that. I haven't figured it all out."

"Lauren!" Matt's voice altered to a hiss, and the squealing ceased. "My father and I both sense danger. It's closing in fast. Don't say anything you don't want anyone to hear."

She flashed the beam both ways, but nothing came into view, only the vast, empty corridor. Now trembling, she pushed the key into the lock. "Let me try one more."

The lock turned. Lauren jerked down on the handle, releasing the latch. When the door swung out, she backed away, aiming the beam at the opening.

Matt, Billy, and Bonnie appeared, their expressions anxious. "Danger is closer," Matt said. "We need to get going."

"Right! Just follow me and—"

A sharp pain stabbed her scalp. Something jerked her backwards. Crying out, she fell and slid. Her flashlight spun on the floor, sending the beam around and around. "Get back in that cell," a woman shouted, "or she's dead! I can pull this trigger faster than you can blast me with fire."

The light's slowing rotations highlighted a pair of shoes and bare lower legs that led up to a calf-length skirt. A female guard clutched a fistful of Lauren's hair with one hand and a gun with the other.

"Okay," Billy said. "We're going."

At the edges of the flashlight's glow, three pairs of shoes shuffled back into the cell.

"And close the door!"

As a hand reached out and pulled the inner door, a flashing ball rolled near the guard's feet. Then, the lock engaged with a click. The ball emanated dozens of beams, illuminating the corridor.

Grumbling an obscenity, the guard nudged it with her shoe. "No matter. We can put it back later."

Lauren lurched to the side, but the guard yanked upward, stretching Lauren's neck, lifting her bottom off the floor.

"Augh!" Lauren clenched her teeth, gasping for breath.

"Will you cooperate now?"

Bonnie's voice reached Lauren's ears. "It's Stella. That's bad news."

A whisper followed, Billy's voice, likely too quiet for Stella to hear. "Lauren, try to figure out a way to leave the outer door open."

"I'll cooperate," Lauren squeaked.

"Good." Stella lowered her to the floor and released her hair. "Get the flashlight, and come with me. There is someone who wants to see you. And don't think about trying to escape. I'm good with this gun."

Lauren grabbed the flashlight and turned the beam down the hallway. She had to distract Stella. With the cell lit up by the flashing ball, she would notice the external door. "That way?" she asked.

"Yes." Stella gave her a shove with her shoe. "Get up and get moving."

Lauren climbed to her feet, and, keeping the flashlight aimed down the hall, she marched ahead at a rapid clip.

"Not so fast!" Stella called.

Lauren kept up the pace. *Just follow, Stella. Don't look at the door!*

"Slow down or I'll shoot!"

Lauren slowed and aimed the beam at the turn in the hallway ahead. With her hands likely glowing, taking off would be risky. She would be an easy target, especially with the strange ball shooting its own beams her way. But did that really matter? She *had* to do this. It might be the only way to keep Stella away from that door.

After sliding her sleeves over her hands, she turned off the light and ran.

A gunshot cracked behind her, and the wall ahead popped. Lauren flinched but kept running. When she reached the corner and turned, she slipped in the blood and slid sideways, smacking her shoulder and head against the wall, but she managed to stay upright.

Pushing away, she looked back. A light flashed. A second gunshot rang out, and a bullet ripped into the wall inches from her nose, splattering plaster fragments over her face.

Lauren took off again. The sound of running footsteps trailed her own. When she reached the stairway door, she shoved it open and dashed up the steps. The door slammed behind her, then opened again. Another shot rang out.

Ducking her head, Lauren sprinted up the stairs. Surely she could outrun that hefty woman, but if she reached Ashley's level, that would put her in danger. Maybe level two would be a good place to hide. By that time, Stella might be close enough to see the door swing, keeping her from continuing up the stairs, but far enough away to lose the trail.

When she reached the second level, she jerked the door open, turned on the flashlight, and swept the beam through the hallway to the left. The light struck several doors on the right side of the corridor. She jogged, pausing to check each knob. The first two were locked, but the third opened. She closed it again and hurried on. The first available door would be the obvious place to hide.

She stopped at the second unlocked door and turned off the flashlight. The stairway door opened, and Stella barged through, looking in the opposite direction.

Ducking low, Lauren slid into the room and quietly closed the door. She turned the flashlight back on and pointed it at the knob. There was no manual locking mechanism—only a keyhole.

Slow, squeaking footsteps drew closer. A doorknob rattled nearby, then another. Lauren grabbed her knob and held it tightly. Maybe she could make it appear to be locked.

With fear mounting, her skin tingled once again. Every squeak, every breath, every heartbeat pounded in her ears.

A third knob rattled, and a door banged open. Then, Stella's voice came through. "I'm chasing her, but somebody needs to get back to the cell. Stupid girl took off before I had a chance to close the exterior door. I shot at her, but she still wouldn't stop."

Another voice came through, distant and tinny. "Did you hit her?"

Lauren held her breath. It sounded like Colonel Baxter.

"Of course not," Stella said. "I made sure I missed. I wouldn't want you-know-who to cut my heart out."

"If you're sure about what you heard, then Tamiel needs to know. I have to check on the reinforcements. They should have been here by now. The storm must be holding them up. Then I'm going out to check the elevation shaft to make sure it isn't icing over."

"Okay. I'll call Tamiel. Maybe he can help me find Lauren."

The footsteps resumed, along with more knob rattling. Finally, the squeaking stopped in front of Lauren's door. "Tamiel, it's Stella. I found Lauren trying to break the anthrozils out of the dragon cell. She got away, but I'm on her trail. Everyone's on attack alert, so I need someone to check on the cell. I chased her instead of taking the time to close the secondary door."

"Why are you calling me for such a menial task?" Tamiel's tone was smooth, yet condescending. "The interior door is strong enough to hold them. They are not dragons."

"Yes, I know, but something I overheard got me worried. Lauren said Bonnie emanates the purity ovulum's song."

"Bonnie?" Tamiel let out a long humming sound. "I see. A mobile song is much harder to find."

"So if Lauren's right, maybe Bonnie has more power than we realize."

"You have done well to inform me. I will go there myself and see if Bonnie possesses what I have been seeking for so long."

"Good. I'll keep looking for the brat. She's on the second level somewhere, and the only way to the stairs is past me."

The doorknob rattled. Lauren gripped it tightly, keeping it from turning, but would that be enough?

M att pressed both hands against the door's left panel and shoved. It wouldn't budge. Billy and Bonnie joined him, all three bracing their feet and lunging. It bent outward slightly, making the metal squeak, but nothing more.

"It's designed to keep a dragon in here," Billy said. "If I try any more fire on that lock, I'm afraid it'll just weld in place."

"Makes sense." Matt turned and leaned back against the door. The creeps had Lauren. The situation seemed to be getting worse by the hour. At least he had been quick enough to roll the eye bomb out before he closed the door. Now they could talk without worrying about its snooping eyes and ears.

After Billy relit the rope with a quick puff of fire, Matt held it close to Bonnie. "Okay, let's think about this. Lauren said that you're emanating the ovulum's song. Can we use that information?"

"Maybe," Bonnie said. "I've been having this dream about two children of Methuselah who are trapped inside an ovulum called the purity ovulum. It's kind of fuzzy, but I think I remember Methuselah saying its song can break shackles that keep the ovulum imprisoned."

404

"So, do you have a special song?" Matt asked. "Something that might break this lock?"

"I do have a favorite song." Bonnie rubbed her wrist. "Whenever the Healers strapped me to the bed for tests, I always sang a psalm Gabriel taught me when I was little. When I woke up, the straps were always loose. And a few times recently, the guard found our cell door unlocked, but I don't remember if I sang the song that day."

"But if you learned that song a long time ago," Billy said, "why would it be the song of the ovulum now?"

"After I became an Oracle of Fire, I altered the tune to match a melody that kept running through my head. I had to change the words to fit, but it still has the same meaning."

"Then that explains everything," Billy said. "Let's see if it works."

Bonnie stepped up to the door and bent toward the locking mechanism. After clearing her throat, she sang.

Oh where can man escape from God,
To fly from hope, to leave this sod?
To Heaven's door? Nay, you are there.
To beds in Hell? You hear his prayer.

I fly at dawn and dwell at sea,
And there you lead and comfort me.
If darkness covers me at night,
Behold, you're there, my shining light.

Yes, darkness cannot hide from you;
The night casts off her blackened hue.
No darkness dwells within your sight,
My God who gives eternal light.

The moment she finished the song, a loud click sounded, and the door swung open a few inches, creaking along the way. Billy grabbed the handle and pulled it back, careful not to let it latch. "I need the shirt."

Matt picked up Bonnie's discarded T-shirt. "The eye bomb?"

"Right. The guards will probably guess who covered it, but at least they won't know which way we went."

Matt handed him the shirt. "We could throw it into the cell and lock it in when we leave."

"Good idea."

"Do you sense any danger?" Bonnie asked.

Billy nodded. "But it's strange. I can't tell how close it is. It's like nothing I've ever sensed before."

The door jerked open, letting in flashing light. A winged man aimed a gun at Billy and pulled the trigger. A popping noise erupted, and a tiny dot of radiance shot from the muzzle and pierced Billy's forehead, raising a splash of blood. He arched and fell on his back. Writhing on the floor, he called out, "Bonnie! Matt! Run!" Then, his limbs fell limp, and he lay motionless.

405

Matt lunged at the winged man. He fired again. Another sparkling dot rocketed out and slammed into Matt's left bicep. He staggered backwards into Bonnie's arms.

As she held him upright, the man stepped into the cell and straddled Billy, pointing the gun at him. "Come with me, Bonnie, or I will finish him off."

Bonnie glared at the gunman. "I know who you are, Tamiel. You're a coward who is so weak, he has to threaten a downed man to apprehend an unarmed woman."

While Tamiel returned Bonnie's stare, a stalemate of violence and defiance, Matt eyed the gun. Light from the eye bomb swirled into its transparent casing. He glanced at Billy. No new blood seeped from his head wound, as if the glittering projectile had cauterized the wound.

"I am not a coward. I am simply careful." Tamiel fired the gun a third time. The dot zinged into Bonnie's hand. A tiny stream of blood spurted, then immediately ceased. Letting Matt go, she grasped her wrist, groaning.

Matt dropped to a crouch and squinted at his jacket's sleeve. Although the pain in his arm wasn't nearly as bad as he expected, it might be better to stay put and be ready to pounce at the first opportunity. Obviously this monster wouldn't hesitate to shoot again.

"That should make you more compliant," Tamiel said to Bonnie. "And this weapon serves another purpose. I can't have you breaking your bonds with your song."

Bonnie's brow wrinkled. Her face paled. Sinking to her knees, she swayed from side to side. "I ... I feel terrible."

Matt slid close and grasped her arm, whispering, "I've got you."

"You will feel it soon," Tamiel said. "Since your jacket slowed the projectile, it will take a little while longer for you."

A hundred insults erupted in Matt's mind, but he swallowed them down. He had to push aside the hatred and concentrate. Since this winged freak expected him to succumb to pain, could that weapon be some sort of candlestone shooter? If so, maybe it was time for a bit of acting. Grimacing, he spiced his voice with a groan. "What did you shoot into me?"

"It is a predator that will consume your energy, a radiant vampire that feeds on the light in anthrozil blood. I assume that the one in Billy penetrated his brain, so he will likely die. Yours will merely incapacitate you."

Matt laid a hand over his chest and wheezed. Rolling his eyes upward, he blinked rapidly and collapsed to a fetal position, his cheek against the floor and one eye slightly open. He let out a low groan, loud enough to communicate pain, but not so loud that it sounded phony.

Tamiel jerked Bonnie up by her arm and forced her to walk to the cell door. She staggered at his side, her legs unsteady. "It is time to go."

At the doorway, the eye bomb pulsed light around Bonnie's frame as she looked back over her shoulder. "I love you, Matt," she called with a tortured voice. "Tell Billy I love him, too."

As soon as Tamiel and Bonnie turned into the corridor and disappeared, Matt pushed up to his knees and crawled over to Billy. Light flashed across a pinhead-sized depression just above his left eyebrow. His respiration seemed strong and even.

Matt slid his hand into Billy's. "Dad? Can you hear me?"

Billy squeezed his hand in return. "Must be … a candlestone."

"Yeah. That's what I was thinking. It looks like it's embedded inside you, maybe in your brain."

Billy's words came out slow and fractured. "They must have created … synthetic ones. … Candlestones are light seekers … and my blood has … photoreceptors."

"Right. If it's in your brain, it'll kill you. I have to get you out of here."

"No. … You have to help your mother. … Don't worry about me."

The flashes of light grew stronger. Matt glanced at the door. The eye bomb rolled in and stopped within inches of his knees. Faking a convulsion, he collapsed on top of it, grabbed Bonnie's discarded shirt from Billy's hand, and wrapped the eye bomb with it.

As it squealed, he leaped to his feet and dragged Billy by his wrists out to the corridor. Keeping his footfalls quiet, he ran back into the cell, grabbed the candlestone from under the chains, and stuffed it into his pocket as he hurried back.

He slammed the inner door and slid the outer one closed, muffling the squeal and flooding the corridor with darkness. Grabbing Billy's wrists, he began dragging him again, but he stepped on something that spun out from under his foot, making him fall to his side.

An explosion rocked the floor. As the vibrations subsided, Matt rose to his knees and ran his fingers across Billy's head until he found his cheek. "Dad, are you still with me?"

Billy choked out, "Yes."

He grasped Billy's hand and scooted to his side. "With the explosion, they probably think we're both dead. That should help."

Billy tightened his grip. "I saw … what you did. … Good thinking."

"I'll try to find Mom, but I'm coming back to get you, too."

"Never forget. … Your mother … is more important … than I am. She is … " He exhaled and said no more.

"Dad?" In the darkness, the silence made it feel as if someone had closed a coffin over both of them. "Dad?"

He laid a hand over Billy's chest. His heartbeat stayed strong, though erratic. How long could he last with that energy-eating vampire in his brain?

Rising to his feet, he pulled the candlestone from his pocket and used its light to search for the object he had tripped on. A black rod lay near a wall. Similar to a policeman's baton, it could come in handy as a weapon.

He snatched it up and, leading again with the candlestone, jogged in the direction Tamiel had taken Bonnie, opposite from the way he had come in. With a few open and empty cells passing by as he plunged through the dark, cavernous hallway, the entire scene was surreal. He had found his parents after all this time, anthrozils no less, in a prison constructed to incarcerate dragons. Now both were in mortal danger, and saving either one seemed impossible.

As he continued, he reached under his shirt and probed for the candlestone's entry point. Feeling a small lump under his skin, he pushed it back toward the wound and squeezed it out. It felt like a BB, smooth and round. He stuffed it into his pocket, not bothering to look at it.

After finding a door to a stairway, he shoved it open and climbed the steps, his legs heavy. As he ascended, a siren began to wail, muffled, as if coming from outside or from another floor. Something big had to be taking place somewhere, but what? The dragon attack? If so, maybe there was hope after all.

Summoning a burst of energy, he ran up the stairs, skipping one with each step as he clutched the baton tightly. It was time to go to war!

DRAGON ATTACK

After flying low across a sparse forest, lights from the prison facility came into Walter's view, including a search lamp that swept the sky, apparently looking for approaching dragons. According to their plan, it should have been disabled by now.

"Sir Barlow," Walter barked. "What happened to taking over the searchlight?"

A whispered voice replied. "I was delayed. I'll have it done in a moment."

Seconds later, the searchlight swung wildly, then stopped, pointing at a field inside the facility. Barlow's voice returned, low and strained. "You are ... all clear."

"Sir Barlow! Are you hurt?"

"We had a scuffle ... and the guard fired a shot. ... I hope ... no one heard it."

"Just stay where you are. We'll pick you up."

"No." Barlow strained with every word. "Do not ... jeopardize the mission. ... I will not ... be here."

"Barlow!" Walter shouted.

411

Silence ensued. After a few seconds, Lois interrupted. "I have registered this anomaly. Will you proceed?"

Walter nodded. "Proceed as planned."

While Legossi and Gabriel broke away to the right, heading toward the tarp-covered weapons, the other three dragons continued straight ahead. When the research wing's rooftop came into view, Makaidos's voice buzzed through Walter's tooth chip. "I sense danger at your landing point."

"I do as well," Thigocia said. "Walter, shall we shift to the alternate plan?"

"There's probably danger everywhere. Why would this be different?"

"It is a pinpoint danger," Makaidos said. "Perhaps an explosive trap. If there is one at the rooftop access, there might also be one at the main entry. Perhaps they have intercepted our plans."

Walter called through the tooth transmitter. "Sapphira and Elam, pull back and make a slow orbit at treetop level. Give me a minute to think."

All three dragons swung around and began a low, curving flight pattern.

"Walter," Lois said, "shall I patch an emergency phone call to you?"

"Is it Jared?"

"No. It is your wife."

Walter's heart thumped. "My wife! Yes! Send her through!"

A crackle sounded, then a scratchy, faraway voice. "Walter, it's Ashley. No time for kissy talk. Listen. I'm at the top of the stairs leading to the research wing's roof, and—"

"Be careful! Makaidos detected danger there. We're orbiting over the forest until we figure out what to do."

"Danger? There's nothing up here but a pile of snow."

"You're on the roof now?"

"Yes, I … Wait a minute. I think I found the problem."

Walter twisted to look back. As Thigocia swung around, the rooftop came into view again, veiled by the blowing snow. A woman dressed in jeans and a dark sweatshirt stood in the midst of a drift, a phone to her ear as she leaned over, apparently picking something up.

"It's a candlestone," she said, rising again.

Walter gazed at the woman. Although thinner than ever, Ashley still cut a lovely profile he could never mistake. His heart pounding, he cleared his throat to keep his voice in check. "That's a bad sign. Why would a candlestone be there?"

Ashley set a fist on her hip and looked toward the interior of the compound. "Fuel for their secret munitions, maybe."

"Secret munitions? What kind of—"

"Shhh! Just listen. Lauren and I picked up some chatter, so we know quite a bit, and I called the facility's headquarters, mimicking a guard's voice. I gave them the idea that your attack will be delayed, so they're not too worried about their reinforcements getting through the blizzard on time. Maybe they'll slow their pace. Anyway, I confirmed that they have some kind of underground munitions that'll pop up when you attack a decoy."

413

"A decoy? What decoy?"

"That's what I was going to ask you. The Colonel seemed to think I should know what it was, so I didn't want to risk blowing my cover."

"I know what it is," Walter barked into his transmitter. "Gabriel! Can you hear me?"

Gunshots sounded, coming from the direction of the targeted weapons cache.

"Gabriel!"

No one answered. A strange popping noise pierced the snowfall, then a wailing siren.

Ashley waved from the roof. "Go back! It *is* a trap!"

In the prison yard beyond Ashley, the snow pushed up in a rectangular shape, as if a platform elevator were rising from a subterranean shaft. Underneath the former ground level, cannon-like barrels aimed toward the sky and shot laser beams into the storm.

Legossi ducked under a searchlight beam and flew low over a series of one-story barracks-like buildings. Ahead, in a football field–sized gap between two sets of barracks, tarp-covered protrusions came into view. Two men in heavy parkas with fur-lined hoods swept snow from the tarps.

"Do you see them?" Gabriel asked as he drew a handgun.

"I do." Legossi beat her wings harder, accelerating against the brutal winds. "We cannot allow the men to warn anyone of our arrival. They will be our first targets."

"Just go for the weapons. When we destroy them, our arrival will be obvious. No need to kill if we don't have to."

"Very well. I will try to blast through the tarp." Now within range, Legossi blew a torrent of flames at the closest weapon. The fire splashed against the side, instantly melting a thin layer of snow and igniting the tarp. The two men threw down their brooms and pulled short-barreled rifles from underneath their parkas. Sparkling white radiance swirled within the semitransparent guns, as if they were absorbing the surrounding light and pulling it into a whirlpool.

Before they could fire, Gabriel shot at both men, striking one in the thigh, then used his wings to lift away from Legossi's back. While Legossi continued blasting the weapons, Gabriel flew straight at the men, but before he could aim, the uninjured soldier discharged his gun, making a hollow popping sound. A sparkling dot flew out and thumped into Gabriel's shoulder. He snapped backwards and fell to the tarp. Legossi charged toward the soldier, leading with a wave of white-hot flames. Just before the fire reached him, the solider shot again and dropped to avoid the blast.

Legossi fell, rolling over both soldiers and dragging the tarp and Gabriel along. When she finally stopped, Gabriel climbed to his feet and ran toward her. A siren blared, and the noise seemed to penetrate his skin and shake his bones. His shoulder ached, but it felt more like he had been punched by a fist than pierced by a bullet.

When he reached Legossi, she swung her neck around and cast her eyebeams on him. Both soldiers lay motionless next to her. "How bad is your wound?" she asked.

"Not bad. It looks like we succeeded."

"Look again. It seems that we have been duped." Her eyebeams shifted to one of the protrusions, a burning heap of pasteboard wrapped around a wire frame.

"Fake?" Gabriel took a step toward the phony gun, but the pain in his shoulder spiked and shifted toward his spine. He dropped to his knees, gasping. "Legossi, it must be one of the candlestone bullets. It feels like it's crawling around inside me."

"He shot me at the base of my neck. How it penetrated my scales, I do not know, but I feel the same kind of crawling pain." She spread out her wings. "Use your wings to help you mount. We must do all the damage we can before the candlestones cripple us."

415

Lauren held the knob as tightly as she could. As Stella twisted it from the other side, the metal slowly slipped through Lauren's fingers. Finally, she flung the door outward, slammed it into Stella, and shoved her against the wall. She smacked Stella in the face with the flashlight and sprinted toward the stairwell.

A pop sounded, and a sparkling sphere flew by, narrowly missing her head. Guided by the flashlight beam, she ran through the doorway and down the steps. When she reached the first floor, she dashed into the hall, then slowed to a jog as she searched for an exit.

After a few seconds, a door came into view. Digging for another burst of speed, she flew out the door and into the snowstorm. With everything coated in blankets of white, it took a few seconds to get her bearings. A jeep sat to her left, and a fence with a gate stood straight ahead. That had to be the fence separating the maximum and minimum security areas, and she was standing on the road she had crossed to get to the alley between the two buildings.

She ran to the gate and whispered the numbers as she punched them in. "Five, seven, four—"

A voice from her tooth transmitter interrupted. "Is it Jared?"

Lauren touched her jaw. That sounded like Walter.

"My wife!" Walter shouted. "Yes! Send her through!"

Lauren shook her head. No time to answer. She had to ignore the chatter and get away.

She tapped her jaw twice, silencing the voice, then restarted the combination, again whispering, "Five, seven, four, one—"

A stab of pain shot across her scalp. She flew backwards and slid in the snow. With her back to the research wing, Stella let go of Lauren's hair and set a heavy boot on her shoulder, a gun pointed at her. "If you move a muscle, I will stomp you."

Lauren shivered but managed a tone of defiance. "You won't kill me. I heard that Tamiel would cut your heart out."

"Oh, not Tamiel. And it's true that I won't kill you, but I don't mind disfiguring you until you submit. Someone wants your—"

A thud sounded, and Stella lurched to the side. Matt stood where Stella had been, a baton clutched tightly in his hand. He grabbed Lauren's wrist and pulled her to her feet. "Are you okay?"

"I'm fine. Just cold and wet." Lauren raised her hood. "How are you?"

"No serious injuries." He rotated his left arm. "Sore here and there from a couple of bullet wounds."

"Bullet wounds?"

"I'll explain later. I heard more guards inside." He nodded at the fence. "Ready to climb?"

"I know the combination." Blinking at the windblown flakes, she punched the numbers again—five, seven, four, one, three. When the gate popped ajar, she shoved it through a pile of snow just enough for her and Matt to squeeze through. They ran together along a road between two sets of barracks, heading toward the Colonel's office. Ahead, an open field lay beyond the barracks, and a searchlight's beam illuminated the center, as if stuck in place.

They stopped and looked around. As Matt scanned the sky, his face grew pale and anxious. "Have you seen Bonnie? Tamiel took her. I have to find them."

"Tamiel took her? That's terrible!"

"Tell me about it." Matt waved the baton toward the medical wing. "And my father's hurt back in the dungeon. Everything's falling apart, and fast."

"*Our* father," Lauren said, taking Matt's hand.

"Yeah, I guessed that. But I haven't told them yet." He compressed her hand gently. "Dad told me finding our mother was more important than helping him."

"If Tamiel has her. Definitely." A sharp pain radiated up her arm. She jerked her hand away. "Do you have a candlestone?"

"Two, actually." He dug into his pocket and withdrew a closed fist. "One is just a little bullet, but they'll both probably hurt you." He threw the stones toward one of the barracks.

"That's better." Lauren reached into her pocket and felt for the leftover granola bar. "If you're hungry, I have a—"

Gunshots sounded to the right. A popping noise followed, then the wail of a siren.

"Go back!" a woman shouted. "It *is* a trap!"

Lauren and Matt whirled toward the voice. Someone stood on the research wing's roof, waving toward the rear of the prison.

417

A squealing noise made them spin again. In the field, a section of the snow-covered ground began to rise, as if powered by a hydraulic lift. As snow cascaded over the edge, a supporting column came into view, a black rectangular shaft, maybe ten by twenty feet. Since the sod on top was somewhat longer and wider than the shaft, it looked like a wide-brimmed hat riding on a vertically standing brick.

After rising about ten feet, the column stopped. Three long gun barrels protruded out of the side facing Lauren and Matt, like cannons on a sci-fi space cruiser. Aiming toward the sky, they shot beams of light through the falling snow. More beams emanated from the back and sides, maybe eight in all.

When the beams reached a point about a hundred feet in the air, they stopped abruptly, as if striking a barrier, and the light spread out to form a radiant sheet that widened until it covered and illuminated the entire facility in a shimmering dome. Snowflakes melted as they struck the top and streamed down the curved sides, but the wind continued blowing through, as blustery as ever.

Lauren pointed at the research wing's roof. "That's Mom's friend Ashley, warning someone about a trap, but I didn't see anyone else."

A dragon swooped down and crash-landed on the lab's roof, spraying snow all around. Ashley climbed up its side and sat behind a drooping winged man. Then, with Ashley propping the man up, the dragon took off again. As the wind beat against its body, it flew erratically. Heading directly toward Lauren and Matt, it crossed over the fence dividing the two sections of the prison, then crashed again and slid, sending high arcs of snow cascading over their heads.

The man toppled to the side. The dragon caught him with a wing and set him gently on the snow. With limp arms and legs, he appeared to be unconscious or dead.

"This is my brother, Gabriel," Ashley shouted as she leaped from the dragon. "He has a candlestone embedded under his skin, and Legossi has one somewhere beneath her scales. I have to cut them out somehow."

"I have a knife," Matt called as he ran toward her, digging into his pocket.

Lauren followed and stopped next to one of Gabriel's splayed wings. Ashley straddled Gabriel's body, a knee planted on each side, and ripped open his shirt. "Are you going to do surgery right here?" Lauren asked.

"No choice." She took the knife from Matt and opened the blade. "Legossi, do you have enough fire to sterilize this?"

"I believe so." Legossi snaked her neck around Lauren. Lauren sidestepped, gaping at the amazing creature as the scaly head passed by. At any other time, she would probably have been scared out of her wits, but after seeing so many bizarre things lately, a dragon seemed mild.

419

Legossi blew a thin stream of fire on the blade. Ashley turned it, allowing the other side to catch the flames. "The candlestone isn't deep, and we have to get these warriors back in the air. The other dragons can't penetrate the Excalibur rays."

"Excalibur rays?" Lauren hugged her body, shivering. "I can't read your mind right now, so tell us what you know."

Ashley ran her fingers across a lump on Gabriel's pectoral. "When the Enforcers took the two of you from your parents, they also stole Excalibur. It's a sword that shoots out a beam that changes matter into light energy, a process called translumination. It can also create a shield, like an umbrella of energy, so it looks like they've replicated the beam. I know it can be done, because I did the same thing with a device I invented." She cut into the lump. Gabriel winced but didn't cry out. As blood streamed, she pushed her finger inside and withdrew a tiny sphere, coated red. "I left one of the candlestone guns on the roof. It's a clever and damaging weapon, but now its ammunition will help the healing process. If Legossi can provide more fire, we'll be in business."

"I think so," Legossi said, "but I am weakening."

Matt pointed at the research building with the baton. "Billy's on the lower level. He's got one of those candlestone bullets in his head and can't move. The hallway was designed for dragons, so maybe Legossi can get down there. In the meantime, I have to find Bonnie. A demon abducted her."

"A demon?" Ashley shook her head. "Tell me later. I'll take Gabriel inside, and we'll look for Billy. When I get everyone on their feet, I'll be back."

"So what do we do?" Lauren asked. "I don't think we can find Bonnie. Tamiel's probably long gone by now."

Ashley pointed at the laser guns. "Disable those."

Lauren pivoted toward the raised platform. "With what?"

"A mechanism that creates a transluminating beam is susceptible to cold temperatures. That's why they're under cover. Probably only the barrels are exposed." Ashley slid her arms under Gabriel and grunted as she lifted. "Expose the machinery, and you'll probably freeze it up."

Matt helped Ashley push Gabriel onto Legossi's back. While Legossi propped Gabriel with a wing, Matt gave Ashley a boost. Once both had settled, Legossi beat her wings and skittered along the path toward the lab, her back claws scratching at the ground. With a flap and a leap, she vaulted over the fence before descending again and continuing her awkward run.

"She took the knife," Matt said as he slapped the baton against his palm. "This is the only weapon we have left."

"She probably needs the knife more than we do." Lauren bounced on her toes. It was so cold! How could Matt stand there without a hint of a shiver?

Grabbing her elbow, he leaned close and shouted through the strengthening wind. "Ready?"

Lauren tapped her jaw twice. "Can you hear me through your tooth?"

"Now I can. Loud and clear."

"Good. We don't have to shout." Heaving a sigh and a cloud of white vapor, she gazed at the laser guns. "Do you have a plan?"

"Not really, but they probably don't expect someone on the ground to—" His brow lifted. "Maybe we should follow that guy."

A man wearing a parka and prison guard pants staggered across the field from right to left, holding a hand against his chest and carrying a coil of rope over his shoulder. White plumes rising with his heavy breaths, he stopped at the edge of the weapons column and looked up at one of the gun barrels several feet above his head.

"That looks like Sir Barlow," Lauren said. "He's on our side."

"Then let's go!"

As they ran toward the snow-laden field, Sir Barlow threw his rope over a gun barrel, caught the end, and tied it to a bolt at the base of the column. When they arrived, he spun toward them and staggered back a step. "Oh! Lauren and Matt! You startled me!" His eyes narrowed. "Where is Ashley?"

Matt pointed with his thumb. "Back in maximum security. She's doing surgery on the wounded."

"Good. A stitch in time saves lives." Sir Barlow reached the rope toward Matt. "Can you climb? I think I have lost my strength."

"Sure." Matt took the rope. "What happened?"

"I was shot while disabling the searchlights. He got me in the shoulder, so I doubt that I can climb that high."

Matt laid the baton down and pulled on the rope with both hands. "What do I do when I get up there?"

"You can use these." Sir Barlow withdrew a pair of gloves from his parka, both designed for a right hand. "They are supposed to control this gun and the one next to it, but I couldn't get them to work. I think we're too far from the control panel. Perhaps if you get closer, you can alter their aim enough to break the shield."

"I'll give it a try."

Lauren nodded. "We both will."

"The gloves have sensitive electrodes," Sir Barlow said, "so you shouldn't grip the rope with them. I will toss them and my gun once you're up. If all else fails, just do whatever damage you can. There is likely no one inside. Since I took the control gloves, the gun operators have nothing to do in there."

"Sounds good." Matt leaped and scrambled up the rope hand over hand, then swung onto the barrel, straddling it with his face toward the muzzle. Barlow sent his gun flying into Matt's waiting hands, then tossed one of the gloves.

As Matt began sliding backwards toward the support shaft, Lauren grabbed the rope and pulled it down. With a quick spin, she whipped it over the adjacent gun barrel and began climbing. When she reached the top and straddled the barrel, Sir Barlow threw the second glove. After catching it and putting it on, she started her slide. "What do you see?" she whispered.

Matt touched the column. "It's some kind of hard plastic. It might be bulletproof."

"Let's try the gloves."

"Shhh! Wait a second! I sense danger."

Underneath them, Sir Barlow hurriedly untied the rope and reeled it into a loop. With a quick turn, he saluted, knocking back his parka's hood. "All is clear, sir."

Colonel Baxter, also wearing a parka, returned the salute. Portia stood next to him, hugging herself and shivering. With only a hooded sweatshirt over her prison jumpsuit, the wind had to be biting through to her skin. "What are you doing out here, Sergeant?" the Colonel asked.

Lauren flattened her back against the support column. Matt did the same. Fortunately, the structure's "brim" provided shade,

though not much. There seemed to be no escape from the surrounding dome's radiance.

"The searchlight stopped," Sir Barlow said, his voice strained,
"so I came out to see what might be wrong."

Lauren looked at her glove. It had a tiny rocker switch on the
side of the index finger, easily accessible by the thumb. The activation switch? Maybe. But should she try it with the Colonel
standing so close?

"Didn't you get the word that we're under attack by dragons?"
the Colonel asked. "You're supposed to be gathering with the others in maximum security. We have to repel the beasts!"

"I heard the order, but I also heard gunshots, so I thought—"

"You thought?" The Colonel pressed a thumb against his chest.
"I gave that order, so I will take the risks. That's why I am personally checking on the searchlight."

"Lauren," Matt whispered. "I found the switch that turns the
glove on."

"Same here. Should we try it?"

"Yes. Just keep that hand still and test it slowly."

"But that's not all," Sir Barlow said, waving a hand, as if reen-
acting. "This gun battery behind us rose out of the ground. I must
say, sir, that I was quite shocked to see it."

Lauren flipped the switch. The glove vibrated slightly, raising
a tingle that rode up her arm and across her body. The sensation
was sure to activate her scales.

The Colonel put on a condescending smirk. "You weren't supposed to know about it, but now that it's in service, I can tell you.
It's a top-secret weapon we're using to deflect the dragons. It activated automatically when the attack began, and the operators are
on their way now. They should be inside in a matter of minutes.
Then they will drop the shield and use the guns as offensive
weapons." He nodded at the rope coiled around Sir Barlow's
shoulder. "Why do you have that?"

Lauren turned the glove counterclockwise less than an inch. The gun shifted a hair to the left but not enough for anyone to notice.

"I found it lying on the ground next to the searchlight tower," Sir Barlow said. "I was taking it back to storage."

"Did you check on the tower guard?"

"I did, sir. There's a malfunction in the turning motor. The weather, I suppose."

"Not likely. Those motors were tested in subzero conditions." The Colonel looked toward the tower. "Could another dragon have gotten through?"

"Did one get through the shield, sir?"

"Never mind. Get to maximum security with the others. I have to check on something." The Colonel walked a few steps toward the tower, lifted a phone to his ear, and barked into it. "Stewart! What's going on up there? ... Stewart? Can you hear me?" Cursing, he pressed a button on the phone. "Control room, this is Colonel Baxter."

"Lauren," Matt said. "I think I have the glove figured out."

"Me, too. Should we wait for them to leave?"

"Yeah. Hold tight for a minute."

Portia scooted up to Sir Barlow and whispered. The words rode across Lauren's back and entered her ears. "Leave ... now ... fast."

"Why, Miss?" Sir Barlow asked. "If you are in danger, I cannot leave you behind."

"He ... kill you." Her face brimming with fear, she slid to where the Colonel stood, his back still toward them.

The Colonel pivoted and faced Sir Barlow. They stood about five steps apart, their profiles in Lauren's view. "Stewart's not answering."

"He isn't?" Sir Barlow's brow lifted. "Well, perhaps he is trying to repair the—"

424

"Cut the nonsense!" The Colonel reached under his parka and pulled out a handgun. "I've been watching you, Hoskins. I've seen you meander off the patrol route too many times, and now I heard from the weapons unit that the control gloves are missing. What did you do with them?"

"Control gloves?" Sir Barlow spread out his bare hands. "I have no control gloves."

"If you don't, then who did you give them—" The Colonel's eyes darted toward the laser weapons. "Ah! I see your coconspirators!"

He aimed the gun toward Lauren and Matt. Sir Barlow heaved the rope coil at the Colonel's chest and leaped at him. The two rolled in the snow, punching and kicking. Portia grabbed the Colonel's hair with one hand and gouged at his eyes with the other.

Lauren gripped the laser barrel with her bare fingers, shivering harder than ever. "What can we do?"

"Stay calm," Matt whispered as he aimed Sir Barlow's gun. "I'm using my left, but if I can get a clean—"

A muffled gunshot sounded. The Colonel threw Sir Barlow to the side and climbed to his feet. Portia backed away, hugging herself as her body quaked.

"So the two of you were in on this together." The Colonel aimed his gun at her. "After all I've done for you."

"No," Portia said, still backing away. "I have ... daughter. Don't kill."

"You should've thought of that before you turned traitor." He pulled back the gun's hammer. "No need to waste time with a trial."

26

THE GREEN OVULUM

A shot rang out. The Colonel toppled over onto Sir Barlow. Matt's laser barrel lurched downward, and the beam ripped into the ground, sending a streak of radiance that melted the snow in its path and washed over Sir Barlow and Colonel Baxter.

As Matt slid forward, he threw his smoking handgun to the ground and manipulated the glove, raising the barrel again. The beam lifted back to the sky and joined the others.

A cloud of vapor rose from the point where the two men had fallen, hiding their bodies from view. Portia staggered toward them and fell on her knees at their side.

Lauren gasped. "What did you do?"

"I must've disintegrated them!"

"Now what?"

"I'm turning off my glove." Matt leaped to the ground. "Let's go!"

Lauren switched off her glove. Grasping the barrel with one hand, she swung down to a hanging position before dropping into

427

Matt's arms. After steadying her, he picked up the handgun and slid it behind his waistband.

As they ran to Portia, a gust blew the vapor away, revealing a gap in the snow and a small collection of metallic objects—two handguns, one of them a semitransparent weapon similar to Catherine's; two belt buckles and name tags; several coins; a gun clip; various buttons and rivets; a cell phone; a brass box; and a gold ring. The rope lay in the snow several feet away, still coiled.

Portia covered her face and sobbed. Lauren bit the fingers of her control glove and pulled it off. Dropping to her knees, she laid an arm around Portia.

As they wept together, Matt stripped off his glove. His hands shaking, he opened the brass box and pulled out a piece of paper, unfolding it as he drew it close. After clearing his throat, he read it with a shaky voice. "To whoever reads this, I hope you found my humble will and testament on my corpse on the battlefield. I am over a thousand years old, and although I can name a hundred glorious days in which I have witnessed God's wondrous miracles, if I died in valor, then this is the finest day of my life. I can ask for nothing better. I have no dependents, so kindly see to it that my meager belongings are given to a worthy charity, preferably one that cares for needy children. To you, my good fellow or lass, I hope to see you in Paradise, my new home. My battles are finally over. In the name of Jesus Christ my Savior, Sir Winston Barlow, formerly of Hinkling Manor."

Lauren reached into the pile and picked up the cell phone. After sliding it into her pocket, she lifted the ring, the rubellite ring she had dropped in the stairwell. Her hands trembling, she slid it over her finger. It fit perfectly. "Thank you for rescuing us, Sir Barlow." She brushed a tear from her eye. "You are a gallant knight, indeed."

Matt returned the note to the box. After helping Lauren and Portia rise, he picked up the semitransparent gun. "Just what we need—a candlestone shooter."

Lauren rubbed a finger across the smooth, glass-like casing. "What are you going to do with it?"

"I'm going to shoot at the dome and see what happens. I'm hoping the bullets will break the dome down enough to let the dragons through."

"More dragons are out there?"

"Yes, I can see three shadows flying overhead. I think the shield is keeping them from communicating with us, so maybe punching a hole will help with that, too."

"Why don't we try the gloves again?" Lauren asked. "If we lower two guns, maybe it will be enough to knock out the dome."

Matt aimed the gun nearly straight up. "We'll do both."

"I take them." Portia scooped up the control gloves and ran toward the Colonel's office.

Lauren opened her mouth to shout for her to stop, then closed it again. "Portia's deaf. Should I run after her?"

"Let her go. She's obviously on our side, and maybe she knows something we don't." Matt squeezed the trigger. The muzzle made a popping sound and sent a glittering sphere rocketing toward the sky. The bullet hit the dome and stuck there, as if embedded in the wall of light. Like a termite gnawing through wood, it attached to the dome and ate a small hole in the shield, its attraction to light overcoming the pull of gravity. As the bullet inched along, the hole grew bigger, only to be closed off from behind as the laser guns continued pumping energy into the dome.

Matt shifted his aim from place to place and fired six more spheres before lowering the gun. "I think it's out of ammo."

Above, seven holes drifted, enlarging and shrinking as the pattern of consuming and refueling continued.

Walter's voice broke through in Lauren's tooth. "I see openings, but they're not big enough for a dragon. Maybe I could jump through one."

"They're too small for you," a female said. "And they're way too erratic."

429

"That might be Sapphira, Queen of Second Eden," Matt whispered. "I heard she'd probably come with them."

"Joran might be able to break the shield completely," Lauren said. "Joran?"

Blinking, Lauren shook her head. "Sorry. It's just from my dream. Joran can use his voice to create energy walls that destroy tanks, but when my dream ended, he was trapped in a green ovulum." She shrugged. "Like I said, it's just a dream."

Walter spoke up. "Did you say a green ovulum?"

"Yes," Lauren said, touching her cheek. "Why?"

"We have one."

Lauren held back a shriek. "You have a green ovulum?"

"Right. According to Elam, there are a couple of people inside—"

"I know! I know! Joran and Selah. They could definitely help."

"Elam says we're not supposed to break it, and even if we did, how could they drop through the shield?"

"Will the ovulum fit through one of the holes?" Lauren asked.

"Give me a minute. I'll see."

During the pause, she looked at Matt. Stooping, he picked through the pile of metallic remains where Sir Balow died. He sniffed, maybe because of the weather, or maybe because of the tragedy. Either way, he was clearly moved by the noble sacrifice.

The tingling sensation on her back returned. A barely audible voice rose to her ears, sounding like thoughts coming from Matt's direction. *Now there's a hero. Why couldn't I have saved him? Maybe I should've shot the guy sooner. And it's my fault that laser disintegrated him. Maybe I could have—*"

"Don't blame yourself," Lauren said. "We all did what we could."

He looked up at her. "Mind reading again?"

"Sorry. I was just—"

Walter's voice broke in. "I think we can fit the egg through a hole, but how will you catch it? With the holes moving, you won't know where to stand."

A new voice barged into the transmissions. "I'll catch it!"

"I hear you, Gabriel," Walter said. "Where are you?"

"I'm on my way." A winged man zoomed over the barracks, then nearly straight up. Seconds later, he flew in a tight circle under one of the holes in the dome. Above him, a dragon-shaped shadow flew in a similar orbit.

"Ready?" Walter called.

Squinting at the radiance, Gabriel held out his cupped hands. "Ready!"

Something dropped through the hole. With a quick shift, Gabriel caught it. Then, folding in his wings, he plunged. Just before landing, he fanned them out again and sailed to a stop in front of Lauren and Matt, a green ovulum in his palms.

Lauren touched the smooth glass. "It's just like in the dream."

"Well, whatever you're planning to do," Gabriel said as he rolled it into her hands, "you'd better do it fast. A bunch of armed guards and three tanks are lining up over in maximum security, and we don't have any dragon help. Ashley's with Legossi and Billy in the dungeon. She got the candlestone out of him, but since she had to take it out of his brain, he's too weak to walk yet. Good thing it was shallow. Anyways, she's working on Legossi now, but she's having trouble digging between her scales."

Lauren held the ovulum close to her face. The sound of a lyre rode up her spine, soft and lovely, though melancholy in mood. "Joran," she said sharply, "since you're holding the lyre, I know you can understand me. We need you out here. You can break through the shell."

"Why aren't we allowed to break it?" Matt asked. "We need to do this fast. I sense danger big-time."

"According to the dream," Lauren said, "the mists that transport people won't return unless he sings a song in response to something he hears outside. If we break the shell, he won't be able to transport, and his refuge will be destroyed."

"Well, Joran or no Joran, we need a plan." Matt pulled his jacket closed, hiding the gun in his waistband. "We have company."

431

Lauren looked toward the fence in front of maximum security. At least twenty men with parkas and boots filed through the gate, each gripping a rifle. "Joran!" she shouted into the ovulum. "Soldiers are coming to get us! Hurry!"

Matt grasped Gabriel's arm. "Can you fly Lauren out of here?"

"Sure. Then I'll come back and help you." Gabriel stepped behind Lauren and wrapped his arms around her waist.

"No!" She broke loose from his hold. "Joran has to sense my danger, and no one else can hear what's going on in there."

"Then go see if Billy's able to come," Matt said. "Walking or not, we could use his firepower."

"Billy is doubtful, but Legossi might be ready." Gabriel launched into the air, zigzagging in the blustery wind.

Several of the soldiers aimed their rifles at him, but a man at the front of the line shouted, "Hold your fire! Four in the rear, go after him. The dome will keep him from getting away."

As the soldiers marched within a hundred feet, the lyre's notes grew louder. A song came through, filling with energy as a feminine voice joined in.

Alone here singing day by day,
I wondered who could hear my cry;
No answers came from Heaven's doors,
Just echoes sung in warped reply.

While Selah sang a lilting descant, the soldiers formed a semicircle around Lauren and Matt, their rifles tucked under their arms as if ready to fire at a split second's notice.

The commander, now at the far end of the formation, waved a hand and spoke in a calm tone. "At ease, men. They're not going anywhere."

As the rifle muzzles shifted toward the ground, the commander strolled in front, his parka hood down and a phone at his ear. "It's Captain Boone. ... Yes, Major, we got the kids, and I have a detail chasing the winged man. We'll have him soon. ... The Colonel?" He stooped at the scorched grass plot where the Colonel and Sir Barlow had disintegrated. Rising again with a name tag in his fingers, he shook his head. "It looks like one of the lasers killed him. There's nothing left of him but a pile of metal scraps, so I guess you're in charge. ... Yes, one of the men told me the dragon got plugged with a candlestone. I saw it flying like a wounded duck. It's probably out cold somewhere. ... Sure. How long? ... Not a problem. The beams are keeping the others out. We can wait."

"Everyone stay where you are," the Captain called in a louder voice. "We will receive further instructions in a moment." While the Captain studied his phone's screen, Lauren refocused on the ovulum. Joran's voice grew stronger, and Selah's blended perfectly.

433

With diligence we kneel once more;
Until you heed, we will not stand.
Remember blood, remember tears,
The red and white of mercy's hand.

"Joran!" Lauren called out. "We're in great danger! Please hurry!"

"Joran?" The Captain scanned the area, first the surrounding field, then the air between the ground and the overhead dome. "I've heard of Jesus and Jehovah, but who is this Joran you're praying to?"

"You might call him an invisible friend." The ovulum grew warm in Lauren's palm, and a cracking noise reached her ears. With no sound coming from within, maybe Joran had finished his song. She set it on the ground, and it sank out of sight under the snow. "I have a lot of weird idiosyncrasies."

"Speaking of weird," Captain Boone mumbled as he nodded toward the Colonel's office.

Lauren swung in that direction. Wearing a form-fitting black trench coat and sleek black gloves and boots, Semiramis strolled toward them with a cocky gait.

Pulling Matt by his sleeve, Lauren whispered. "Stay close. I think the egg's about to hatch. We might be in for a wild ride."

Semiramis stopped within Lauren's reach and folded her arms in front. "It has been a long day for you, hasn't it, my dear?"

Scowling, Lauren focused on Semiramis. Since Ms. Ghost hadn't noticed the ovulum, keeping her distracted might be a good idea. "Too long, thanks to you."

"We merely did what we had to do to get you to comply." Poison laced her tone. "You found what we were looking for much more quickly than we expected, and now that it is in our possession, I have been granted permission to do as I please with you."

434

Lauren kept her stare fixed. Fear instincts screamed at her to run, but since Semiramis lacked a physical body, she couldn't do any harm. "Did you come out here just to brag? You could have done that in front of a fireplace while sipping witch's brew."

"I hope you can keep your sense of humor. You will need it." Semiramis withdrew a gun from under her coat, grabbed Lauren's arm, and pressed the muzzle against her chest. "I came out here to collect my prize." Glaring at Matt, Semiramis pulled the hammer back. "Move out of reach, hero."

Raising a hand, Matt slid away three steps. "Okay. Okay. Just stay cool."

Lauren looked at Semiramis's tight grip. Pain ripped from elbow to shoulder. "How did you—"

"Surprised?" Semiramis laughed. "Thank your friends from Second Eden. They provided the magic. But their arrival won't help you at all. The shield will keep the lizards at bay until our reinforcements arrive, so I suggest that you put away all thoughts of resistance and make this easier for both of us."

Lauren glanced at Matt. His fingers slid toward the gun hidden behind his waistband. He whispered, "Stay calm. I'll look for an opening."

"Major," Captain Boone said, smiling nervously, "this young lady isn't likely to overpower my men. If you'll lower the gun—"

"You have no idea what she can do!" Semiramis nodded toward the scorched grass. "I see rope. Have one of your men bind her wrists. That's an order!"

The Captain heaved a sigh. "Very well." He waved for one of the men. "Tucker, get the rope and tie the girl's wrists."

A beefy soldier broke from the ranks and scooped up the coil. As he passed by, the Captain whispered, "If you get a chance, disarm her." Without acknowledging the command, Tucker hurried on.

Lauren tried to stay expressionless. She barely heard the Captain's whisper herself, so Semiramis likely didn't hear.

While keeping the gun aimed at Lauren, Semiramis backed away a step, giving Tucker room. "Make sure it's tight," she said.

Tucker looped the rope around one of Lauren's wrists and fashioned a tight knot. Keeping her lips as still as possible, she whispered, "When I get her to look away, that'll be your chance."

He gave her the slightest of nods.

Lauren pointed at the ovulum with her free hand. "Look! That green egg's cracking open!"

"What?" When Semiramis looked down, Lauren leaped toward Matt. Tucker spun and grabbed Semiramis's gun, grunting as he tried to wrestle it away. The gun discharged, sending Tucker lurching backwards. After staggering a few steps, he collapsed.

Now aiming at the Captain with a smoking muzzle, she shouted, "Lower your weapons and march away, or I will kill him!"

The soldiers looked at the Captain as if waiting for his command. He nodded at them. "Do as she says."

As they began a march toward the maximum security area, a pop sounded. Thick green mist shot out from the depression and

435

rose in a violent swirl that split into two cyclones, miniature tornadoes spinning and scattering the snow.

At the weapons column, one of the barrels shifted downward, and its beam began a slow descent. The dome thinned, and its holes grew wider. Radiant droplets and sparkling candlestone bullets drizzled from the sky, raising vapor when they hit the snow.

Semiramis shifted the gun toward Lauren. "Now pick up the rest of the rope and get over here!"

Matt gathered the coil and laid it in Lauren's arms. As he guided her toward Semiramis, he whispered, "I'm hiding my gun behind you. When I get a good shot, I'm taking her down."

"Matt. No. Her gun's already aimed. She'll kill you."

"You stay back," Semiramis shouted, "or I'll shoot through her to get to you."

As sparkling rain continued, the descending laser beam shut off, and the gun next to it darkened as well. Raising his hands, Matt stepped to the side. Lauren glanced at him. The gun was now out of sight.

"You're too dangerous to leave alive." Semiramis aimed directly at him. Just as she fired, Lauren shoved Matt to the snow. The bullet struck the side of Lauren's bound wrist, slicing into both bone and skin. As blood oozed, Lauren grasped the wound and fell to her knees. Pain roared up her arm and sent shock waves to her brain.

"Hesitation is purchased by blood," Semiramis said as she picked up the end of the rope and looped it around her wrist. "Hero boy, you and the Captain stand together and turn your backs."

Matt rose to his feet and helped Lauren to hers. "If you're going to shoot me," he said, "you'll have to look me in the eye when you do."

"As if that would stop me." Semiramis pulled the hammer back.

436

Lauren jerked the rope, twisting Semiramis away. The gun went off, sending a bullet into the air. Lauren bolted toward the maximum security area, pain throttling her senses. If only she could get to Billy or Legossi, maybe their firepower would keep her safe. Since Semiramis wanted her prize so badly, she would follow right away, wouldn't she?

A hard pull on the rope brought her to a sliding halt. Semiramis called, "You fool! You can't get away."

Lauren spun and looked back. The wicked witch gave chase, the rope in her grip. Matt stood next to the Captain, aiming his gun, but he didn't fire, apparently worried about hitting the wrong person.

Letting out a relieved sigh, she waited for Semiramis to catch up. The pain was so awful, she wouldn't be able to escape anyway. At least she had saved Matt, and now Joran and Selah could materialize without interference.

When Semiramis arrived, she slapped Lauren across the cheek and barked, "Follow me!"

Lauren staggered behind her and trudged through the snow toward maximum security. When she gained her balance, she looked over her shoulder. The green cyclones congealed, forming Joran and Selah, both shivering in the cold wind. When they fully solidified, Selah picked up the fractured egg, fitted the two halves together, and slid it into her pocket.

Lauren slipped, nearly falling. Semiramis jerked on the rope again. "Keep your eyes on the path! We can't waste even a second!"

Blinking away tears, Lauren marched in front of Semiramis. What could Matt, Joran, and Selah do now? Joran's gift would have been perfect for breaking down the dome, but that was already taking place. The only hope was for the holes to grow and allow the dragons to enter, but would they come in time?

As more radiance dripped, it seemed that fire rained from the sky, bringing sheets of snowflakes in behind the flames—impossible weather, but perfect for this bizarre, twisted reality.

437

With her fingers wrapped around the rope and her wound, she whispered into her transmitter. "Matt, the two who came out of the egg are Joran and Selah. They're called Listeners, son and daughter of Methuselah. Ask them if they can create a protective sound barrier. When the prison's forces show up, you're going to need it."

"Okay. I'll ask." His voice sounded tense. "Are you all right?"

"Not really, but don't worry about me. I can take it."

"As soon as I talk to the Listeners, I'm coming to get you."

"It's too dangerous." Lauren's voice dropped even further. "She'll kill you."

"Like a little danger is a problem? I've been risking my life ever since I met you. Why should now be any different? Nothing's going to stop me."

She took in a breath, trying to force the pain out of her voice. "Okay, I'm counting on you. If anyone can get us out of this mess, you can."

27

CHAPTER

THE FIRESTORM

As Lauren and Semiramis approached the fence between the prison sections, Matt slid the gun behind his waistband and hustled to where Captain Boone knelt at Tucker's side. "How is he?"

"Dead." The Captain looked up, cursing under his breath. "If I get my hands on that—"

"Exactly." Matt pushed some bite into his words. "Semiramis is a she-devil! She shot my sister and took her away, and she was ready to kill you, too!"

"Hang on, kid. I'll see what I can do." The Captain hustled away, following the path Semiramis and Lauren had made through the snow.

Matt blew out a stream of white. He couldn't go with the Captain until he took care of the new arrivals. Laying a hand on Joran's shoulder, he looked him in the eye. "I'm Matt. My sister, Lauren, called you here. Do you understand?"

"Yes, we both know your language." Still shivering, Joran held a lyre in both hands. "What can I do to help?"

"Lauren wondered if you're able to create a sound barrier that can protect people."

"Our barriers destroy." Joran withdrew two metal rods from a pouch in his pants. "But there is a song we heard recently that might reverse the effect."

"We can try it," Selah said as she took one of the rods. "We'll know soon."

A tank slammed into the fence in front of maximum security and bulldozed it down. Two more tanks followed, each one crunching the fallen chain links as it passed. Carrying rifles, dozens of men marched in the tank's tracks.

Atop the lead tank, a man sat behind a mounted machine gun. As he swept it from right to left, a hail of bullets sprayed the sky above Matt and the two Listeners, apparently warning shots.

Above, a dragon dove through one of the gaping holes, then two more. The first dragon zoomed straight toward the lead tank. It blasted a fireball that narrowly missed the gunner and splashed into the hole at the top. As the dragon flew past, Walter leaped from its back and tackled the gunner, sending them both flying to the side. Smoke poured from the lead tank, and it stopped in its tracks. The other tanks halted, unable to pass on the narrow path between the sets of barracks.

As the ground troops shot at the dragon, it swung around and blew fiery streaks at them, staying in a wide orbit to avoid their bullets. From that distance, the dragon's flames did little damage, but they kept the soldiers distracted.

Matt touched his cheek. "Lauren, what's going on? I can't see you anymore."

"She's going to put me in one of the tanks." Her whisper was barely audible. "She said something about keeping her prize safe. With all the dragons and bullets flying around, I don't think I'm going to argue too much."

"Listen. I'll see if I can call off the dragons and—"

440

"Don't! If you do, we'll never get out of here. I'll hunker down. Don't worry about me."

The other two dragons orbited the laser weapons column, blasting fountains of fire at the guns as they beat their wings to fan the flames. One of the riders, a white-haired female, threw fireballs into the furious cyclone. With all but two of the guns still shooting laser beams, the blend of flames and radiant light created a dazzling display of pulsing, swirling energy.

While the Listeners lifted their rods and began a song, Matt eyed the two darkened guns, the same two he and Lauren had mounted. Since Portia had taken the control gloves, she had to be the one who shut the guns down. She might still be inside the weapons column.

Before Matt could shout a warning to the dragons, a loud pop sounded. The column vanished, leaving a rectangular hole in the ground. The remaining dome of light collapsed, and the entire compound dimmed, now lit only by the single searchlight and a few flood lamps attached to the buildings.

Matt took a heavy step backwards. The entire column had disintegrated, and Portia with it!

As snow pelted Matt's head, the two dragons broke away from their orbit and flew toward the tanks. A male rider stood on his dragon's back, leaped to the ground, and rolled in the snow. When he popped up to his feet, he ran to Matt. Snowflakes fell from his mop of tawny hair as he gasped through his words. "I'm Elam, and the white-haired woman riding on Roxil is Sapphira. I think the lasers and flames created a portal where the weapons were. If we can get the soldiers close enough to the portal, Sapphira and the dragons might be able to transport them somewhere else."

"Where?" Matt asked.

"Another world, I hope. At this point, we'll take anywhere but here. While we were in the sky, I saw a convoy of vehicles coming down the road. They're stuck behind a snow plow, so we have

441

some time, but not much. We just need to get everyone out of here as fast as possible."

"How are we going to draw the soldiers close enough? They can't go anywhere right now."

"If we can keep them where they are, we can try to move the portal to them. With the dragons' help, I think Sapphira can do it."

"Then we have to get Lauren and Walter out of there first," Matt said.

Walter's voice buzzed through Matt's tooth. "I've been listening." Grunts peppered his words. "Get it started. I'll try to find Lauren."

Matt looked at the oncoming troops. One of the trailing tanks had smashed two of the barracks on the right side. While several women fled from the ruined buildings and began pounding on nearby doors, the tank rumbled back to the path.

While two dragons continued the onslaught around the tanks and soldiers, slowing their progress, one flew back and landed next to Joran and Selah.

"Makaidos!" Joran lowered his rod. "It's you!"

Makaidos bowed his head. "Shall we go to battle again?"

Joran looked at Matt. "We will probably do more good as a sword than as a shield."

Waving a hand, Matt nodded. "Sounds good. Go."

Joran gave Selah the lyre, scrambled up Makaidos's back, and helped her climb to a seat behind his.

The new lead tank fired. A glittering ball shot out and thumped into one of the circling dragons. Sapphira grabbed a protruding spine to keep from falling off.

"Roxil!" Makaidos called.

Wobbling in flight, Roxil reversed course and headed toward Makaidos. She crashed and slid through the snow, stopping almost within reach. Sapphira leaped off and knelt close to Roxil. Flames erupting from her hands, she massaged the dragon's neck.

Elam smacked Makaidos's flank. "Go! Join Thigocia. I'll look after Roxil."

Now within two hundred feet, the lead tank stopped and fired again. The shining missile zinged by, narrowly missing Makaidos. Beating his wings, he launched toward it. Dozens of men swarmed around the tank and shot at him. Bullets clinked against his scales and ricocheted, driving him into a faltering flight pattern.

The tank's gun shifted, following Makaidos and Thigocia. The two dragons blew a storm of flames at it and began an orbit around the entire company. A riderless dragon joined the fray, also blowing a fury of orange.

"Legossi is here," Elam said as he helped Sapphira to her feet. "They should be enough to move the portal. Sapphira can begin the migration from the old laser weapons site."

"Start the process." Matt drew his gun. "I'm getting Lauren." He took off down the path, keeping his head low. When he reached the tanks and soldiers, a ten-foot-high wall of fire surrounded the entire company, swirling as the three dragons flew in an orbit that hemmed in all three tanks and every soldier.

443

From a foot or so above and outside the cyclone, they spewed torrent after torrent of fire into the spin, their wings fanning the upper part of the flames and their tails whipping the wall close to the ground.

Matt halted near the wall. Shots rang out from within. Bullets and candlestones flew at the dragons, but they zipped by so quickly, the projectiles either missed or glanced off armor. A soldier leaped through the wall. With his clothes on fire, he dove into the snow and rolled. White vapor flew upward, and after a few seconds, he lay motionless.

"Walter," Matt called. "Where are you?"

A reply buzzed in his transmitter. "Standing on top of the middle tank. After I fought the gun operator, I hustled back to see if Lauren was here, but no luck. Not even the driver's inside. It's a madhouse down on ground level. It's so hot, the soldiers all stripped down to their uniforms. They're in a state of panic, and they're shooting wildly. If they settle down, they might figure out that they can drive a tank through the flames and break the firestorm."

Matt looked back at the field. Sapphira stood in front of the former weapons column site, her hands raised. An instant later, a spinning cocoon of flames surrounded her. A tongue of fire shot out in an arc, spanning the two-hundred-foot gap, and melded with the dragons' swirling flames. Sapphira and her flames drifted toward them, melting the snow as she advanced.

"Where's Gabriel?" Matt asked. "He could fly in there and help you get Lauren out."

Walter grunted, as if throwing a punch. "No idea. I haven't heard a word out of him."

"Legossi!" Matt shouted. "Where's Gabriel?"

As Legossi zoomed by, she spoke through her transmitter. "Gabriel and Ashley were carrying Billy out of the research wing's lower level. The transmitters do not seem to work well there, so I doubt that we can reach them."

"They're still jamming communications in that building. We'll have to rescue Lauren without them."

When Makaidos swung around on their side of the cyclone, Joran and Selah leaped from his back and into the circle, disappearing behind the flames.

"Makaidos!" Matt called. "What are they doing?"

"They think they can rescue Walter and Lauren with a sound shield. Joran said something about a mercy song."

With noise hammering his ears, Matt pressed a hand against his jaw. "I can't count on two kids and a song to rescue them. I have to get in there."

"I understand. Joran was concerned that he might not be able to remember the song."

"Well, then, pick me up the next time you come around and drop me in there."

"No! That would be madness."

Matt looked back at Sapphira. Now about thirty paces away, she would arrive soon. He slid his gun behind his waistband and watched the dragons zoom by. Walter had mentioned how dangerous a tail mount could be, a feat requiring perfect timing whether from the ground or in the air.

As a sharp, spiny-topped tail whipped by in a blur, Matt's heart thumped. Perfect timing? Probably. Insanity? Definitely.

When Makaidos flew by again, Matt sucked in a breath, jumped as high as he could, and grasped the tail with both arms. A sharp pain jabbed his hand, a spine piercing the heel. The wall of flames zoomed past. Hot wind whistled in his ears. He slid his arm up, freeing his hand from the spine. As the muscle cramped, blood flowed and dripped to the scales. "I'm not letting go!" he called. "Flip me to your back with your tail."

445

"I see that I have no choice," Makaidos grumbled. "Very well."

Makaidos's tail flipped, slinging Matt forward. He flew in a somersault and smacked against the dragon's neck, facedown and riding backwards. Hugging the neck with both arms, he squirmed toward the back, swaying with every blast of fire Makaidos spewed. Fortunately, the spines bent toward the tail as he pushed over them, but any sudden bump might send him lurching in the opposite direction, and the spines would impale him.

Finally, he grasped a spine at the base of the neck and pulled himself down. Still riding backwards, he set his feet and rose to a standing position, a hand gripping the top of the spine. His legs wobbled, and his feet shifted as Makaidos's body rode up and down with his wing beats. Soon, he steadied himself and looked inside the cyclone.

At ground level, at least a dozen men aimed their rifles at the dragons, constantly sweeping the barrels in arcs as they fired useless rounds. A few soldiers trembled, either wounded or terrified. Others lay in blackened heaps, smoke curling up from their charred bodies.

Walter, Joran, and Selah stood atop the middle tank. Joran and Selah locked arms and held their sonic rods and the lyre while they sang. Joran shook his head, apparently frustrated.

Outside the cyclone, Sapphira approached, now visible within her firestorm, her arms high as she waved them in a circle. She was only seconds away. Next to one of the barracks, the Captain braced himself against the building's frame while he helped a female prisoner to her feet. It seemed clear that he was no longer in a position to command the troops.

Matt eyed the last of the three tanks, motionless, apparently nonoperational. A five-foot-long section of rope dangled from its open hatch. He picked out a spot to land and leaped as far as he could. As he sailed over the fire, inertia carried him beyond his target. He landed feetfirst on a charred body and rolled with his momentum through the mud and against one of the rear tank's tracked wheels.

446

A soldier aimed his rifle at him. "Get up!"

As Matt rose, he scooped a handful of mud and slung it in the soldier's face. He caught the gun barrel and ripped it away, spinning the soldier around. With a kick to his backside, Matt shoved him into the mire.

Dripping mud, he dropped the rifle and scrambled up the tank. Staying out of view of whoever might be inside, he picked up the dangling rope and peered in. Semiramis and Lauren crouched together, looking through the front viewport. Now dressed in a camo uniform, Semiramis kept her stare locked straight ahead.

Coiled at the floor, the rope hung close to Semiramis's head. If he could loop it around her neck and jerk back, maybe he could disable her, but with throbbing pain in the heel of his hand, could he pull hard and fast enough?

Bullets zinged all around. One nicked his jacket, ripping a hole in the sleeve. No time to think about it. Stooping low, he wrapped the rope around his waist and tied it as tightly as pain would allow. He peeked into the hatch again, spun the rope around Semiramis's neck, and leaped off the tank.

He halted in midair, his back scraping the tank's side. After a quick spin, he braced his feet and climbed the rope. Keeping the line taut, he knelt at the opening. Semiramis hung inside, her head caught at the hatch's lip. Gagging and spitting, she clawed at the makeshift noose.

Matt reached in with his good hand and hauled her out by her collar. He threw her down on her back and planted a foot on her chest. "Don't move!"

She closed her eyes, and her arms fell limp. Lauren climbed out of the hatch, her wrist still tied and the rope coil in her arms.

"Are you all right?" Matt asked.

447

She showed him three long scratches on the back of her hand. Blood trickled down her wrist and behind her sleeve. "She clawed me, and the bullet wound hurts like crazy, but I think I'll be okay."

Matt pushed her to a crouch. "We'd better get back inside. I've never operated a tank before, but if I can figure it out, we can break through the ring of fire."

"That might take too much time." Lauren touched her cheek. "I heard the chatter. Joran's trying to sing the mercy song. A protective shield might be the only way to save us all."

Atop the tank in front of theirs, Walter stood next to Joran and Selah, his gun extended. As Walter shot at anyone who dared aim their way, Joran again shook his head in frustration.

"It looks like he's having trouble," Matt said.

"I need to get to him. I might be able to help him remember the song."

Matt spotted the rifle he had dropped. "When we get down, you take off, and I'll guard your back."

"What about the rope?"

He pulled at the knot, but the fall from the tank had tightened it. "Can't get it loose." He showed her the heel of his hand. "Dragon spine speared me."

"Same problem. The knot's too tight, and I can't grip it."

Matt touched his pocket. Ashley had taken the knife. Cutting the rope with a sharp edge of the tank would probably take too long. "Just go for it. I think there's enough rope."

After unwinding the loop from Semiramis's neck and dropping the coil to the ground, they joined hands and jumped. While Lauren ran to Walter's tank, Matt snatched up the rifle and flattened himself against the tank. As the coil fed the rope out smoothly, he watched the soldiers. Still distracted by the dragons, they barely looked at her. After all, why shoot an unarmed girl? Yet, if he sprang out with a rifle, they might take deadly notice.

Matt studied the gun's firing mechanism. Coated with mud, it looked suspect. Aiming at the sky, he pulled the trigger. Nothing. Jammed. He threw the rifle down. Now what? Maybe it would be better to stay put until Joran and Selah created the barrier. If they failed, he could try to commandeer the tank. With only moments remaining, it might be their only hope of escape.

CHAPTER

THE MERCY SONG

auren rushed to the tank. Standing on top of the wheel track, Walter met her with an outstretched arm and hoisted her up. "Stay low," he said. "The soldiers are leaving us alone for the most part, but we can't take any chances."

Lauren steeled her body to ward off the shakes. "Does Joran remember the song?"

"Not enough of it." He touched the rope. "Want me to untie it?"

"No time. Let's go."

When they reached the top, Walter shouted. "Matt! Get the gunner!"

A new gunner had taken the seat behind the rear tank's mounted machine gun and aimed it at the dragons. Matt scrambled up, jerked the soldier out of his seat, and tumbled with him down the tank's side and into the mud. The slurry covered most of the rope, hiding the section on the ground from view.

As they fought, Walter took aim at Matt's opponent. "I can't get a good shot." He touched Lauren's arm. "Just do what you have to do. I'll help him."

449

While Walter climbed down, Lauren shifted in front of Joran and Selah. "How much of the song can you remember?"

"Only a few notes."

"Give me the lyre," Lauren said, reaching for it. "Keep trying. I'll see if it comes to me."

After Joran handed it to her, Lauren set her fingers on the strings and closed her eyes. The roar of swirling fire, shouts of angry men, and sporadic gunshots combined in a riotous swell in her mind. *Concentrate! You have to remember the tune. You just have to.*

She began plucking the strings in turn. With each note, thoughts and images took shape. The sounds around her slowed, as if played well below their normal speed. With the violet and indigo strings, Bonnie and Ashley appeared, risking their lives for her sake. With the blue string, Walter came to mind, leaping from a dragon to tackle a tank gunner. With the green and yellow strings, her dreams about Joran and Selah repeated. They toiled within the ovula trying to help others while being in a prison themselves. When she played the orange string, the image of Matt appeared as he faced the prison guards while Bonnie flew her to safety.

When she plucked the red string, the dream image of the woman in the courtyard flashed in her memory. She stood there weeping, stones scattered around her feet, the very stones that other sinners hoped to dash against her head. Then, she sang her mercy song. The resurrected tune flowed through Lauren's soul, stirring the flood of beautiful images the lyre's strings had summoned, reflections of the great mercy God had shown to her through the love of others. New words emerged in her mind, her own mercy song, and the passion within her soul erupted, bringing with it the pain, the heartaches, and the fears and doubts of restless uncertainty. Even though she had spent years in foster care, even though her adoptive parents and best friend had been brutally murdered, even though she had suffered horrific torture in recent hours, hope rang true. She was loved, and she was forgiven for ever doubting the one who loved her.

Opening her eyes again, Lauren sang the words, and Joran echoed them while Selah added a harmony.

Your love protects my soul within
And shields my heart from shameful sin;
No flames or fear can steal my love;
It's safely stored in God above.

So now I ask with mercy's song,
Unfurl a banner, safe and strong,
The sound of love's enfolding grace;
We trust in mercy's warm embrace.

Although the tempest tosses seas,
And evil men encompass me,
Let grace and mercy be my shield,
And love and truth the sword I wield.

451

The gap between the sonic rods rippled. The sound barrier was taking shape, but two of the people they needed to rescue were no longer close.

At ground level, Walter stood next to Matt, a foot on the gunner's chest. Several other soldiers closed in on them. His fists flying, Walter plunged into the line. Matt did the same. As the pops of knuckles striking chins and grunts of pain combined with the roar of fire and gunshots, Joran sang on without words, repeating the melody.

A burst of flames shot up at the field side of the dragons' firestorm. Sapphira appeared in the midst, still waving her arms. Like a slow fuse, the burst spread out, following the perimeter in both directions. The scenery beyond the newly energized part of the wall changed from the snowy field to bare, blue sky. Sapphira vanished, apparently having stepped back after finishing the portal migration.

As the dragons continued orbiting, whenever they flew around one leading edge of the spreading fireburst, they disappeared, only to reappear at the other edge. Near the opposite side of the firestorm, a circle of five soldiers surrounded Matt and Walter as they lay in the mud. One aimed a rifle at them, while the others glanced around frantically, apparently terrified as they pointed their guns at every passing shadow.

"The sound barrier is ready," Joran said. "We could take it down there and wrap them all up, but if they fight us, the barrier would likely fail."

Lauren nodded. "Can we wait just a little while longer?"

"I think so. It should last a few minutes."

452

The portal-shifting fire continued its circular march in both directions, now reaching three-quarters of the way around the dragons' cyclone. In seconds, they would all be transported into open air, perhaps hundreds of feet above the ground.

A dragon spewed a stream of flames at the soldier aiming a gun at Matt and Walter. While he burned and two others dodged fireballs, Walter jumped up and decked a fourth soldier, and Matt swept a leg under the fifth. After gaining traction in the mud, Walter ran toward the tank, apparently not noticing that Matt had stayed behind, a rifle once again in his hands.

When Walter climbed to the top, dripping muddy water, he panted. "Thanks for waiting. Let's do it!"

"Matt didn't come," Lauren said, pointing. "He doesn't know the barrier's ready."

Walter touched his cheek. "Matt! Did you hear Lauren? We're all set! Get up here!"

"On my way." Matt hustled toward the tank, but one of the fallen soldiers reached out and tripped him, sending him sliding through the mud. The soldier scrambled up and held a rifle to Matt's head. "Don't move," he called out, "or I'll put a bullet through him!"

Walter picked up the rope. "Keep holding it, Lauren. It might be Matt's ticket back up here."

She held up her wrist. "I don't think I could untie it if I wanted to."

Semiramis dropped down from the top of the tank, apparently fully recovered. Grabbing Matt's collar, she jerked him to his feet with strength that belied her size. She set a dagger against his throat and called out, "Give me Lauren. If you do, she and hero boy will both live. If you don't, I will kill him immediately."

"Wrap them in the barrier!" Matt shouted. "Don't trust a word she says!"

The rear tank dropped out of sight, apparently swallowed by the portal. A vacuum slurped the surrounding men into the void. Walter and Lauren tightened their grips on the rope. Still attached to Matt's waist, the lifeline kept him from getting sucked in. Semiramis hung on to his arm, the dagger poised.

As the ground around them continued to crumble, she locked her fiery stare on Walter. "What is your answer?"

Walter made a twirling motion with his finger. "Joran, wrap Lauren and Selah and yourself up."

"We can't leave Matt!" Lauren strained against the rope. "I *won't* leave Matt!"

The wind swept the remaining men away, leaving only one tank, its riders, and Matt and Semiramis.

With dragon fire still swirling, Walter shouted at Lauren. "Do what I say! Now! I'll hang on to the rope."

"But—"

"No buts." Walter turned to Joran. "I'm counting on you to save Lauren and Selah. Like I said, wrap them and yourself in your barrier."

453

"Not you?" Joran asked.

"Of course not. I'm going to try to save Matt." Walter shifted his focus to Semiramis. "Ease up on that dagger, and we'll talk. In the meantime, I'm going to protect the kids."

Joran unhooked his arm from Selah's and, holding his sonic rod high, began walking around Lauren, wrapping her in the vibrating ribbon. When he finished the circuit, he guided Selah and himself inside and touched the rods together, completing the shield.

Lauren checked the advancing fire. Only a few feet to go before the edges met, maybe fifteen seconds. With the melodic wall singing the Listeners' lovely hymn, all other sounds fell silent.

Walter kept both hands on the rope, leaning back against the pull, easing the tension on Lauren's wrist. He appeared to be talking to Semiramis, but even Lauren's sensitive ears couldn't pick up the conversation.

454

Lauren looked at the expanding portal. If Walter didn't hurry, he and Matt would fall into open sky. Was Semiramis blind to what was going on? Was Walter playing a high-stakes game of "Who will blink first?" Whatever he had in mind, she wasn't about to untie the rope. If Walter slipped, she would remain Matt's lifeline.

"Open the barrier," Lauren whispered to Joran. "Just a little so I can hear."

Joran moved his rod away from Selah's and shifted his body, allowing Lauren to squeeze between them.

"There must be a reason you want Lauren so badly," Walter said, shouting to compete with the wind. "I can't believe you're going to let yourself plunge into an unknown world."

"I know what I'm doing." Semiramis dug the blade into Matt's throat. Blood streamed around the edge. "You have five seconds to decide."

As tingles spread across Lauren's back, a whisper entered her ear. "Lauren, the rope's still tied to my waist. You and Walter can reel me in. Don't worry about Semiramis cutting me. I've been trained to handle this. Just do something that'll distract her for a split second."

Lauren jumped between the rods and shouted, "Semiramis!"

When Semiramis flinched, Matt shoved her arm, snatched the dagger from her hand, and elbowed her in the ribs. She fell away, sucked into the growing hole.

Lauren grabbed the rope behind Walter's gripping point. The advancing edges of the portal joined, and the circle of fire disappeared. The ground under Matt crumbled, and he flew back, hanging in midair, the dagger still in his grip. The knot at his waist held firm, and his body pulled against the rope like a kite battling a gale.

As the tank began to sink beneath them, Lauren and Walter strangled the rope and pulled, but the suction was too strong. "It's slipping!" Walter called. "Hang on!"

Wind whipping her hair, Lauren set her feet and leaned back. "I am!" The rope slid through her fingers until only the loop around her wrist kept it from breaking free.

"Stay here!" Joran shouted at Selah. He, too, joined the pulling effort, while Selah held both rods.

"Let me go!" Matt flailed his arms. "Save yourselves!"

The tank now nearly submerged, Lauren strained with all her might. "Never! If you go, I'm going with you!"

As Matt gazed at her, a new whisper rose into her ears. "I love you, Lauren. It was great being your brother, even for just a little while."

With a flick of Semiramis's dagger, he sliced through the rope and flew away.

Lauren, Walter, and Joran fell backwards, nearly colliding with Selah. Lauren scrambled up and looked for Matt in the blue expanse, but he had already disappeared. "Matt!" she choked out, barely able to breathe.

"Get in!" Walter grabbed her arm and pushed her and Joran into the barrier. He reeled in the rope and shouted, "Now, Joran!"

Joran took one of the rods from Selah and closed the barrier around them, blanketing everyone in silence. They stood on solid ground instead of metal. Somehow the foundation had closed after the tank submerged.

Lauren sobbed. "Oh, Matt! Why did you do that? Why did you cut the rope?"

As if a door had opened to the outside air, cold wind assaulted Lauren's face and lifted her hair. She opened her eyes. Two dragons appeared, flying in a tight orbit but no longer blowing fire. The barracks and field beyond them lay quiet under a mounting blanket of snow. The tanks, the soldiers, and the world of open sky were gone.

Holding his sonic rod, Joran hustled around the group, stripping away the sound barrier. When he joined his rod with Selah's, the melody silenced, and all was quiet except for the whistling wind.

"Is all well?" Sapphira asked as she walked toward them, her white hair aglow.

Lauren fell to her knees and sobbed. She couldn't answer, not even a word. She just stared at the loosely hanging rope, still tied to her wrist.

Walter crouched and laid a hand on Lauren's shoulder. "We lost Matt. He sacrificed himself to save the rest of us."

"Could you see where he went?" Sapphira asked.

"No. He just flew into open air. I had to hustle everyone into the barrier, so I couldn't watch for long."

Legossi flew down with Ashley and Gabriel on her back and landed with a slide in the snow. "The military convoy is closing in," Legossi said. "They have more tanks and men. We do not have enough healthy dragons to carry everyone away."

"And Billy's in no shape to ride," Ashley added as she slid down Legossi's flank. "We left him in the research building with Elam."

Walter stared at Ashley. He swallowed, but just as he was about to speak, a new voice broke in.

"I'll take care of the convoy." The Captain limped from between two barracks, a phone at his ear. Sooty burn marks and a pained expression covered his face. Now without his parka, he wore only a long-sleeved T-shirt and muddy camouflage pants. "This is Captain Boone. Call off the mission. Everything is taken care of. I have all the anthrozils in custody, and the dragons are under control. ... Verification? Why? ... Colonel Baxter was killed in battle. I'm in charge. ... C'mon, Charlie, it's me. I wouldn't steer you wrong. ... Yeah, it's a terrible night. Get the men home while you can. ... Sure, I'll keep you up to date."

He tucked the phone into his pants pocket and scanned the remaining crowd. Setting a hand on his hip, he offered a weak smile. "If only I knew an hour ago what I know now, I could've spared a lot of young lives. It's going to be hard writing letters to bereaved mothers and spouses, and I still have to carry Tucker's body from that frozen field."

457

"Speaking of hard," Walter said as he helped Lauren rise, "telling parents that they lost a son they recently found after fifteen years might be hardest of all."

"Lost a son?" Ashley glanced around. "Where's Matt?"

Walter's face flushed. "Gone. Swept away in the portal."

As their eyes met, Ashley's face twitched. Her lips trembled as she whispered, "I think my brain is choking."

"I had hoped for a happier reunion." Walter spread out his mud-coated arms. "But we're finally together again."

She walked into his embrace and pressed her cheek against his. Sniffling, she rubbed his back. "Will these days of sadness never end?"

Walter kissed her, then touched her nose with a finger. "Knowing you, you're already planning a way to get to wherever this new portal leads."

Ashley stepped back and began counting on her fingers. "I'll need a spectral analyzer and the Apollo device. Then when Sapphira opens the portal, we can look into it safely and—"

"First things first," Gabriel said as he flew from Legossi's back and landed next to Ashley. "From all the bleeding cuts I see, it looks like you have quite a bit of stitching to do. We can ask Carly and Shelly to send the technical stuff you need, but for now, we'd better get everyone inside." He laid an arm around Ashley and drew her close.

She returned the hug and kissed his cheek. "I think I can do more surgery."

"Just a second." Walter touched his jaw. "Jared, you can fly right into the prison to pick us up. Land wherever you can. ... That's right. The area is secure. ... That's fine. We can wait. If Larry says the storm will be over in a few minutes, you can believe him. We'll see you soon."

Selah slid her hand into Lauren's. "Joran and I were taken into another world long ago, and it saved our lives. There is still hope."

Lauren kissed Selah's cheek. "Thank you both for all you've done."

While Joran played a melancholy tune on the lyre, they trudged to the research wing. Makaidos and Thigocia helped Roxil through a dragon-sized hole at the front door. Once everyone made it inside, Elam, Sapphira, and Gabriel rode Makaidos, Thigocia, and Legossi away to Second Eden. With Tamiel unaccounted for, they wanted to make sure the new portal to that world remained secure. They would keep it open for now and guard it well.

Captain Boone brought all the necessary supplies to the Healers' Room—scalpels, bandages, suture thread, and topical anesthesia.

With the storm settling, the power came back on, providing plenty of light and heat.

While Ashley removed the candlestone from Roxil, everyone else showered, though Ashley insisted that Selah stay with Lauren in the female wing's community shower room to make sure she didn't pass out. While warm water poured over Lauren's head, Selah stood at a nearby sink where, after learning how to operate the faucet, she washed her hands and face.

Their conversation began in a somber mood with Lauren lamenting her adoptive parents' deaths, the fact that she had killed a guard, and especially the loss of her brother. Selah, her attitude as effervescent as ever, sang a beautiful song about freedom from bonds and flying above sorrows and strife. As her words echoed in the room, they seemed to try to massage Lauren's soul but without much effect. Grief crushed her heart, and no song was capable of easing her pain.

The men showered in another wing, and Captain Boone provided prison-issue clothing while one anthrozil-friendly staff member laundered the soiled garments. With the Captain now in charge, the prison felt like a hotel, though one remaining guard seemed wary. During the cleanup time, the Captain ordered that guard to drive Stella, still unconscious, to a nearby hospital. Both would be out of the way, at least for a while.

Soon, Ashley had everything she needed to begin stitching the human warriors. It seemed that everyone who had stayed behind suffered a significant wound somewhere. By the time Lauren lay on one of the hospital beds for her turn, loss of blood had taken its toll. Dizziness made the walls turn around her. With the door propped open, it seemed that the bed might spin right out of the room.

The sway added to an unsettled feeling. So much remained to be done; so many mysteries lay unsolved. Finding Matt, Bonnie, and Portia, of course, stood as the top priorities, but what about

Mardon's role? Just moments ago, Walter had filled her in on Mardon's scientific know-how and his relationship to Semiramis. If Semiramis was able to transform to a ghost whenever she wanted to, could Mardon have the same power? With his expertise, he might put more obstacles in their way.

While Ashley prepared to work on Lauren's wrist, Walter, Joran, and Selah looked on. The son and daughter of Methuselah stared, apparently mesmerized by yet more new revelations—hypodermic needles, modern beds, and electric everything.

Billy lay on the adjacent bed, his face clean-shaven, though pale and gaunt, and his ragged hair freshly washed. With his upper body propped against pillows behind him, he looked at the cell phone Lauren had taken from the Colonel's remains. "So is this Portia?" Billy asked as he studied the screen.

Lauren nodded. "She was in the weapons control room when the dragons attacked, and we haven't seen her since. We're wondering if she got transported somewhere."

"Well, her name isn't really Portia." Billy turned the phone around so Walter could see the photo. "Do you agree?"

Walter squinted at the image. "Looks like she's lost quite a bit of weight, but there's no doubt about it. We've been wondering where she's been."

"Her name is Tamara." Billy turned the phone toward himself again. "She was once Sorentine, the first dragon-turned-human Devin killed."

"And also the first *pregnant* dragon he killed," Walter added. "A few years ago, Tamara begged to help with our rescue efforts by going into the prison undercover, but I thought her ... um ..."

"Speech impediment?" Ashley offered.

"Right. I thought her speech impediment would get her in trouble, so I said no." He shook his head sadly. "Maybe I should have done more to discourage her."

"Don't beat yourself up," Ashley said. "From what I heard, she's the reason the dome dissipated. When the spectral analyzer gets here, we'll find her."

Lauren cast a thought at Ashley. *Not to be a pessimist, but you didn't see what I saw. Matt flew into midair. There's no telling how far he fell.*

Ashley lifted a blood-stained finger. *I once fell into a bottomless chasm and still survived. With portals, you never know what's going to happen.*

That helps. Lauren touched her ear and spoke out loud. "If my supersensitive hearing is a dragon trait, could Tamara's deafness be from dragon genetics?"

"Deafness?" Billy began punching numbers into the phone. "Tamara's not deaf. Her speech impediment is real, but her hearing is fine."

An image of Portia's face entered Lauren's mind—intense, dedicated, loving. "Then she's a great actress. She had me fooled."

"I met Tamara," Joran whispered to Lauren. "I know Devin killed her. How did she resurrect?"

"I wish I knew. I'm looking forward to hearing that story myself."

A tear glistened in Joran's eye. "An actress," he said softly. "She lived her dream."

"Hey, Dad," Billy said into the phone. "Can you contact Elam? ... Great. Get a message to Listener that we're on Tamara's trail. She was posing as a prisoner here. If Elam can let Listener come to Earth for a little while, she might be a big help. ... No. There's no news on Bonnie. I don't sense danger anywhere, so we think Tamiel's long gone. We don't have any idea where he took her. ... Right. Tell Walter's folks that he's fine. ... Of course he nearly got killed. That's normal for him. ... Tell his dad that he'll give him a call later. He's cooking up a great way to tell the story.

It might be sadder than usual, but it'll be worth a listen. ... Any news on the disease?"

During the pause, Lauren studied her new father's worried face. Even with a bandage wrapped around his head, his furrowed brow was clear. One word he said reverberated in her mind—*Listener.* How interesting that her name reflected the gift Joran and Selah shared. Could she be the same Listener the viewing wall showed?

"This will numb your skin," Ashley said as she pricked Lauren's wrist with a hypodermic needle. "I don't want you feeling like a pin cushion."

Lauren smiled and cast another stream of thoughts her way. *Don't worry. It can't hurt more than a bullet.*

"Then you probably have the disease now," Billy continued, his tone growing somber. "Are the others getting sicker?" After another pause, he whispered at Walter. "They're pretty bad off. Dr. Conner is running out of options."

Walter and Ashley locked gazes, both with worried expressions.

Billy turned his attention back to the phone. "You heard right, Dad. Sir Barlow died in battle. Apparently he got transluminated, and there wasn't a candlestone around to catch him, so we don't even have a body for a funeral. ... Sure. We'll have a ceremony after we get Bonnie and Matt home." His voice cracked. "Yeah. I agree. Sir Barlow was the cat's pajamas."

"What was that about a candlestone catching him?" Lauren asked.

"Hold on, Dad. Lauren has a question." Billy looked over at her. "A candlestone can absorb a person who gets disintegrated by Excalibur. It's happened to Sir Barlow before. He was trapped inside of one for over a thousand years."

"We had candlestones out there." Lauren held her thumb and index finger close together. "Shiny little bullets. But the Colonel shot Sir Barlow. He might have died before he was ... what was the word?"

"Transluminated." Billy threw the bedsheet back. "Dad, there still might be hope for Barlow. Land on the prison's sports field. I'll see you there in a few minutes." He swung his legs and sat on the side of the bed. "Can someone get my shoes?"

"Just hold your horses," Ashley called. "Even if Barlow's alive in one of those candlestones, we won't be able to get him out until I build an extraction device. The search can wait till dawn."

"I can track them down in the dark. After all the time I spent with a candlestone in my cell, it shouldn't take long. Then I can concentrate on looking for Bonnie."

Carrying the lyre, Joran walked over to Billy's bed, hand in hand with Selah. "Maybe we can help with finding her."

"Really? How?"

"With this." Joran showed him the lyre. "It belonged to Enoch, my grandfather."

Billy eyed the strings. "What does it do?"

"When I play the right notes, I can create images of people I hope to see, sometimes from the past and sometimes from the present. Maybe it can show us where Bonnie is."

463

Billy leaned forward, wincing at the sudden movement. "How can you tell the difference between the past and the present?"

"We should be able to communicate with images from the present. I was able to talk to Selah when she was trapped inside a string, but this might be different since Bonnie's not physically near."

"Let's see what it can do."

Joran ran his finger slowly along the strings. As each note played, a dim halo pulsed, radiating the string's color. "This is a tune my sister taught me, and she learned it from my father, who learned it from Enoch. It's a ballad about love between brothers and sisters, and each generation makes up new words in keeping with their love for their siblings."

Touching the lyre, Selah gave Joran a hopeful look. "May I sing? I have new words of my own."

"That's fine. I think it's the melody that matters." Joran played while Selah sang.

My brother loves, my brother gives;
He lifted me with gentle hands.
No matter where the dangers lurked,
He carried me through lonely lands.

Lauren laid a hand over her chest. Such beautiful lyrics! They reflected exactly how she felt about Matt.

O why do some forsake such gifts,
A brother's sword, a sister's shield,
And turn their weapons on their friends,
The ones for whom they ought to yield?

464

The lyre projected a full-color image of Bonnie sitting with her knees propped up, her wings spread behind her, and her hands tied at her back. Her face seemed pained and worn.

Joran stopped playing and held the lyre close while Selah sang the traditional refrain in a whisper. "Bonnie," he called, "can you hear me?"

Bonnie looked around as if searching for the source of the voice. "I'm here. Who are you? Where are you?"

Billy got up and stood opposite Joran. "Bonnie, it's Billy. Can you tell us where you are?"

"Hello?" Bonnie looked around again. "Is someone there?"

"Maybe only a Listener can talk to her." Joran cleared his throat and called out again. "This is Joran, son of Methuselah."

"Joran?" She stared straight ahead. "I've been dreaming about you! Are you inside an ovulum? I can't see you."

"Selah and I escaped, and now we're with your husband and your friends."

Bonnie smiled through her pain. "Can Billy hear me?"

"Yes. He's watching you. We're all hoping you can help us find you. What have you seen? What have you heard?" Joran again plucked the strings, slowly playing the tune while Bonnie answered.

"Tamiel blindfolded me until I got to this place. We rode in a car for a while, but I don't think he was driving. I heard Mardon's voice from the driver's seat. Then Tamiel carried me in the air. It was very cold for the first part of the flight, and I felt snow, but then I heard a dragon, and a warm wind swirled around me. Maybe the dragon was Arramos, and he might have created a portal. I'm not sure. Anyway, when the wind died down, I was standing on soft turf. It was cool and damp, but not cold. I heard water, but not a stream. It sounded like a pond with something hopping into it, maybe frogs or bugs. Then we climbed a hill. I smelled blossoms—gardenias, I think. For a while, I thought I was back on Morgan's island, but that all changed when we walked into a building. It didn't feel or smell like Morgan's castle at all—none of that dank, musty odor or the feeling of deadness. It reminded me of what Heaven felt like while I was there—light and carefree, smelling fresh, clean, and alive.

465

"Then Tamiel said, 'You start in Paradise, and you will slowly descend into Perdition. Every second of suffering will help me corrupt this world, and Elohim will have no choice but to administer justice, this time with a judgment far worse than a flood.'

"I asked him what that judgment might be, and his response still makes me shudder. He said, 'Abandonment. A world without the divine presence. Yet, what will be the worst of worlds for humans will be the best for my kind. I leave the details to your imagination." She shivered hard before settling. "So now I'm sitting in a small, empty room that has a floor and walls made of stones and mortar, like something from the Middle Ages. There's a waist-level window across the room in front of me, open and big enough to crawl through except for vertical black bars. There's a heavy wooden door to my right. I can hear a fire crackling, and I smell wood smoke, so I think there's a fireplace nearby. Outside I see a lawn, mostly green but with weeds and brown splotches, like it hasn't been tended in a while. It slopes down almost right away, and thick mist hangs in the air, so I can't see much beyond that."

Ashley patted Lauren's shoulder. "You're all stitched. You can get a closer look."

Lauren rose and squeezed around Joran and Selah. She took her father's hand and watched Bonnie through the strings.

"Mom," Lauren said. "Can you hear me?"

Another weak smile emerged. "It's good to hear you call me that, Lauren. I thought you might be my daughter, but I wasn't sure. You had blonde hair when you were a baby."

Lauren touched the ends of her dark locks. "It changed when I was about four."

"Well …" Her voice quaked. "I love you, sweetheart. I'm looking forward to telling you face-to-face."

466

"I love you, too." Lauren swallowed. The lump in her throat had never been this big. Obviously no one wanted to say a word about Matt. Their mother was already suffering enough. "I was wondering about something I heard Tamiel say. He mentioned keeping two others until they could be tested. I got the impression he was talking about anthrozils. Have you seen them?"

"I haven't seen anyone else, but I have an idea they might be Thomas and Mariel. Billy can tell you about them."

"I'll tell you later," Billy said. "Right now, let's concentrate on Bonnie while we can."

Joran continued playing the melody, more quietly now. "Bonnie, are there any other details you can tell us?"

"I don't think so. I didn't give you much to go on, but it's all I have. I tried singing my way out of the bonds around my wrists, but I think the candlestone embedded in my skin has weakened me too much. I think there's a lot of pain in my future."

When she stopped, she leaned her head back against the wall and closed her eyes. "Billy," she said softly, "I was in your arms only a little while ago, and it already feels like it's been another fifteen years. I didn't give up hope during the first fifteen, and I'm not about to give up now, but it hurts …" Tears seeped between her eyelids and streamed down her cheeks. "It hurts a lot. Tamiel says my suffering will smother my song and help him corrupt the world, so I'll try to resist, but I'm so weak, so sick. I need you to pray for me. I can't do this alone."

"I'll pray for you," Billy said, his own tears flowing. "And I'll search the ends of the …" He let his voice trail into a whisper. "I forgot. She can't hear me."

"Shall I tell her what you said?" Joran asked.

Billy clasped his arm. "Please do, and tell her I love her with all my heart." His voice strengthened. "And I *will* get her out of there."

While Joran relayed Billy's message, Ashley joined them. She and Walter sandwiched Billy and Lauren, each laying an arm around the pair. "We've been through tougher situations than this," Walter said. "I mean, think back to when you carried Bonnie's dead body through Hades. And now you have one of your kids here to help. Things could be worse."

467

"I know. I know." Billy took in a deep breath. "We *have* been through worse. We'll get through this, too."

Joran stopped playing. Soon Bonnie's image began to fade. Lauren set her ear next to the strings and listened. Bonnie's tune emanated, not as clearly as before, but still strong enough to be heard. Finally, she disappeared.

Lauren leaned away. With her rising emotions, the tingling surged along her back. Sounds filled her ears. Even though the strings' projection had vanished, Bonnie's emanating tune continued, the mercy song riding the air like a faraway fragrance. Yes, she would be able to track it. She had to, no matter what.

"Excuse me."

The voice came from the hallway. A man wearing silver-dollar glasses poked his head through the entrance. Burn scars covered his oval face. "Please allow me the favor of a parley."

"Mardon?" Billy let go of Lauren's hand and strode toward him. "If you come in peace, we will grant a conference."

Mardon lifted a hand. "No closer, please."

Billy stopped within a few paces of the doorway. "Okay, what's on your mind?"

"I know you want to locate and rescue your loved ones." Mardon took off his glasses and stepped inside, blinking at the fluorescent lights. Wearing a tattered brown jacket and jeans with patches at the knees, he looked like a beggar. "I want to find my mother. You have extraordinary talents, and I have knowledge that you need, including the location of where I drove Tamiel and your wife, as well as information regarding the disease that inflicts the original anthrozils. If we work together, I think we will have greater success than if we strive alone."

"Do you have Excalibur?" Billy asked.

"It is not in my possession, but I know where it is, though obtaining it might prove to be difficult."

Ashley crossed her arms over her chest. "Why should we trust you?"

Mardon put his glasses back on. "As my burn scars attest, I am no friend of Arramos, so Tamiel is also my enemy. We went along with him, because my mother wanted Lauren."

Lauren studied Mardon's pathetic face. Of course, she already knew Semiramis wanted her. Based on the conversation in the limo, the reason probably had something to do with using her skin for restoration. This mad scientist likely could provide the details. "What's so special about me?"

"I think I will hold that information for now. The more I give away, the less I have to bargain with." He bowed his head, revealing more scars on his balding scalp. "I will retire to the hallway so you can discuss my offer in private." With that, he backed away and exited the room.

For a moment, a profound silence reigned, communicating confusion, sorrow, and skepticism. Lauren scanned each troubled face. Their expressions reflected the silence, yet, like mercy, hope hung in the air. No one was about to give up.

"We don't have much choice," Billy said as he walked back to Lauren.

"Nope." Walter pulled Ashley to his side. "And we have our own genius to counter Mardon."

A distant sound entered Lauren's ears, the whipping blades of a helicopter. Her new grandparents were near. "I hear a chopper," she whispered. "What are we going to do?"

Her father grasped her hand again, his finger rubbing across the rubellite on her ring. "We'll take Mardon with us. But don't worry. We've dealt with him before. He's not as unstable as Semiramis."

As he pulled her closer, she leaned against his chest. Images of Matt flashed again in her mind, especially his love-filled eyes as he cut the rope and sailed away. No one had ever shown her so much love. No one.

Her throat tightened, pitching her voice higher. "I ... I need to find my brother."

"We'll find him, Lauren." He kissed the top of her head. "You and I will move Heaven, Earth, and every world in between to find him and your mother."

She let the words sink in. His voice seemed so calm, so soothing. And he called her *Lauren*, not *Karen*, allowing her to maintain the identity she had known for so long, a gift of familiarity and security during these hours of life-shattering upheaval. After only a few moments together, he had proven himself as a father. She could trust him. She could love him.

She pulled away, grasped both of his hands, and gazed into his glistening hazel eyes. "I am Lauren Bannister, daughter of Billy and Bonnie Bannister." As tears trickled down her cheeks, she smiled. "And we *will* find them ... Dad ... I know we will."

469

Recap of *Dragons in our Midst* and *Oracles of Fire*

Jason Waguespack

Enoch, son of Jared the patriarch and prophet of the Most High, extends greetings to all who read this account. For the sake of brevity, I will tell you only the broadest possible strokes of a much longer tale. Yet I know this will be enough for you to understand the extraordinary events that are about to take place.

Back in the days just after Adam and Eve sinned in the Garden of Eden, a group of high-ranking demons called Watchers came to Earth and took beautiful wives for themselves. One of them, a sorceress named Lilith, plotted with Lucifer to use seeds from two trees in the garden—the Tree of Life and the Tree of the Knowledge of Good and Evil—as part of an elaborate scheme to rule the entire world. Using genetic material stolen from her demonic husband, Lilith implanted within her sister, Naamah, the ability to produce a hybrid race of humans—a cross between normal humans and fallen angels. Lucifer then ordered Naamah to marry Ham, a son of Noah, ensuring that she would ride on the ark and escape the flood.

Lilith attempted to board the ark herself by taking the alias Morgan, but her deception was unmasked during a cataclysmic battle between the Watchers, who wanted to destroy the ark, and a host of dragons. The dragons safeguarded the ark's inhabitants, including two dragons who would ensure the survival of the dragon race, while the Watchers were banished to Tartarus, the lowest level of Hades. While on the ark, Naamah gave birth to Ham's son Canaan, a hybrid who carried the genetic code of the Nephilim.

Morgan died in the flood, but her sorcery allowed her to become a wraith, a quasi-physical phantom who could change her shape. However, her form was unstable enough that she had to take up primary residence in the realm of Hades, which was called Sheol at the time. There, she worked with a brilliant scientist named Mardon, who used Canaan's genetic material to fashion a new genome, a cross between a plant and a human. Morgan also took Mardon's mother, Semiramis, the wife of the king of Shinar, under her wing.

In the caverns beneath the third circle of Hades, Morgan, Naamah, and Mardon created creatures that started as plant seedlings but later matured into humans. Many of the males blossomed into giants, new members of the Nephilim race, while the females became simple laborers called underborns who toiled under the merciless whips of Naamah and the evil giants.

One of those laborers was Mara. She was unusual due to her special traits—intelligence superior to the other laborers, eyes that shone with an unearthly blue radiance, and stark white hair. Her sister, Acacia, another laborer with the same traits, had been cast into a river of magma, punishment delivered by Morgan, though Acacia did nothing to deserve it. Mara worked with Mardon in

472

the lower realms of the underworld. While Mara helped Mardon as a laboratory assistant, the other girls dug in the cavern, mining for magnetite ore. One of those girls was the young and verbally challenged Paili, whom Mara protected from Nabal, their cruel taskmaster.

At a lower level in the maze of underground tunnels and chambers, two boy laborers fashioned and baked bricks. One of those boys, Elam, had been kidnapped from his father, Shem, son of Noah, and forced to work in the mines, barely surviving on the morsels he could scrounge. Mara befriended him and later, when he was near starvation, fed him by hand through a hole in the wall. From that time forward, whenever they wiggled their fingers at each other, they were reminded of her gift of love.

Elam found the tree of life Morgan had grown from the seeds she discovered in the Garden of Eden. After eating its fruit, he no longer hungered and never aged. Mara, since she was born and lived in the land of the dead, also never aged, so she and Elam retained the appearance of teenagers. He later stopped showing up at their meeting place at the hole in the wall, so their friendship seemed to have abruptly ended.

473

It was then that Mardon discovered my ovulum. I spoke through the egg that I would communicate only with a maiden of nimble mind, and Mardon guessed that Mara could be that maiden. When he showed her the ovulum, I told her to visit Nimrod, Mardon's father, an idea to which Mardon readily agreed. The two of them traveled through a portal to Shinar and met King Nimrod atop the Tower of Babel, a structure designed to reach Heaven. When King Nimrod met Mara, he was so taken with her beauty and sparkling sapphire eyes, he called her Sapphira Adi, a blue gem, a name she took as her own.

When Sapphira showed Nimrod the ovulum, I spoke a prophecy of destruction upon the king and his tower. Moments later, the judgment came in the form of an attack by several dragons.

Their fire created a spinning column of flame that caused the bottom third of the structure to sink into the ground. Nimrod and Mardon perished in the attack. Sapphira, still carrying the ovulum, raced away from the destruction and escaped back to Hades. She felt, however, that she was a hideous freak incapable of being loved. She wished to die, and it was then that I introduced myself as the Eye of the Oracle, the prophet within the ovulum. I taught her about Elohim, the God for whom I spoke. Despite the fact that her knowledge of Elohim was minimal, she came to love him in a way that was pure and very real.

Mardon returned to Hades as a dead spirit and returned to his work with the Nephilim. In an underground chamber called the mobility room, he taught the maturing giants how to walk and become powerful soldiers, including a seedling Sapphira had raised on her own, a plant she named Yereq. Sapphira and Yereq had grown fond of each other, but Morgan taught Yereq to hate Sapphira and recruited him into Mardon's army.

Centuries passed. In the world of the living, Roxil, the dragon daughter of Makaidos and Thigocia, rebelled against her father's commands to serve mankind. Her brother Goliath, also a rebel, took her as his mate and produced a son named Clefspeare, who sided with Makaidos when he came of age. Morgan hatched a plan to create war between humans and dragons, using Sir Devin, one of King Arthur's knights, as a dragon slayer. Devin murdered Makaidos and Roxil and claimed that the dragons wanted to kill all humans. However, Merlin, a prophet of God, convinced the king to wage war only against the dragons who were not loyal to Makaidos.

In Hades, Sapphira learned that she and Acacia were Oracles of Fire, twins who were supposed to disrupt Morgan's plans. After opening a portal to Morgan's domain, Sapphira searched for Elam in a castle-like house on an island surrounded by a snake-infested swamp. Through her searches, she eventually found a portal to the

474

sixth circle of Hades, where Morgan held Elam prisoner. Naamah sang songs of hatred for Sapphira that constantly repeated in Elam's ears in an effort to sway Elam to betray Sapphira. He refused to betray his friend and spoiled Morgan's plans to obtain Sapphira's blood for her wicked purposes. Sapphira then escaped the circle with Elam.

Their travails took them to a place called Dragons' Rest, where they found Paili and the spirits of Makaidos and Roxil. While there, Sapphira used her power as an Oracle of Fire to withdraw her laborer sisters, including Acacia, from an ovulum where they had been trapped for centuries.

Although Makaidos was friendly to the humans, he told them they had to leave, because Dragons' Rest was meant only for dragons. Sapphira and Elam departed, taking Acacia, Paili, and the other underborn girls with them. With the help of the ovulum, Elam escaped to the world of the living. Sapphira, however, had to return to her caverns in Hades, but she was comforted when she learned that her underground portal could expand into a viewing screen that allowed her to watch Elam and follow his adventures.

475

Merlin gathered the remaining twelve dragons he believed were loyal to Makaidos and asked God to transform them into humans. Theoretically, they would be safe in their disguises, and since they retained their dragon genetics, they would survive for centuries and outlive Devin and any other slayer who thirsted for their blood. Unfortunately, Devin learned of the plan and began searching for and killing these newly formed humans. Merlin then assigned Elam the task of following and guarding Hannah, who had once been Thigocia.

While the dragons tried to remain hidden, some of them marrying normal humans and bearing children called anthrozils, Devin spent centuries hunting them down. Gabriel and Ashley were born to Hannah and Timothy, who was once the dragon Makaidos. Bonnie Conner, the daughter of another dragon-turned-human, had dragon wings as well as an amazing gift of eloquence. After Devin murdered her mother, she changed her name to Bonnie Silver in an attempt to hide her identity. Billy Bannister was born to Marilyn, wife of Jared, who was once the dragon Clefspeare. In time, Billy's gift of fire breathing manifested itself.

Unfortunately, the slayers remained on the trail of the former dragons. In addition to Bonnie's mother, Timothy and Hannah fell to the slayer's sword, and their daughter Ashley had to live with her grandfather. Billy Bannister eventually uncovered the truth of his lineage, and through a series of dramatic events, he met Bonnie Silver. Jared transformed into Clefspeare again, and the slayer Devin became trapped in a light-absorbing gem called a candlestone. Billy's adventures continued, in which he and Bonnie met Ashley, Bonnie's mother was revived as the dragon Hartanna, and Billy finally embraced the Christian faith that Bonnie had known since she was a child.

476

Merlin received a plan to retrieve the spirits of deceased dragons from Dragon's Rest and usher them into Heaven through the coming of the dragon messiah, who turned out to be Billy Bannister. His journey was aided by his best friend Walter, as well as Ashley, Bonnie Silver, and Professor Hamilton. I had kept my own watch over them all, even exchanging a few words with Walter and Ashley as they traveled to England to aid Billy and Bonnie. Together they worked to free the spirits of the dragons who had been turned into humans.

As a result of his travails in Hades, Billy restored those dragons to life, including Thigocia, who had once been Hannah. Billy went on to fulfill Merlin's prophecy, and the exodus of dragon spirits from Dragons' Rest brought about its destruction. Morgan was finally defeated and taken to her ultimate judgment at the Lake of Fire.

As for the dragons who still lived, each of them had the opportunity to become human again, if they wished, and all but Thigocia chose to do so. She believed she could more easily search for

Gabriel and Makaidos in her dragon form. Thigocia and Ashley set off to find their lost family members, taking Walter and a teenage girl named Karen along with them. Their journey, however, met with danger. Arramos, who had seemingly perished in the floodwaters thousands of years ago, returned and forced Thigocia to separate from her riders by throwing Karen into a dark tunnel that reached into the tunnels of Hades.

Walter and Ashley followed after Karen and eventually found her, along with Sapphira, and Ashley's long-lost brother, Gabriel, and sister, Roxil. Unfortunately, they were not in time to stop Mardon's army of giants from awakening and tunneling to the surface. Mardon himself reappeared and revealed that he had not given up on building a tower to Heaven. Now he planned to unite Earth and Heaven into a single dimension, just as he had done with Earth and Hades. Unfortunately, due to his efforts, the dead that were in Hades now walked the Earth, terrorizing people.

477

The next part of this story requires me to reveal a dimension that had remained hidden from most eyes in creation, Second Eden. Timothy awoke in a hospital in this world, greeted by a woman named Angel, her son, Candle, and her daughter, Listener, a frail and silent girl. Timothy saw that the people in this world were accompanied by floating, ovulum-like objects called companions that provided the people with wisdom and moral instruction.

Timothy met the leader of this world's people, Father Abraham, whom he would later learn was the real Arramos, returned to life in human form in this world. The people of Second Eden were born from plants in birthing gardens, and many of them had actually been gestating humans on Earth, but had been slain before they could be born. He also noticed they possessed innocence, uncorrupted from the sinful ways of Earth.

After an encounter with my ovulum, Timothy's memories of his identity as Makaidos resurfaced, and with it, the memories of his two daughters, Ashley and Roxil, whom he learned were both on the Earth. However, an earlier meeting with Acacia revealed that their eternal destinies hung by a thread, unless a soul could be traded in a sacrifice. Acacia said an innocent lamb had already been prepared.

Meanwhile, in one of his last acts on Earth, Merlin sent Elam on a journey through Hades to the realm known as the Bridgelands, with the goal of reaching Heaven's Altar. Elam survived tests of his character to reach his goal, and I met him personally to discuss the next step in his journey. I instructed him to gather ten wandering souls from the Bridgelands. His observations of their character, however, made him question their reliability. Ultimately, they proved as faithless as the ten spies who fled from the giants in the Promised Land, and despite my appeals, they deserted us at a crucial moment.

Fortunately, faithful courage similar to that of Joshua and Caleb showed itself in the hearts of two who stepped forward to stop Mardon's tower at the cost of their own lives—the young teenager named Karen, and the former harlot Naamah who once served Morgan's evil plans, but gave herself over to Christ in repentance and obedience. Meanwhile, Timothy learned that the lamb Acacia spoke of was Listener. He could not bear to allow this frail young one to sacrifice herself, so he took her place, dying for the sake of his daughters. In the process, his body was burned up, leaving only his bones.

Although Mardon's efforts to merge Heaven and Earth were thwarted, I knew the danger was only just beginning. I proceeded to shepherd groups of brave heroes from the Earth to Second Eden to prepare for a coming war. Elam, who was prophesied to be the warrior chief of Second Eden, arrived first, along with Acacia and Paili. Walter, Ashley, Thigocia, and Roxil arrived next. Billy; Billy's father; Sir Patrick, who was once the dragon Valcor; and Sir Barlow, a knight from the time of King Arthur, then arrived in an airplane belonging to the Bannisters.

In Second Eden, Abraham and Angel gathered Timothy's bones and placed them in a birthing garden. Paili, who was also Sir Patrick's wife, Ruth, was to call forth Makaidos with a song when the bones were energized during an eclipse. By adding Makaidos's name to the heavenly empowered call, Makaidos would be resurrected in the garden. Sadly, the effort ended in disaster. Angel's deceased husband, who was also the evil dragon Goliath until he came to Second Eden, appeared to her and instructed her to change the name in the song from Makaidos to Dragon, to summon him instead. He said to claim that I instructed her to do so, which was a lie.

The changed song released Goliath and brought about a chain of events that allowed an army of Mardon's Nephilim to enter Second Eden and join forces with Flint, a member of Abraham's village who had rebelled against Abraham and had been exiled. To stop Flint's army from destroying Abraham's villages, Abraham and Angel sacrificed themselves to create a wall of fire that secluded Flint and his allies for four years. This gave Billy and the others time to gather the other dragons and strengthen their army. Over time, they brought more dragons to Second Eden, including Bonnie's mother, Hartanna.

At that time, Semiramis, Mardon, and Arramos, who was actually Satan in Arramos's body, put their plan into motion. Mardon had secretly attached an invisible dimensional rope to Bonnie, which brought the dimensions of Second Eden and Earth together. Arramos blasted Mardon with a fiery jet that scarred his facial features and gave him the visage of a pathetic burn victim. He and Semiramis then went to Second Eden and offered themselves in assistance to Elam, Billy, and the others, a ruse that allowed them to plant a sinister seed in the birthing garden.

Meanwhile, Bonnie and Sapphira ended up in a place called the Valley of Souls and encountered an angelic dragon named Abaddon. Bonnie also met her deceased father, and the two made

479

a heartfelt reconciliation. Listener had been seriously wounded by a Vacant's spear, and Dr. Conner's medical assistance was needed in Second Eden. He agreed to submit himself to Abaddon's authority and was resurrected in Second Eden where he saved Listener's life with the help of Semiramis. Bonnie and Sapphira, however, remained in the Valley of Souls, in the care of a teenage warrior named The Maid.

Despite Semiramis's help, Billy and Elam did not trust her. Semiramis then presented Billy with a gruesome sight, a severed finger from Shiloh, and a warning from Arramos not to continue their battle against Flint's forces. They discovered an odd plant growing in the garden, and Semiramis warned Billy and his friends not to uproot it. The plant—growing from a seed placed there earlier by Mardon—was likely linked to Shiloh's life, and they could not know what in fact was growing there. If the plant were to be plucked, Shiloh could die. Billy set out with Acacia to rescue Shiloh, but the effort failed, and in the process Acacia and Shiloh both vanished into the Bridgelands. Semiramis and Mardon then disappeared from the village.

Four years passed. Billy was able to bring more of the former dragons to Second Eden, including Tamara, also known as Sorentine, and Dorian, who was also Yellinia. Thanks to the energized garden, the two were restored as dragons. Billy had his mother brought to Second Eden, along with Yereq, the giant who successfully resisted efforts to make him hate Sapphira.

With another eclipse finally occurring after four years, Billy thought they could summon Sapphira and Bonnie. Ruth had taken ill, but as it turned out, Listener was able to sing the song, and in the process of learning the words, she discovered that Sorentine was her mother. Listener had died in Sorentine's womb, both victims of Devin's blade. Billy had Listener sing to summon Sapphira, and she appeared in the garden. Sapphira then urged Billy to call for Bonnie's return. Billy did so, and Bonnie, four years older and battle-trained, appeared. At that very moment, however, Goliath arrived and took Mardon's planted egg from the garden.

Meanwhile, the wall of flames finally dissipated, and Abraham and Angel departed for Heaven, exposing the Second Eden villagers to Flint's army. Billy and Bonnie discovered that a disease had struck Flint's village, killing much of Flint's forces and rendering Flint himself too weak to fight. In a show of mercy, Billy had Flint brought back to their village.

Shiloh and Gabriel had just arrived in Second Eden along with Mardon, escaping the destruction of the Bridgelands. As it turned out, Bonnie's earlier arrival had also brought the dimensional rope with her, and in the process, she pulled the dimensions of Second Eden, Earth, and Hades together, destroying the Bridgelands and allowing for unencumbered travel between the three worlds. Worse, Devin, the evil dragon slayer, returned in a new body that seemed almost invincible. He had been in the egg during the past four years, regenerating with the garden's assistance.

I arrived in Second Eden to warn Billy, Elam, and the others that Satan had gathered an army of dead souls from Hades, and that the aim of Satan was not Second Eden, but the gate of Heaven. Flint and his forces were mere pawns in the deceiver's greater scheme to attack Heaven. Since Satan did not use his demonic host but rather an army of deceased, mortal servants, we countered with the human and dragon forces of Second Eden.

Devin then appeared and attacked Bonnie, in the process killing Yellinia, but Bonnie fended him off and returned to Abraham's village. Devin followed and tried to kill Billy, but Acacia jumped in front of his blade. Since anyone who spills the blood of an Oracle of Fire is subject to a curse, Devin lost his invulnerability, and Bonnie slew the slayer once and for all.

Sapphira, though devastated by her sister's death, applied Acacia's blood to the garden so they could finally bring Makaidos back. The king of the dragons joined the battle, and the forces of

Second Eden rallied to beat back the undead army. Walter, however, was wounded severely, and without the energy of the garden he would die.

Makaidos volunteered to die again and allow his energy to stimulate the garden's healing power, but Goliath intervened and vowed to sacrifice himself instead. Although possessed by Nephilim spirits, Goliath broke from their hold when he remembered his Second Eden identity as Dragon—Listener's father and Angel's husband. Goliath's sacrifice allowed Walter to live and also restored the dragons, if they so wished, to their human forms.

The forces of Second Eden prevailed. Flint joined the side of Abraham's army and fell in battle, but the light of his companion gave us great hope that he finally repented of his rebellion. At the end of the battle, we captured Mardon and Semiramis and imprisoned them in Second Eden.

482

Bonnie Silver then split the dimensions apart, returning the realms to their rightful places in the universe. A glorious marriage ceremony followed, with three couples at last joined together—Elam to his beloved Sapphira, Walter Foley to Ashley Stalworth, and Billy Bannister to Bonnie Silver.

A year later, Bonnie and Billy's happiness blossomed into parenthood, as they welcomed their twins Karen and Charles into the world—a world at peace with Second Eden, where there were no slayers to thirst for dragon blood, and anthrozils were accepted by society.

At least that is how things seemed at the time.

The **Dragons in our Midst®** and **Oracles of Fire®** collection
by **Bryan Davis**:

RAISING DRAGONS
ISBN-13: 978-089957170-6

The journey begins! Two teens learn of their dragon heritage and flee a deadly slayer who has stalked their ancestors.

THE CANDLESTONE
ISBN-13: 978-089957171-3

Time is running out for Billy as he tries to rescue Bonnie from the Candlestone, a prison that saps their energy.

CIRCLES OF SEVEN
ISBN-13: 978-089957172-0

Billy's final test lies in the heart of Hades, seven circles where he and Bonnie must rescue prisoners and face great dangers.

TEARS OF A DRAGON
ISBN-13: 978-089957173-7

The sorceress Morgan springs a trap designed to enslave the world, and only Billy, Bonnie, and the dragons can stop her.

EYE OF THE ORACLE
ISBN-13: 978-089957870-5

The prequel to *Raising Dragons*. Beginning just before the great flood, this action-packed story relates the tales of the dragons.

ENOCH'S GHOST
ISBN-13: 978-089957871-2

Walter and Ashley travel to worlds where only the power of love and sacrifice can stop the greatest of catastrophes.

LAST OF THE NEPHILIM
ISBN-13: 978-089957872-9

Giants come to Second Eden to prepare for battle against the villagers. Only Dragons and a great sacrifice can stop them.

THE BONES OF MAKAIDOS
ISBN-13: 978-089957874-3

Billy and Bonnie return to help the dragons fight the forces that threaten Heaven itself.

Published by Living Ink Books, an imprint of AMG Publishers
www.livinginkbooks.com ✦ www.amgpublishers.com ✦ 800-266-4977

Now Available from Living Ink Books

MASTERS & SLAYERS

(BOOK 1 IN THE <u>TALES OF STARLIGHT</u> SERIES)

Bryan Davis

Expert swordsman Adrian Masters attempts a dangerous journey to another world to rescue human captives who have been enslaved there by dragons. He is accompanied by Marcelle, a sword maiden of amazing skill whose ideas about how the operation should be carried out conflict with his own. Since the slaves have been in bonds for generations, they have no memory of their origins, making them reluctant to believe the two would-be rescuers. Set on

For purchasing information visit

www.LivingInkBooks.com

or call 800-266-4977

Coming in 2011 from Living Ink Books

THIRD STARLIGHTER

(BOOK 2 IN THE <u>TALES OF STARLIGHT</u> SERIES)

Bryan Davis

Adrian and Marcelle continue their quest to free the human slaves on the dragon planet of Starlight. While sword maiden Marcelle returns to their home planet in search of military aid, Adrian stays on Starlight to find his brother Frederick, hoping to join forces and liberate the slaves through stealth. Both learn that reliance on brute force or ingenuity will not be enough to bring complete freedom to those held in chains.

For purchasing information visit

www.LivingInkBooks.com

or call 800-266-4977

Coming Soon from Living Ink Books

PRECISELY TERMINATED

(BOOK 1 IN THE CANTRAL CHRONICLES SERIES)

Amanda L. Davis

ISBN-13: 978-0-89957-896-5

It is 800 years into the future, and the world is being oppressed by the ruling class. Millions of slaves toil under the Nobles' oppressive thumb, but because of microchips implanted in their skulls at birth, there can be no uprising. Monica, a young slave girl, escaped the chip implantation process. She is able to infiltrate the Nobles' security and travel where no one else is able, but can one girl free the world?

Precisely Terminated is the debut dystopian novel by Amanda L. Davis, daughter of bestselling inspirational fantasy novelist, Bryan Davis.

Now Available from Living Ink Books

SWORDS OF THE SIX

(BOOK 1 IN <u>THE SWORD OF THE DRAGON</u> SERIES)

Scott Appleton

ISBN-13: 978-0-89957-860-6

Betrayed in ancient times by his choice warriors, the dragon prophet sets a plan in motion to bring the traitors to justice. On thousand years later, he hatches human daughters from eggs and arms them with the traitors' swords. Either the traitors will repent, or justice will be served.